The Hitler Progeny

Steve Dimodica

To all the men and women who heard the call to duty, and volunteered to don a uniform of the United States military. Theirs is a special experience the protected will never know.

'Those who cannot remember the past are condemned to repeat it.'
(George Santayana-1905).

Author's Note

This is a work of fiction. In many cases the names of existing people, places, political parties, military units, police organizations, educational institutions, religious or ethnic groups, intelligence agencies, and governmental departments are used as a tool to flesh out the story, but the reader is reminded that this is a novel, and the context is solely a product of the author's imagination.

In addition, please bear in mind that any physical or personality resemblance between characters and historic or prominent persons, is clearly coincidental.

Finally, there are many events, conversations, and activities that take place between people, that are interspersed to serve a fictitious plot line throughout the novel. Pay them no heed as they only serve to foster a narrative created to entertain.

Spring 2017

Chapter 1

Hamburg, Germany

The delegate for the European Commission of Trade sat in the rear seat of the fleet Mercedes-Benz. He was en route to the American Consulate on Alsterufer, to meet with the U.S. Consul General and the German Trade Minister. The delegate hoped to conclude a bilateral agreement that had been negotiated for a year.

The Mercedes turned onto Kennedybrucke and the delegate leaned back in his seat. His boss, the EU Trade Commissioner, would be pleased. This deal was good for everyone. It offered the United States, the EU's largest trade partner, a tariff reduction platform for three years. This coincided with the Port of Hamburg's ambition to regain its leadership as the largest deep sea port for container shipping in Europe. Given the fact that Germany was the European Union's dominant economic member, the contract was a win for all sides.

Two Audis sped by the Mercedes as it turned right onto Warburgstraße. Suddenly the first car darted in front of the delegate's sedan and pumped the brake lights, forcing the Mercedes to slow. Then the second car swerved sideways and rammed its right front fender into the driver's side door and forced the Mercedes to the curb.

Instantly four men bounded from the Audis and circled the delegate's vehicle. The first pair raised MP5K submachine guns and fired through the windshield, stitching the driver's torso with a double line of 9mm Parabellum bullets. He died instantly. The second pair circled to the rear, flung open the door, and grabbed at the delegate who cowered in the back seat.

They taped his mouth, shackled his wrists with plastic handcuffs, and covered his head with a hood. Then they dragged him from the Mercedes and stuffed him into the trunk of the first Audi. One of the men went back and

1

dropped a red arm band emblazoned with a white crescent on the rear seat. Then the four assailants jumped into the two Audis and sped from the scene.

***

Timbuktu, Mali

Terry Solak walked the dusty streets of Timbuktu. It was everything one expected in a desolate desert town; a scorching sun, a bleak landscape, arid weather, and poverty. He turned a corner and followed a dirt road to the left.

Solak had learned that in the Sahara, Bedouins became one with the sand. It swirled, constantly shifting in disparate patterns as it enveloped the traveler in a film of coarse granules; finding openings to penetrate, irritating the eyelids, the ears, the neckline and the long sleeves of their flowing tunics. There was no respite from the sand. One did not conquer the desert, but rather bent to its rhythm.

Terry looked around. The stifling heat had baked the ochre-colored walls and the mud-caked homes that clustered in a jagged line along the ridge. He swallowed hard. Thirst was the constant. Solak had flown into Bamako, the Mali capital, three days earlier before hiring a guide to transport him on a twenty-hour trek across the country to the former salt trading outpost. His parched throat, scratched raw from the windswept dunes, ached for a drink. In the desert water was gold.

A few steps more and Terry unwrapped his keffiyeh and exposed a thick beard and long, unkempt hair. There was a swarthy look to Solak's features, but he covered his eyes with dark, wraparound aviator sunglasses. The rest of his attire, including the long tunic worn by the locals called a zerebou, drawstring cotton pants, and covered-toe sandals, helped to blend him into the Mali wardrobe.

Solak ducked under the archway to an adobe mosque of mortared stone inscribed with Qur'anic phrases. He knew that the legacy of this once-great city of the caravan trail with its rosewater-flowing fountains had disappeared. Now, Timbuktu's only hope for survival was in preserving its distinction as an Islamic center for scholars.

During its golden age, Timbuktu had a flourishing trade in gold, ivory, salt, and slaves. Soon the money flowed, and the Muslim Emperor spearheaded the collection of sacred texts. Eminent scholars traveled from Cairo, Baghdad, and

Persia as all the great teachings of Islam were relocated to this remote, mysterious, forbidding corner of the desert, at the end of the civilized world, in the middle of nowhere. Timbuktu held 300,000 books of Islamic importance.

At the walled entrance to the Ahmed Baba Institute, a uniformed guard halted Solak. Terry addressed him in French, knowing that the European colonists from the north had imprinted their language and some customs on the North African nation. In any event, Terry did not speak any of the local dialects. He was ushered into a large, light-filled courtyard filled with empty, wooden library stacks and a pile of gray and black ashes in the middle of the floor.

A few years earlier the Tuareg rebels had invaded Timbuktu. They set up a strict process of Sharia Law, burning books, destroying religious shrines, and flogging immodestly dressed women. They cut off the hands of thieves. In a few weeks, a combined force of French and Mali soldiers arrived to restore order. Fortunately, the ancient families of the town had managed to smuggle away and hide most of the irreplaceable documents and an uneasy calm settled over Timbuktu.

Solak removed his sandals, padded barefoot towards a small oriental throw rug and sat cross-legged with his feet tucked to the rear. He faced the remnants of the long-extinguished bonfire. Terry tugged at his tunic, loosening the garment at the hip, offering easy access to the Glock pistol tucked into his waistband. Then he removed his sunglasses, set down his shoulder bag, and sat with open hands resting on his knees.

Chapter 2

Langley, Virginia

The Director entered the SCIF on the seventh floor of CIA headquarters and closed the door. It was a special conference room, constructed under strict security measures, designed to prevent all methods of visual, audio, and electronic eavesdropping. He took a seat at the head of the table, and looked around.

There were three other people seated at the conference table; two deputy directors, and a petite, dark featured analyst of thirty, dressed in a business suit with a colorful hijab wrapped loosely around her head and neck.

The Director nodded to the man on his left. "Let's get started."

The deputy director for Analysis reached forward and touched several buttons on the electronic console. The lights dimmed, an extra layer of sound-proofing slid into place along the walls, and a flat screen television descended from the ceiling.

"We have an update on the kidnapping of the EU trade delegate," said the deputy. "This video was picked up by NSA on an Islamic website one hour ago." He paused as the screen blinked into focus.

A man sat bound to a chair, his head covered by a hood. A voice in the background began to speak, an unseen narrator, as the camera lens focused solely on the prisoner.

The language was Arabic and the enunciation polished. It exhibited a nuanced training in a difficult dialect. Two men entered the camera frame dressed in black clothes and masks. They circled behind the seated captive. The first man ripped the hood from the prisoner's head. The second turned his body sideways and raised a pistol to shoulder height.

4

The prisoner stared at the camera, blinking, his eyes adjusting to the sudden light. He tried to focus. It was clearly the face of the kidnapped EU trade delegate from Hamburg. A flashing red dot on the camera caught his attention and he started to swivel in the chair. Then the screen went blank and the video blinked off.

The conference room lights came back on and the television screen retracted into the ceiling. It gave everyone a moment to digest that the video had abruptly ended. "That's it?" asked the Director.

"Yes." The deputy opened a folder and slid a three-page, typed, double-spaced transcript to each person at the conference table. "The trade delegate's body was recovered yesterday with three bullet holes in the back of his head." He nodded at the transcripts. "This is a verbatim translation of the narrator's words. He spoke in standard Arabic."

The Director nodded before settling on the man to his right. "Art?"

The second deputy director in the room led the CIA's National Clandestine Service. He cleared his throat and spoke. "The initial signals are an Islamist group, but we are unclear as to exactly who. We have nothing on the books to indicate any relationship between known Islamic groups and this abduction. We have reached out to the German BfV, but they have no explanation."

The Director frowned. As a former U.S. Senator, he was a quick study in geopolitics but unafraid to ask questions. "Please clarify."

"In the final statement," said the first deputy, "the narrator makes reference to the Dar al-Harb, the House of War."

"Yes," replied the Director. He touched his glasses and looked towards the woman seated at the far end of the table. "Your name is Havva, correct?"

She leaned forward. "Yes, Director. I go by Evie."

"Well, Evie," said the Director in a conversational tone, "you're our resident expert. Any insights?"

Evie touched her hijab self-consciously and then folded her hands together on the conference table before speaking. "The use of the term Dar al-Harb, or House of War, has previously referred to a spiritual place; a place that depicts an abode of permanent conflict."

"Like a concept?" asked the Director.

"More like a mindset," replied Evie. "It could be attributed to any parts of the world not yet conquered by Muslims. It will only end when Islam triumphs and all countries are ruled by Sharia."

Her response initiated a short silence in the room before the Director pulled a photograph from the file. It depicted the red armband with a white crescent left at the scene of the kidnapping in Hamburg. "Is this an Islamic symbol?"

"Actually," said Evie, "this construction is often identified as such, but unlike Christianity or Judaism, Islam has *no* central symbol." She paused. "This resembles an early flag of the Ottoman Empire, which controlled most of the Muslim world for seven centuries—but it is missing a star."

"What does it mean?" asked the Director.

Evie hesitated before answering. "I don't know."

***

Timbuktu, Mali

Ten minutes elapsed before a well-dressed man with a tightly groomed beard entered the courtyard from a hidden door. He wore a silk-embroidered cotton shirt known as a thawb, covered by a flowing full-length outer cloak called a bisht. On his head was a white keffiyeh held in place by a silver-encrusted cord. One wrist dangled expensive gold bracelets studded with garnets, turquoise, and amber stones. The other displayed a diamond-encircled Vacheron Constantin wristwatch. Two bodyguards followed the man. They carried Italian-made Beretta model 12 submachine guns.

Terry remained motionless, slowing his breath as they circled to his rear. This was the mad minute, when adversaries sized each other up to determine if there was hostile intent. Solak kept his poise, and allowed the contact to walk behind his dusty, disheveled body. He felt the well-groomed man regard his pose of piety the way a scientist might study a sample in a petri dish. Finally, the man sat across from Terry and struck a similar cross-legged pose. He waved the two protectors away, motioning them to a corner of the courtyard beyond earshot.

"They do not speak English," said the man with a shrug. He spoke in standard Arabic. "But why take a chance."

Solak and his host looked at each other in silence. This was a test, so Terry responded in Arabic. "Caution is a virtue in our world."

The man smiled. "I am known as Sharif Ali."

"And I am known as Helios."

"You are not what I expected," said Ali.

Terry switched to English. "With respect, I do not know what you were told."

The wealthy Saudi smiled again. "You act like a Muslim."

"I am a Muslim."

The information seemed to surprise Ali. Another moment of silence passed before he asked, "And you represent Washington?"

"I do."

A seed of doubt crept into Ali's expression before he reluctantly asked, "What have they told you?"

"That you are a scholar, who has ventured far at great risk to come to Mali."

"As have you, Helios." The Saudi waved a hand over the pile of rubble to their front. "You see, they have destroyed irreplaceable manuscripts central to the study of Islam." A hint of despair flickered in Ali's eyes. He pointed at the mound of ashes that lay between them. "I needed you to see the destruction of these holy books for yourself."

"As a Muslim," replied Terry, "I am offended."

Ali leaned forward, "Are you religious?"

"Yes," said Solak, "and there can be no rest for any man who defiles our heritage in the name of purity. Allah the merciful will guide our journey."

Ali bit his lip and leaned back. Terry knew he was a minor prince of the House of Saud, the ruling family of Saudi Arabia. This made him incredibly wealthy by any reasonable measure. Connected, rich, and over-educated, Sharif Ali traveled the world in a life of privilege; fearful—as all in his family were—that the extremists would overthrow their rule. Saudis losing their money and power was anathema to the pampered children of the oil-rich nation.

"You are a man accustomed to hardship," said Ali. "You traveled a difficult road to arrive here."

"Yes."

"I sense you are a learned man."

"There are levels of knowledge," replied Solak deferring to the prince's status. "We each serve as we can. Inshallah." As Terry spoke the final words, he bowed his head and touched an open hand to his chest.

The Saudi smiled a third time. Then he looked up and snapped his fingers. Suddenly an attendant entered from behind the hidden door. He carried a metal, cylindrical tube across the courtyard. The prince took the tube and examined the outside. It was four inches long and an inch in diameter. He checked the seal. Satisfied, he waved the attendant back towards the corner with the two bodyguards. "The information you seek." He held the metal tube in the air, not handing it to Terry, but not setting it down. "You realize what would happen if anyone knew of our meeting?"

"Yes, and for that reason we agreed to meet at a place of your choosing, at a time of your comfort."

"Far from prying eyes and ears," said Ali.

"To demonstrate the respect we have for your decision."

The Saudi nodded. He was used to being flattered. Money created a layer of sycophants throughout the kingdom. Ali was an aristocrat immersed in a life of leisure and scholarly pursuits who had entered a dangerous game.

Chapter 3

Frankfurt, Germany

The administrator of the ESRB Secretariat strolled from the Euro Tower on Kaiserstraße. He had developed the habit of dining alone once per week. Each Wednesday, the administrator took a briefcase filled with information and escaped for an early lunch. He found the respite from meetings and technical conversations peaceful. It enabled him to sit quietly and think about macro issues without interruption. It improved his vigilance. The administrator was an economist by training and Dutch by citizenship. He crunched numbers for a living; analyzing data, reviewing financial statements, and studying formulas. As the Eurobank executive overseeing the systemic risk department for the member nations, he absorbed mathematical printouts for a living.

Unbeknownst to the administrator, two men followed him five steps to the rear. They were young, rough looking, wearing leather clothes with long hair and scruffy beards. They timed their walk to ensure a distance of ten meters.

The central business district was relatively quiet. It would be another hour before the high-rise skyscrapers emptied and Kaiserstraße clogged with pedestrians.

The administrator turned left at Neue Mainzer Straße. He shifted his briefcase between hands when suddenly, to the rear, the roar of high performance motorcycle engines ruffled the morning calm. Then he heard the patter of rubber soled boots on the pavement. The administrator turned. Two handguns pointed at his forehead.

A second elapsed as the administrator's face turned ashen and a lump clogged his throat. Then the two men started to shoot. They fired fifteen rounds into the Eurobank executive at point blank range, alternating bullet wounds between his head and chest. He collapsed backwards.

The first man dropped a red arm band emblazoned with a white crescent on the sidewalk next to the administrator. Then two Ducati motorcycles raced up Neue Mainzer Straße and screeched to a halt. One assassin hopped on to the back of each motorcycle, they donned helmets, and sped away.

***

Timbuktu, Mali

"Look into my eyes," said Ali, as he handed Solak the metal cylinder. "I place my life in your hands."

Terry hesitated, and then reached forward. He held the tube as he met the Saudi's eyes.

"If this were to become known," said Ali, "not only would my family disown me, but I would die a most gruesome death."

"I understand."

"What I do is not for money, or to curry favor with your government. It is for the glory of Islam." Sharif Ali swept his hand theatrically across the pile of burned books between them. "It is to prevent *this* from ever happening again."

Terry made a slight bow with his head and tucked the metal tube under his tunic. Then Ali snapped his fingers and the attendant took two steps forward. The Saudi looked at one of his bodyguards and motioned. The protector pulled out a curved jambiya knife, stepped behind the attendant, and cut his throat.

Solak jumped in reaction but managed to control his movements. He slid his right hand into his lap closer to the Glock. Then Ali waved at the second bodyguard. The man turned and fired a burst from his Beretta into the side of his knife-wielding partner. A dozen bullets penetrated the protector's ribcage. He crumpled to the floor.

In a blur, Terry drew his pistol and aimed the Glock at the second bodyguard. Then he swept the barrel of the automatic back towards Ali.

"I am unarmed," said the Saudi, holding up his hands, "but now you see my position." He nodded towards the remaining bodyguard. "There can be no witnesses. Only two men can leave here. I prefer it is you and I. Do you understand?"

Solak studied Sharif Ali. He calculated the various scenarios in his head. As always, there was a very gray area in hard operations. It was a murky world filled with lies, deceit, and double-crosses set on the fringe of chaos. This prize was too valuable to ignore, but it would take a deft hand to recover the information.

The second bodyguard pointed his Beretta at Solak. Then he looked to Ali for instructions. Terry shifted his gaze between the Saudi and his bodyguard.

"I leave you no choice," said Ali, "you cannot leave here with the cylinder if he is alive." The Saudi nodded at the second bodyguard. "Either you kill him, or I will have him kill you."

Terry remained silent for a few seconds. Then he lowered his hand holding the Glock. "Call him off."

The prince motioned at the bodyguard. The man lowered the muzzle of his submachine gun and pointed it at the floor. Instantly Solak swiveled, raised his pistol to shoulder height, and fired twice from his sitting position. The .40 caliber bullets tore two holes in the bodyguard's chest an inch apart, and the protector toppled backwards.

Sharif Ali stood and surveyed the three bodies. His men were dead. He turned back towards Solak. "Go with Allah, my Muslim friend. Make this sacrifice worth the price."

The prince disappeared through the hidden door, leaving Terry to quietly consider what had just occurred. A minute elapsed. Then Solak stood, wrapped the keffiyeh around his face, and touched the metal cylinder tucked into his waistband. He took a final look around the courtyard, retrieved his shoulder bag, and exited.

Chapter 4

Langley, Virginia

Bob Colman stopped outside the deputy director's office.

"He's on the phone, Bob," said the assistant. "It won't be long."

Colman turned away. He was mid-fifties, short, balding, with a hint of mid-drift paunch, and black framed eyeglasses. He carried an unlabeled file folder. At first glance, Bob was the antithesis of the slick, ultra-smooth 'James Bond' caricature, but in fact, he ran the CIA's most secretive black ops section, the Special Activities Division. Functioning under the National Clandestine Service, SAD delivered the hard edge of covert U.S. intelligence capabilities.

A minute elapsed.

"He's ready now, Bob," said the assistant, "go right in."

Colman turned and entered his boss' office. Unlike his own modest layout two floors below, Kent enjoyed a spacious, well-appointed set up. It conveyed power.

"Robert," said Kent, standing to greet his subordinate. The deputy director always referred to underlings by their formal names. It was part of Kent's style. He waved Colman to a conference table. "Coffee?"

"No thanks, Art." The SAD chief sat and folded his hands together on top of the file folder.

Kent circled from behind his huge desk, cup of coffee in hand, and sat next to Colman. "I just got off the phone with the Director. He wants me to brief the President tomorrow at sixteen hundred Pennsylvania."

Colman bit his lip. Kent had a pronounced habit of name dropping. It was some banal insecurity displayed by the deputy director to inflate his importance. Bob could care less. He learned years earlier that politicians came and went, but the core players in Washington lingered under the radar. "Congratulations, Art, I'm sure you'll do a fine job."

"Have you met the President?"

"Can't say that I have," replied Colman shifting uncomfortably in his chair. "Our paths don't cross."

"By design," said Kent, acknowledging the obvious. Black ops and elected officials made for uncomfortable bedfellows.

Kent was tall, handsome in a preppy sort of way, and political. He wore tailored suits and had perfectly coiffed hair. By all accounts his presentation was first rate, but what nagged Kent, his glaring weakness, was a lack of operational experience. He had never worked a day in the field. The deputy director had spent his entire twenty-four-year career on the Agency's analytical side. He was a desk jockey, an information processor, one who plied his trade working with a computer.

Kent crossed his leg at the knee and motioned towards Colman. "So, tell me who you selected for the German assignment."

Colman opened his folder. "Terry Solak will be our lead on the ground."

Kent looked across his office, trying to place the name. "Is he the one you call the Turk?"

"That's him."

"He took a hit somewhere in Europe. Was it Rome?"

"Paris," said Bob. "He went down hard, so we kept him on ice for a while. He's bounced back."

"Sounds tough." Kent settled in his chair and sipped at his coffee. "Tell me about him."

This was the deputy director's way to appear involved. He treated mission decisions like a labor-sensitive HR rep. The fact was, Kent would no more understand appropriate operational qualifications than would a history teacher.

"Born and raised in New Jersey," said Colman, reciting Solak's bio from memory, "Rutgers, Army, Afghanistan."

Kent sipped his coffee. "Is that where we found him?"

"Yes. He was a Team Leader in Fifth Group."

"Special Forces?" asked Kent.

"Yes, he did some work with several of our SAD officers. We got a tip to keep an eye on him."

The deputy director set his cup down and crossed his arms. "How old?"

"Mid-thirties…eight years with the Agency."

Kent stood. He seemed to quickly lose interest in their discussion, as if suddenly something more important had caught his attention. "If he's your choice, fine. Just make sure he's on his game."

"Understood."

Kent paced back towards his desk. "Keep me posted."

The words signaled that their meeting was over.

***

Munich, Germany

The head of the European Commission Regional office strolled the streets of Munich. He ambled along the pedestrian zone that connected Kaiserplatz and Marienplatz, searching for a birthday gift for his wife. The bright sun warmed his face, making for a delightful excursion as he browsed the eclectic mix of specialty shops.

He never noticed the three men to his rear, nor did he hear the muffled scuttle of their feet. They closed fast, surrounding the commissioner just as he paused to admire the display in a large picture window. He turned.

The first man stuck a double-edged dagger into his abdomen. He gasped. The second plunged a knife into the commissioner's back and the third drove a stiletto into his throat. He gurgled, stumbled sideways, and fell.

A woman inside the shop screamed and a crowd started to gather. Two of the assailants furiously withdrew their knives from the commissioner's midsection. The third dropped a red armband emblazoned with a white crescent on the sidewalk. Then the trio turned and fled to the left, taking a moment to drop their weapons into an open canvas bag propped on the ground.

Several bystanders pointed at the fleeing assassins as others rushed to the executive's aid. A fourth man, standing off to the side, stepped forward, plucked the canvas bag from the ground, and walked in the opposite direction.

Chapter 5

Langley, Virginia

Evie walked down the short, secluded corridor of the Special Activities Division. This was new ground for the analyst, as SAD's array of deep cover operators were intentionally kept separated from everyone that didn't function in their dark world. She stopped in front of Bob Colman's office and addressed the assistant who typed an e-mail.

"I'm Evie Khazemi, here to see Mister Colman."

The assistant peered over the top of her glasses and studied the petite brunette. Evie was poised, slim of frame, attractive, and polite. She dressed in a pinstripe business suit and wore a colorful hijab that partially covered her black hair. Then the assistant looked at a list of Colman's appointments for the morning.

"You're Havva, the analyst?"

"Yes, I go by Evie."

The assistant nodded, reached over, and put a check mark next to Evie's name. "He'll be a few minutes. Take a seat." The assistant motioned at several chairs in the small anteroom.

Evie sat and politely tugged her skirt below her knee before folding her hands in her lap. Several minutes elapsed. The assistant finished her e-mail and turned back from the computer.

"Your first time here?"

"Yes," replied Evie. She was nervous and welcomed the conversation. "Have you been with the Agency long?"

"Fourteen years," said the assistant, adjusting her eyeglasses, "nine with SAD and three with Bob."

"What's he like?"

The assistant considered her reply before answering. "Demanding, very direct, no pretenses. What you see is what you get."

Evie digested the information and then asked. "Any suggestions?"

The assistant leaned back in her chair. "Be prepared, he has a short fuse for careerists, and never try to spin him. He'll smell it a mile off."

The two women looked at each other in silence, and then the assistant leaned forward at the waist and placed her elbows on the desk.

"It's like this," said the assistant. "If other areas of Langley drop the ball, someone gets an earful and the Agency is embarrassed…if *we* mess up in SAD, someone dies."

Colman's door opened and two rugged looking operators, dressed in casual attire and sporting facial hair, exited the chief's office.

"Later, Marge," said the first man as he passed the assistant's desk.

The second man gave Marge an innocuous pat on the forearm and waved. Both men glanced at the seated Evie and then quickly looked away.

The assistant swiveled towards the office and called over her shoulder. "Bob, your ten o'clock is here."

The short, balding Colman came to the door and looked at Evie. "You're the analyst?"

"Yes, sir."

"It's Bob. Come in," Colman waved her through the door and pointed at a chair next to his desk. He checked his watch. "I've only got about fifteen minutes." He sat and slid a stack of manila folders sideways so they could face each other. "I've heard a lot about you," said Colman in a flat tone.

Evie stared at the SAD chief, unsure how to respond. Her anxiety cloaked a touch of curiosity. Colman looked nothing like she expected. Evie had it in her head that the chief of SAD, the leader of the CIA's most covert and highly trained operators, would be a tall, chiseled physical specimen. Bob was anything but…he was so bland and utterly unassuming in appearance, that one would pass him in the street without a second glance.

"I've read your two-oh-one file," said Colman. "I know you are fluent in several Middle East languages and that you have been working in the Analysis Directorate for six years."

"Yes, sir…Bob," replied Evie.

"You are ethnically Persian and you grew up in Irvine, California?"

"Yes."

"You are a practicing Muslim?"

Evie self-consciously touched her colorful veil. "Yes."

16

Colman bit his lip in a noncommittal expression. "Do you understand what we do here?"

"Only in general terms."

It was the correct answer, because SAD was heavily involved in the hard side of black operations, and few outside of those directly involved in the missions knew the whole story.

"As you know," said Colman, "the Special Activities Division is divided into Special Ops and Political Action. The two sides often work together, depending upon the assignment."

Bob paused and watched as Evie listened. She was polite and attentive, a picture of comportment. If she had any concerns, they didn't show.

"From this point forward," said Colman, "you do not communicate with your old friends in Analysis. No coffee, drinks, or buddy lunches. You see them in the hall, you smile, say hello, and keep walking. Understand?"

The mandate caught Evie off guard, but she nodded.

"We are placing a deep cover officer in Europe to probe these German assassinations," said Bob. "We are convinced that the Islamic twist is an important distinction. Do you agree?"

"Yes."

"The officer's code name is Helios. You will be his personal contact here at Langley, twenty-four-seven. He is now your *only* assignment. Understand?"

Evie leaned back in the chair. She was slightly overwhelmed. It was clear that the black ops of SAD was a different world from the collegial groupthink of analysis work.

Bob removed his glasses and stroked a flat palm over his balding pate. He leaned forward and asked again. "Evie, do you understand?"

"Yes."

"Do you have any questions?"

Evie shuffled her feet on the carpet. "I guess that since we'll be working so close together, I would like to know when I can meet him?"

"That's not possible," said Bob.

Evie hesitated, not sure about the protocols. Finally, she asked, "What can you tell me about him?"

Bob replaced his eyeglasses. He could read the concern in her expressions. This was all new turf for Evie to assimilate. "Suffice to say, Helios is very capable…and very resilient." Colman glanced at his watch. "Anything else?"

"No."

Colman stood and Evie followed his lead. He walked her to the door.

"My assistant, Marge, will get you situated here. We'll send a security officer over to clean out your desk and pick up your personal possessions. Don't go back to the Analysis Directorate."

Evie waited as Bob opened his door and extended a hand to shake. "Welcome to SAD," said Colman.

Evie leaned forward and grasped Colman's palm in a firm grip. "Bob, thank you for selecting me for this opportunity. I appreciate the confidence."

The SAD chief tilted his head sideways in an odd pose. Then he smiled for the first time. "I didn't select you, Evie, my boss did."

***

Berlin, Germany

There were twenty professionals in the room, a mixture of men and women, some old and a few young. They represented the Federal Uniform Police (BPOL) as well as the Federal Criminal Police (BKA), the domestic security agency (BfV), the foreign intelligence service (BND), the Ministry of the Interior, and the chancellor's office.

It was the kind of meeting that appealed to the orderly German mind. The agenda was precise, thorough, and organized. The purpose was to create a structure where information could be coordinated and acted upon despite the haze of overlapping mission statements.

The difficulty was that each of their respective agencies had some jurisdictional claim to the recent rash of murders. Yet the lack of a clear motive or a defined antagonist complicated the matter. Despite the internet blogs and videos of the attacks, no perpetrators had stepped forward to accept responsibility. The only thread, which was nebulous, was an armband that depicted a white crescent on a red background.

A tall man wearing a uniform stood and cleared his throat. He had close-cropped gray hair, a square jaw and deep blue eyes. His epaulet insignia designated the gold stars and wreaths of a police director—equivalent to an army general.

"Three attacks in two weeks," said the police director in a deep voice, "in three different locations."

A murmur floated around the conference table as the other participants to the meeting reflected on the obvious: Germany was under siege, by an unknown but highly adept adversary, and thus far, no credible leads had surfaced despite the combined efforts of their federal departments. The sense of frustration in the room was palpable.

"We are fully engaged, Herr Director Geiger," said a man seated to the left. He was the vice president of the domestic security agency, often referred to simply as the 'BfV.' "There are limits to our ability to act." The VP leaned forward in his chair and pointed a finger at the tall police director. "We are under judicial control, and you know very well that *all* of our activities can be legally challenged in court."

It was the German conundrum. To prevent a repeat of heavy-handed Aryan ideologies prevalent during the Second World War, the government constrained its police and security services under strict constitutional guidelines. The goal was to prevent a reoccurrence of overt nationalism. The effect, however, was to create bureaucratic, cautious organizations that were either afraid or unable to act when necessary. Protection of the citizenry took a back seat to the rights of foreigners. Then a million 'Schengen' migrants crossed the nearest EU border and beelined it to German soil.

Europe became a magnet for the dispossessed, the homeless, and the secretly subversive. The great social experiment of a unified Europe was imploding in the laps of the liberal elite, as vast groups of migrants refused to integrate even as they sucked their host countries dry of financial resources.

"Rape and sexual assault are increasing at an alarming rate," said Geiger, as he turned to face the domestic security VP, "even as gangs of unemployed youths roam our streets and defile our culture." The police director raised a hand in the air to match the pointed finger. "This, Herr Vice President, is *not* what Germans expect as a response for our beneficence."

The police director's words echoed through the conference room. His tone, and his erect posture always exuded confidence. He was law and order, a policeman's policeman.

"Perhaps," replied the woman from the chancellor's office, "you could offer a suggestion, Herr Director Geiger?"

The police director turned to face the woman before speaking, "Ja, Frau Steir, we should pursue *any* lead available, *even* if such an inquiry is incomplete."

"You refer, of course, to the armband left at each location," replied the woman.

"It is our only thread, the only constant in all three attacks," said Geiger. "We cannot ignore the implication because it makes us uncomfortable."

The police director took a moment to scan the faces of the other delegates in the room. He noted several nods, the unspoken agreement of some of his peers. Then he sat down.

Chapter 6

Terry Solak sat at the rooftop restaurant of the Les Oliviers Palace Hotel and sipped an espresso. The last vestiges of the warm Mediterranean day had diffused into an early sundown, and now, as the tall Gantry Cranes of the harbor ended their workday, the port city of Sfax fell into a quiet calm.

Solak stroked his chin. His recently cut hair and trimmed beard allowed Terry to more easily blend into the citified Arabic culture of the North African nation. The trek to the seaport community from Mali proved arduous. For just as difficult as Timbuktu was to enter, it was equally difficult to depart. There was just no easy way to cross the grand Sahara without tripping choke points along the route. Yet, given the nature of Terry's assignment and his orders to 'hand-deliver' the information to a designated courier team, he took five days to traverse the distance. Each step in the process saw a further depletion in the sack of gold coins he carried in his shoulder bag. Baksheesh ruled the world.

Now thirty hours after the hand off of the metal cylinder, Solak started to relax. This was his post-op wind down; a chance to reduce the operational antenna for a few hours and reprogram his mental acuity.

His boss, Bob Colman the chief of SAD, had spent many years in the field; so Bob instinctively understood the need of his officers to decompress after a dangerous assignment. Terry followed his instructions and stayed in Sfax, killing time by wandering the streets of the walled city and acting like a tourist for a couple of days. Finally, a security officer from the embassy in Tunis made contact and traveled down to Sfax.

"My name is Quinn," said the security officer without preamble. "My job is to escort you to a safe house in Sousse where you'll be debriefed on this most recent assignment. You doing okay?"

Solak shrugged. "A little wear and tear, nothing a few days of rest hasn't helped."

Quinn nodded. "I was told to inquire as to the injury from Paris—any repercussions?"

Terry squinted, not suspecting that the security officer knew the details of that mission but that Bob would be checking on Solak's bounce back from an almost fatal experience. "No, fully engaged, nothing to slow me down."

"Good," replied Quinn. "I'll give you an hour to pack and check out of your hotel. I'll be waiting downstairs in a blue Citroen." With another nod the security officer stood and moved towards the elevator.

***

Berlin, Germany

Frau Steir of the chancellor's office strode at a quick pace through the sprawling Tiergarten. The large multiuse park in the center of Berlin was filled with adults and children alike, all enjoying the pleasant weather of a warm spring day.

Steir scanned the crowds as she walked, and spotted her contact standing in front of the Goethe Monument. She picked up her gait, angled right, and approached the tall statue circled by a wrought iron fence. "Sorry about the time," said Steir with a nod. "It was unavoidable."

The VP of the BfV, the domestic security agency, glanced at his wristwatch and shrugged. "Thank you for meeting me on short notice." He paused and took a quick look to their rear before continuing. "I did not want to raise any alarms, but I felt you needed to have some important information before tomorrow's meeting."

"It couldn't wait?" asked Steir.

"With Herr Director Geiger pushing for a more aggressive posture," said the VP, "it seemed wise to *not* let the chancellor be caught off guard."

The woman frowned and then relented. "Please continue."

"Our counterparts at the BND passed along two separate leads they picked up on electronic surveillance. One was a speech in Arabic fed through a Turkish website. It referenced the Dar al-Harb, or House of War—same as the videos that followed each of the three murders."

Steir turned to her left and reached out to casually touch the low fence. The BND, Germany's foreign intelligence service, was very adept at collecting and evaluating international communications. "And the second lead?" she asked.

"More complicated," said the VP.

Steir fixed him with a steady gaze and motioned.

21

"There was a speech broadcast in Austria by an unknown source over the internet."

"Unknown?" asked Steir.

"The speaker was not visible. It was only a voice—a man's voice."

"What did he say?"

"He promoted the usual extremist views; racism, xenophobia, the danger of migrants, and the threat posed by foreigners."

Steir raised her hand in a diffident way. She wasn't getting the point. It all sounded so routine.

"It was *the voice*," said the VP in mild exasperation, "the cadence, the tone, the very *same* use of modulation."

Suddenly the woman's eyes opened wide and she stared at the VP. "*His* voice?"

"As if we were back in time…as *if* eighty years had not transpired."

Chapter 7

Sousse, Tunisia

Terry Solak sat on the balcony of the safe house, stretched his legs across the coffee table, and sipped a cold beer. He shielded his eyes from the strong North African sun with a hand and gazed out across the Gulf of Hammamet. The contrast of a chilled brew and the vast waters of the Mediterranean Sea did wonders for Solak's desert decompression. It was as if the Agency shrinks back in Langley knew that small rewards paid big dividends. First in Sfax and now in Sousse, Terry experienced the calming effects of a seaside city. It was an opportunity to disengage the vast, suffocating blanket of sand known as the grand Sahara.

Solak's debrief went smoothly. He was questioned by a seasoned interrogator who taped several sessions and then compiled Terry's narrative into appropriate after-action report format.

Reports were the lifeblood of the Agency. Yet Terry, like most operational personnel, hated the process of committing memories, recollections, and impressions to paper—despite understanding the need for analysis and mission continuity. The interrogator helped the process. Terry smirked. It felt good to be spoiled with small stuff.

A knock on the door interrupted Terry's reverie, and then Solak watched his boss step onto the balcony carrying a briefcase.

"Bob?" Solak stood, surprised, as Colman offered a hand. They shook.

"Sit," said the SAD chief. "Relax."

"What brings you here?"

"A change in plans," replied Colman. He motioned at the Styrofoam cooler next to the table, and Terry pulled out a bottle of Celtia lager. Solak popped the top and they clinked glass in a toast. "First, the Timbuktu assignment…"

Colman removed his eyeglasses in a moment of reflection as he parsed his words.

"…if the information provided in the metal cylinder proves accurate, then we have the intel hit of the decade." Colman paused before adding. "And we owe it all to *you*."

Terry nodded. The verbal accolade was the sum total of the praise he would receive. "You came a long way to give me a pat on the back," said Solak with a smirk.

"You're right." Colman leaned back in his chair. "But you deserve it."

They sat in silence for a few minutes, each taking a measure of the moment. It was a game of poker, and one of them had to either up the ante or call.

"Something has come up," said Bob finally.

"Oh?" Terry gave his boss a noncommittal look.

"Can you manage switching gears on short notice?"

"I'd prefer to avoid the desert for a while."

Colman laughed and took another sip of beer. "I think I can assure you of that."

"Where?"

"Germany."

Solak sat forward in his seat. "Anything to do with those murders?"

"Yes," answered Bob, "I see you have managed to keep abreast of world events."

"Thank the BBC. Is there an Islamic connection?"

"We think so, but at this point, the facts are still disjointed. That's where you come in. The Germans need help. The BND asked for a fresh face."

The mention of their German counterpart, the foreign intelligence service, or BND, touched a nerve. "So we are working with them, but on their turf."

"In a nutshell," said Bob. He handed Terry the briefcase. "Everything you need is here, including plenty of euros. Standard procedure, after you review and memorize all the information, destroy the flash drives."

"Got it," said Terry as he took possession of Colman's briefcase. "Anything else?"

"Yes," replied Bob after another long swallow of beer. "I managed to assign you our newest collections officer back at headquarters."

"Really?"

"All the details are there," said Bob as he pointed at the briefcase. "Call her from a secure line before you leave."

"How experienced?"

"She's an analyst by training; new to SAD, but she is *very* sharp. Her name is Evie."

***

Stuttgart, Germany

The Stuttgart Spring Festival, known to the locals as Wasen, is an annual event that attracts one and a half million visitors. It is the largest spring festival in Europe.

In addition to a chandler market that features jewelry, spices, leather goods, textiles and articles for the home, there is also a Ferris wheel, a roller coaster, a fruit column, various side shows, confectionary stands, and four huge beer tents.

The tents are a constant draw. Each is a football field in size, festooned by brightly colored walls, pitched canopies, hanging chandeliers, and a large stage for the band. Boisterous revelers shared long, wooden, picnic-style tables stacked end to end, as young waitresses delivered a constant flow of German lagers in crystal glass beer steins.

A middle-aged man representing the Stuttgart Chamber of Commerce guided a group of six visitors to a reserved table in the third tent. They were delegates of the European Economic and Social Committee. The delegates were in the historic city of Stuttgart to review business models, as the industrial center was renowned for high-tech and prominent companies. Names such as Daimler AG, Porsche, Bosch and Celesio dotted the landscape and could prove a beacon to other EU members' cities if the process could be replicated.

At an hour past noon, the third tent was packed, and many patrons stood and swayed, singing popular songs along with the band. German women frolicked in their bosom-hugging trachten dresses, and young men sported alpine hats and lederhosen breeches. Frivolity reigned.

Just as the band signaled a break, a huge explosion rocked the tent, spiraling the EU delegates' picnic table skyward towards the roof canopy, splintering wood, shattering glass, and severing body parts in a mass of mixed debris. The noise itself deafened and stunned the crowd and seconds elapsed as the patrons tried to assimilate what had just occurred. Then the screams began.

Chapter 8

Langley, Virginia

Evie sat in a large cubicle deep in the SAD wing and studied the condensed history of Germany. The transition from intelligence analyst to collection management officer was a whirlwind. There was a guidebook for reference, but the formal training course had been suspended due to the urgency of the situation. Fortunately for Evie, she was organized and efficient. These attributes helped her assimilate loads of information. The strength of any good analyst was the ability to scan reams of data in search of hidden threads in order to locate a pattern, and piece together the puzzle.

Evie swiveled in her seat. Her cubicle was like a mini control tower, filled with computer screens, telephone consoles, television viewers and a world clock. SAD clearly operated on a different plane than the more academic world of Analysis. Yet, as exciting as the new challenge was, there were moments where Evie felt she had been thrown into the deep end of the pond and told to 'swim' on demand.

Her phone buzzed, and the console light indicated an overseas line processed through a scrambler in North Africa. She flipped her headset switch and answered. "This is Evie."

"This is Helios," said Terry in a deep voice. He let the codename settle. "I guess this call will serve as our introduction."

Evie nodded to herself before answering, "I was hoping to say hello in person."

"Our time will come," replied Solak casually, "don't let the protocols throw you."

"I won't," said Evie, feeling reassured by Terry's confidence.

"Do you understand your new job?"

"Yes, I think so. In short, I should collect and manage information pertinent to regions, target countries, and areas of interest that will support current operations."

"And now?"

"Help pull it all together so that we can connect the dots."

"That's pretty much it. If you have questions regarding procedure, check with the boss."

"Bob?"

"Yes. He won't steer you wrong, and he won't let you get caught in a bureaucratic shuffle."

"Good to know." Evie paused for a moment before asking. "Do you have my background?"

"I do. I read through your file."

"Any concerns?"

"No."

"Any suggestions?"

"No, just keep your head down…and try not to read into everything. The fact that I know more about you right now than vice-versa is not relevant. This is not about status, it's about function. We work *together*. Make sense?"

"Yes," replied Evie, appreciating his attitude.

"My only suggestion," said Terry with an air of finality, "is to stay focused on the mission. The *mission* is the key. Be conscientious. Do that, and everything else will fall into place."

"I understand," replied Evie in a quiet voice. As she started to ask a question, she heard the line disconnect.

***

Berlin, Germany

Director Geiger of the federal police stood at the window on the eighth floor of the chancellery building. The huge, modern, glass-enclosed structure is the largest governmental headquarters in the world. It is part of the complex of buildings around the Reichstag that was built to house federal institutions following the reunification of Germany and the relocation of the capital from Bonn to Berlin.

The tall police director watched in silence as a crowd of demonstrators walked through the middle of Berlin along the Unter den Linden. Thus far they seemed peaceful, yet that could change in an instant. The numbers swelled as bystanders, marchers, and curiosity seekers entered the gathering along Pariser Platz facing the Brandenburg Gate. This was the very heart of Berlin.

Geiger's jaw tightened as he clasped his hands behind his back and watched the scene from a distance.

"Herr Director Geiger," said the VP of the domestic security agency sitting at the conference table, "we are ready to begin."

The police director turned and paced across the room in his pressed police uniform. Before taking a seat, he turned and addressed the deputy president for the Berlin State Police, the Landespolizei. "The crowd is growing by the minute, Holger, traffic is snarled, and the protesters are taking over the plaza."

"Thank you, Herr Director, but we have it under observation."

Geiger looked at the state police counterpart through penetrating blue eyes. "At least set up blockades and move the water cannons into position."

"Thank you, Herr Director," said the deputy in an irate tone. "I *know* my job."

The difficulty for the two police officials was the strict separation of powers. Ever since the fall of the Nazis at the end of World War Two, law enforcement in Germany was relegated to the sixteen states of the German federation. The federal police, Geiger's organization, was responsible for border security, ports of entry, and special duties. The feds were relegated to a supporting role unless the state police requested assistance.

"Then you should do it," replied Geiger with an air of indignation, "we are looking at a repeat of the G20 riots in Hamburg from last month."

"These are *Germans*," said the deputy in a loud voice, "not left wing radicals from other countries."

"How do you know?" asked Geiger, his tone matching that of the state police deputy president. "Our citizens cry out for protection as our long-standing cultural institutions are being attacked—maybe by Islamists, or maybe by left wing radicals, and yet we sit and *watch*."

"Enough," said the VP of the domestic security agency. "We have no information to confirm that the demonstrators in the plaza are anything but peaceful."

Frau Steir of the chancellor's office pointed at the typed agenda laying on the table. "Let us suspend this conversation for the moment, and focus on the beer tent attack in Stuttgart."

Chapter 9

Berlin, Germany

The apartment was in a condominium complex on Corneliusstraße, south of the Tiergarten, in the exclusive embassy neighborhood. It stretched across the entire third floor of the building; the front faced a manicured internal courtyard, the rear an access canal to the Spree River. The only sound was the chirping of birds.

Gerhardt entered the living room and set a small, palm-size Dictaphone on a side table. He had just recorded a ten-minute monologue for the ever-expanding viewership of his political webcasts. It would be disseminated through the internet.

Gerhardt took a long swig of bottled water, settled into a cushioned chair, and played back the oration through an earpiece. He was a student of rhetoric, more involved in the medium than the message. What Gerhardt understood, was that people responded viscerally to the spoken word. Broad themes and a populist ideology, when delivered in an evolving cadence, could mesmerize a crowd. It touched an emotional nerve. It propelled people to act.

Gerhardt played back the monologue several times, picked spots to stop the tape, and made a notation of the elapsed time. It helped him refine the delivery.

A blonde woman entered the apartment followed by a huge, bald-headed man wearing a tight-fitting suitcoat that hid several tattoos. He nodded at Gerhardt and then receded towards a rear hallway.

"You are home early," said the woman.

"Ja, I needed to record the special address," replied Gerhardt. He turned his attention back towards the Dictaphone. "It is important, Nora."

"How does it sound?" she asked.

Gerhardt did not answer. Rather, he slid the Dictaphone across the table towards the blonde. She sat, adjusted the earpiece, and started the tape.

Her attention focused on the monologue as she studied Gerhardt. He was forty, tall, slim, with straight brown hair and a distinct mustache that suddenly stopped inside the edge of each corner of his upper lip. Gerhardt's eyes seemed to shift between greenish brown and dark gray. He sat in silence, exuding patience, unaware that Nora marveled at his uncanny physical resemblance to history's most evil personification, Adolf Hitler.

***

Berlin, Germany

Terry Solak stepped from the taxi in front of the Intercontinental Hotel. He paid the driver and waited until the cab sped off. Then he turned right and headed back towards the sidewalk. It was a throw off.

He was en route to a meet with his local contact, a man known simply as Otto. The meet was set for a public, easily accessibly forum. These precautions permitted both parties to check for unwanted surveillance.

Terry saw the Bikinihaus on the right. It was a concept mall, converted into an eclectic shopping center in city west. It combined boutiques, flagship stores, restaurants, and distinct modular exhibition boxes. It also housed a hotel, office space, and a landscaped rooftop terrace that looked down on the Berlin Zoo.

Solak mounted several steps and entered the atrium. Then a few minutes later he exited an elevator at the terrace level wearing a red handkerchief around his neck.

Terry took his time. He pretended to be interested in the various animals dotting the zoo below but, in effect, he was studying the other pedestrians strolling the green garden. A man carrying a folded newspaper and an unlit pipe approached.

"Pardon," said the man in English, "would you know what time the rooftop closes?"

"Ten p.m.," answered Solak.

"And on Sundays?"

"Every day."

The man took a puff on his unlit pipe and turned. "I am Otto."

"Helios," replied Solak. "I'm clean."

"Yes, I checked as well. Thank you for helping out."

"Friends and allies," said Terry, "we understand that you have some internal constraints."

Otto handed Solak his folded newspaper. "Flash drive inside. Our counterparts at the BfV have undercover assets in several mosques. There are two mosques with Turkish imams that are not penetrated. As you know, the internet voice narratives all emanated from Istanbul."

"And the BfV does not approve of your involvement?"

"No," said Otto, "they are caught in a mode of judicial constraint—even though we brought them the Dar al-Harb videos."

"It's now a domestic security matter, so you guys are out."

"Officially," replied Otto with a nod, "we have been sidelined."

"Which leaves outside friends to help."

"Some of us fear the ramifications of this massive Schengen migration. The chancellor acts calm, but many in the service worry that if we don't control the issue, time will work against us."

"I'll do what I can. I will only be in touch if I need something or I develop something."

"Agreed," answered Otto with a wave of his pipe. "Good luck, Helios." The German foreign intelligence officer turned and headed towards a different section of the rooftop garden.

Chapter 10

Langley, Virginia

Evie immersed herself into the symbolism of the Islamic world. She contrasted and compared flags, murals, and ancient etchings over centuries. Then she studied photographs of the red armbands with a white crescent deliberately left behind at the location of each attack. She was searching for a historic link. Something that the perpetrators wanted the world to discover.

"How goes the battle?"

Evie looked up to see Bob Colman leaning over the top of her cubicle partition. "The battle goes," answered Evie with a bright smile. It was a good smile, one without guile or hidden meaning. One that highlighted her already attractive features.

"Any news?" asked the SAD chief.

She shook her head. In the first few days of her transition Evie learned that Bob regularly walked the corridor. He pushed, prodded and questioned; stretching the process to assure that information flowed to his operators without preamble. Colman's demeanor set the tone: SAD was about function, not form. Looking good *only* counted when they won.

"Helios made contact with the German foreign intelligence officer," said Evie. "The leads and background info were passed. He is immersing himself in two separate locations. One is a prayer hall, one is a mosque, but both have suspect imams."

"His cover is intact?" asked Bob.

"Yes. He is backstopped as a recent Turkish migrant from Istanbul seeking work, and arriving under Schengen."

Colman removed his eyeglasses and wiped them with a handkerchief. Then he pointed at a series of colored flags on her computer screen. "What are your thoughts?" he asked.

Evie looked at the side by side comparisons on the screen. "The intentional clues, the arm bands left at each location—including the beer tent—are an anomaly. They contain parts that resemble the old Ottoman flag, but they are incomplete."

"How so?"

"A white crescent on a red background but no star," said Evie.

"And if a white star had been added?"

"It would be an exact replica both of the old Ottoman flag and of the current Turkish flag."

"What about the internet feeds?" asked Bob.

"The post attack narratives all emanate from Istanbul, but the unseen speaker uses standard Arabic, not Turkish."

Colman considered the information before speaking. "Each of the four attacks occurred on German soil but did not target German citizens. The victims were foreign nationals employed by the European Union. It doesn't sync."

"Another anomaly. For the record, the last caliphate was in Turkey under the Ottoman Empire. The caliph was sent into exile with his family in 1924. Many Muslims believe that the return of the caliphate will directly correspond to the Dar al-Harb, the House of War."

***

Berlin, Germany

Terry stood in the middle of the prayer hall at the Sehitlik Mosque surrounded by long rows of Muslim men. There was a practiced ritual to their movements— bowing, hands on knees, standing, prostrating, sitting in a special position; not on their heels and not on their buttocks.

It was Friday, the Muslim holy day, and Salat, or prayer, was obligatory. It was a good time to be seen and remembered. This was the essence of a probe mission; to introduce an undercover agent into a group or organization, and allow them to earn acceptance by the membership, thereby gaining access to information previously unavailable.

Solak bent over his prayer rug and tapped his forehead on the floor. He faced the Mihrab, the semicircular niche in the wall that indicated the direction of the qibla. All Muslims faced Mecca when they prayed.

The Sehitlik was Berlin's most beautiful mosque. Built on the grounds of an old Turkish cemetery, the complex was both a cultural and a community center. It welcomed all Muslims, and during the holy month of Ramadan, the mosque would accommodate as many as fifteen hundred worshipers under its roof. If Terry was to uncover radical tendencies in the percolating waters of the Turkish diaspora, the odds were strong that the Sehitlik would be a factor. Today was his third visit to the mosque.

Hands on thighs, Solak slowly lowered himself to a kneeling position. He touched his forehead, nose and palms to the ground, careful to bend his toes so the tops of his feet faced the qibla. Then he chanted in Arabic, in a quiet voice, reciting the memorized phrases.

Fifteen minutes elapsed and the prayer interlude concluded. The Turkish imam took some time to lecture the participants on their responsibilities as good Muslims. Only briefly did he touch on the violent attacks and gathering protests of the last few weeks in Germany.

As Terry rolled up his prayer rug two men approached from the far side of the prayer hall.

Chapter 11

Berlin, Germany

The lights in the conference room at the chancellery dimmed as the video began. The camera focused on a fading, yellow, three-story building. The lens paused and then zoomed in for a close-up. The voice of an unseen narrator began to speak in standard German.

"This is a building on Salzburger Vorstadt in Braunau, Austria, a small town on the south bank of the Inn River which separates Austria and Germany…"

The camera swept the ground floor of the building as the narrator spoke. After a few seconds the lens settled on a granite memorial stone positioned on the sidewalk in front of the building. The camera made a point to pause long enough for the viewers to read the inscription on the stone before continuing upward.

"…an important man was born here," said the narrator, "on the evening of Easter Sunday, at 6.30 p.m. on April twenty, 1889…"

There was something in the narrator's voice that transfixed the listeners in the room. It radiated a quiet power, a restrained modulation that used tone and timed pauses to emphasize rhetorical points.

"…the child grew to be a man of stature, a man who believed in Germany's place in the world. He was a man prepared to *lead* Germans in a quest for self-determination. A democracy whose politicians and elected officials would *serve* her *citizens*…"

The speech seemed to grow in ardor. The camera scanned the top floor and then fixed on the ground level double door and iron grill work. The narrator gradually infused his words with increasing emotion, small verbal flourishes that cascaded and grew.

He recounted the recent spate of terrorism perpetrated in German cities. Then he suggested the likelihood that radical Muslims led the attacks. He railed against the European Union, and the reality that bureaucrats in Brussels decided the fate of Germany.

"…*Schengen*, what is this Schengen? Who empowered the politicians to saturate our cities with undocumented foreigners, to fill our streets with lawless bands of marauding youth…"

He urged the speech forward, increasing the volume, sharpening the pitch, rising the intonation on broad themes.

"…join us in Dresden. *Unite*. Take to the streets and show our elected officials, that they must *not* ignore our concerns…"

Finally, in a frenzied moment of passion, he implored:

"…Germany is *not* for Schengen. Germany is *not* for foreigners. Germany is *not* for the European Union. Germany is *for* Germans!"

The video blinked off and several of the committee members leaned back in their seats as the overhead lights turned on. Everyone was a little stunned.

"This video," said the VP of the domestic security agency, "was picked up on a known internet site for right wing extremists."

"Where was it posted?" asked Director Geiger of the federal police.

"Munich," said the VP.

A collective sigh circled the conference room. Finally, Frau Steir of the chancellor's office spoke. "As you can see, we have a problem; but one that just took on a decidedly more dangerous overtone."

***

Berlin, Germany

Gerhardt sat alone in the small office at the rear of the condominium on Corneliusstraße. He had just concluded watching—for the third time—his voice-over narrative of the yellow, three-story building in Braunau Austria. Ever the perfectionist, Gerhardt watched the video on the internet the same way the viewing public would experience the speech. So much of the style and sounds simulated the audio-only medium of decades long past, when radios ruled the airways, and the physical appearance of the speaker did not influence the perceptions of the listening audience. The goal was to seduce the masses by voice alone, tweak their emotions, and then propel them forward in a decisive act.

Gerhardt reached forward and halted the video on his laptop computer. Then he initiated a recorded speech made decades earlier during a Nationalist

Socialist Party rally. He compared the two, seeking to match the recently created video voice-over to the dated radio speech.

Suddenly his office door flew open, and Nora motioned in excitement, "Are you watching?" asked the blonde.

"Watching what?" said Gerhardt in an agitated tone. He started to wave her off when she motioned again.

"The news on Das Erste," she said. "Turn on the television." Nora spun and charged from the office.

With a sigh, Gerhardt stood and followed her into the living room. He found Nora perched in front of the television, sitting on an ottoman two feet in front of the flat screen.

She was immersed in the process. The cameras followed several reporters who floated between the throngs of protesters in an attempt to talk over the din of the crowd. She could see a huge bonfire in the foreground dwarfed by the Dresden Opera House. German flags fluttered, and then the camera zoomed in on the blue and white decals of a Saxony State Police cruiser burning as the crowd danced.

Then the camera shifted to a different location and a different reporter. The lens focused on an immense crowd of anti-immigration marchers that vastly outnumbered the much fewer pro-immigration supporters. They were forcing their way into the Neumarkt towards the Church of Our Lady. The riot police, clad in their Kevlar armor and helmets, held the line as the mob grew more boisterous. It chanted, waved, and threatened. Then the police began to reposition the mobile barriers and water cannons. From the rear of the anti-immigration crowd several flaming bottles arced over the police line. The Molotov cocktails shattered in the square, the pieces of the fuel-soaked glass bursting into flames.

"How many?" asked Gerhardt.

Nora held a finger in the air as she absorbed the content of the reporting. A few seconds later she jumped in the air, excited, with an expression of deep satisfaction etched across her face. "Thirty thousand!"

"Really," replied Gerhardt. He was surprised at the number. "*That* many?"

"Ja!" She crossed the room in a few quick steps and hugged him in a moment of elation. "You did this Gerhardt. *You.*" Then she aggressively stuck her tongue in his ear and whispered, "I am going to do things to you."

Nora grabbed his wrist and led him into the bedroom.

Chapter 12

Irvine, California

Evie dialed the memorized number and listened patiently as the telephone rang. A male voice with a pronounced accent answered. "Hello?"

"Baba," said Evie in a quiet voice. "I got your message, you sounded concerned."

"Are you okay?" asked her father.

"Yes of course, I just got home."

"Home," said her father in an incredulous tone. "It must be midnight on the east coast."

"I worked late. I have a new job."

"You left the government?"

"No, Baba, it's like a promotion, but it's the same place."

"Havva," said the father, lowering his voice to a whisper. "You don't need to make more money. I will pay you to run my store. Come back to California."

"Baba," replied Evie, she continued to use the informal term of endearment for 'father', just as he used her formal name, Havva. "It's not the same. I can't explain, but this is important work."

"Yes, yes, yes," replied the father in a pique. "They are all parasites." Twenty seconds elapsed and they slid into a quiet pause over the phone. Finally, the father spoke. "Have you met anyone, Havva?"

"No, Baba," said Evie in a whisper.

"Why not? You are such a beautiful girl. Are the men in Washington all blind?"

"No," said Evie with a laugh, "but I am so busy, I rarely meet anyone."

"You need a different job."

"I just changed my job."

"It sounds like the same thing," said her father with a deep sigh. "So many Persians here would love to meet a beautiful, educated woman from Tehran."

"Baba, I am from Irvine."

"And you should be *here* to meet all the successful men I know."

"Baba…"

"Okay," answered the father in frustration. He paused before adding, "your mother's anniversary is in a few weeks. I will buy tickets and mail them to you."

"I have money. I'll get my own tickets—but thank you."

The conversation lulled before Evie asked, "Are you watching your diet?"

"Yes," answered the father in a bored voice. "I eat vegetables every meal…can you stay a few days when you come?"

"I hope so, let me check."

"Surely you have vacation saved."

"Yes, Baba, but its more about the assignment. There are people counting on me to be available."

"Havva…"

"I know, Baba. Give me a little time. I will call you as soon as I have a clearer picture."

"Be careful, all those hush-hush people…too many secrets…"

"I love you, Baba. I will call."

The telephone disconnected.

***

Berlin, Germany

They sat for thirty minutes at a restaurant in Kreuzberg. Terry was being tested. He knew he was being tested, and they knew, that he knew, that it was all a test.

The goal, of course, was to determine if he was who he said he was, and if so, could he be recruited.

The difficulty was the two competing sides in the probe. One was the extremist elements of radical Islam that wished to draw everyone into their dark world, to rain death and destruction down on the West. The second side was the undercover elements of the BfV, the domestic security agency that regularly infiltrated the mosques with agents to collect information on plans to attack inside Germany.

Terry was a 'new' migrant, recently arrived from Istanbul, seeking work and stability for himself and his family back in Turkey. Or so he appeared. The difficulty, was that no one trusted anyone. The Turks feared the German domestic security agency, and the Germans feared the Turkish migrants that targeted their country for a terrorist attack. Either side could be sponsoring the new arrival.

"I heard that you arrived from Turkey," said the Muslim. "Why here?"

Terry shrugged. "Germany has a long history of welcoming Turks to their country. Everyone in Istanbul knows the stories of the guest-worker programs offered by Germany after the Second World War."

"And you lived in Istanbul?"

"Yes." Terry reached forward and sipped some tea. He knew that the Agency had backstopped his cover with multiple layers. Any checks would confirm the same.

"Are things settling down?"

"Slowly," answered Solak. "Many people are still out of work. Many others are under arrest. It has led to a great feeling of uncertainty."

"And you?" asked the interviewer leaning forward at the table.

"I lost my job at a restaurant in Bebek when the owner had to hire his out-of-work cousin."

"Why?"

"The cousin had been forced from his position at a newspaper when the government demanded its closure."

The interviewer remained expressionless as he considered Terry's responses. He was a trained interrogator; calm, thoughtful, easy to like, and he spoke excellent Turkish. It all appeared routine and collegial.

"How do you feel about the president?"

"In Ankara?" asked Terry.

The interviewer nodded.

This was the planted question to assess tendencies. The current president of Turkey had a controversial reputation. He demonstrated dictatorial attributes in his administration as well as Islamic sympathies. Many believed he wanted to restore the caliphate in Turkey, the home of the Ottoman Empire.

"I am sensitive to Islam being respected throughout the world," answered Terry. "I believe that if the Dar al-Harb is upon us, if the return of the caliphate is possible, then we need a stable platform in Turkey in which to receive it."

The interviewer sat back in his chair and permitted himself a smile. Then he motioned to the waiter for more tea.

Terry had baited the hook with a noncommittal answer that could be interpreted several ways. The interviewer would hear what he wanted to hear. There was a method to Solak's words. He cracked the door open far enough so that they could risk making the next move.

Chapter 13

Berlin, Germany

Frau Steir of the chancellor's office waited patiently at the Goethe Monument in the Tiergarten. The events of the last few weeks had put everyone on edge. First the assassinations of a lone European Union employee at each of three different locations, followed by a beer tent bombing in Stuttgart, and now a massive riot in Dresden. The emotional tide was turning, and the powers in government were no closer to ferreting out the perpetrators of the crimes than when it all began.

"Frau Steir," said the VP of the domestic security agency in a clipped voice.

"Any news?" she asked with a half turn.

"Nothing definitive. We have our best people working on the problem. We can verify with certainty that the speaker is *not* Hitler, but even the engineers agree that the voice bears an uncanny resemblance to him."

"Well of course it's not him. He would have to be over a hundred and twenty years old."

"But," replied the VP adding to his explanation, "the scientists could not rule-out a physiological connection."

"What?"

"A relative," answered the VP. "Someone who shared a partial DNA match to the original speaker."

"A family member?"

"Perhaps. Voice analysis can measure the vocal folds and the laryngeal musculature that controls them. I have pressed our technicians on voice biometrics. There are acoustic patterns in both anatomy and learned behavioral patterns."

"What does all this mean?"

The VP shrugged. "It means that much can be taught through training and practice—right down to the style of delivery and the ability to change or modify accents. Even to the way the speaker rolls his 'r' in the Bavarian fashion."

"The German speeches are all posted from Munich," said Steir with a frown.

"Yes," said the VP, "and I'm also told that speaker diarization identifies when the *same* speaker is making an address."

Steir paused to consider his words before changing topics. "The riot in Dresden started as a typical joint demonstration. It was peaceful, a Monday night candle vigil by groups who have shown no propensity towards violence...what happened?"

"The visitors arrived by the busload," said the VP. "They joined the peaceful protesters and there were neo-Nazis amongst them. The mobs grew and the right wing extremists agitated the crowd. They overwhelmed the police."

"The question that the chancellor will ask is: did they see an opportunity and take advantage of events *or* was that their plan all along?"

The VP shrugged but did not speak.

"We are shifting from criminal acts, to Islamic terrorists, to right wing extremists very quickly," said Steir.

"Ja," said the VP in agreement.

"I feel our country slipping," said Steir. She fixed the VP with a steady gaze, turned, and walked away.

***

Berlin, Germany

Terry felt submerged under layers of darkness. He lay motionless, scanning the room as he controlled his breath, letting his eyes rotate around the bed in a counter-clockwise fashion. Blurred images seemed to move in the shadowy netherworld that filled the blackened corners.

A brisk motion and Solak felt a sharp pain in his back. He gasped, thrusting upward, swinging his right arm in a swift blow as the stiletto withdrew and quickly struck again.

His instincts were to fight, to survive, but he couldn't identify the wave of unseen attackers. They hid in the shadows. In a desperate move Terry flung his body upwards. It catapulted him from the bed, into the air, before he crashed on the floor with a thud. The landing jarred him awake. Thick beads of perspiration soaked his neck and rivulets of sweat curled down his chin. It was the dream again.

The dream, a nightmare actually, had plagued Solak since the Paris operation of three years earlier. It had left him feeling helpless. The idea of being caught off guard haunted Terry. Not the fear of dying so much, but more the fear of dying without a fight. *How* he died, mattered.

Solak refocused on the small room as his mind cleared. Like all Schengen immigrants, Terry was granted temporary housing, food, medical attention, schooling, and a monthly stipend of cash for basic needs. This was Terry living his cover as he probed the Turkish community in Berlin. They were flying blind. In the absence of stronger leads, they were playing the odds. Turks were by far the dominant ethnic minority group in Germany. In addition, people of Turkish descent were overwhelmingly Muslim. It started with the broadest possible net, trying to catch someone's attention, hoping for a break that would open a door for deeper analysis.

Terry twisted and checked his back for knife wounds. There were none. Then he stood, and took a minute to look around the small area to assure he was alone. He sat on the bed and closed his eyes. He knew he needed rest, but he was afraid to disengage. Dreams.

Chapter 14

Berlin, Germany

The mood in the conference room was somber. The members of the group were feeling the pressure. They didn't know if a shifting, events-driven, pre-election inertia had taken control of their country, or if they confronted a deep state scenario where unseen hands pulled levers in a pre-determined direction.

The VP of the domestic security agency called the meeting to order and began to update the attendees on the video with voice-over narration.

"We all saw the video. The similarity in the speech was unmistakable. Our experts agree that there was professional training."

The foreign intelligence service delegate spoke. "Our contacts in Austria confirm the obvious: that the three-story structure in Braunau is, in fact, the house where Adolf Hitler was born. As many of you know, the property was seized by the Austrian government following disputes with the owner. The issue is before their highest court."

Director Geiger of the federal police raised his hand over the conference table. "And while their courts debate the issue, the site has become a place of pilgrimage for neo-Nazis. They use it to glorify their extreme ideology."

"It was a prop," said Frau Steir. "A means to introduce the speaker and to tie his narration to the past."

"And it worked," replied Geiger. "Look at the size of the crowd."

"It was Dresden," said the VP, "the valley of the clueless."

"Ja," answered Geiger in an elevated tone. "Dresden is different, but you cannot dismiss out of hand the obvious."

"Which is what?" asked Frau Steir.

Geiger took a moment to look around the long conference table. He stood and focused on Steir before speaking in a quiet voice. "Maybe Frau Chancellor is wrong."

A murmur emanated from the other members in the room. The three-term elected leader of Germany was not only a force at home, but also throughout the European Union and the world.

"What are you suggesting?" asked the VP in a snarly tone.

Geiger turned on the VP with a venomous demeanor. "I am suggesting, that our chancellor is a politician, and there is an important general election in a few months."

"Do you believe, Herr Director, that our chancellor would subvert the needs of our nation to the needs of her party?"

"I am saying that the expediency of the moment can cloud one's vision. It is easy to dismiss—out of hand—the size of the crowd because it was Dresden, but that would be a mistake. There were similar anti-immigrant protests in several other states and in Sweden, Austria, and Switzerland. The video played a role as a catalyst to help mobilize the crowds. The internet is a tool; the Hitler voice and birthplace symbolic: people descended on Dresden by buses, autos, trains, and foot from multiple locations."

"Foreign nationals as well?" asked the VP.

"Ja," answered Geiger. "Professional provocateurs, financed by outside sources. The problem is the Schengen asylum rules."

"The chancellor," said Steir, "feels very strongly about our need to lead the EU in this matter."

"As I said," continued Geiger in a quiet voice while remaining erect, "maybe the chancellor is *wrong*…the enemy is *not* the Pied Piper of Hamelin, reincarnated as the embodiment of Adolf Hitler. It is our own failure to enforce *real* border controls, obligatory integration programs, and strict asylum accountability. If we don't act *now* the participation will grow. We must speed up the deportation process and permit the federal police to immediately restore border control tasking on *all* borders."

Geiger sat back down and folded his hands together on the table.

***

Munich, Germany

The apartment was modest by Bavarian standards; small, unobtrusive, out of the way, tucked into a quiet corner of Schwabing, just beyond the Englischer Garten.

A white-haired lady fidgeted with the tulips in the window boxes of the apartment; she watered, then fertilized and pruned, allowing the seasonal warmth to coddle her flowers.

Frau Fuchs was spry in appearance, not tall, but erect, moving with a sureness that belied her seventy-plus years. Her telephone rang, and for a moment she hesitated, debating in silence whether to answer the landline. Then she turned from the open shutters and picked up the phone.

"Call G," said the mechanical voice message.

The woman turned, wiped her hands on a kitchen towel and reached into a drawer under her carving station. Frau Fuchs pulled out a burner cell phone. Then she walked into the living room and dialed a memorized number.

"Ja," answered the familiar voice in German.

"Gerhardt," said Fuchs in a quiet voice.

"Mutti, did you see the news?"

"Yes, it is wonderful, and now the success of Dresden will grow. They are spreading our message by their reporting. Pieces of the video with your speech have gone viral on the internet, and everyone wants to know *who* is the man behind the voice."

"When do we show them, Mutti?"

"Patience, Gerhardt, we do not want to reveal too early…the elections are still three months away. Discipline. Do you understand?"

"Ja," said Gerhardt with an expulsion of air.

A quiet lull passed between them before Frau Fuchs asked, "How is Nora?"

"She is well, Mutti, but very busy." His voice was despondent. She could tell he was lonely.

"Nora is a *good* woman Gerhardt, please give her my regards."

"I will."

After a pause, Fuchs said, "We should stop now, it isn't safe."

"Ja, Mutti."

She sensed the disappointment in his voice. He clearly wanted to talk. "I am so proud of you, Gerhardt. Stay strong. Just a little longer." Fuchs disconnected the telephone before he could respond.

Chapter 15

Berlin, Germany

Terry walked the streets of Kreuzberg, the location of his new home. He continued to memorize various trip points, absorbed with the sights, sounds, and smells of the Turkish quarter.

His initial immersion into the Muslim neighborhood several weeks earlier began with a trek through the south-eastern section of the borough known as 'Little Istanbul.' Since then, he had made multiple prayer visits to several mosques, spreading the glue, acting the part of devout believer, trying to penetrate the veil of trust in an abbreviated timeframe.

Everywhere Terry looked he saw street art, from tiny, colorful graffiti to building-size wall murals. For just as Kreuzberg wore the bohemian mantle for nonconformist Berlin, it was also a breeding ground for left wing politics—including Islamic fundamentalism.

Solak turned at Maybachufer and entered the Turkish Market. He threaded between several sidewalk tables decorated with posters of Turkish pop stars and multiple kebab stalls. Turkish hip-hop music played in the background. He pulled out a cell phone and dialed a coded number.

"This is Evie."

"This is Helios," said Terry.

She quickly sat and scanned the computer screens in her cubicle. Evie never knew when he would call, and therefore she wanted to assure that nothing important was missed. "Go ahead."

"One, I have had three meetings since my immersion. I documented everything in a sitrep, and loaded the primary drop. It was serviced and unloaded. You need to assure that the sitrep gets to Langley from Berlin Station." Solak's use of the term sitrep was shorthand for a situation report, a more detailed dump of information.

"Got it," said Evie, scribbling on a legal pad as he spoke.

"Two, I have not, repeat *not*, been approached by the interviewers. The discussions have been very defensive."

"No attempt to recruit you?"

"None," answered Terry as he side-stepped a fruit stand in the outdoor market. "They are on edge."

"The attacks," said Evie, "have caused an anti-immigrant backlash. There are general elections in a few months. Many politicians are getting vocal."

"Still, something doesn't feel right," said Terry. "They act like they are being set up."

"Can you give me an example?"

"They mentioned the armbands."

"Yes," replied Evie, "I think it's an anomaly. They resemble Islamic symbols, but they are *not* Islamic symbols."

"And the goal?" asked Solak.

"Not sure," said Evie, "but the videos that follow the attacks are all posted from Istanbul. In addition, the unseen narrator speaks in standard Arabic."

"Do the videos *show* the attacks?"

"Only the aftereffects. They do not show the murders, only the corpses— and there is no attribution; no claim of responsibility, just a reference to the Dar al-Harb."

"The House of War," replied Terry.

"Yes, it's odd, as I said, an anomaly."

"Okay," said Solak. There was a pause before he added, "get over to the German desk and see what their read is on the Dresden riots."

"Okay," said Evie as she continued to jot notes on the legal pad.

"And get their take on the Hitler sound-alike. It's quite the buzz over here."

"Will do," responded Evie.

They fell into a quiet moment for a few seconds before Terry said, "I'm on the clock. I have to run," and the line disconnected.

Evie clicked off her headset and sat back. She knew that Terry's parting thought referred to operational security. He was using a burner cell phone to communicate. This was necessitated by the risks of infiltrating under deep cover while possessing weapons, burst transmission devices, and one-time cipher pads. Solak expected to be searched, and carrying specialized equipment would expose his cover, and threaten his life. The only reasonable alternative was an international burner cell phone that he could discard at will. The risk was staying 'on air' long enough for an experienced surveillance team to pick up on his call through their counter measures.

As Terry exited the Turkish Market, he approached a five-story building with a worn, wooden door on Graefestraße. He keyed the lock and mounted the rickety stairs that led to the third-floor walkup in the rear.

Then he entered his one room studio and confronted four men sitting in his apartment.

***

Berlin, Germany

Three of the men jumped to their feet as the door opened. The one on the right made an aggressive step forward and Terry reacted. He snapped from the hip with a short, hard chop that caught the man flush in the face. The intruder went down.

Instantly Terry threw his shoulder against the partially opened door, and slammed the wooden barrier against the man on the left. A muffled groan and Solak was already attacking the man in the middle. He used a series of clawed fingers to the face and low kicks to the shins to cause pain and confuse the intruder. The man immediately stopped and backed away into a defensive posture.

There were broken bones and blood as the intruders tried to regroup, when the oldest man, seeing the carnage inflicted on his young associates, held up a hand and yelled: "Enough!"

Everyone in the room paused as Terry's eyes shifted from side to side, waiting for the next reaction. There was none.

It was the classic mistake of judgment. The intruders, confident in their superior numbers, expected Terry to flee, huddle backwards, or engage in nervous dialogue. Instead, he attacked.

The old man, still seated across the room, swept his arm sideways and motioned for the three younger men to cease their aggressive behavior. He waved them to the far side of the studio apartment so that Terry could sit and face him directly, while still watching the others. "Please forgive my associates," said the older man, "the exuberance of youth." He gestured towards an empty chair.

Terry nodded, but kept a suspicious eye on the three wounded intruders. He also continued to stand. The older man sighed before asking in a quiet voice, "Where did you learn to fight?"

"The streets," said Solak. "My father died when I was young."

It was a lie, but it helped explain Terry's obvious skill at hand to hand combat.

"They call you Tuncay," said the old man, using Solak's Turkish first name, which few knew and he rarely used.

"Yes."

"You traveled here from Istanbul?"

"Yes...what is *your* name?"

"They address me as Maulana," said the older man as he stroked his beard. "I have the privilege to be an imam at the Dar as-Salaam mosque in Neukölln."

Terry knew that the term 'maulana' was an honorific title bestowed on prominent Islamic scholars. He had not visited this particular mosque, but it seemed that curiosity of him, of the new migrant, had spread. It signaled that he was penetrating deeper under their veil of secrecy.

Solak scanned the room and noted several clues that the intruders had performed a quick but thorough search of his possessions. He kept the aggressive posture. "With respect, Maulana, you are in my room with strangers, and I do not remember extending an invitation."

The imam stared hard at Terry. He knew he had intruded into Solak's personal space without permission, and yet he was unprepared for the chastisement.

Solak had quickly calculated that to be too pliable, too permissible to inappropriate behavior, suggested someone too willing to be recruited—and therefore most probably a deep cover operator seeking to penetrate a cell. By acting disinterested and offended by their intrusion, Terry in fact deepened their interest.

"Perhaps," said the imam, "we can try again."

For a moment, Solak said nothing. Then in a conciliatory tone he offered: "Each day, I pray in a mosque. Perhaps this Friday I will join you for Jumah in Neukölln." Terry had referenced the special prayer session held each Friday by Muslims.

"It would be our privilege, Tuncay."

The older man stood and motioned across the room at his three associates. They gathered together in a circle, still nursing their wounds. There was a mumbled conversation and then, with a wary eye on Terry, the four men exited.

Summer 2017

Chapter 16

Munich, Germany

Gerhardt's mother sat at an oval table in an apartment across town, sipping tea, and waiting for the other two women to finish their whispered conversation.

"It is settled," said the woman on Fuchs' left. She gestured. "I will make the arrangements." She stood and walked to the far side of the room while tugging out her cell phone.

"Thank you for your patience, Frau Fuchs," said the younger woman to the mother's right. "I am afraid these precautions are necessary."

"I understand," replied Fuchs as she sipped at her tea. "But, of course, my son will ask, and I need to have an answer for him."

"Ja," answered the younger woman. She leaned forward, closer to Fuchs, and whispered as if they were not alone. "We received a call from Berlin. There are two busloads of asylum seekers who have been processed and the government is transporting them from the induction centers to Bayreuth."

"When?" asked Fuchs.

"In two days' time," said the younger woman. "Under cover of darkness. They are sneaking them into a hostel that was prepared for resettlement. The town folk do not know—only the mayor."

"How reliable is the information?"

"Our contact works at the Federal Office for Migration and Refugees. She confirmed the dates and times."

Fuchs nodded before asking, "Are we planning an intercept?"

"Ja, it is important to see how quickly we can mobilize our supporters in a short window."

"Wunsiedel is nearby…"

"Ja," said the younger woman. "Our tactician studied the available routes. He said that the federal three-oh-three runs two kilometers south of Wunsiedel. It joins the A-nine motorway from Berlin to Munich, near Bad Berneck."

"Wunsiedel could work very well."

"Ja," replied the apartment owner. "This is a test of our pipeline."

"Is it time to introduce our new colors?" asked Gerhardt's mother.

"We think so," said the younger woman to Frau Fuchs, "do you agree?"

"Maybe...let me give it some thought."

The apartment owner turned in her seat. "I thought you would be in favor."

"I am, but we have waited so long, that I just want to be sure."

"Why the hesitancy now?" asked the younger woman.

Gerhardt's mother sat up straight and said, "I have learned, over the years, that it is better to play your cards well, than it is to play them fast."

***

Bayreuth, Germany

The two yellow school buses drove in tandem as they carried sixty-four men, women, and children in a midnight relocation from Berlin. Two federal police cruisers provided an escort, bracketing the buses to the front and rear, creating a four-vehicle single file line along the inside lane on the A9 autobahn. Thus far, the low-profile, semi-disguised, late-night migrant resettlement had proven uneventful. Things changed quickly.

They came from all directions, using every mode of public and private transportation, descending on the Exit 42 interchange as a mass of cars, vans, trucks, and buses. Crowds of pedestrians carrying signs clogged the off-ramp just as the sparse vehicular traffic slowed.

The lead police cruiser stopped as several trucks braked to a halt and angled sideways blocking the road. Immediately tail vans hemmed in the rear and closed the highway ramp to additional traffic. The convoy was trapped. Railroad flares were lit, and strategically placed to either side of the exit ramp.

The crowd, which started with a handful of sign-carrying protesters, grew to dozens of loud and exuberant youth. Inside the buses, men yelled and children cried. The crowd carried sticks which they put to use by pounding on the metal flanks of the yellow buses. Eggs and fruit flew through the air, smashing on the windows. Women screamed.

The federal police realized the migrants were in danger. They exited their cruisers and bulled their way through the crowd, pushing and shoving the ten

54

meters distance to the buses, taking up position outside and assuring that the mob could not enter the yellow transports to harm the occupants.

The protesters ballooned to a hundred and they appeared to be well organized. Several rough-looking men carrying sticks and wearing a red armband emblazoned with a white circle entered the fray. They pounded on the buses, smashing windows, painting graffiti, and splintering the glass into a cracked spider web of crooked lines. They chanted in German, "Immigrants go home, Germany is for Germans."

The mob started to tear apart the unprotected police cruisers, first stripping the cars of valuables and electronics, and then damaging the autos to render them useless.

To add an exclamation point, the men wearing the armbands tossed flaming Molotov cocktails into each of the open cruisers. Bonfires erupted.

Helicopters buzzed overhead as both police reinforcements and television news crews descended on the exit ramp. More people arrived. The crowds that surrounded the buses started to rock the yellow vehicles side to side, threatening to tip the occupied transports over.

The migrants began to panic and traffic at the highway intersection ground to a halt. More pedestrians streamed to the scene. There were now several thousand protesters in the mob. Threading their way through the crowd were the men and women with the armbands. They were shouting and pointing. They seemed to be directing the attacks against the buses.

In minutes, the four federal police were overwhelmed and dragged from their position outside the bus doors. The mob pulled the police deeper into the frenzy, kicking and stomping, as crow bars were produced. Then the bars were thrust between the accordion-like door frames and the entrances to the buses were pried open.

Chapter 17

Berlin, Germany

The VP of the domestic security agency made his way through the Tiergarten towards the Goethe Monument. He walked with a pronounced limp.

Frau Steir of the chancellor's office was already waiting, a deep furrow etched in her brow. "Are you injured?" she asked.

"Arthritis," answered the VP. "It flares up a couple of times each year depending upon the humidity or the rain."

Steir nodded, accepting the explanation without further comment. Her focus was squarely on current events. "The Bayreuth migrant transfer was a disaster," she said.

The VP twitched. There was an element of edge in his tone. "Was this not under Herr Director Geiger's responsibility?"

"Ja," said Steir, "but of course he suggests that there were too many hands in the kitchen. The time and place of the transfer were designated and controlled by others. Geiger further stipulates that using four police officers in two cars would not provide sufficient escort had he suspected any en route transfer issues."

"Of course not," said the VP with a sarcastic attitude, "and therefore he points the finger of blame elsewhere."

"At you," said Steir. She turned to face the VP. "Geiger was very vocal in pointing out that it is the responsibility of the BfV to predict and warn the government of these risks."

The VP swallowed before asking, "And what responsibility, Frau Steir, does the chancellor's office bear in this?"

She gave the VP a stern look before saying, "Don't go there, Herr Vice President. The chancellor is very much committed to leading the EU on the Schengen issue, and she has a fifteen-point lead in the polls."

The VP turned and faced Steir with a grimace. "Her position is tearing apart the republic. It is too much, too fast. There is no integration, and we are putting our citizens at risk."

"Now you sound like Geiger," said Steir. "He is ready to deploy his army of federal police to the four corners of Germany, and to start dragging every migrant back to the border." She paused for a moment to let the VP digest her words, and then added, "Fascism."

"What do you suggest," asked the VP.

Steir whispered, "I fear we have a leak; someone informed, someone who was aware of the migrant transfer process and the specific logistics for the Bayreuth resettlement. It was hardly an 'open' event."

The VP bit his lip as he pondered her statement. "That would suggest someone in our group."

"Ja," replied Steir, "it is rather disconcerting. Someone with knowledge but who is also sensitive to the emotional urge that exists in places like Bayreuth and Wunsiedel."

***

Berlin, Germany

Gerhardt looked at Nora, hiding his anticipation, waiting for her critique. The speeches were a laborious process, yet so very important. If done correctly, they pulled the listener into the discussions; crafting an outline, laying out a pattern of concern, suggesting important fundamental themes, and then offering corrective solutions. The speeches culminated in an emotional call to action.

Nora stopped the dictation machine, reversed the tape, and then played it aloud for both of them to hear. Some of the words were selected, quite intentionally, from the Beer Hall Putsch speech of November 1923. "…until the criminals have been overthrown…until we have risen once more, a Germany of power and greatness, of freedom and splendor."

The similarity in speech was uncanny; the sound and timbre of the voice quite remarkable. The twelve-minute voice-over recording would be merged with preselected footage of the Dresden riots and the Bayreuth bus attacks. These would be spliced together with recordings of EU delegates spending lavishly. Finally, the video would showcase several different Islamic-inspired terrorist incidents in neighboring countries, and then each host nation's death toll.

"It is remarkable, Gerhardt," said the blonde. "I will call the courier to transport the audio down to Munich."

"How long will it take?"

"Maybe a day, two at the most."

"Then it will hit the internet?"

"Ja," said Nora with a smile. She stood and reached out for Gerhardt's hand. Then she took his fingers in her mouth and seductively started to lick them, one by one.

Gerhardt's eyes rolled back and his breath started to shorten. Then he stood and followed Nora from the room.

Chapter 18

Langley, Virginia

Evie entered the seventh-floor SCIF and took a seat at the conference table. A minute later the Director entered the room, followed by the deputy directors for Analysis and the National Clandestine Service.

"Let's get started," said the Director. Within seconds the electronic insulation and countermeasures were activated and the room sealed. He held up a hand, "Where's Colman?"

"He got pulled away at the last minute," said Arthur Kent. "Something hot broke in Pakistan."

The Director frowned. "I wanted his take on the German situation."

"Yes, Director," replied Kent. He touched the knot on his club tie. "Bob briefed me on the SAD efforts to date. I will be able to cover his portion of the briefing."

The Director nodded at the NCS deputy directory. "Go ahead."

The screen slid down from the ceiling and a twelve-minute video showed various scenes of rioters in Dresden, and then the bus attacks in Bayreuth—all timed so that the speech, which started as a German news narrative, became a political rally. The Director caught the nuances in the speaker's voice and noted the armbands displayed on several of the protesters. The video finished and the lights turned back on.

"I feel like this is all a repeat," said the Director, "of two years ago when the EU first opened the Schengen doors."

"Except that general elections are coming," said Kent.

"Yes," said the Director, "in late September. My question would be, *why* attack EU delegates?"

"Because," said the deputy director for Analysis, "to attack the EU delegates in Germany, is to attack the EU's strongest member at home."

"Is all the anti-immigrant protesting focused on the Muslim migrants?"

"Yes, Director," said Kent. "There is a powerful anti-immigrant backlash taking place, but the Muslim population is bearing the brunt. The demonstrators see the European Union as the cause of the Schengen border rules. To disrupt Schengen is to slow the migration pattern, and by so doing, stop the terrorism."

"I understand," said the Director, "ISIS and other radical groups are planning attacks and encouraging lone wolfs, but are we convinced that it is the *Islamists* that are attacking EU delegates?"

"Yes," said Kent without hesitation.

"No," replied Evie in a quiet voice.

Arthur Kent gave Evie a very stern look across the conference table. It was the kind of glare that asserted one's position without words.

The Director looked at Kent and then Evie. He motioned towards Kent.

"First," said Arthur, "we have the brazen aspect to these attacks; not gruesome in the typical ISIS fashion, beheadings and immolation, but flashy in a braggadocio kind of way…slick, showing off, taunting authorities in broad daylight—tactically proficient."

The Director considered Kent's words and then beckoned him to continue.

"Second," said Kent, "we have an armband that is an incomplete flag—white crescent on red backdrop—that resembles both the Turkish flag and the ancient Ottoman Empire flag, home of the last caliphate."

The Director leaned back in his chair and sifted through his file folder. He held up photos of the armbands. Then the Director looked back at Kent and rolled his index finger.

"And third," said Kent, "the Arabic narration that follows each of the EU delegate murders always refers to the Dar al-Harb, the House of War. The Islamists are attacking the EU delegates specifically on German soil, to foment a reaction. They fear a united economic front in the European Union, and a united military front in NATO."

The Director leaned back in his chair and let his eyes settle on Evie. She sat at the conference table with her hands folded. "Well," said the Director, "as is often the case in our world, opinions vary. Some of us think that the attacks on the EU delegates are Islamic inspired—even though their pattern of provocation is different. Could a group be evolving?" The Director asked the final question in a rhetorical way.

He sat forward as his attention focused on the young collection manager. "You are over at SAD now Evie, correct?"

"Yes, Director."

"And your boss is not here; but I wonder, you are a Muslim…do you have any thoughts that might add some clarity?"

Evie swallowed. She was not one to pick a political fight with Arthur Kent, her boss' boss, a senior officer. She hesitated for a moment, and then said in a nervous voice, "Actually, Director, I do."

***

Berlin, Germany

Terry entered the meeting room at the rear of the Dar as-Salaam mosque in Neukölln and paused. Ten men sat gathered in a circle, shoeless, and sipping tea. For a moment he questioned the wisdom of accepting their invitation to join them following Jumah, the special prayer session reserved for Friday, the Muslim holy day. Then he relaxed as he realized the mosque itself would not be the site of a bloody interrogation. Solak recognized the older maulana from his apartment. The man smiled and motioned for him to join their group. Terry removed his shoes and sat cross-legged in the open space on the rug.

Religious rituals and cultural courtesies came easy to Terry. Born in Paterson, New Jersey a first generation American of Turkish and Scottish descent, he was raised with equal parts Islam and Christianity. The truth was, his family was not particularly religious, and although Terry spent some Fridays at the mosque and some Sundays at the Presbyterian Church, his psych never filled with any fervor.

The group around the circle were serious looking men, elders to the mosque, and as Terry soon learned they were very concerned with both their status in the local Turkish community, as well as the larger demographic of Berlin.

"Please, Tuncay," said the maulana. He gestured with an open hand for Solak to accept some tea. Then he continued, "It is our pleasure that you accepted my invitation. I have explained to these men how we first met, and the unfortunate incident that ensued. May I take your presence here as forgiveness of our intrusion?"

Terry looked around the circle and met each man's eyes before speaking, "As Allah the merciful is my judge, I assure you that the incident is forgotten."

61

A smile broke across the maulana's face. "You are very respectful for a young man, and for this reason, we would like to share with you an explanation, as you are new to Berlin."

Terry nodded as he sipped tea.

"The history of Turkey and Germany is a long and at times contentious one," said the maulana. "It goes back decades. Some times have been more difficult than others…of late, there are many concerns that exist between our homeland and this, our new home."

Solak remained silent and allowed the maulana to lecture him on the current state of affairs. The slant of the monologue would expose the speaker's bias.

"Both Turkey and Germany are democracies. As you know, Ankara held a national referendum this past April. It was very controversial and created an executive presidency in Turkey. Now, in three months' time, Germany will have a general election. There is much at stake, to include the status of Muslims in this country."

"And you fear that this upcoming election will affect our status?"

"We fear," said the maulana, "that there are forces in play that seek to cast blame on migrants. Muslims are by far the dominant religion of these new immigrants seeking asylum—and Turks are heavily represented by a wide percentage within the Islamic minority. *We* are a target."

Chapter 19

Langley, Virginia

From the beginning, Evie sensed that the cross-current of unrelated clues were, in fact, related. Her goal now was to offer a different interpretation, hopefully one that didn't directly refute Arthur Kent's position.

She leaned forward and cleared her throat. "I believe, Director, that deputy Kent is correct in his assessment of an Islamic signature, but…" she paused as she thought about her wording, "…my instinct also tells me that the perpetrators of the attacks intentionally left the footprint open, so that *we* would see, what *we* wanted to see."

The Director leaned forward. "Can you give us an example?"

Evie stroked at her hijab, and pulled the veil back from her face. She opened her file. Then she tugged at several colored photographs and pointed. "Note the armbands from each attack: Hamburg, Frankfurt, Munich, and Stuttgart, all against EU employees, but targeted in Germany." She paused. "A white crescent on a red background. *Almost* an Ottoman flag, home of the last caliphate. *Almost* a current flag of Turkey. In either case the same, but neither is complete without the addition of the white star."

"So, to your point?" asked Arthur Kent.

"No one came forward to take credit, and there is no one to blame."

"What about the Arabic videos following each attack?" asked the Director.

"Suggestive, but again, *no* attribution; and ISIS craves credit, it serves their recruiting needs."

"So Ankara has complete deniability."

"Tensions between Turkey and Germany are high. We are left with an Islamic footprint," said Evie, "but one that is incomplete. We read into the clue and we *see* what we fear."

Everyone paused to let the information settle. It was disconcerting to have evidence that did not fit, as so much in the world of intelligence was developed conjecture.

Evie then passed around colored photographs of the armbands worn at the Bayreuth bus attacks. "Note these," she said. "The white circle on the red backdrop. What is it missing?"

The deputy director for Analysis sat forward and studied the photographs. A few minutes elapsed before Evie offered an answer. "In the migrant bus transfer to Bayreuth, the *Muslims* were attacked. The most visible protesters wore this armband." She pointed at the photos.

The Director shook his head and sat back in his seat. He took the opportunity to cross his legs at the knee. "So, tell us, Evie."

"A Hakenkreuz." She plucked the final photo from her file, a black swastika, centered on a white circle, on a red backdrop. It was the universal symbol of the Nazi Party.

"To what end?" asked Kent. "Why would the neo-Nazis perpetrate these actions and then leave us disjointed clues? The Nazis are thugs, but not subtle."

"Yes, Evie," said the Director, "they are not known for keeping a low profile."

"The publicity," replied Evie, "was the selection of the sites. Dresden is a hotbed of latent dissent. It holds a collective grudge going back to the reunification of Germany twenty-five years ago. A vein of right wing extremism exists."

"And Bayreuth?" asked Kent.

"The home of Richard Wagner, Hitler's favorite composer."

The Director leaned forward with a spark in his eye—he was intrigued. "And Wunsiedel?" he asked.

Evie turned in her chair. "The hometown of Rudolf Hess, Hitler's deputy Fuhrer. The number three man in the hierarchy after Hitler and Goring."

The deputy director for Analysis considered her speculations before asking, "Evie, why would a neo-Nazi group go to such efforts and *not* seek credit?"

"To buy time," replied Evie with a touch of sureness. "They are using secure locations to test the appetite. The clues—anomalies—send a message, but the infrastructure is still protected as they build their organization. The anomalies tie up our personnel, our focus, and our resources. They feed our suspicions. We are propelled by our own concerns. Somehow there is a connection between the EU murders and the migrant attacks—and the symbols used for both."

"But you believe that an Islamic signature exists," said Kent.

"Yes," replied Evie. "I believe there are Islamic overtones and that Muslims—either wittingly or not, played a part…" She paused at mid-sentence, and considered her words. "…but I also believe that the Islamic angle is a secondary play. Something deeper is in the works, and there is Nazi involvement."

***

Berlin, Germany

Frau Steir circled the Goethe Monument in the Tiergarten. She waited for her contact, the VP of the domestic security agency, to arrive. Finally, she saw him shuffling in the distance, his gait an uncomfortable hobble. The arthritis seemed to be in full flair-up.

"My apologies on the delay," said the VP as he approached.

"You're still limping."

"Ja."

There was a pause in the conversation before Steir finally said, "We have seven weeks before the general election and the AfD is creeping up in the polls."

"The Alternative for Germany Party is preaching," replied the VP, "that they are the only party sounding the alarm about what they see as an existential threat posed by Muslim immigration. They are extremists."

"Yes," answered Steir, "but at the risk of feeding the fear, I must admit that its pending entry into parliament will mark a turning point for the country."

"Right wing populism has always been a fringe element," said the VP, shifting his stance to offset the leg pain.

"The country is on edge," said Steir. "There is a great feeling of unease, and an undercurrent of distrust. This discontent threatens to unsettle our political system. I worry that we are one incident away from losing major support."

The VP looked at Steir for a moment, and considered the gravitas of her comment. Then he added an unsettling remark. "Yesterday the *voice* posted another speech on the internet."

"Oh?" Steir was surprised.

"The IP address was, again, Munich."

"Can you narrow it down?"

"We are working on it. They are using sophisticated routing methods to cloak their specific location." The VP paused before adding the final point. "As of this morning there were over a million downloads."

"A million? Good god, someone is paying attention," replied Steir. Her expression turned very serious. "Tell me about the speech."

"The same pattern. News releases of EU financial excess mixed with a heavy dose of Muslim immigrant crime. He matched the rhetoric to the scenes on the screen. He even selected and re-used many memorable words and phrases from Hitler's past speeches."

Steir remained quiet for a few minutes before saying, "We have made a decision on the leak. The chancellor needs your help. We are constructing a false narrative in an attempt to expose the responsible party."

"Is that prudent?" asked the VP.

"We can*not* be undermined by any group that seeks to disrupt our government. We must preserve stability."

"Yet the AfD is gaining momentum."

"Yes, and if the chancellor is forced to partner with the Social Democrats in a grand coalition government, then the Alternative for Germany Party would emerge as the largest opposition force in our parliament. We would be pulled to the right."

The VP considered Steir's solution to exposing the leak before nodding. "Let me know what you need," he said in a frustrated tone. Then the VP turned and walked away.

Chapter 20

Berlin, Germany

The Long Night of Museums summer festival was celebrating its twentieth anniversary. The cultural evening was founded in Berlin. It was an annual event to take advantage of seasonal warmth and long daylight hours while also introducing many institutions to potential new patrons. The concept proved so popular, that in two decades' time it expanded to 120 other continental cities.

Two European Union delegates, a man and a woman, exited the EU country representation office on Unter den Linden and turned east. With an air of excitement, they melded into the foot traffic of the late-night crowd. It was nearly midnight and the participants in the anniversary celebration had three more hours to review museums, concerts, street performances, sculptures, and art work—all displayed in unique settings.

The couple planned to take a leisurely stroll along the picturesque boulevard, past Humboldt University, and on to Spree Island. Here they would then decide which of Berlin's famous five museums they would visit on the festive night.

Tailing the EU delegates were three young women in their twenties. Each was dressed in a colorful Muslim abaya dress that covered her torso from neck to ankle. Wrapped around their heads were matching silk hijabs that partially obscured their hair. The women walked in unison, three abreast, their arms interlaced in a Muslim sign of friendship. They whispered in quiet conversation.

Thirty meters ahead, a dance troop began to prepare for a performance in front of the equestrian statue of King Frederick II. The dancers used the broad stone walkway as a stage, gathering their props, and exhibiting feathered costumes and brightly applied makeup.

The EU couple slowed as the show began. They watched as the dancers mixed a combination of modern dance and ballet. The crowd grew as more pedestrians marveled at the dexterity of the performers.

The three Muslim women edged forward, closing the distance between themselves and the EU delegates, assuring that they were positioned directly behind the two Europeans.

Then as the audience bunched together four-deep, a silent signal was passed from across the audience to the far side. A lone, male voice cried out from behind the huge bronze statue, "Allahu Akbar."

People looked across the boulevard, suddenly alert to the danger of the phrase. The man held up both hands, stretching for the sky, chanting even louder as he repeated the haunting words, "*Allahu Akbar.*"

The dance performance stopped and everyone looked around. The crowd focused on the man, when suddenly, the three Muslim women in the crowd unzipped the front of their abaya dresses and removed long, sharp, hunting knives. They plunged the knives into the EU delegates backs, first the man, then the woman, repeatedly stabbing the defenseless couple as people began to scream.

The man chanting the Arabic phrase held up a portable fog horn and gave a loud blast of the compressed air device. The noise jolted the audience and everyone started to run.

Three men emerged from the rear of the crowd. Under the cover of panic, they guided the women attackers to a dark corner in the shadow of the buildings. They kept watch as each of the Muslim women stripped off their dresses and head scarves to reveal European style pants and blouses. Then they dropped several red arm bands emblazoned with white crescents on the ground. The chanting decoy turned and joined the circle. He gathered up the abayas and hijabs and stuffed them in a black bag with the knives. Then he pointed, and each of the three men quickly paired off with one of the Muslim women. The decoy gave a final nod, and the three couples ran towards the anonymity of the mob, quickly blending in, and moving away from the scene of the attack.

***

Langley, Virginia

Evie leaned back in her chair, closed her eyes, and pressed her three middle fingers against her forehead. The most recent terrorist attack in Berlin left her feeling numb. The whole scenario was fraught with contradictions, and yet she knew that, somehow, the answer she sought was right in front of her. The anomalies. There was something she wasn't seeing.

Bob Colman peeked over the side of Evie's cubicle as he walked to his office. He stopped and looked at the former analyst before whispering, "Are you okay?"

She paused, her reverie interrupted, and smiled. "Sorry, I was just thinking."

Bob held her gaze for a moment and then took it upon himself to sit in the empty chair inside her cubicle. Colman was as strong in EQ as he was in IQ. The SAD chief sensed a need, and long ago he learned that people were social beings, and that discussing some things out loud often helped to frame the issue. "So, try me," he said as he folded his hands together.

The relaxed pose caused Evie to sit forward. "I think we are chasing a false flag," she said.

"How so?"

"All the obvious indicators around the attack in Berlin suggest an Islamic signature, but again, there is no attribution."

"No claim of responsibility?"

"None, and just as ISIS is cornered in Syria, just as they *need* fresh recruitment, they are silent."

"Maybe it's not ISIS," said Colman.

"Agreed. It could be a splinter group such as the Taliban, maybe Al-Qaeda."

"The question is," said Bob, "who, and how deep?"

Evie paused before saying, "Deputy Kent feels strongly that Islamists are involved."

Colman shrugged. "Maybe he is wrong."

Evie didn't respond, but instead flipped to a page on her computer. Multiple icons appeared on the screen. Each of them depicted a different portion of the Berlin museum night attack, taken by several closed-circuit surveillance cameras mounted along the Unter den Linden Boulevard.

"Evie," asked Bob in a quiet voice, "before we study these, tell me, what do *you* think?"

"I think," said Evie in a quiet voice, "that someone is replicating a political blueprint from eighty years ago. I think the perpetrators are acting on a template."

Chapter 21

Berlin, Germany

Terry stood in the center of Potsdamer Platz and waited. The busy shopping district, the glass and steel crossroads of Berlin, was filled with restaurants, specialty shops, and theaters. It easily mixed office space, retail establishments, public transportation and automotive traffic. It also created a hide-in-plain-sight anonymity that was hard to replicate.

Solak swiveled his head, casually scanning in every direction until his contact, Otto, entered the plaza from the north. The German foreign intelligence officer made a point to puff on his unlit pipe and then gave a cursory wave with his folded newspaper. Terry nonchalantly touched the red handkerchief wrapped around his neck.

The actions were almost imperceptible to an onlooker, but to the two men this was standard procedure. Each had confirmed that the far recognition signals were accepted. It was safe to proceed.

As Otto strolled past Terry standing in front of the Sony Center, Solak turned left and fell in step beside the German. They never looked at each other, yet they walked in unison. To an observer, they appeared to be strangers that shared a crowded sidewalk.

"Good day, Helios," said the German. "You appear to be holding up well."

Solak shrugged. "Some days are better than others."

The German puffed on his unlit pipe. "I have read the sanitized reports of your probe into our Muslim community. Your efforts are greatly appreciated."

"But…"

Otto permitted himself a sly grin before answering. "…*but* there has been a change in focus."

"To where?" asked Terry.

"Everything is explained, Helios. As before, the flash drive is in the folded newspaper."

They slowed a little to permit threading between pedestrians and window shoppers.

"Whose decision?" asked Solak.

"I don't know, but both sides apparently agree that the change in focus is warranted. You are to call home for verification." Otto handed Terry the folded newspaper. "I'll break here."

Solak didn't respond, but at the next intersection he continued to walk straight ahead as Otto made a sharp turn to the left. They never exchanged a glance.

***

Munich, Germany

Six women sat around the oval table in the small apartment. The owner of the flat spread her hands face down. She seemed to be studying her fingernails. After a short pause she looked up and spoke. "It's time."

"Are we ready?" asked the woman to her right.

"Will the country ever be ready?" said their host. "We have been preparing for this day for decades."

"The populist trend is surging throughout the world," replied the woman to her left. "Look at the American election, Brexit in London, the protest amongst European Union members in France, Austria, and the Netherlands. We are *not* alone. Schengen has opened a dangerous door."

"Ja," said an elderly woman across the table. "There is tremendous resentment throughout Europe. *This* is the time."

A short silence ensued before the host said, "The Nazi-era guilt must stop. The Army is dissatisfied. Several pockets of soldiers have been arrested for plots to assassinate senior politicians. Is it enough?"

"The European Union's top court has ruled that member states have no legal grounds to reject refugee relocation programs."

"Brussels takes our money and determines policy," said the sixth woman, who had previously been silent. "The Muslims are the problem. Schengen is the problem, and this makes the EU policy the problem."

Finally, the other women turned towards Frau Fuchs as the host asked, "Is Gerhardt ready?"

"My son is a man of destiny," said Fuchs. "In the next day you will hear his response to the Muslim attack in Berlin during the Long Night of Museums. You judge for yourself."

Chapter 22

Landsberg, Germany

Terry sat alone on the fast train from Berlin. The five-hundred-kilometer trip would take six hours to Augsburg. There he would be met by one of Otto's assets who would turn over a rental car for the final leg of the trip to Landsberg.

The focus had changed but the mission continued. Solak was still in the hunt for the perpetrators of the EU assassinations. His job was to develop intel as a deep cover operator. He sought the identity and intent of the terrorists, so that the Germans could better protect their own country.

Solak stroked his now clean-shaven face. After four months of scruffy facial hair, it felt good to touch skin. When added to a business suit and a fresh haircut, Terry looked rejuvenated. More important, he looked different.

The abrupt change of focus made sense in light of new developments. Between Otto's USB flash drive information, and Evie's cryptic telephone details, Terry was comfortable that the players had good reasons to alter course. The bosses understood the risk of pulling Terry from the Muslim migrant scene in Berlin, just as he was making inroads in several mosques. The new focus would take a different path, but hopefully one that proved fruitful. The gamble was that the new direction didn't end up a diversion. The nation of Germany suffered from a collective guilt that spawned an institutional paralysis. They equally feared political agitators from the left as well as those from the right.

Terry closed his eyes and went over the memorized information provided by both Otto and Evie; people, places, dates, times. He reviewed the line item bullet points in his head, and when confident he had the logistics down, took the opportunity to gather some rest.

***

Berlin, Germany

The VP of the domestic security agency cleared his throat and referenced the wide-screen closed-circuit television. The group watched the most recent video posted in Istanbul, and narrated in Arabic, that followed the murders of an EU couple on the Long Night of Museums festival. The film posted scenes of the corpses wrapped in sheets under the statue of King Frederick II.

"As in previous attacks," said the VP, "there is no attribution or claim of responsibility, but a clear reference to the Dar al-Harb, the House of War. There is also the placement of several familiar arm bands—white crescent on red background. We suspect an Islamic orientation."

"Of course they are Muslims," said Geiger. The tall police director stood and pointed at the VP. "Why do you waste our time with intentional avoidance? Multiple eye witnesses confirm that the attackers chanted, 'Allahu Akbar.'" Geiger's square jaw was set at a rigid angle, challenging his peer group to refute his conclusion. The VP frowned and motioned to the far end of the conference table.

Frau Steir leaned forward and spoke. "We have several more migrant transfers planned. They are mostly Muslims being resettled. Due to the Bayreuth incident and the sensitivity of the operation, it is imperative that we keep the information as discreet as possible. Therefore, effective immediately, logistical knowledge of the transfers will be restricted to the persons in this room, and not provided until the very last moment."

"How do we effectively execute our responsibilities without proper notice?" asked the Berlin State Police deputy president.

"This is your notice," replied the VP. "Be ready. Have your personnel prepared to fulfill their functions."

Frau Steir and the VP exchanged a cursory glance before both looked away.

Chapter 23

Landsberg, Germany

Terry slowed his rental car as he entered the colorful town square of Landsberg. It was a typical Bavarian settlement, more known for medieval walls, stone towers, and a picturesque river than for lofty skyscrapers.

The drive south from Augsburg took less than an hour. Solak took his time to check for surveillance, and to reacquaint himself with the German countryside. He drove past the apartment building and parked his car several blocks further down the street. Then he retraced the distance along the cobblestone by foot.

Terry knocked on the door, and heard a noise inside just as the heavy oak portal swung inward. An elderly woman barely five feet tall with cropped white hair stood looking up at Solak.

"Ja?"

"Frau Jokols?"

She nodded.

"Otto, hat mich geschickt," said Terry.

"Yes, I know that Otto sent you." She motioned for Terry to enter the foyer before closing the door. "You are not from here."

"No," answered Solak in English, "is my German that bad?"

"No," replied Jokols, leading him into the living room. "Your accent is." She pointed at two cushioned chairs separated by a table. A pot of coffee with utensils sat ready to be consumed. As the elderly woman sat in the larger of the two chairs, she took a moment to adjust a small pillow. Then she looked at Terry with clear, pale eyes. "I am a Jew," she said.

Terry was a bit surprised by her admission. He held his hands up and asked. "Is that relevant?"

"Of course," replied Jokols as she looked across the room. "To understand modern Germany, one must first comprehend her historic ideology. The Nazi Party came to power as an embodiment of their leader."

"Adolf Hitler."

"It all started here," she said.

"In Landsberg?"

"Yes. Hitler failed in his attempt to overthrow the government in 1923 during the Beer Hall Putsch. He was sentenced to jail here, in Landsberg Prison. It was here that he dictated his autobiography, *Mein Kampf*, and described the process by which he became anti-Semitic. In jail he formulated his political ideology and future plans for the country."

"And the Jews were the victims."

"Yes, but not by coincidence," said Jokols. "In some regards all of Europe was the victim of the German war machine. The Jews, however, were specifically targeted."

Terry leaned forward in his chair. "Why?"

"Ah," replied the woman in a thoughtful tone, "that's the question." She sipped some coffee. "Historians and psychologists have struggled with the elusive answer."

It was clear to Terry that Otto had selected the elderly Jokols for an important briefing. Solak guessed her age as mid-eighties, and it was apparent to Solak that her firsthand knowledge added an emotional bridge that helped Terry 'feel' the moment. "What do you think?"

Jokols poured more coffee. "First, I will touch on the various theories."

Solak stretched his legs as she began.

"One, Hitler had a childhood friend who betrayed him and that boy was a Jew…two, Hitler carried Jewish blood in his veins courtesy of his biological father Alois' ancestry, and he was embarrassed…three, a Jewish professor at the Academy of Fine Arts in Vienna rejected his application for admittance, preventing Hitler from pursuing his lifelong dream of being an artist…four, Hitler contracted syphilis from a Jewish prostitute…"

Terry held up his hand in submission and Jokols paused. "I think I get the point," he said.

"There are many theories," said the old woman, "most have a degree of credibility, but *none* are conclusive."

"Back to my question, Frau Jokols," said Terry. "What do *you* believe is the underlying reason for Hitler's targeting the Jews?"

Jokols leaned forward and lowered her voice. "As humans, we find it easier to accept an emotional break, some deep-seated hatred developed from one's past. We seek explanations that we can understand—even if we don't like them. But when the answer is elusive?"

Terry stood and paced for a moment as he wrestled with her explanation.

"What if," asked Jokols, "the reason was coldly pragmatic?"

"A convenient target?"

"Ja," said the woman. "Did Hitler invent hate or use it as a tool? The Jews were unpopular, different, successful in business…bind a people together against a common enemy. Acquire all their assets. Choose a target that could not possibly achieve equal status in the population's mindset. How many tall, blonde, blue-eyed, Aryans are an ideal that Jews can aspire to? We are a Middle East people by ethnicity."

Terry stopped his pacing and turned to face Frau Jokols. "So, Adolf Hitler, the world's foremost genocidal monster, made a decision to exterminate a whole race of people based on political calculus?"

The woman gave Solak a slow but perceptible nod, as if to say, 'now you get it.' She sat forward. "Accept that as a temporary premise," said Jokols. She sipped some more coffee, before adding, "It will better prepare you for the next thing I say."

***

Munich, Germany

Sharif Ali entered the expansive suite on the top floor of the Vier Jahreszeiten Hotel and set his briefcase on the coffee table. He had just concluded a long meeting with several German women.

In the past few months, the country of Saudi Arabia had led a coalition of Gulf states against Qatar. They accused their wealthy neighbor of providing financial support to Islamic terrorists. Qatar denied the allegation and appealed to the United States. The U.S. remained neutral, but to calm the Saudis' concerns, they asked for proof. Sharif Ali traveled to Timbuktu to supply that proof. He gave Terry Solak a closely guarded list of wealthy terrorist benefactors. Terry then hand delivered that list to his organization, the CIA.

Middle East intrigue always suffered from duplicity and shifting winds. Turkey picked sides and supported Qatar in the diplomatic crisis. Saudi Arabia was livid.

Beyond the economic issues surrounding gas exploration and production, Saudi Arabia and Turkey were also quarreling over influence. Turkey claimed the distinction of being home to the last caliphate during the Ottoman Empire, and Saudi Arabia wore the mantel of being custodian to Islam's two holiest shrines.

The prince took a sip of bottled water before pulling one of six unused burner phones from his briefcase. He dialed an international number and spoke in Arabic. "I have met with the women. They are on schedule." Then he disconnected the call, pulled apart the phone, removed the SIM card and flushed it down the toilet. Finally, he smashed the burner into little pieces and wrapped the remnants into a plastic bag for disposal.

Chapter 24

Landsberg, Germany

Frau Jokols looked up at Terry and spoke in a whisper. "It's happening again."

Solak looked at the diminutive woman and squinted before asking, "What is happening?"

"The Nazi rise to power."

Terry gave Jokols a skeptical look and then shook his head dismissively. "They have nothing left. They were eliminated at the end of World War Two."

"Not eliminated, forced underground. They *never* ceased to exist."

"Aren't they outlawed by the German Constitution?"

"Not exactly," said Jokols. "In fact, earlier this year, Germany's highest court rejected a bid to outlaw a far right neo-Nazi party. To be outlawed, the government needs conclusive proof that the party is explicitly subverting the constitution. The Nazis are careful. They are building momentum."

"Towards what?"

"The election."

"Can they win? Everything I read suggests that a fringe party may—at most—only pick up a few percentage points," said Terry.

"They don't need to win. They only need five percent to have standing in parliament."

"That's a small start."

"You miss the point. That *start* will be a sea change in Germany. Adolf Hitler took a decade to rise to power following his release from prison. Then he lost the election in 1932. The very *next* year he was appointed chancellor. He had standing, and it didn't take long for him to amass power."

"He was one man," said Terry. "A charismatic orator who pushed emotional buttons. A cult of personality."

"He preached an ideology that appealed to the masses. He was positioned; the right man at the right time."

"So, who on the German political scene could command that stature?"

"The narrator."

Solak paused for a moment and sat back down across from Jokols. "The voice we keep hearing over the internet, the Hitler sound-alike?"

"The same," replied Jokols.

"But we don't know who he is."

"Yet."

Terry raised his cup of coffee. His thoughts drifted. "You think there is more to come?"

"I am not alone," replied Jokols. "All the signs are there. The current pattern replicates the birth and the growth of the Nazi Party from eighty years ago."

"For example?" asked Terry.

The woman leaned forward. "The end of World War One was instituted by signing the Treaty of Versailles. It forced Germany to accept all the blame, to give up territory, and to pay massive war reparations. Germany was punished by the allies. It treated us harshly and was hugely unpopular."

"And the equivalent?"

"In terms of effect, Schengen," answered Frau Jokols in a quiet voice. "The EU is dictating policies and penalties that are having a vast, negative impact on our country."

Terry considered her explanation and then nodded. "Anything else?"

"Yes, the Jewish issue."

Solak shook his head. "That couldn't happen again—not *here*. There is still anti-Semitism in Germany and Europe, but I don't see that issue coming back in Germany. It's too obvious as a weak point. Everyone is on guard."

"Of course," replied Jokols, "but go back to my previous comment. The pattern is repeating itself. If the Jews were a convenient target the first time, who is the expedient target *now*?"

There was a slight pause, and then Solak raised an eyebrow. "The Muslims."

"Yes," said Jokols as she sipped her coffee. "They are being honed as a tool for hatred. The Muslims are an unpopular minority in our midst. The migrants have a different language, religion, and culture. They soak up our tax dollars and then create problems that disturb our way of life. The vast majority of Germans *resent* the Muslims that arrive under Schengen. Many harbor a grudge that grows by the day—even as the EU places greater demands on member states."

Terry leaned back and frowned. "It sounds like a self-serving theory."

"Is it," asked Jokols, "or is it a model? What are the chances that so many well-planned attacks would occur on German soil, but *only* against EU employees?"

Terry remained silent.

"What are the odds," continued Jokols, "of an Arabic linguist posting a warning on the internet to reference the Dar al-Harb or 'House of War' each time there is an attack?"

Terry shrugged, trying to organize the various leads and clues that continued to bracket the mission. If Jokols' theory was accurate, the Nazis were on the move and they had a plan to bind together the political climate to the anger of their citizens.

"Then the only step that remains is a catalyst," said Terry.

"What if one is waiting in the wings?" asked Frau Jokols.

"Is someone biding their time?"

"Ja," said the elderly woman.

Terry bit his lip in silence. It all sounded plausible, but it may also have been a touch of fear run wild. The German mindset was one that welcomed order and stability. In many ways these character traits helped propel the chancellor to her current status in office. "Is that a shared perspective?" he asked.

"In some quarters. Most in official government circles will not discuss it. But there has been a gnawing apprehension over the years that at some point, the shadow of our Nazi past will resurrect."

"Does Otto share this fear?"

"Of course," said Jokols with a slight smile. "Why do you think you are here?"

***

Munich, Germany

It was a speech for the ages, a throwback to a time and place when radio—as a medium—ruled the airways. Gerhardt had polished and pruned the substance to reflect a nostalgia for the past. He lifted whole paragraphs from Adolf Hitler's most memorable orations, substituting words and phrases to update the rhetoric to the current time and situation.

He spoke with an incredible power, the echo of his words propelling listeners to a different era when German pride infused her politics.

For weeks Gerhardt's videos had gathered interest. Older Germans watched with concern and apprehension, as younger voters watched and listened in curiosity. At first it was a forbidden fruit, drawing in a new generation of adults precisely because their parents and grandparents hid their own interest. The taboo of Gerhardt's addresses drove the popularity. Something denied was something coveted. It was emotive, a secret salve that solved the political pressure applied by Schengen, EU policies, and their financial burdens. Muslims and politicians were to blame.

Gerhardt painted a portrait with broad strokes, coaxing the buried frustrations of the listener to the surface, exposing the wounds of political neglect. Germany's bureaucrats had made decisions and forced an invasive migration on the nation.

At no time did Gerhardt ever mention the Nazi Party. There were no symbols or references to the National Socialists—or for that matter, any political party. Instead, he turned every phrase into a focus on the enemy. Muslims were the target. He recounted how, in the most recent incident, the female attackers wore traditional Turkish Islamic clothing. The male decoy chanted in Arabic the phrase 'Allahu Akbar.' Another Arabic video was posted in Istanbul warning of the Dar al-Harb, the House of War. The signs were obvious, the pattern consistent. What more did the people need for proof?

Gerhardt preached a new nationalism, with pride in their language, their culture, *and* their history. The guilt must cease. The overreaching, punitive policies of the EU must end. The mandate of Schengen must stop.

The video displayed a well-timed collage of photographs beginning with the Brandenburg Gate, the Reichstag, and the towers of the Oberbraumbrucke in Berlin, all matched as visual aids to the essence of his speech. Then the video expanded the photographs to include the most celebrated architectural gems from Germany's other major cities: Hamburg, Munich, Cologne, Frankfurt, and Stuttgart. The final five minutes of the video was the narrator's parting words, set against the backdrop of the German flag.

"…Germany of pride and strength…a nation dedicated to democracy, that adheres to the goals of their citizens…say *no* to Muslims…say *no* to the European Union…say *no* to Schengen…we are an industrious nation…on the cusp of a new era…." Gerhardt paused before offering the final thought, "…in the next few weeks, I will introduce myself—in person—to the noble, the brave, the willing…the keepers of the flame…our future, Germany's future and her greatest days, lie ahead."

Chapter 25

Landsberg, Germany

Terry exited Frau Jokols' home and turned right on the sidewalk. His head spun with a muddled blend of questions. The old woman had been a fount of insight and information, as much for her perspective as for her near computer-like memory of details.

She had escaped from Latvia with her family only to be caught and incarcerated at the Landsberg Concentration Camp. Her parents were soon taken away and never seen again. Fortunately for young Jokols, the prison was soon liberated by U.S. troops and she was saved from execution. The camp was then converted into a displaced person camp consisting mostly of Jewish refugees. During this period, the orphan turned her attention to the war crime trials held in Landsberg, and the full weight of the Nazi 'final solution' fell on Jokols with a thud. She grew up with a profound first-person sense of the Holocaust.

Terry took a look over his shoulder as he walked along the cobblestones. A young couple, walking arm and arm, seemed to be matching his stride at a distance. He picked up his pace.

Frau Jokols saw her calling, stayed in Landsberg, and dedicated her efforts to working with the Simon Wiesenthal organization. It would signal a profound change in her life, while also helping to eradicate the emptiness of losing her family at such a young age. She became a unique repository of all things Nazi, which in turn led her to an odd grouping of professional contacts. This led Terry to her front door.

Abreast of his rental car, Terry hesitated before glancing sideways. The couple was now twenty meters to his rear. He made a small twist and then accelerated his gait, passed his parked car, and continued at a fast clip. The couple matched his speed.

At the corner of the square Terry took a hard right and ducked into a clothier that specialized in Bavarian attire. He waded into the store and mingled between the racks. Then he moved towards the corner of the large picture window where he could keep an eye on the street. Forty seconds later the couple walked by. Their eyes rotated in all directions, searching for the now elusive quarry.

***

Berlin, Germany

Nora straddled Gerhardt in their bedroom, naked, using her tongue and teeth to leave little love bites on his flesh. Then she reached forward and raked both hands down his chest. Her manicured fingernails scratched with just enough pressure to sting without breaking the skin. He moaned, and she fluttered her eyes in response.

It was a complex relationship; sexual, but also highly emotional. They had been together for three years, ever since his mother's friend made the introduction. From the beginning, it was obvious that Gerhardt was attracted to the blonde. He had needs, and the best way to protect the sheltered son from outside influences, was to control his circle of contacts. Nora became the solution. This in turn increased their leverage over the developing orator, and permitted him a level of independence as the pretty blonde kept him close with a watchful eye.

"I am so proud of you, Gerhardt," said Nora as she panted, short of breath. "You will change Germany." She kissed his chest and slid down to his abdomen, using her lips to circle Gerhardt's manhood. The anticipation caused him to shudder, and she whispered in a quiet voice, "The whole world will *know* your power."

Autumn 2017

Chapter 26

Berlin, Germany

Frau Steir stood beside the Goethe Monument and watched several children at play. She had activated an insider's alert to the special committee, advising of two migrant transfers from the Berlin reception facility to Gottingen, a large college town in central Germany. This was the intentional leak designed to expose the senior government official who was feeding information to right wing sympathizers.

Her associate, the VP of the domestic security agency, approached from the far side of the Tiergarten. He seemed to be limping less.

"How is the leg?" asked Steir.

"Not good," said the VP with a nod, "but better."

"Anything to report?"

"We've primed the system," said the VP, "yet none of our agents-in-place have noted any increased activity."

"How many extremist groups have you targeted?"

"All told," replied the VP, "three on the right are under direct surveillance. The real concern is when these groups cross-pollinate. It makes it difficult to close the net."

Steir turned towards the monument and grabbed at the black handrail fence. "I worry," she said, "that they could mobilize sufficient crowds on such short notice."

The VP shrugged. "Maybe it isn't an attractive enough transfer. Gottingen is not a hotbed of right wing discontent."

"If anything," replied Steir, "it's left-leaning with all those university students. It was selected so that we could control the logistics. The false narrative is key."

"I understand," said the VP. "The transfers were easy interceptions—if they were interested."

Steir turned and gave the VP a curious look. "What are you driving at?"

"The timing. It's auspicious, especially when one considers that the voice has had over twelve million downloads on his most recent video release."

Steir frowned.

"Maybe," said the VP as he continued his thought, "they are holding back, stockpiling reserves for a bigger forum."

"What forum?" asked Steir.

"The voice made a point of saying he would meet his supporters—in person—in the next few weeks."

The conversation lapsed as Steir exhaled. "Thank you for the update. Please contact me if any of the target groups mobilize to interdict the migrant transfers."

"Do you think someone will take the bait?"

"Maybe. The objective is to see who reacts and how they handle the information." Frau Steir turned and walked away.

***

Munich, Germany

The six women sat around the oval table in quiet anticipation. They had prepared for this opportunity for years, and now that it was in their grasp, there was a nervous energy that effused the group. Their dream, the dreams and hopes of so many, was about to become a reality. They were at the tipping point, and a successful reveal would change Germany and Europe for years to come.

"Our preparations are in place and, as the election nears, we gain momentum," said the apartment owner.

"Our political advisors assure us," said the woman to her left, "that the deep resentment felt by the voters is changing the balance."

There was a murmur of satisfaction amongst the other women as the leader raised a hand in the air. "There is, however, a potential problem that has developed."

The group grew silent.

"We had discussed, that as our influence grew, agencies of the current administration would likely become more aggressive. To protect our interests, we placed several known antagonists under our *own* surveillance."

"For example?" asked the woman across the table.

"Frau Jokols in Landsberg."

"That old Jew," replied the woman to the leader's right. "Is she still alive?"

"Yes. She had a visitor. A man, but not a suitor, he was fifty years her junior. Our team followed him into the square and then lost him."

The woman to the leader's left set down her teacup with a noisy clatter. She frowned. "Did we get a photograph?"

"No," said the apartment owner, "but we have stepped up surveillance on Jokols. She is well connected to the apparatus in Berlin."

"Yes," said Frau Fuchs speaking for the first time. "My son is about to generate a good deal of increased attention. We must control our adversaries *before* the reveal."

Chapter 27

Berlin, Germany

Terry walked past several trendy boutiques in Prenzlauer Berg on his way to Otto's safe house. The upscale, gentrified neighborhood hung on to the last vestiges of an early fall sunset. Young couples still crowded the streets eating, drinking, and socializing, but they did not appear to notice the preoccupied Solak. It had been a long day.

Terry exited Landsberg within minutes of slipping his tail. Instead of taking the train, from Augsburg he drove the entire distance to Berlin. This provided increased flexibility in his travels—and control over possible events. The old maxim was, when in doubt, change the routine.

Terry had abandoned his apartment and his identity that morning when he shifted gears on the probe. His small wardrobe with few accessories were all left at the migrant studio apartment in Kreuzberg. Anyone checking on the Turkish asylum seeker from Istanbul would dead-end.

Solak looked forward to speaking with Otto. If a Nazi-oriented group was moving toward a deadline, it seemed to coincide with the German general elections. Terry considered the beliefs of Frau Jokols, a Jewish historian and Holocaust survivor, and wanted to compare her analysis with that of Otto, the foreign intelligence officer.

Terry walked past an organic restaurant, a café, and several art galleries before stopping in front of a five-story building on Saarbrücker Straße. He buzzed his way past the outside door through the intercom. In minutes he was greeted by Otto's security team on the second floor.

"Helios," said the German standing to greet Solak as he entered the apartment. "You've managed a busy agenda." The foreign intelligence officer guided Terry towards a small side table and offered refreshments with an open hand.

"You won't stay long," said Otto, "just a quick debrief before your next appointment."

Terry reached for a bottle of Lowenbrau and sat. "First thing I would offer is that I picked up a tail outside of Jokols' home."

Otto fumbled with his pipe as he sat across from Terry and leaned forward so they could not be heard. "Interesting. They must have assigned surveillance in advance."

"They expected someone?"

"I don't know," said Otto with a frown. "No one knows about you, and we only set up the brief with Jokols at the last minute."

"Do you have a leak?"

"Not on this issue. We are more concerned that our counterparts at the BfV find out about our involvement."

"Will they raise hell?"

"The domestic security agency is very turf conscious," replied Otto. He paused for a moment. "It does suggest, however, that our concerns are grounded. The extremists would not expend the resources if they didn't have something to hide."

***

Berlin, Germany

Sharif Ali entered the ramshackle warehouse in the Marzahn section of Berlin. The Saudi prince was followed by two bodyguards and all three men were dressed in western clothes. The building itself, like most structures in the rough neighborhood, was a Soviet-style cement block of precast concrete slabs. A huge skinhead covered with tattoos stepped forward and made a motion towards Ali.

"I need to check you," said the skinhead.

"No," said Ali in a calm voice. "You will not touch me."

The skinhead bristled at the remark. He was a bruiser in size and therefore conditioned to intimidating an adversary. He took a step forward and Sharif's two bodyguards moved to the front.

"Step aside," said the prince.

A steel door to the rear opened and a second German appeared. This man was dressed casually, but in European attire. He immediately called over to the skinhead. "Rolf, he's expected." Then the second man escorted the three Saudis through the door and locked it behind them.

They entered a small, private room that functioned as an assembly area. In the center of the concrete floor sat a three-year-old Volkswagen Golf compact car.

Ali stepped forward, opened the driver's door, and examined the interior. Then he repeated the process, of opening and closing each of the other doors and the hatchback. Finally, he stepped back and asked, "Did you test drive the vehicle?"

"Ja," answered the second man. "It drives well and can handle the added weight."

Sharif nodded. "Show me the Semtex."

The German led the prince over to the corner and pulled aside a waterproof canvas from atop a stack of wooden pallets. Piled in neat bundles were dozens of burnt orange colored squares, each the dimensions of an oversize brick. The packages were labeled in Czech SEMTEX 10.

Sharif took a few moments to inspect the package. He nodded and the German re-covered the plastic explosive with the canvas.

"The primers and det cord will be here within a week," said Ali. "The specialist will survey everything and then customize the charge. Stay on schedule."

The German nodded and watched as Ali led his two bodyguards from the warehouse.

Chapter 28

Landsberg, Germany

Two women, one in her sixties, the other in her fifties, knocked on the heavy oak door of Frau Jokols' apartment.

The spry octogenarian answered the door and looked at the strangers with a curious expression. "May I help you?"

"Frau Jokols," said the older of the two women, "I am Friedel Schulz and this is Frau Keller. May we take a few minutes of your time?"

Jokols examined the two women. "What exactly does it concern?"

"I teach at Heidelberg University," said Keller, "and I am writing a book on the history of Bavaria following the war. I understand that you had quite an experience here, and I wanted to include as many firsthand references as possible."

Jokols considered the explanation. "I was just a child," she replied.

"Yes, and I understand you witnessed the war crime trials held here in Landsberg."

"Yes."

"May we come in for a few minutes?" asked Schulz.

Jokols hesitated and then invited the two women into her home.

The visitors settled in the living room as Jokols turned to the older woman. "Are you an educator as well?"

"No," said Schulz with a laugh. "I am a widow with time on her hands, and since I am from Munich, I know the area. I offered my companionship as a guide."

The three ladies laughed and then Jokols stood. "May I offer you some coffee?"

The two visitors exchanged a glance.

"That would be lovely," said Keller, "but we don't wish to take too much of your time."

Frau Jokols waved a hand in a dismissive fashion. Then Keller pulled a notepad and a small tape recorder from her briefcase.

In a few minutes they settled around the table with a pot of freshly brewed coffee and three cups. Schulz casually scanned the room and suddenly stood. "That photograph," she said with an air of excitement, "may I?"

Jokols turned in her seat and looked at the black and white framed photograph on the wall. It depicted a late autumn forest.

Keller winked, and spoke in a whisper. "Go ahead, she's an amateur photographer. I'll prepare the coffee. How do you take it?"

"A little milk," replied Jokols. She stood and walked over to Schulz in front of the photograph.

Keller's interview lasted thirty minutes. She asked questions from a prepared list, took notes, and recorded several interesting episodes of Jokols' life. Then the diminutive woman suddenly sat up in her seat and touched her abdomen. The visitors looked surprised.

"I'm sorry," said Jokols, "I seem to have a little indigestion." She stirred uncomfortably. "The coffee tasted a little sweet. Did you add sugar?"

"No," said Keller, "just a little milk as you said. Maybe it was the milk, was it fresh?"

Jokols' mouth felt dry, and her heart started beating fast. She stood and felt a little lightheaded. Then Jokols motioned at her two visitors. "I'm afraid I will have to interrupt the interview."

"Of course," said Keller, "can we get you something?"

"No, no," replied Jokols, "I'll be fine. I just need a little rest. I'm sorry, but can you show yourselves out?"

"Certainly," said Schulz. The two women stood and gathered their belongings.

"May I call you direct if I have some follow-up questions?" asked Keller.

"Yes," said Jokols as she started for her bedroom. "My number is listed in the directory."

The visitors exchanged a glance, shook hands with Frau Jokols and exited the apartment.

Langley, Virginia

Evie was nervous. They had been summoned to Arthur Kent's office and she suspected it was due to the abrupt change in focus of the German assignment. She had staked out a position on the EU terrorist attacks, and believed the perpetrator was a Nazi inspired group. This oriented their efforts away from Islamic extremists and, in so doing, angered the deputy director.

Bob Colman was already sitting at the conference table. He looked up as she entered Kent's office and gave her a calming motion. Finally, the deputy director stood, circled his desk, and joined them at the conference table.

"Some coffee, Havva?" asked Kent.

"No, thank you, sir," replied Evie as she placed several file folders on the table.

Kent nodded. "Let's get started." He shifted his attention to Colman. "Bob, was it your call to reorient the focus of the German probe mission?"

"It was," answered the chief of SAD.

"Why?"

"Analysis of the facts in the EU member murders indicate that there is an inconclusive Islamist footprint. If anything, it looks like a setup, a false flag, whose intent is to blame the Muslim community, primarily Turks."

"Why?" asked Kent again, pressing the issue. The deputy director was irritated and unconcerned that it showed.

"Because there is a general election in a few weeks and Germany is on edge. The European Union has a Turkey problem and it isn't going away."

"Can you be more specific?"

Colman sat up in his seat. "Many EU leaders want to punish the Turkish president for the erosion of democracy in Turkey. The authorities in Ankara have swept up European Commission nationals in raids, specifically targeting German journalists and human-rights activists. There is a great deal of pressure on the German chancellor to take economic and political action."

"What kind of economic action?"

"The most recent suggestion was that the EU should slash and redirect the six hundred million euros in annual funding extended to Turkey as a candidate to join the EU."

Kent paused before turning to face Evie. "Your opinion? Do you agree?"

"Well, we take educated guesses," she said, "and the pending election, when coupled with the EU member attacks seems to feed their frustration."

"Time is critical," said Bob. "I made a decision to shift the resources from Muslims to Nazis." Colman was not easily intimidated by his boss, and he didn't want Evie to catch flak for his decision.

"We are providing assistance to an ally," said Kent. "Did you discuss the change with our German counterparts?"

"Of course," replied Colman, "and they agreed."

"Did they?" asked Kent with a theatrical flourish. The deputy director opened his file and began to read: "Islamist terrorism is the biggest challenge facing the BfV, and we see it as one of the biggest threats facing the internal security of Germany." He closed the file. "That was delivered two months ago by the head of their domestic security agency."

There was a short silence in the office as Kent considered his options. Colman had made an operational decision that ran at odds with the deputy director's position. He allowed the chief of SAD to make such a call, but Kent was enough of an Agency insider to scope out the playing field and protect his flank. If the new focus proved valuable, Kent would get the credit. If it proved worthless, Kent would avoid the blame.

"How many Islamic extremists are in Germany?" asked Kent, turning towards Evie.

She answered from memory, "Nearly ten thousand Salafists, and almost as many Turkish Milli Görüs,"

"So, twenty thousand?"

"Yes," answered Evie. She had identified the most virulent, committed Islamic terrorists groups embedded throughout the country.

"And how many Nazi extremists?"

"Less than six thousand," replied Evie.

"So call it six…the odds are twenty to six, is that correct?"

"Yes, sir."

"And we are basing this decision upon inconclusive evidence, anomalies from planted clues. Is that right?"

"For the record," said Colman, "the Germans agree with this call."

"Well I should hope so," said Kent in a terse manner, "it's *their* country. Who at the BfV did you speak with?"

Colman hesitated before answering. "It wasn't the BfV…it was the BND."

The deputy director's eyes opened wide in surprise. He now saw the landmine. The foreign intelligence service of Germany was providing cover for a domestic operation for which they had no authority. Kent leaned forward in his chair. "I will *not* let us get dragged into a pissing contest over their constitution. We have enough turf battles here." Then Kent raised his right hand and pointed at Bob and Evie with his thumb and baby finger at the same time. The motion made it clear that although he was speaking to Colman, they both accepted responsibility. "You *own* this decision," said the deputy director. "Don't let it take you down."

Chapter 29

Berlin, Germany

It was nine at night and Terry was alone, dozing in a cushioned chair at Otto's safe house in Prenzlauer Berg. It had been twenty hours since his visit to Landsberg and the briefing by Frau Jokols at her home. So much to think about, so much to consider. Her parting words haunted Terry as he exited her apartment, "Don't listen to anyone that denies it could happen again."

There was a resolute fix in the old woman's demeanor. Something deep and foreboding as if she knew secrets that no one was willing to discuss. Now, the German intelligence officer was setting up a second briefing for Terry with a confidential informant.

A sharp, distinct rap on the door and Solak was on his feet pointing a SIG Sauer P6 at the entrance. The pistol had been supplied by Otto.

"Helios," said the familiar voice from outside.

"Yes," answered Terry.

"Ja, Helios, open up."

Solak checked the peephole and then unbolted the door.

"Quickly, Helios," said the German barging into the apartment. "Change in plans. We must go now."

"We're leaving?"

"Yes, relocation, I will explain when we are on the road."

Terry felt the intensity in the intelligence officer's voice. He grabbed a pre-packed duffel bag filled with a change of clothes and toiletries. Then he followed Otto downstairs.

"My people will sterilize the apartment," said Otto. "Into the car."

Solak jumped into the back seat and the Audi sped away. "Are we made?"

"Maybe," answered the German looking over his shoulder, "something has come up. It's not worth the risk."

The driver was skilled and he demonstrated a keen sense of the neighborhood and the local streets. He initiated a series of abrupt turns and last-second changes in direction designed to expose a tail, all the while watching in the mirror. After a few minutes he nodded and spoke over his shoulder to his boss. "We're good."

Otto relaxed and patted the driver's arm. He turned to face Terry who waited patiently for an explanation. "Well?" asked Solak.

The intelligence officer spoke in a quiet voice. "Frau Jokols is dead."

***

Berlin, Germany

The Brandenburg Gate was the symbol of a city and the icon of a nation. The huge triumphal arch was one of the most recognized landmarks in the world. Topped off by a large bronze statue of the goddess of victory driving a chariot of four horses, the monument bore witness to three centuries of German history. Now it proudly boasted of post-cold war reunification.

The Volkswagen compact slowed. It was half past three in the morning, a Wednesday, in the middle of the work week. Traffic was sparse and the streets deserted. The vehicle was packed front to rear and top to bottom with ten rows of plastic explosives, six stacks deep. The Semtex bricks were lined up end to end, assuring that everything had physical contact. Covering the entire rear seat and the electric firing system was a green canvas, on top of which sat a dozen potted plants, all of which were easily visible to anyone using a flashlight to examine the inside of the car without wishing to open the door.

A young couple strolled through the Pariser Platz towards the huge monument, crossed the famous square walking west, and locked their arms in an affectionate embrace as the man talked on his cell phone. They passed under the middle arch and angled sideways along the cobblestone pedestrian zone; just two late-night revelers returning from an evening of dancing and music at one of Berlin's vast array of night clubs. Within minutes they blended into the thick forested silhouette of the Tiergarten.

Five minutes later, when the pedestrian couple was out of sight, the Volkswagen drove along Straße des 17 Juni and picked up speed. It approached the Gate heading east. At the last moment the driver jumped the curb, avoided the Beton armor blocks, and sped the VW the last few feet towards the middle of the five Arches. He jammed the VW between the Doric column and the vehicle impediment post, scratching and scraping both sides of the car into the narrow portal until it stuck in the opening, directly under the eighty-foot-high triumphal arch, pointing northeast. The Volkswagen contained long, steel inserts to bind and guide the placement of the plastic explosives so that the car itself became a massive shape charge.

The driver jumped from the car and ran back towards the Tiergarten. A taxi idling in the turn-around circle spun into action. It picked up the VW driver, dropped a satchel on the ground, and sped west along Straße des 17 Juni. Two auxiliary police raced across the square to give chase by foot.

Ten minutes later both sides of the Brandenburg Gate were flooded with police. Sirens blared and lights flashed. Television crews responded. Within twenty minutes, the center of Berlin, the very heart of the city, was bustling with night owls, curious onlookers, and hundreds of police. Helicopters buzzed.

Something was off, and official minds quickly determined that it was improbable that an intoxicated driver would attempt to squeeze through such an insufficient opening. They played it safe. Under the glare of Klieg lights the police set up a very wide perimeter, using road blocks, crime scene tape, and makeshift barriers to control the crowd.

The Brandenburg Gate stood tall, bathed in artificial light, a solitary edifice of pride and stature. The news reporters faced the cameras using the brightly lit monument as a backdrop to their sound bites. The focus of the lens honed in on the rear half of the VW Golf stuck protruding from beneath the middle arch. Four minutes later a huge explosion rocked the square.

Chapter 30

Heidelberg, Germany

Terry walked along the Bahnstadt housing project in Heidelberg. Events were moving fast, and the sudden death of Frau Jokols only added to the urgency. Despite the appearance of 'death by natural causes,' it was hard to ignore the intimation of the elderly woman's demise immediately after meeting with Solak. Otto reacted, changed Terry's safe house, and stepped up logistics for the second asset briefing.

Now, strolling the paved sidewalk of the passive settlement, far from the charming baroque-style architecture of the old college town, Terry considered the implications for the general election. Voter discontent was high, fear and anger were prevalent, and Germans sought calm in a river of chaos. As Jokols said, the desire for order lay the foundation for political change.

Solak slowed his gait as he surveyed the cookie-cutter, cubed apartment blocks that populated the energy efficient neighborhood. He spotted the address, crossed the narrow, man-made pedestrian canal to a stairwell, and climbed.

"Otto sent me," said Terry in German as the door opened.

The old man took a long, appraising look at Solak and then took a step back. Terry crossed the threshold and waited as the host then took a quick peek into the hallway, glancing left and right before closing and bolting his door.

He led Terry into a small sitting area filled with newspapers, periodicals, maps, textbooks, and stacks of printed e-mails all gathered around a desktop computer and a half-full cup of coffee. He lit a cigarette and exhaled a long stream of smoke. "Do you mind?" The question was asked as an afterthought as he pointed at an empty chair.

"No," said Terry as he sat.

In the middle of the table placed between the two men, was a steel, over-flowing ashtray filled with dozens of half-smoked filter cigarettes. "You don't smoke."

"No," replied Terry.

"But you don't mind?"

"Your home," said Solak, "your rules."

The old German broke into a smile, flashing a grin of nicotine-stained teeth. "I am always curious as to the visitors that Otto sends me. He has such a varied group of contacts."

Solak shrugged, and managed a small smile. "I wouldn't know."

"Are you an American?"

"What did Otto tell you?" asked Terry, leaning back in his chair.

"He didn't say, but your features are inconclusive."

"In what way?"

"You are ethnically mixed, hard to read…but you carry yourself like an American."

"Which is how?"

"Confident. There's a certain conviction in your walk."

Terry didn't respond. He didn't want to lie, but there was a degree of trust necessary to get information, and he realized that this old host was a curious sort—which was probably why he excelled at his work.

"Does it matter?" asked Solak, managing a grin to take the edge off the question.

"No," said the host with a laugh. "But for the record my name is Dieter."

"Thank you, Dieter, I am Helios."

Dieter took a long drag on his cigarette and considered the Greek name. Then he shrugged and turned his attention to the pile of papers on his table. "So, you have an interest in the Nazis?"

"Yes."

"Which means you are interested in our unseen impersonator."

"You've seen the videos," said Terry. "What do you think?"

"I think," replied Dieter, "that someone has gone to a good deal of trouble to impersonate a man dead for seven decades."

"Is it viable?"

"To the extent that it sounds exactly like Adolf Hitler, in both style and substance, and pushes at the same emotional buttons—yes." Dieter exhaled a long stream of smoke.

"So what is the end game?"

"Political power," answered Dieter. "What else?" He mumbled the final words in a self-evident manner.

"So, a reincarnated Adolf Hitler returns to lead Germany to a new world order?"

Dieter leaned forward and stubbed out his cigarette. "These are difficult times. Do not underestimate the loyalty of Hitler's adherents."

"The Nazis?"

"The Schutzstaffel," said Dieter. "The SS controlled the party."

Terry leaned back and absorbed the clarification before saying, "The SS did his bidding."

"They swore a personal oath of loyalty to Hitler—not the party, not the nation. The members of the Schutzstaffel were fanatics."

Solak shifted in his chair. "You seem to know quite a bit about the Third Reich."

"I should," replied Dieter, taking the opportunity to light another cigarette. "My father was an SS officer."

***

Berlin, Germany

Sharif Ali entered an appliance store on Ritter Street followed by two body-guards. The small, family owned business, like so much in the neighborhood, contributed to the Kreuzberg nickname the 'export quarter.' Many similar shops and retail outlets dotted the bustling street. It was a secure setting for Ali, as business people of all types crowded Ritter Street day and night, taking advantage of Germany's economic prowess and broad international connections. No one noticed the Saudi prince, who dressed and acted like a westerner. The only qualifier to do business on Ritter Street was cash.

Inside the appliance store Ali threaded between rows of toasters, microwaves, and espresso machines. He caught the eye of the shop's owner who waved him to a rear hallway. The prince knocked twice before entering a storage room to find three men seated around a square table. One of the men was the driver of the explosive-laden Volkswagen Golf compact car.

The driver stood as Ali entered the room, a glint of excitement in his young face. He bowed his head in respect before laying a flat hand on his own chest. Then he looked up at the prince with nervous eyes.

Sharif relaxed the moment by opening his arms wide in a welcoming embrace. Ali hugged the young man and kissed him platonically on each cheek. Then they sat and Sharif pulled his chair closer to the driver.

"You have done a great service to Allah, my young friend," said the prince in a quiet voice. "The whole world is watching television replays of your courageous act." Ali permitted the driver a moment to bask in the glow of his accomplishment. "And now we need a believer with special skills to help with our next phase. Can we ask you to serve Allah one more time?"

"Of course," answered the VW driver in an excited whisper. "What do you need?"

"For now," said Ali with an approving smile, "I need you to leave with my associates." He nodded at his two bodyguards. "They will take you to a safe house. I will join you there later tonight."

The driver stood and bowed in an obsequious manner, as Ali patted the man's forearm.

"Now go," said the prince with a smile. He sat and watched the driver exit the small storage room accompanied by his two bodyguards.

Chapter 31

Heidelberg, Germany

"In August of 1944," said Dieter, "when it was clear that the fortunes of war had turned, a group of German industrialists and bankers attended a secret meeting in Strasbourg." He paused in his narrative to exhale a long stream of smoke. "The purpose of the meeting was to insure a future for the Nazis."

"What happened?" asked Terry.

"An organization of former SS officers was formed. It was known as the ODESSA."

Solak nodded as he shifted in his seat. "I've heard of them. They helped fugitives obtain false papers and setup escape routes to flee Germany."

"Yes," replied Dieter, "the short-term goal was to preserve the party infrastructure. The long-term goal was to finance the new Reich."

"And it worked."

"Quite well," answered Dieter. He stood to refresh Terry's coffee. "ODESSA built a large and reliable network. Contacts were established. Many influential Nazis vanished as they were smuggled out of Europe. New lives under false names cropped up in foreign countries."

"And by the end of the war?" asked Solak.

"Only a handful of high-ranking Nazi officials stood trial for war crimes. The ODESSA had managed to sneak the vast majority of the hardcore SS out of reach."

Solak leaned back in his seat. "And your father?"

"They say he was shot trying to escape," said Dieter in an ambiguous tone.

"Do you have doubts?"

Dieter shrugged as he bit his thumbnail. "I was a child. My father was young and aggressive, thirty years old and totally committed to the cause. He may have

105

provoked the captors, he certainly wouldn't have submitted willingly, but…" The old man looked off into the distance. "It is hard to reconcile. We heard many stories that the allies would just execute the prisoners if they were SS."

"How did you get to this point?" asked Terry.

"Through my mother's intercession."

"I don't understand," said Terry.

Dieter smiled and lit another cigarette. "For all the historians that have tried to analyze the blinding loyalty of the SS officers, the unwavering devotion of the Nazis, no one *ever* saw the obvious. It was right in front of them."

"What did they miss?"

Dieter leaned forward and spoke in a quiet voice. "It's the women, Helios. The women were the force behind the Schutzstaffel."

Terry stood and walked around the small apartment, digesting the information. "Help me understand."

The old German leaned forward. "The women—wives, mothers, sometimes sisters or aunts—*they* propelled their men to join the SS and pledge fealty to Hitler. The party appealed to them as recruiters. Success in the Schutzstaffel was first and foremost based on loyalty. Germans of modest backgrounds, void of university educations, family contacts, or wealth could rise to powerful positions, unlike in the regular Wehrmacht. Ambitious women saw the opportunity. They plotted and guided their men's careers, becoming the perfect, dutiful force behind their men. Their spouses, sons, and brothers received the recognition, but it was the women who paved the road. The women banded together and setup an informal support system, a warren of committed members. They called it simply 'das Netzwerk.'"

Terry looked at the old man, seeking further explanation. "Forgive my German," said Solak.

"It translates," said Dieter exhaling a stream of smoke, "as *the Network*."

***

Berlin, Germany

The group of twenty gathered in the eighth-floor conference room at the chancellery. The mood was somber, a frost in the air that suggested a collective frustration. As the caretakers to the republic they felt inept, unable to calm the waters; yet they were unwilling to cede control. The most important democratic process of their country lay just ahead, a general election for national office. Yet these attacks propelled a broad awakening of a disgruntled electorate, as the persons entrusted with the safety of the citizens could not protect their people.

A peaceful insurrection would manifest in actions at the voting booth, and politicians would lose their jobs.

The VP of the domestic security agency cleared his throat and stood, resting his portly frame on his good leg. "The final tally," said the VP, "are two dead, eleven wounded, and massive structural damage to the middle Doric column and sandstone base of the center arch." He looked around the table and focused on Geiger of the federal police. The police director sat expressionless, looking down at the pad of paper on his blotter.

"Three weeks," said Frau Steir, "before the general elections. We must assume that between now and then there will be more disruption." She turned towards the deputy president of the federal investigative police, "Herr Deputy Ludwig?"

The deputy stood. "The initial indications are the use of weapons-grade plastic explosives and a remote firing device. We should consider that the perpetrators have a high level of expertise and sophisticated bomb-making skills."

"Military training?" asked the VP.

"It appears likely," said Ludwig. "We have reached out to our counterparts at the FBI and Scotland Yard."

"And the explosive itself?" asked the VP.

"Semtex," answered the deputy, "confirmed by detection taggants."

The conference room grew silent before Frau Steir spoke again. "We are in a defensive posture. The events of the last few days are shaking our confidence. The chancellor asks that all of you step up your presence to preserve a sense of structure."

To emphasize her point, Frau Steir stood and walked to the large windows that towered over the center of the city. She gazed into the distance and studied the carnage of the Brandenburg Gate, the cracked and partially crumbled monument, the debris, and the defaced facades of other buildings in the square. Together, the view told a story of the destructive nature of the attack, and the ability of the adversary to challenge Germany's very foundations—both literally and symbolically.

Geiger stood, stretching to the full height of his tall frame. He looked down at the pad of paper on the blotter and then over his shoulder at Frau Steir. She continued to look out the window. "Order," said the federal police director. He read the only word written on the pad as he addressed his peers in a loud voice, "Order. Our citizens crave order!"

Chapter 32

Berlin, Germany

Otto played with his pipe as he leaned back in his chair at the second safe house in four days. Things were moving at a rapid clip and the German intelligence officer wanted to assure that he had his arms around as many variables as possible. "So, when you reported that a tail had picked you up after leaving Jokols' home, I sent my own man down to check things out."

"You were suspicious."

"Of course. I've never accepted coincidences as being without consequences."

"And in Landsberg, what did you find?" asked Terry.

"An eighty-six-year-old woman dead of an apparent heart attack in her own apartment."

"Nothing overly suspicious in that."

"Agreed," said Otto. "But it appeared that she had some guests just before she died. We found a half-full pot of stale coffee on the table with three cups. I didn't like the coincidence."

"Especially after she had just met with me for several hours a day or two earlier."

"Precisely," answered Otto.

Terry took a sip of bottled water and shifted in his chair. "What did you do?"

"I suspected foul play, so I insisted on an autopsy."

"How did that go over?"

Otto shrugged. "Thankfully, Frau Jokols had no family members alive to protest. Since we have no standing on domestic issues, I used a friend over at the BKA."

Otto's reference to the federal criminal investigative police made sense. The BKA was the German equivalent of the FBI.

"And what did the autopsy prove?"

"Frau Jokols had been poisoned."

Terry paused as he absorbed the information. "What was the agent?"

"Ah," replied Otto, "there it gets interesting. This was no accident; a sweet poison, odorless, from the Himalayas in West Bengal, India. It's called Aconitum ferox."

"Poison is usually a woman's preferred method."

"My experience as well," said Otto. "In any case, this poison causes ventricular tachycardia and fatal arrhythmias, which paralyzes the heart."

"We must have hit a nerve with Jokols," said Solak.

"Yes, Helios…I sense we are causing them distress. Needless to say, you should be extra aware of your surroundings. If this is a compressed schedule centered on the general election, it will only get more intense as the time nears…especially following their attack on the Brandenburg Gate."

Terry shuffled his feet for a moment and stretched. Then he fixed Otto with a curious gaze and asked, "What can you tell me about 'das Netzwerk?'"

***

Berlin, Germany

The three-year-old Mercedes-Benz minivan approached the intersection of Kreuzberg Straße and Grossbeeren Straße. It was late at night, and the streets around Viktoria Park were sparse with traffic.

The Kreuzberg neighborhood location was important. It was close to the Islamic center of Berlin, as well as to a heavily traveled tourist destination. Across from the intersection was the street level access to a man-made waterfall that extended upward for sixty-odd meters to a hilltop crowned with the cast-iron monument of a Prussian King. Few tourists to the public park missed the special photo op.

The van screeched to a halt and two men jumped from the vehicle. They opened the sliding side door, grabbed at a gray, canvas bundle soaked with a dark stain, and dragged it to the pavement. Then they dropped several armbands on top of the bundle, climbed back into the van, and sped away.

Chapter 33

Evie placed a scratch pad on her desk. The left-hand column listed several important historic events in the rise of the Nazi Party during the 1920s and 1930s. The right-hand column listed a series of important events that occurred in the last several months leading up to the recent bombing of the Brandenburg Gate. The dual lists were sequentially connected by a half dozen horizontal lines. Each political event from the past had a corresponding and equally important incident from the present. The pattern was full.

Evie stood in her cubicle, gathered the information, and walked down the hallway to Bob Colman's office. In three minutes, she was peering over the SAD chief's shoulder as he examined her busy, scribbled spreadsheet. She pointed. "See here, the Reichstag Fire was the seminal event of the election cycle of 1933. Many believe the Nazis initiated the attack themselves to assign blames to their political rivals, the Communists."

"The German Reichstag, their parliament."

"Yes, at the time, their most important building, highly symbolic to the German people. Today, most historians would assign that distinction to the Brandenburg Gate."

Bob leaned back and pondered her analysis. "So, you believe the recent bombing is political subterfuge to affect the election?"

"Yes," answered Evie. "The signs are consistent. A massive destructive attack against a symbolic structure. A minimal loss of life due to a middle-of-the-night initiation. I believe we will see a steep climb in political rhetoric. The Muslims will be implicated. In the 1930s the Nazis used the Reichstag Fire as a tipping point for German bitterness. *If* it was a false flag operation—it worked.

There was an emergency decree, evidence was procured, communist party delegates in parliament were arrested, and their seats were filled by Nationalist Socialists. Hitler had successfully manipulated the elections."

Bob Colman looked back down at Evie's notes and managed to follow her connective hand-written matrix. "Okay, put this in some type of a clearer format, so we can present a simple picture."

Evie plucked her notes from under Bob's nose and beelined it from the SAD chief's office.

***

Heidelberg, Germany

Twice each week, Dieter would exit his cluttered apartment in Bahnstadt and take the local train down to Old Town. He would walk around the romantic shops, marveling yet again at how the baroque architecture and historic charm of the medieval city could seduce a visitor. Narrow streets, picturesque houses, and ruined castles all contributed to the energy and flavor of the college town on the Neckar River.

Ostensibly, Dieter's walk was the German's concession to his doctor's advice: "Quit smoking and get more exercise." But in truth, it was his excuse to socialize and treat himself to an early dinner.

Dieter watched the crowds of youth and the tourist couples with equal interest, absorbing their energy while he made several routine stops to purchase supplies, including more cigarettes, along his route.

After forty minutes of a leisurely stroll around the neighborhood, Dieter turned down a side alley onto Bauamtsgasse. He angled towards the Schnitzel Bank, a casual restaurant serving traditional fare on work benches. A couple of beers, a good meal, and some casual conversation would top the day.

Twenty meters to his front, Dieter saw a small, very fast-looking Opel GT sports car idling along the curb. As Dieter shifted his packages, the coupe crawled into the middle of the street and activated the distinctive pop-up headlights. Dieter froze. Then the driver gunned the engine and the Opel screeched forward.

The car rammed Dieter flush in the knees at thirty miles an hour. Both legs snapped and the force flung his torso headfirst over the contoured hood, crashing his skull on the windshield. Then his limp body slid to the stone pavement and the GT continued to accelerate down the street.

Chapter 34

Munich, Germany

Munich, the capital of Bavaria, the third-largest city in Germany, a major center for art, finance, publishing, culture, education, advanced technology, beer production, the counter reformation, and the home of the National Socialist German Workers Party, also known as the Nazis. Of course, everyone knew that the Nazi Party no longer existed.

Terry strolled down Sendlinger Straße, the wide pedestrian-zone boulevard in the heart of Munich's shopping district. In his pocket was a recent photograph of a local woman in her mid-thirties named Ronja, along with the name and the address of the boutique craft shop that she managed in Stachus.

Terry was on the move again, traveling from Berlin to meet another asset on Otto's list of confidential informants. It surprised him a little that the intelligence officer would have such a well-developed inventory of local assets domiciled within the country. This of course ran contrary—at least on paper—to the stated mission of the BND, the foreign intelligence service. Not that Solak cared, because under any scenario, he was there at the invitation of the Germans. It was their country. They could settle the internal squabbles on their own.

Halfway between Marienplatz and the medieval city gate, Solak entered a small shop and recognized the woman who matched Otto's photo.

"Guten morgen, Ronja," said Terry using her name to convey knowledge, "Otto schickte mir."

Ronja's pleasant smile turned into a frown as she realized Solak was not a potential customer but had arrived at the shop with a different intent. She studied Terry for a minute before waving a finger towards the door. Then she spoke to a second woman in the rear before she led Solak out of the craft shop onto the cobblestone boulevard.

"Who are you," asked Ronja in an irritated tone, "you are not a German."

"No," replied Terry, "I am called Helios."

"Are you a Greek?" she asked. There was an edge to her question.

"No," replied Terry honestly, but he didn't offer any further explanation.

They walked in silence for a few minutes before Ronja turned down a narrow side street and led them into a small coffee shop. She chose a table in the rear.

"What do you want," she asked without preamble.

"Clarification."

"About what?"

Terry glanced around the shop before lowering his voice. "Das Netzwerk."

Ronja's eyes popped in surprise. Her irritation turned to anger, and she made no pretense to hide her mood change. "This is *not* right," said Ronja through clenched teeth. "He promised me."

Solak looked at the woman who appeared to be about his age. Obviously, Terry was not privy to the dialogues or the agreements Otto had made with his confidential sources. All he knew was that this woman was a bona fide provider of information.

Ronja nibbled at a strudel without really enjoying the pastry. A tear crept into her eye as she stirred her coffee. "These are dangerous people."

Solak nodded. He remained silent as Ronja processed the request, giving her some space to deal with the sudden intrusion to her life. Finally, after several sips of coffee, Ronja gave Terry a long and appraising look. "You don't know anything about me, do you?"

"No, but it's that way by design."

Ronja exhaled. "I was in prison."

Terry hid his surprise, but quickly accepted the information. Otto was an experienced intelligence officer, and professionals used a full array of enticements or pressure to gain information and advantages. "Where?" he asked.

"Right here in Munich at Stadelheim Prison." She gazed off into the distance, remembering her experience. "It has quite the history. Ernst Rohm was executed there, as were many supporters of the White Rose Resistance."

"Before your time."

"Yes," replied Ronja. "I was sentenced to five years for Volksverhetzung."

"And that means?"

"German law," said Ronja, "defines it as the incitement to hatred...anyone who tries to rouse hatred or promote violence against a group or individuals."

"And for this you received a sentence of five *years*?"

"Yes, and most of my friends were first time offenders like me, and they only received a three- to six-month sentence."

"What happened?" asked Terry.

"Otto happened. Somehow they determined that I was the leader because I was the oldest—mind you I was all of twenty-six years old."

"He put you there?"

"I don't know, but they made an example of me," replied Ronja, "and I soon realized my friends would be back to their carefree existence, and I would be in Stadelheim Prison. Five years is an eternity when you are young."

Terry nodded in agreement. He recognized the leverage in the turn of events. Maybe the intelligence officer initiated the process or maybe he took advantage of the situation. Either way, Otto gained another source.

"So what did he do?"

"He made a proposal," answered Ronja, "and I accepted. My sentence was reduced, from five years, to one year and two months."

"And now?"

"I have been out of prison for seven years. In the interim, I met someone, got married, then divorced, and had two children—I can*not* put my boys at risk."

"I understand," said Solak.

Ronja leaned forward and whispered in a quiet voice, "Do you? Das Netzwerk has resources and contacts that extend beyond Germany."

"Beyond Germany?"

"Of course," said Ronja. "Why do you think Otto made the approach? He had better information than the other federal agencies."

"About das Netzwerk?

"Yes," said Ronja in a thoughtful tone. She scribbled an address on a piece of paper and slid it across the table towards Solak. "I cannot talk now. Meet me tonight at this address at nine o'clock."

Ronja stood and walked from the pastry shop.

***

Berlin, Germany

Gerhardt was nervous. On the eve of his coming-out party, the Great Reveal, the trained orator was about to confront his biggest challenge. Could he measure up? Everything he had learned, practiced, and prepared for was about to culminate in a fifteen-minute speech that personified the German ethos. It was his duty to set the parameters, present the facts, and lead the electorate by outlining their choices. Everything that Gerhardt had been schooled for had pointed towards this moment in time, and his mother and the other members of the organization had plotted their schedule, patiently awaiting the precise moment when Germany would win back her identity and her country.

Nora approached Gerhardt with the patience of a monk. The difficulty with all highly talented individuals were bouts of self-doubt. They needed a stream of constant reinforcement to augment their output. She had plenty of help, but the day-to-day push and pull from Gerhardt's psych was a combination of outward confidence and bluster, and inward insecurity. He had been sheltered from his youth; groomed, educated, and indoctrinated for a unique moment in history. That moment was now.

She wrapped her arms around Gerhardt from behind as he sat and stared at the black screen. Then she started to nibble on his neck. "It is wonderful," said the blonde, taking a moment to hug Gerhardt warmly. "Come to bed."

"This is our last chance to edit or change our video," said Gerhardt. "We should review the finished product one more time."

Nora hesitated and then agreed. "Of course, my love, one more time, but then I need you close to me, because starting tomorrow, I will no longer have you to myself. Starting tomorrow, you will belong to all of Germany."

He looked at Nora with hopeful eyes. She reached forward and turned on the desktop computer and initiated the video.

"Tomorrow," said Nora, "the world will meet Gerhardt, our leader, the savior of a nation."

Chapter 35

Munich, Germany

Terry departed the pastry shop a few minutes after Ronja returned to her craft boutique. The pedestrian zone in Munich was crowded, and it offered Solak the chance to test for unwanted foot surveillance. He wandered and window shopped for twenty minutes and then hailed a cab and applied the same concepts in a car.

He traveled around the inner city in Munich, circling the Deutsches Museum, before instructing the cab driver to travel the area around his hotel.

Earlier that day he had checked into the Sofitel on Bayerstraße, a centrally located, historic hotel in the heart of the city. He had used a fake Canadian passport supplied by Otto. Now, following his initial contact with Ronja, it was time to eyeball the streets in daylight that he would be traveling at night.

Terry instructed the cabbie to perform three expanding concentric circles around his hotel before finally relenting and dropping Solak at the front doors of the Munich Bahnhof. Then Terry paid up, entered the front doors, and immediately walked out the side doors of the station. The Sofitel was a mere hundred meters away.

Solak used the next couple of hours to get in a workout at the hotel fitness center as well as study several street maps. He used the time to contrast the visual memories of his long cab ride with the lines and photos on the maps. Terry sat back and rubbed tired eyes when his cell phone rang.

"Helios," said the familiar voice, "did you meet our mutual friend?"

"Yes," replied Terry, "but she had to break-off. We plan to reconnect." He could hear Otto sigh on the other end of the phone. A moment of silence passed. "Is that a problem?" asked Terry.

"Maybe," said Otto. "I am calling because we've had some unexpected news."

Solak could sense the seriousness in the German's demeanor. Otto was struggling with how much information to share over an open line, even one that used a burner cell phone. "Can you talk?" asked Terry.

Otto hesitated, choosing his words carefully. "The elder gentleman that you met, the one who liked to smoke, he's had an unfortunate accident."

Terry bit his lip, "What kind of accident?"

"The fatal kind," answered Otto. "It appears there was a hit and run incident using a stolen car. The driver is unidentified, and the police are short on leads."

Solak felt the walls closing in on his probe. The improbability of Dieter being murdered in Heidelberg, following the poisoning of Frau Jokols in Landsberg, raised the stakes. Terry took a breath as he pondered the upcoming meet with Ronja—if, in fact, he was not being boxed. He and Otto both understood the implications.

"Alright," replied Solak.

"There's more," said Otto before Terry could disconnect. "We've located the body of the driver who attacked the Brandenburg Gate."

"He's dead?"

"Yes, when he didn't blow himself up with the car, we disregarded the act of a suicide bomber."

"Who is he?"

"A Syrian national traveling on a Turkish passport. A Muslim. He was executed with two bullets in the back of his head. His body was left in a public park."

"Sounds like he got set up."

"I agree," said Otto, "and at the same time, our attention is being directed. He was wearing an arm band of the Turkish flag."

"You mean a similar pattern to the flag."

"No," said Otto, correcting Solak's statement. "An *exact* replica of the current Turkish flag."

For the next thirty seconds, the two intelligence officers remained silent. They had already violated security time limits for an open-air communication. Finally, Otto said in a quiet voice, "Keep your wits Helios, Munich is the belly of the beast."

The line disconnected.

***

Munich, Germany

The location selected by Ronja for their meet was a noisy tavern a short walk from the Deutsches Museum. The 'Wirtshaus in der Au' was a mainstay on the popular local scene, attracting both regulars and tourists alike.

Terry arrived early, using the opportunity to scope out the tavern as well as to secure a private seat. It didn't matter. The raucous crowd was already in a boisterous mood. He was able to identify the last corner booth in the rear and convince the maître d' to let him settle in with his back to the wall. Solak immediately ordered a beer and a plate of traditional dumplings.

He took the next few minutes to survey the vaulted ceiling, the beer stein collection, and the eclectic chandeliers. Most of all Terry studied the people. The Bavarian-style restaurant was the type of establishment where one needed to sit close and speak into each other's ear to be heard. This of course made the telling of secrets appear normal. The din of the crowd offered its own protection.

After thirty minutes, Solak saw Ronja pass by the garden fountain and enter the Wirtshaus. Her eyes scanned the crowd with a practiced motion before settling on Solak in the corner. Terry gave her a nod, they locked eyes, and Ronja weaved her way towards the booth.

As a courtesy, Solak stood and motioned to the empty seat he had saved. Ronja brushed away the offer and squeezed her way into the bench next to Terry. Then she grabbed his forearm with her right hand and raised her lips to his ear. "This way, no one can overhear our private conversation." She wrapped their arms together.

It was a good move. They looked every bit a romantic couple. The message to onlookers said their contact was social. Terry appreciated the guise. "What can I offer you?" asked Solak quietly in her ear.

"Beer," said Ronja with a smile.

He nodded. "Are you hungry?"

"No." She smiled again, and the motion served to brighten her attractive features. Terry couldn't determine if her smile was for the effect of others or if it was genuine. Ronja leaned towards Solak so that their bodies touched and she raised her lips to his ear as he signaled the waiter.

"The Network is very powerful. They have existed for years. Some say they go back to Bormann's wife."

"Really." The admission caught him by surprise. Ronja may not have been trained as a professional, but she seemed to have natural instincts. "That would be quite a legacy," said Terry. "Do they have that kind of reach?"

"Yes," nodded Ronja speaking into his ear. "I'm terrified."

Solak leaned back and studied her features. "Were you followed?"
"I don't think so," replied Ronja. "Otto taught me a few tricks, but I still worry."

"A lot is going on," said Terry, thinking about the most recent news given to him that very afternoon by Otto.

"Something big is in the wind," said Ronja. "The rumor is that the news will shake the very foundation of the Republic."

Solak sipped his beer and pushed away the plate of half-eaten dumplings. "Is it another attack, something overwhelming?" Terry's mind wandered as he tried to guess at the extent of the pending event.

Ronja shook her head and snuggled closer to Terry's ear before whispering, "Only that it is unexpected and it will affect the election."

Solak thought about her response as he leaned back and took a slow appraising look around the tavern. He studied the patrons as if somehow the German Zeitgeist would leap to the surface, identify itself, and solve the secret dilemma.

Ronja turned away as Terry pondered her response. "Do you have children?" she asked.

Solak shook his head.

"It changes everything," said Ronja. There was a melancholy aspect to her comment that served to hide her smile. She took a long drink of beer. "A rumor has circulated for years, that the Network would surface when the time was right."

"Is that time now?"

"I don't know," answered Ronja, "but a friend of mine once said that there is a fatalism deep in the German soul that craves a sign."

"A sign?"

"Some type of signal," said Ronja in Terry's ear. "Something that will release the pent-up emotion, the guilt, the frustration that resides deep in every German."

Solak pressed closer to Ronja and asked, "This signal will act as a prompt, a catalyst?"

"An excuse," replied Ronja, "for Germans to follow their instincts—not the collective homogenization of the European Union. We are a proud people."

Ronja studied Terry as he considered her thoughts. She could see that her words had opened a previously closed door. It was difficult for an outsider to grasp the crosscurrents that competed in the psych of postwar citizens; the institutionalized guilt buffered by a bristling pride in all things German.

"What are your thoughts on the narrator?" asked Terry.

The question caught Ronja off guard, and she studied Solak's features from a few inches distance before answering. "He has developed a strong following in a short period of time. He uses historic references. The question one must ask is: with the general election two weeks away, can this voice, this narrator, complete the circle? Can he convert emotions into votes?"

"What do you think will happen?"

"I don't know," replied Ronja, "but if the narrator is tied to this pending event, it could have a dramatic impact on Germany."

Terry frowned and half turned in his seat so that he could look at Ronja. "Will you help us?"

A look of fear flashed across Ronja's face. "I can't." A serious expression followed, and her hand started to shake.

"Do you owe them?" asked Solak.

"No, it is *not* loyalty or debt." Ronja gripped Terry's hand and pressed the back of his hand against her cheek. Solak noted a tear creep into her eye. "Do you understand?" she asked.

Terry remained silent, letting Ronja work through the process by herself.

"They will take my boys," said Ronja in a desperate whisper. She blotted away her tear and stood. "I have to go."

In seconds she twirled and exited the crowded tavern.

Chapter 36

Twelve days before the German general elections, Gerhardt's special video hit the internet. It immediately went viral. Expectations had built since his last release, and the promise of a face-to-face introduction of the unknown narrator proved overpowering.

The followers were a diverse collection of hopeful citizens, curiosity seekers, fearmongers, and undecided voters. Everyone sought clarity from the good, to the bad, to the indifferent. The narrator with the magic voice, who matched the style, sound, and substance of Germany's most notorious politician, had promised to reveal himself in the days leading up to the election. That time was now.

The video began with a short history of Germany as a nation, dating back to Otto the Great, King of Germany and the Holy Roman Emperor. Select photographs were projected with sweeping scans of castles and the medieval countryside.

Gerhardt modulated his narrative, drawing in the viewers with broad points of historic significance, laying an irrefutable foundation of how deep the German roots penetrated the soil.

It was a tempered discussion, calm, measured, and factual; broad strokes on which to build. He had struck a chord deep in the heart of the populist movement. Something had to change.

Then Gerhardt extolled important world events led by Germans from the proclamation of Martin Luther's ninety-five thesis to the defeat of Napoleon at the Battle of Leipzig. In each frame of the narrative, visual images accompanied the speech. Gradually Gerhardt led the viewers to the modern age, omitting any discussion of the two World Wars, sidestepping Germany's failures until the fall of the Berlin Wall and then to the year 2002, when the euro replaced the Deutsche Mark as the nation's currency. He paused and let the fact settle. His voice changed as the narration picked up steam. There was now an edge to the voice, a clear shift in demeanor as Gerhardt allowed the sound of frustration to creep into his tone.

He mentioned parliament's ratification of the European Union's constitution three years later, and then the approval—again by parliament—in 2010, of twenty-two billion euros to bailout the Greek economy.

His voice became irate. Gerhardt was moving towards the crest. Photos of newspaper headlines crossed the screen, interspersed with film of protests. He reminded the viewers of the government's offer to accept a million refugee asylum seekers; and how hundreds of German women were assaulted by Muslim migrants on New Year's Eve. He highlighted the continued attacks in Wurzburg, Ausbach, and Berlin, as well as the recent spate of assassinations throughout the country. Finally, he focused on the heavily covered car bombing of Germany's most honored symbol, the Brandenburg Gate.

He paused before summating in a call to action, "…when leaders stop leading, when our politicians place their own interests before those of their citizens, it is time to get *new* politicians…the nation comes first, a Germany for Germans…*this* is our time…vote for a party that will work for *you*, for your interests…*we* control our destiny…"

The voice-over reached a fevered pitch as the German flag fluttered on the screen, and then suddenly a head and shoulder close-up of the speaker zoomed in, and the incredible likeness of the Fuhrer appeared. "…join me in a vote for *change*. My name is Gerhardt, and I *am* the grandson of Adolf Hitler."

***

Berlin, Germany

The group of twenty was in an uproar. For the first time in over a decade, the chancellor's center right party could win the most votes but lose control of parliament. It was a disquieting thought. The risk was in the rise of a new far right populist party that displayed overtones to Germany's dark history. If such an event occurred, then to preserve the ability to govern, the chancellor would be forced to reconcile with less desirable fringe parties, which would then demand special policies to gain their support. This threatened the entire postwar order.

Prompting this reassessment of the parliamentary obstacles was the new star of the disaffected, a man named Gerhardt. And ground zero for the looming power struggle was Munich, the wealthy, Catholic, tradition-infused capitol of Bavaria, and home of the long-dead dictator Adolf Hitler.

"Who is he?" asked Frau Steir in an exasperated tone. "He can't possibly be related to Hitler."

"This is some type of populist insurrection at the eleventh hour," said the VP of the domestic security agency.

"Someone is trying to influence the election by introducing an emotional pull at the last moment," replied Holger of the Berlin State Police.

The conference room broke into a cacophony of noise as several of the delegates all became animated at once. Suddenly, Director Geiger of the federal police stood and asked in a rhetorical tone, "Is it possible?"

"Is *what* possible," said Ludwig of the Federal Criminal Police, "that Adolf Hitler had an heir? Do we even want to entertain such a notion?"

"Make this Gerhardt *prove* his lineage," said the VP of the domestic security agency.

"How," asked Frau Steir. "Do we have time? Is it his motive to prove his bloodline or our responsibility to disprove it? We don't even know who he is."

"We need to silence him," said Holger. "His rhetoric is inflammatory."

"Be very careful," replied the VP of domestic security. "To arrest him without clear proof that he has violated constitutional protections, is a dangerous precedent."

"He is espousing Nazi ideology," said Ludwig, "without the symbols or the language. He is walking a fine line. We need to expose him as a fraud, not make him a martyr."

"He is not a candidate for office," said Steir, "and he has not supported any political party. I ask again, who is Gerhardt?"

"It is obvious," said deputy Ludwig, "that the far right stands to benefit from this development."

"If we find the man," said the VP of domestic security, "we can find the truth. The burden falls on us to stifle this problem."

"Pay heed," said Steir, "this issue threatens our stability."

"Find him," said Holger. "We must locate and apprehend this Gerhardt before the election. He needs to be identified."

"He needs to be questioned," replied Ludwig. "His very assertion poses a danger to the republic."

The conference room broke into a free-for-all of opinions, warnings, and recriminations as the noise escalated to unprecedented levels. The normally collegial group of professionals turned their focus inward, mired in caustic debate, over the presence and the handling of the populist ideologue called Gerhardt.

Chapter 37

Munich, Germany

The whole world was watching, and the sudden shift in the playing field was spurred by the live introduction of Gerhardt. The timing was superb; the Hitler sound-alike was also a Hitler look-alike, and also claimed direct descendance to the deceased dictator.

Terry's cell phone rang. The only person that had his number on the burner phone was Otto.

"Ja," answered Solak.

"Helios," said the foreign intelligence officer, "have you seen the news?"

"Couldn't miss it."

"The cat is out of the proverbial bag," said Otto, "now we know what we sought to know, although I must admit, this one is a bit of a shocker."

"Is it possible?"

"That Hitler had children? I don't know…in the grand scheme of things, does it even matter?"

"The people believe it."

"They will believe what they want to believe," replied Otto. "The question is, will it affect the election?"

"Is Gerhardt positioning the far right party for inclusion in parliament?"

"Yes, Helios, if they succeed in gaining five percent of the popular vote, they will be admitted to the Reichstag."

"They would have standing."

"Yes, and for the first time in postwar Germany, there will be real Nazis as members of parliament. That is a sea change in our world." Otto paused for a moment before asking, "How did you leave things with the asset?"

"She's scared, she's a mother, and the organization has her spooked. She broke contact."

Otto exhaled. "Give her some space, Helios, I will recheck her file. Maybe there is some leverage I can dig up."

Otto's attention seemed to digress as the foreign intelligence officer focused on activities taking place back in Berlin. A minute passed, then he made an observation. "I must admit, Helios, no one believed it would lead to this…give me an hour. I will call you back."

The cell phone disconnected.

***

Munich, Germany

Friedel Schulz and Frau Keller sat in the Ozdeveli restaurant on Preysing Straße behind the Gasteig. The police presence was everywhere, as each major city patrolled their streets with local Landespolizei, state police. They moved by foot near immigrant businesses and tourist spots. In addition, federal police augmented the local presence with teams of three that circled government institutions and landmark locations.

"Do you think he decided the visibility was too great?" asked Keller of her older friend.

Friedel Schulz considered the comment before shaking her head. "No, he is just being cautious. Traffic is clogged with the protesters."

The nation had been gripped in a political vortex as the run-up to the general election pitted the status quo against a quickly expanding populist movement. Protesters and counter-protesters appeared spontaneously, some with, and some without, appropriate permits, as a new wave of civil disobedience surfaced. Traffic snarled, neighborhoods clogged, and crowds formed as sound-bites of Gerhardt's Great Reveal speech focused the electorate on Muslim migrants. The most recent revelation stated that the bomber of the Brandenburg Gate was identified as a Turkish national. The issues of immigration and national sovereignty were propelling a split in the ruling coalition.

A plate of pide, the long, freshly baked flatbread concoction filled with ground meat and spinach arrived at the table. The two German women exchanged a look before surveying the crowd. Friedel hailed the waiter, "There must be some mistake," she said, pointing at the pide.

The waiter politely shook his head and whispered in German that the pide was, "Compliments of the house." Then he walked away.

Neither of the women reached for the flatbread, but rather they took the opportunity to glance around the restaurant again, to study the dining crowd.

A few minutes later Sharif Ali entered the Ozdeveli followed by his two bodyguards. He squeezed into the corner table with white leather upholstery and waited as his men took up a position at the next table, just beyond earshot.

"You are late," said Frau Keller in English.

Sharif looked at the German with an irritated expression. The prince was not used to chastisement—especially from a woman. "I was delayed on an important matter," replied Sharif. He offered neither an apology or further explanation.

"We are on a tight schedule as well," said Friedel Schulz. She wanted to drive home the point of punctuality.

For a moment, the two women held their ground, and then Ali gave a courteous nod. "Your point is well taken," said the Saudi. "What is the status of your list?"

"It is still being developed," answered Keller, "it won't be finalized until after the general election. Much will depend on how things turn out."

Ali nodded. "Just bear in mind, that to properly prepare the logistics, we need sufficient lead time."

"We understand," said Friedel.

"*And*," replied the prince with a single index finger pointed up, "we need a complete rupture with Ankara. Enough of this acrimonious sniping and diplomatic chill between old friends. *We want* a clear break in relations. Both imports and exports between countries stop, reduction of investments, money is frozen, trade comes to a standstill…and Turkey receives no support and no viable path to EU membership."

"We agree," replied Keller.

Sharif leaned back in his chair and motioned at the plate of pide. "This Turkish restaurant serves a wonderful flatbread—you really should try it."

The incongruity of the statement stood in stark contrast to his plans for the Turkish economy. He smiled and gave a polite nod to the two women. Then he motioned at his two bodyguards and the three Saudis stood and exited the restaurant.

Chapter 38

Munich, Germany

Terry entered Stachus from the western end of the pedestrian zone, under the medieval city gate known as Karlstor. He paced the boulevard, retracing his steps by memory to the boutique shop. Ten minutes later he entered the store and Ronja's eyes settled on Solak. She nodded, and then motioned towards the corner before speaking to one of the other female employees. Finally, she grabbed her waist purse from under the counter and led Terry from the shop.

"I've been expecting you," said Ronja, forcing a smile.

"Things change fast. You heard the news?"

Ronja folded her arms across her chest as they walked, and she looked at Terry with clear blue eyes. "The whole *world* heard the news. Is it true?"

Solak shrugged, "You tell me."

"You believe it's possible or you wouldn't be here," replied Ronja. She fell into a silence.

They walked around the corner and then, as Terry started to enter the coffee shop from their first meeting, Ronja tugged at his elbow and steered him away. "We need a taxi."

Solak considered for a moment that he was being set up, but then he dismissed the concern to focus on the woman. If her goal was nefarious, then at least Otto would know where to look. Terry needed to play it out.

They cut through a narrow alley and exited the rear side of the pedestrian zone, making their way toward the well-traveled thoroughfares of Karlsplatz and the East Stachus taxi stand.

"Did Otto tell you to threaten me if I didn't help?" asked Ronja.

Solak hesitated before answering. "Not exactly…but he did emphasize how important this turn of events was for Germany."

Ronja studied Terry as he spoke, watching his eyes, his mannerisms. She was looking for 'tells,' and her own demeanor suggested an ingrained distrust.

"And if I don't cooperate?" said Ronja, pressing the issue.

"That I should remind you of the indiscretion with the narcotics."

"It wasn't my indiscretion," said Ronja with an edge in her voice, "and Otto knows that."

At the taxi stand Ronja gave the driver an address and they tumbled into the rear seat of the cab before speeding away.

After a few minutes of silence, Ronja looked over at Terry and spoke in a quiet voice. "I am sure, Helios, that you are relaying the conversation in a much more diplomatic manner. Otto can be *mean* when he doesn't get his way."

Solak considered her observation but did not answer. Instead, he chose a different tack. "Tell me what happened?"

Ronja looked out the window of the cab. "Three years ago, my husband was caught smuggling a large supply of crystal meth across the border from the Czech Republic. Some of the stash was stored at our apartment in a special compartment in the attic. I knew nothing about this, and I certainly wasn't in-volved—I do *not* do drugs."

"So how did it progress?" asked Terry.

Ronja leaned closer to Solak in the rear seat and whispered. "They impli-cated me as a matter of course and Otto stepped in to save the day. Of course, he *knew* I didn't mess with drugs, and he also knew I would never put my boys at risk."

Terry frowned before asking, "So he leveraged up his value to you."

Ronja gave Terry a smirk. "More like he leveraged up his *control over* me."

"And your husband?"

"My *ex*-husband. I was livid. For him to jeopardize our family was inexcus-able. It was a selfish act. He went to prison and I divorced him."

Solak changed the topic. "Where are we heading now?"

"Bogenhausen," replied Ronja, "the thirteenth borough of Munich, the home of the wealthy elite, filled with castles, large villas, and old German aris-tocracy."

Terry studied the leafy neighborhoods as the cab cruised the residential en-clave. He counted several foreign consulates constructed in the Wilhelminian-style architecture. Then as they drove down Prinzregentenstraße, Ronja pointed at a nondescript police station. "On the second floor of that building, was the apartment of Adolf Hitler."

***

Berlin, Germany

Frau Steir stood motionless at the Goethe Monument in the Tiergarten. There was a seasonal nip in the air as summer faded into the recent past and a mid-September breeze from the southeast settled over the city. From her right, Steir saw the VP of the domestic security agency hobble towards the tall monument, walking better, but still showing a noticeable limp.

"The leg is improving," said Steir.

"Ja, slowly," replied the VP. "I think it has become the repository of all the stress over the last few weeks."

She let the comment pass before offering her own observation. "The AfD, the Alt for Germany, did not exist as a party four years ago, and now they are positioned to win seats in parliament and propel the center into negotiating a coalition."

"The populist message strikes a chord for the far right," replied the VP. "Do you think that this Gerhardt is aligned with the AfD...we have not identified any connection."

"Nor would you," said Steir. "We would never see it, but the fact remains, that by not declaring a party affiliation, Gerhardt has positioned himself as a leader for *all* the disaffected voters of the last few years."

They lapsed into silence before the VP offered, "I worry about Geiger."

"So do I," said Steir, quick to embrace his concern. She waited for the VP to clarify. When no explanation was given, she forced the VP to articulate his concern. "In what way?"

"He has hardline tendencies."

Steir acted indifferent. "He is a law-and-order type. He was former military."

"Yes," said the VP, "but I sense that he has right-leaning sentiments. I believe he agrees with many of Gerhardt's positions."

"You think he's a Nazi?"

"More of a sympathizer. Someone who envisions a very different solution to the immigrant problem."

Frau Steir considered the VP's words and then turned to face her counterpart. "We have had no reaction to the leaks. Everyone is being very careful...is there something we can offer, that would cause Geiger to show his hand? Something significant?"

"Let me give it some thought," said the VP. "We need to assure this reaction to Gerhardt doesn't spread."

"He needs to be stopped," said Steir in a sharp tone. "Last week four British soldiers were arrested in the UK for neo-Nazi membership. That was in England…what do you think is happening *here*, in the home of Adolf Hitler?"

"Muslims are being attacked by roving bands of neo-Nazis," replied the VP, "and several Turkish businesses have been burned and looted. We are close to identifying the instigators, but there has been no clear route to Gerhardt." The VP paused before asking. "Will the chancellor grant emergency powers?"

Chapter 39

Munich, Germany

It was a grand mansion in the finest tradition of old Europe, boasting three levels of polished limestone, a gabled roofline, semi-curved window trellises, wood edgings, and crafted wrought iron railings all surrounded by a high stone wall that occluded vision and impeded access. The manicured lawn boasted a fountain, a circular driveway, and several perfectly maintained antique cars.

Terry raised an eyebrow as the taxi slowed. He turned towards Ronja. "Friend of yours?" he asked.

"My boss," replied Ronja. "Her name is Hedda. She owns the boutique that I manage down in Stachus."

"I see, evidently your little shop does quite well," said Solak with a nod towards the huge villa.

Ronja smiled. "My shop is just a sideline for her. She doesn't know what to do with all her money, so she keeps turning it over and reinvesting. From what I can tell, she has quite a knack for business."

Terry paid for the taxi and they stepped from the cab. It was a short walk to the front door and he sensed they were being watched the entire time. His instincts proved accurate, and before Ronja could knock, the large oak portal swung open.

"Miss Ronja," said a dapper manservant dressed in a tie and herringbone vest. He stepped back as Terry and Ronja entered the large foyer.

"Were we expected?" asked Solak in a quiet voice.

Ronja shook her head as she touched Solak's elbow and guided him inward.

The inside of the villa was every bit a match to the exterior, complete with oil paintings by Dutch masters, crystal chandeliers from the island of Murano, and Parisian Louis XIV gilt and lacquer-veneered furniture. This was old money, generational wealth, the kind of affluence that infused politics, dominated business, and influenced cultures. Somehow Ronja, the activist protester that crossed a line of civil disobedience into the realm of criminality, was on familiar terms with the villa's owner, a world that at first blush appeared wholly divorced from her more prosaic existence. It just didn't fit.

Solak's eyes wandered around the ground floor entrance, quickly studying the layout. Then he noticed an inner parlor where a woman in her forties sipped coffee while reading a newspaper. The manservant led them to the parlor.

"Ronja," said the home's owner, shifting in her seat and appearing surprised by the interruption. She stood. "What brings you around?"

"A friend," said Ronja, "in need of some information. He goes by Helios."

The home's owner studied Terry for a moment, holding her bifocals in one hand, and the newspaper in the other. "That's an odd name."

"A nickname," replied Terry, quickly addressing the observation. "My name is Paul Carter; I am from Toronto." He used the name on the fake Canadian passport supplied by Otto.

"And what is your interest?"

"The developing climate here just before your elections."

"You mean Gerhardt?"

"Amongst other issues. Our concern is not political, actually, it is financial. We are trying to understand how these events affect your economy and, by association, the European Union."

Hedda pointed across the parlor to a sitting area with a divan, two cushioned chairs, and a small table. "Let's sit."

They moved across the parlor and within minutes the manservant reappeared carrying a pot of fresh coffee and a tray of sweets.

"Ask your questions," said Hedda in a diffident manner. The posture didn't match the profile. Ronja's boss didn't seem at all like the timorous type. Solak's antennae went up a couple of notches, and he leaned forward. "Is it possible that this Gerhardt is a descendant of Adolf Hitler?"

"Possible," said Hedda. "A few years ago, a Frenchman named Loret surfaced and told a story relating back to World War One. He asserts that Hitler, who was a corporal in the Germany Army, had a brief affair with his mother, to which she became pregnant and gave birth."

Hedda took a sip of coffee.

"He claimed to be the son of Hitler," said Terry.

"Precisely."

"Was it true?" asked Solak.

"Maybe. There were a number of similarities to include handwriting analysis and a blood type match, as well as some circumstantial evidence like photographs, signed paintings, and cash payments delivered by German Army officers; but in the end, nothing to refute or corroborate the information."

"Where does it stand?" asked Solak.

"Nowhere," replied Hedda. "The Frenchman has been dead for thirty years."

"And now Gerhardt surfaces."

Hedda leaned forward. "Ja, but this poses a very different set of variables."

"How so?" asked Terry.

"Gerhardt is a uniquely German story. If the rumors are true, then the National Socialists finally have their icon. The bloodlines are pure, the resemblance uncanny, and the political orientation unique. He *will* change Germany."

***

Berlin, Germany

They sat together on the couch in the condominium on Corneliusstraße. Both faced the television, as Nora wrapped her legs around Gerhardt's hips and clasped her feet at the ankle in an affectionate embrace. She sat patiently as Gerhardt raised and lowered the remote control, switching channels in random order as the television flashed different versions of the same story. Everything was about Gerhardt.

The narrator was exposed, but was he? Who was the recently revealed Gerhardt, an unknown, unseen political commentator who was *not* running for elective office, but claimed to be the grandson of Adolf Hitler?

Finally, Gerhardt swiveled in his seat and tried to stand. Nora tightened her grip around his hips and hugged him close. "What is it?" she asked.

"I need some air," replied Gerhardt.

The blonde's eyes widened and she pointed at the television screen. "You can *not* go out, you are all over the news."

"I will stay in the neighborhood," said Gerhardt.

Nora gripped his upper body in a hug, as she possessively locked his lower body in a crossed leg squeeze. "You can't go, my love, everyone is looking for you. Stay here with me where it is safe."

Gerhardt pulled away, gently prying Nora's legs apart at the ankle and stood. He stretched. "They think I am in Munich. I *need* fresh air."

Nora gripped at Gerhardt's leg with her bare feet, trying to pull him back to the couch as he gave her the remote control. She looked up and then changed the channel. The story was about Gerhardt. She flicked the button: Gerhardt. And again...Gerhardt. Each channel had a different version of the same news story, all offering a perspective on the hunt for the narrator named Gerhardt. He was wanted by both the police and the federal authorities for questioning, yet news reporters were quick to point out that he had broken no laws.

"It is not safe," said Nora.

"I will wear a disguise."

Gerhardt turned and started towards the rear foyer. Nora hesitated for a moment and then jumped to her feet. "Wait for me," she said, "I am coming with you." Nora caught up to Gerhardt and pulled at his pocket as she followed him to the closet. "We also need security."

"I will be fine," replied Gerhardt in mild protest.

"You are the most wanted man in Germany."

"I have done nothing wrong."

"They will create a reason to apprehend you," said Nora with a look of concern.

"Why," asked Gerhardt, "because of the truth?"

"Because they *fear* you."

Chapter 40

Munich, Germany

Hedda leaned back in her chair and rotated her bifocals in a slow, rhythmic motion. "The rumor behind the Gerhardt narrative is true."

Terry sipped at his cup of black coffee and looked across the room. Hedda sensed that Solak needed context.

"Adolf Hitler," said the home owner, "had no family and no descendants; at least, that is the historic belief. He did not marry Eva Braun, his longtime girlfriend, until hours before they committed suicide in the bunker in Berlin."

Solak nodded. "Were there other relationships?"

"Yes, over the years, Hitler had several romantic affairs, but he was politically ambitious, and women often got in the way."

"Is that accurate?"

"I believe so," said Hedda. "There are many theories that purport to explain Hitler's sexuality and his lack of children. Most of it is dubious content."

"What is your take?" asked Terry.

"Hitler, or Herr Wolf as he preferred to be called, liked women, but only as a diversion. He never involved women in affairs of state. He was quite fond of children, but for propaganda purposes, he positioned himself as the father of Germany."

"So Eva Braun was kept in the background."

"Yes, she was over twenty years his junior, and a bit carefree. They spent a considerable amount of time together—especially when secluded at the Berghof. For political reasons the relationship was kept secret."

"What changed?"

"Gretl, Eva's sister."

Terry looked at Hedda with a confused expression. She leaned inward.

136

"Eva was an important figure within Hitler's social circle, but she did not attend public events with Herr Wolf *until* her sister, Gretl, married an SS staff officer named Hermann Fegelein."

Hedda paused in her explanation to allow the statement to settle. She stole a look at Ronja who sat quietly next to Terry listening to the story.

"In many ways," said Hedda with a smirk, "Hitler fancied himself as the nation's most eligible bachelor, and therefore he felt that Eva should not become the focus of the country's attention."

"So Gretl, her sister, offered political cover?"

"Exactly. Gretl was now around all the time because of her marriage to Fegelein. Eva could be introduced as Gretl's sister, *not* Adolf's girlfriend."

"How does Gretl's presence factor into Hitler's progeny?" asked Terry.

Hedda took another sip of coffee and cleared her throat. "If Eva was carefree, Gretl her sister was an incessant flirt. Her marriage to SS staff officer Fegelein was one of attraction and expediency. He was a notorious womanizer in his own right."

"Gretl and her husband sound well suited."

"It was a political marriage of the first order," said Hedda.

"So, what happened?"

"Fegelein, flirted with Eva and, to an extent, she reciprocated, but there is no evidence that Eva crossed the line."

"So there was no consummation," said Solak seeking confirmation from Hedda.

"It appears she stayed loyal to Hitler, but Herr Wolf noticed."

"What did he do?"

"Hitler had several choices," said Hedda looking across the room as she recollected the options. "One, kill Fegelein outright, but without evidence of an actual affair between Eva and Hermann, that would look like an overreaction, and Hitler was very sensitive to perception."

Solak considered Hedda's analysis before she continued.

"The second option," said Hedda, "was to transfer Fegelein to the Russian Front, which was tantamount to a death sentence, but it also had the potential to make Hitler look weak, as if he had to remove a competitor for his girlfriend's attention."

Hedda shifted in her cushioned chair as Terry considered the nuances of the story.

"Finally," said the homeowner, "Hitler could turn the tables on Fegelein, and make *him* the cuckolded husband."

Terry's eyes widened as he asked, "Did Hitler sleep with Gretl?"

"Yes," answered Hedda. "To get even, he seduced Gretl, his future sister-in-law, and she became pregnant."

"With Hitler's child?"

Hedda took a moment to set down her coffee cup and look directly at Solak. "And there lies the question. Most historians know that Gretl gave birth to a baby girl in May of 1945…but few people know that Gretl actually had twins."

***

Langley, Virginia

Evie had adapted well to the switch from analyst to collection manager. As much as she appreciated the camaraderie and groupthink of the Analysis Directorate, nothing quite compared to the fast-moving, operational mode of SAD. It offered a whole new perspective to critical decision making.

She stood at her desk rearranging a checklist of information pertinent to Terry's probe mission in Germany. The crosscurrents seemed to grow by the day, and part of her job was to keep Terry—the officer she knew only as Helios—a step ahead of the competition.

Her special scrambler telephone line buzzed, and she plucked at the receiver, "This is Evie."

"Helios," said Solak, knowing that the one-word confirmation was sufficient. "How goes the battle?"

"Good," said Evie with a laugh, "but you're the one on the front line."

"Still like the new job?"

"Yes," replied Evie, "I'm starting to feel competent at my work again."

"It's only been a couple of months," said Terry, "sounds like you got your arms around the whale in pretty quick order."

"Thank you," replied Evie as she acknowledged the compliment. "There's a lot at play. Are you holding up?"

"Yes…I'm on the clock, so I'll be quick," said Terry switching gears, "I need you to gather everything you can find on Herr Wolf's romantic life, to include past girlfriends, relationships, and romances over the years."

"Okay," said Evie taking notes as Terry relayed his request. "What else?"

"You need to become an expert on pregnancy, find a doctor, an ob-gyn, and pick their brain on twins and multiple births—especially ones involving different parties in the same time frame."

"Will do," said Evie, writing in her own shorthand. "Is that the supposition?"

"I don't know, but I'm getting an earful on the sisters and the women's club."

Evie knew that Terry was speaking in code about Gretl and Eva Braun and das Netzwerk. "Got it." She paused and then said, "Bob wanted to be sure that you had a handle on the current friction between the German chancellor and the Turkish president."

"I've been picking up enough local news to get the gist. Their rhetoric is off the charts."

"Bob believes that there are other players in Germany pressing the Turkish angle."

"Okay," said Terry, "good to know."

"Anything else?"

"Yes…we know that Herr Wolf's body was burned at the bunker. Are there any DNA-type tests that can be performed to confirm or refute bloodlines or lineage?"

"I'll find out," answered Evie.

"That's it, got to run, thanks for the chat."

A second later, Solak's burner cell phone disconnected.

Chapter 41

Munich, Germany

The SWAT (SEK) team of the Bavarian State Police surrounded the tool and die factory in Erding. They were accompanied by two investigators of the Federal Criminal Police and two agents of the domestic security agency.

The general elections were a week away, and Germany had evolved into a cauldron of bubbling discontent. The long-cherished goal of centrist alliances and consensus-based government was crumbling. The cities became the focal point of the national effort to locate and apprehend Gerhardt. The unknown narrator, a man who claimed to be a direct descendant to Adolf Hitler, needed to be questioned. Every legal precept available to the authorities was employed in a desperate effort to control the sudden appearance of the non-candidate. Gerhardt was dangerous. He resonated with a vast percentage of youth, disaffected citizens, and nonaligned voters. A new nationalism bloomed in Germany, and Europe shuddered.

The police quickly entered the factory and surrounded the machinists. They fanned out amongst the industrial equipment. Then one of the federal criminal investigators presented the shop foreman with a warrant and they took him into custody.

Three dozen similar scenes took place in seven German cities, with a heavy focus on Munich and Berlin. A combination of arrests, detentions, searches, and business closures were initiated across the nation. Places of business, worship, social centers and private residences were targeted as the chancellor's office approved 'emergency powers' in a bid to control civil unrest days before the election.

Munich felt the surge in activity due to its obvious connection to history. The far right nationalism of neo-Nazis and ultra-conservative adherents were a threat. So, too, were the far-left pockets of Islamic extremism. Not only did the president of Turkey openly petition Turks in Germany to vote *against* the current administration, but mounting evidence of the Brandenburg Gate bombing and European Union delegate assassinations all pointed at Muslim-inspired terrorists.

If past was prologue, then a grave danger existed. Gerhardt's presence on the national scene exacerbated community tensions.

The SWAT team marched the bevy of skilled machinists from the factory floor and locked down the tool and die shop. Then they posted orange police closure notices and drove off with the shop foreman.

***

Munich, Germany

Terry excused himself to use the lavatory. His head spun with information. Their host, Hedda, told a narrative that at face value sounded at once farfetched, but also entirely plausible.

Solak used the break to study his surroundings, quietly observing and committing to memory the mansion's layout. The manservant was nowhere to be found, yet Terry still sensed that his trek to the bathroom was being observed. He was careful to appear slightly lost in the expanse of the floor plan to explain his wanderings. Finally, he stumbled his way back to the parlor and sat across from Hedda.

Ronja gave him a curious look and then returned her attention to the mansion's owner.

"Where was I?" asked Hedda.

"Twins," answered Solak.

Hedda set down her coffee cup and fixed her gaze on Terry. "Twelve minutes after giving birth to a baby girl, Gretl gave birth to a second child, a boy."

"The twins you speak of."

"*Fraternal* twins," replied Hedda with a quiet emphasis.

"How do you know?" asked Terry. "Was there some kind of DNA match?"

"No, not then, but I saw the photographs. The children looked nothing alike. Their features and coloring were quite different."

"Different fathers," said Terry.

"Same mother, different eggs," replied Hedda with a nod.

"Is that possible?"

"Of course," replied Hedda. "Gretl Braun was a promiscuous girl. She slept with both Fegelein her husband and Hitler her lover during the same ovulation phase. Two different eggs impregnated by two separate sperm deposits."

"What happened to the daughter?"

"She died in 1971," answered Hedda. "Another chapter in a tragic life. A suicide."

"Did she know about her brother?"

"No," replied Hedda, "it was kept from her. Frau Bormann stepped in and took charge."

"Bormann," said Terry in surprise. "As in Martin Bormann?"

"The same. The men were long gone. They were in Berlin. Gretl stayed behind in the mountains at Obersalzberg to have her baby in a calm environment."

"Did Gretl know she was pregnant with twins?"

"Probably not. Frau Bormann was controlling the situation. No one would cross her—certainly *not* the obstetrician."

Terry leaned forward. "Two babies separated at birth, the daughter stayed with her mother, and the son was taken by Frau Bormann. Do I have that right?"

"Yes," replied Hedda shifting in her chair. "The wife of Hitler's private secretary, Martin Bormann, was a fanatic. She smuggled the son to Wolkenstein, a little village twenty kilometers from Balzano."

"How was the child explained?"

Hedda smirked as she considered the question. She set down her coffee cup. "Frau Bormann was a baby machine in her own right. She bore Martin a flock of children and actually wrote his mistress a letter exhorting her to have many German babies by her husband."

"So she smuggled the Hitler child to Wolkenstein under cover of her family?"

"Yes, she traveled as the director of a children's home. At least nine of the children were her own, one was Hitler's, and five were kidnapped to pose as her cover."

"Then what?" asked Solak.

"A year later Frau Bormann died at a hospital in Merano, Italy…cancer."

"What happened to the children?"

"They survived the war and were cared for in foster homes."

"All of them?"

Hedda took a sip of her coffee and looked off into the distance. "All except the Hitler child. He was raised by a close friend of Bormann here in Munich."

"Was he aware of his lineage?"

"No."

"Was he indoctrinated?"

Hedda gave Terry a tedious look. "He was *educated*," said the mansion owner in a firm voice. "He was raised by a conservative political family to have pride in one's nation."

Terry absorbed the mild rebuke before asking, "Did he marry?"

"Yes. The Hitler child was introduced to several prospective wives, vetted and selected by the organization."

"Women that were suitable."

"Women that were *reliable*," said Hedda, again correcting Solak's choice of words. "He married in 1975 and they had three children. Gerhardt was the only boy, and he was the youngest."

"And Gerhardt's parents?"

"His father, Hitler's son, died of mysterious causes in 1989."

Terry pondered that statement before continuing. "And his mother?"

"She continued to raise Gerhardt on her own with help from the Network."

Chapter 42

Mittenwald, Germany

Sharif Ali sat alone in the rear seat of the three-car caravan and read the coded text message that appeared on his burn phone. Then he spoke quietly to his driver in Arabic. The man nodded and slowed as they shuffled the three cars in a practiced pattern, allowing the first and last Audi sedans to change places in a smooth transition. This permitted the prince's auto to stay securely in the middle. To an untrained eye it was vehicle hopscotch, but to Ali it was a change in pattern that could signal a long-distance car tail that travel changes were imminent.

The Saudi was en route to a forest compound five kilometers outside the Bavarian town of Mittenwald. The sleepy alpine hamlet of seven thousand was a minor tourist destination strategically located along the former trade route that connected Augsburg, Germany and Innsbruck, Austria. Mittenwald's claims to fame were buildings with elaborately painted exteriors and the making of violins.

Ten minutes later, the three autos pulled on to an exit ramp, downshifted gears, and turned into a local hard-ball road. A few minutes later, the three Audis were winding their way through a dense forest. They stopped at a paved driveway that led to a guarded gate secured by a high chain link fence.

Two men, brandishing MP5 submachine guns, exited a small building inside the compound and motioned at the lead vehicle. Words were exchanged and the gate electronically slid open. The Saudi caravan crept forward.

The access road wound through a serpentine pattern of sharp turns that forced the visitors to proceed slowly as they were monitored by numerous closed-circuit cameras. Five minutes later they turned into a circular drive and came to a halt.

Sharif exited his middle vehicle accompanied by two bodyguards from the lead car, as his driver and the three men in the tail Audi stepped to the pavement to stretch. They remained with the sedans. A clean-cut man in a suit stepped through the front door of the reception center and walked forward to greet Ali.

"How was your journey?" asked the man in the suit.

"Uneventful," replied the prince.

"Another few weeks and we could be covered in snow."

Ali shrugged. "Another few weeks and our work will be done."

They turned, and the host led the Saudis through the front door into the rustic mountain lodge.

"Some refreshments?" asked the suited man.

"No," replied Ali in an impatient voice. "I wish to see the training facility, and the students."

"Of course," said the host. He motioned towards a set of double doors at the far end of the reception hall.

They passed through the doors and down a set of steel stairs. At the end of a short hall the host keyed a series of numbers into a combination electronic pad and the metal door slid open.

They entered a large concrete bunker to see a firing line of ten men, each practicing marksmanship with the same model automatic pistol. The target wall was thoroughly padded with sand bags to minimize bullet ricochets. The noise of small firearms echoed through the cement chamber under the watchful eyes of several instructors.

Ali waved off ear protection from one of the instructors and motioned the host forward. The three Saudis followed the suited man into an adjoining room.

A dozen students listened to an instructor as he coached them in the finer points of a knife attack. He used a stiletto, and pointed the weapon at a padded mannequin highlighting special kill zones marked in red.

Finally, Ali and his bodyguards were led into a third adjoining room where a group of men sat in a circle as the instructor guided them through the sequence of constructing a mechanical ambush using various types of explosives.

Sharif studied the students. Many of them bore tattoos but made an effort to hide the body art. In addition, all of the students grew beards and long hair and, when necessary, dyed their hair black.

The prince took his time unobtrusively pacing the room, studying the class setting from various angles. The instructor in the center of the room merely nodded to Ali, but continued the block of information. After ten minutes Sharif turned towards the suited host and asked, "Have you identified the group leaders?"

"Yes," replied the host, "each team of three or four men are led by a group leader, many of which are women."

Ali looked around. "Where are they?"

The host motioned, and escorted Sharif and his bodyguards to a small paneled room to the rear and closed the door. Then he pressed a button and a metal sleeve slid up exposing a one-way window. A classroom with desks, chairs, and overhead projectors was crowded with twenty students, a mix of male and female, all collectively studying urban maps of German cities.

Sharif nodded before asking, "Is there overlap in their training?"

"Yes," replied the suited man, "we have stressed the need for redundancy in skill sets."

Ali looked up, and considered the makeshift classroom facility that sat thirty feet below the forest. "Do you anticipate any delays?"

"No," answered the host. "Our only concern is the arrival of the list."

"It is coming," answered Ali, remembering the assurances given to him by Friedel Schulz and Frau Keller at the Ozdeveli restaurant. "Be patient."

Sharif turned and started to retrace his walking tour back through the underground bunker followed by his bodyguards.

***

Innsbruck, Austria

Otto faced the Golden Roof, one of Austria's most iconic landmarks, and snapped a photograph. The copper tiles, each with a fire-gilded gold plate, stood out amongst the Old Town mix of gothic and baroque architecture. The foreign intelligence officer took a few steps to the left, paused, and snapped another picture. Then he smiled to himself and waited until Terry approached him from his rear.

"Welcome to Innsbruck," said Otto. "Thank you for being flexible." The foreign intelligence officer lowered his camera and reached for his unlit pipe.

"Playing the part of a tourist in the mecca of winter sports?" asked Terry.

"Yes," replied Otto. "Innsbruck offers an easy cover. This little town is a tourist magnet. In truth, it has hosted two Olympics and a slew of international competitions. People love the snow."

"I don't ski," said Terry with a grin.

"Ha," replied Otto, "neither do I...at least not anymore." He turned and whispered. "Besides I don't have any film in the camera." Otto stifled a laugh and turned away from the famous balcony. "Time for a cold Tyrolean beer." Otto made a twist of his shoulder. "I know just the place." The tall German turned and led Terry towards an outdoor café on the far side of the square. They sat and Otto signaled the waiter with two fingers.

"Your flight was good?" asked Terry.

"Yes, how was the train?"

"Simple, a couple of hours on the rails."

"Well, again, I appreciate the meet. These days there are too many eyes and ears in Munich, and Berlin has devolved into a state of mild paranoia."

"And you are, after all, a *foreign* intelligence officer," said Terry in a quiet voice.

"Yes, that too," said Otto with a nod. "Hard to explain sticking my nose into issues outside of our charter." He paused for a moment. "My counterparts on the domestic side are more concerned with protocol than with productivity."

"You're not alone," replied Terry. "We have some of the same issues back in the States."

Otto nodded and took a sip of beer. "Austria to Germany is like Canada to the U.S.; a benign, trusted neighbor with a shared border…but in any event it allows me to download your information while on foreign soil."

Otto let the conversation lag as he reached up and poked the knot on his bowtie. He waited for Solak to begin the briefing.

Terry told him everything he could recall around his meeting with Ronja and the mansion owner named Hedda. It was a long story, starting with the base facts, and then interspersed with various impressions, conjectures, and suppositions. Some things could be verified, others couldn't, and the face-to-face chat gave them an opportunity to sort out pieces of the puzzle or what they could identify as intentional 'throw offs.'

Twenty minutes later Terry looked up, took a long breath, and then an even longer swig of the frothy beer. Then he leaned back in his chair and gazed at Otto.

The German put his empty pipe on the table and frowned. "Quite a story."

Terry's eyebrows raised and lowered in a sign of agreement. "They have made it sound plausible."

"Yes," said Otto, "as in any good piece of disinformation."

A few seconds of silence passed and then Terry asked, "Do you have any insights into Hedda, the mansion owner?"

"Actually yes," said Otto. "Frau Hedda Eckhart, the scion of a wealthy industrial family based in Munich."

"You know her."

"No, I know *of* her."

"Is it feasible she would have the information she shared with me?"

"The information regarding Herr Wolf?"

"Yes."

Otto circled the rim of his beer stein before answering. "Feasible she would have access to the information, not so feasible she would share it—at least not without intent." The foreign intelligence officer looked across the square. "People like Hedda Eckhart trade in information as a commodity. It is the currency of business."

"So, she is playing us?"

"More likely," said Otto, "she is playing both sides. She told you a possible story in a credible way. It sounds *good*. It is believable, except you, Helios, aren't sure you believe it—because of her delivery."

"Do you think that Hedda is a member of das Netzwerk?"

"I would suggest a fringe player," said Otto. "Someone like Frau Eckhart maintains contact with many sources, but commits to few. Her only goal, is to further the strength and the power of her family empire."

"So we only see what she wants us to see."

"Precisely." Otto stood and lay a ten euro note on the table. "I have to check on several issues before I head back to Berlin. The beer is on me. Travel safe."

Chapter 43

Berlin, Germany

Director Geiger of the German federal police entered the elementary school in Kreuzberg. He was accompanied by two commissioners and an inspector. It was Friday, the last business day of the work week, and two days before the general election. This was Geiger at his most demanding. Unannounced visits and snap inspections were the norm.

The German Emergency Acts limited basic constitutional rights in a state of tension or an internal state of emergency. Geiger and his federal police, under the supervision of the Minister of the Interior, were tasked with protecting federal buildings, courts, and border facilities. In addition, with the advent of the national elections, they also dispersed federal mobile response teams and elements of the GSG-9, Germany's crack counter-terrorism unit, to various locations.

There were sixty-one million eligible voters in Germany. They would execute their democratic prerogative by voting in one of eighty-eight thousand polling stations throughout the republic, most of which were in schools and public buildings. Geiger's responsibility was to augment the sixteen state police departments in protecting the voters, and the six hundred thousand volunteers involved in the process.

The police director paused and inspected a pile of sealed voting ballots and unused envelopes being stacked on a special table. Each stack was guarded by three volunteers. Then he pointed across the classroom at several opened windows. One of the two commissioners nodded and made a notation in his memo pad. In Germany, all voting was done by paper and pen. There were no electronic voting machines.

The second commissioner's cell phone rang and a private conversation followed. Then the commissioner grimaced and approached Geiger. "Herr Director," said the commissioner motioning Geiger to the side. "A moment."

The commissioner relayed the information to Geiger. The police director's posture changed and he visibly bristled at the message. Then he motioned and paced towards the classroom door. The three men followed.

The inspector sidled up to the second commissioner and asked in a quiet voice, "What happened?"

"Gerhardt just released another video," said the commissioner, as he quickened his step.

***

Munich, Germany

For nine years, the SKAT club of Munich met once every other week at the Hotel Rothof Bogenhausen. Typically, two dozen avid players arrived in mid-morning, and broke into groups of three or four to begin the player rotation in the German card game. They played for two hours before taking a lunch break.

The members stretched and paced around the Park Conference Room, taking the opportunity to view the beautifully manicured lawns and gardens through the large windows. Then they moved to various card tables and intermingled with the other members.

Hedda Eckhart was an enthusiastic SKAT player, having grown up playing the card game as a child, and continuing with little interruption for the better part of three decades. It was time and a diversion that she could readily afford. In addition, she excelled at the trick-taking card game, which made it all the more fun. Hedda felt that SKAT was, in many ways, a natural extension of her business acumen.

A team of waiters fanned out with plates of pre-ordered food. The lunch was catered by the renowned Kafer Delicatessen on Prinzregentenstraße which served excellent Bavarian cuisine. As a waiter prepared to set down Hedda's lunch plate, a female waitress bumped him aside and set a similar meal on the placemat. Then she leaned forward to take drink orders.

The beverages ranged from bottled water to Bavarian beer, and Hedda ordered her typical cup of coffee.

The members took their time enjoying the meal and discussing SKAT strategy. Many of the members of the club had known each other for years and were seasoned players. Following lunch, they would rotate and play for another two hours with most members sitting in three-player games, while others sat in groupings of four with the dealer required to sit out each hand.

Hedda moved to another table and took her seat. After a few minutes, her face blanched and she heaved forward gripping her abdomen. Her heart fluttered and her eyes rotated in distress. Her breathing turned laboriously. Then Hedda started to shake as she convulsed in spasms.

It all happened in seconds and one of the women at the table called for an ambulance while the second member rushed to Hedda's side. All play in the conference room halted as Hedda bounced in her chair, and keeled forward—face first—into the playing cards.

Chapter 44

Berlin, Germany

Frau Steir stood in silence, looking up at the monument of Johann Goethe, and appearing to wish that the long-deceased statesman would somehow bestow his wisdom upon the huddling masses. It was Saturday, one day before the general election, and the crowds had gathered into a crackling display of competing protests. All over Germany, at any moment, the far right anti-immigration, anti-Muslim crowd threatened to erupt in violence against the left-leaning, Eurocentric counter-protesters, filled with angst that their laissez-faire lifestyle would crumble in a vast default to jingoist nationalism.

The Gerhardt video had implored Germans in a passioned, taped oration to *vote conservative*, and it had gone viral in an hour. Millions upon millions of downloads and 'hits' crisscrossed the internet, highlighting the narrator with a full head and shoulders camera angle. His physical resemblance to Adolf Hitler was uncanny, and when combined with the expressions, movements, and voice modulation on the screen, he captivated the unseen audience. This was the tipping point, when all populist citizens, fed up with the European Union dictates on their time, their money, and their lifestyle, would choose a different course. Germany would vote right or she would erupt.

Steir shifted her stance as the VP of the domestic security agency approached from the manicured path. "Twenty-four hours," she said. "This city is a tinder box…one spark and it could all go up."

The VP considered her words. The polling stations were guarded by an eclectic array of police—both state and federal, posted to assure freedom of movement in the voting lines and an absence of intimidation by the crowds.

The republic was a cacophony of competing currents, and the emotional paradox was fueled by the presence and impassioned rhetoric of a man who claimed to be the grandson of Adolf Hitler.

Frau Steir hesitated before saying, "The neo-Nazis scare me, but I fear our real risk is in the Islamic extremists. Their finger prints are everywhere."

"No," replied the VP. "That is not the worst predicament. The worst case is a nationwide eruption of violence at multiple polling stations that undermines the orderly and accurate voting process. *These* actions could serve to delegitimize free and fair elections."

Steir turned from her counterpart and looked up again at the statue of Goethe. "Where is he?" she asked rhetorically, referring to Gerhardt but seeming to appeal to the monument. "Who is he?"

The VP shrugged and shifted his stance, the discomfort in his leg evident for the first time. "We don't know, even with the Emergency Powers Act. We have used the opportunity to apprehend many questionable persons and close multiple temples, social organizations, and places of business—but the greater threat remains."

"He is a populist."

"A non-candidate. He has no official capacity, no police or military authority to reinforce his status."

"He has been very careful to tread the line," replied Steir.

"You fear we are missing something?"

"Yes." Steir looked up again at the tall Goethe Monument, hoping for inspiration from the historic figure. "Something bigger is at play, and it is right in front of us."

***

Munich, Germany

There was a knock on the door and Terry jumped to his feet. He drew the SIG Sauer P6 pistol from the small of his back and then checked the peephole. It was Ronja.

Solak opened the door with a flourish and scanned the hall. As he stepped back to allow her entrance, she attacked him.

"How could you?" said Ronja in an angry tone. She started to punch and slap at Terry as he backpedaled. She smothered his torso with flailing arms, fueled by emotion, her face a contorted mask of fear and frustration. Terry grabbed at Ronja as she rushed forward, and he bear hugged her limbs to protect himself. Then he pulled her into the room and slammed the door shut.

Ronja collapsed in Terry's arms and he guided her to a chair. She broke into tears, exposing a distraught, bleary mess of frayed edges.

"What happened?" asked Solak. He moved to the hotel fridge and pulled out a bottled water for Ronja.

"My boys," she replied. Then she crumbled backwards into a fetal position and began to breathe in heavy, sporadic gulps of air.

Terry pulled over an ottoman and sat. "Please," he said, "tell me what happened."

"They took my sons."

The statement caught Solak off guard, but he leaned forward and touched her hand. "Who took them?"

"Das Netzwerk," answered Ronja in a distraught voice. "I told you what they would do."

Solak leaned back, a bit puzzled by the turn of events, but then, clear headed in that he had learned to expect the unexpected. "Tell me *exactly* what happened."

In many ways, Terry suspected that Ronja was much closer to the organization than she let on. He also suspected that her boss, Hedda, was an important player—at least he surmised as much, given the apparent openness of the wealthy business woman's narrative to a stranger from Canada. But Otto seemed to dispel that notion, and Solak's instincts trusted the German's insight.

Solak took it down a notch and asked again in a quiet voice, "Can you tell me what happened?"

"I received a call at work from Rolfe," said Ronja.

"Rolfe?"

"Hedda's manservant," replied Ronja between sobs. "He told me that Frau Eckhart had taken sick while at her regular SKAT club meeting."

"SKAT?"

"A card game," answered Ronja. "She was rushed to the hospital, and that I should close the boutique and send everyone home." Ronja fought for control as she parsed out the facts.

"Did you?" asked Terry.

"Yes."

"Then what?"

"At home, my boys were gone but school was out for the day."

"Should they have been home?"

"Always," said Ronja, "and the nanny was not there, either."

"What did you do?"

"I called the nanny. There was no answer, but then I found this on the kitchen table." Ronja pulled out a piece of folded stationery.

Solak read the typed, one-sentence message in German, and then looked to Ronja for an accurate translation.

"It says, be careful, we have your sons."

A tremor gripped Ronja as she recited the message to Solak. She clenched the stationery and fought to maintain control. Then Terry leaned back on the ottoman.

As much as Solak suspected both Ronja and her boss of duplicity, Ronja's grief appeared genuine. Terry believed the Hitler narrative told by Hedda to be either a stall tactic or a ruse to lead German authorities in a different direction. Nothing was ever what it appeared. For this reason, with the clock ticking on the national election, he offered Ronja his support. Yet he also knew that for security considerations, *only* Otto knew his Munich location.

"Wait here," said Terry as he moved to a private corner of the hotel room. He tugged out his burner phone and called Otto.

Ronja looked at Terry with bleary eyes but she didn't seem fazed by his weapon. Terry watched her in the chair while speaking quietly into the cell phone. "It's me."

"Helios, I was about to call you."

"No doubt," said Solak with a tweak of sarcasm. "I have a visitor."

"Yes…apologies on the unannounced arrival, I will accept your recriminations later, but…"

"Go ahead," said Terry.

"Hedda Eckhart is dead."

"How?"

"Poison."

Terry paused before asking, "What's the agent? Was it the same poison as Landsberg?"

"No, this time they used phenol."

"I'm not familiar with the ingredient," said Solak. He glanced over at Ronja who sat motionless in her chair. "What is the angle?"

"Phenol is a nasty poison, Helios, but not subtle. It has *only* been used by the Nazis. For years the SS used phenol to quickly and efficiently execute their concentration camp prisoners."

"They wanted us to know."

"Yes," replied Otto. "This is a warning."

Chapter 45

Evie sat at an empty cubicle in the situation room set up for the German elections. She had worked through the weekend, surrounded by groups of analysts and officers from different Agency branches; the German desk, the Europe Division, the Counter-Terrorism Mission Office—each had a different angle or focus of concern. All wanted to understand the pending political developments for the EU's dominant member.

Listening to cable news break-ins and downloading spot German reports proved difficult for Evie, until her newly developed 'friends' from the situation room offered their country knowledge and language facility to explain various updates.

True to form, Evie gathered up every scrap of information; scribbling notes, collecting facts, absorbing nuances, and seeking explanations. She was a human suction machine who grabbed at a morsel of information and quickly patterned its importance.

It wasn't long before the polite, hardworking, hijab-wearing collection manager from SAD caught many people's attention. Everyone was intrigued that the black ops side of the Agency had such a keen interest in the German general election.

"Amazing," said the situation room monitor, looking up at two different cable news feeds from Germany. "The grand coalition just splintered for the first time in memory."

"What does that mean?" asked Evie, as she twisted to face the man standing in the middle of the room.

"It means that even though the chancellor won, her party was a big loser in delegates. On the far right, the AfD, the Alt for Germany Party, is the beneficiary. Most of their gains came at the expense of the Social Dems and the Christian Dems."

"Without a majority," said a desk analyst, "the chancellor could be forced into a caretaker administration."

"How likely is that?" asked Evie.

"Very," answered the room monitor. "This is unprecedented. Germany has reached a point where a grand coalition can no longer be justified. These results mark a low for the two dominant parties."

"Their worst scores in two decades," said the analyst for Evie's benefit. "This could trigger snap elections for next year."

"It's uncharted waters," said the woman on Evie's right in a quiet voice. She represented the Europe Division. "Everyone in Germany is holding their breath. The political reporters are trying to figure out what happens next."

"What we do know," said the room monitor, "is that the AfD are the new power brokers."

"The ultra-conservative party," said Evie.

"Yes."

"The party of Gerhardt."

The situation room grew very silent as several analysts turned towards Evie. She had voiced what the others had only thought.

"Well, not officially," replied the desk analyst. "They have been very coy about admitting their relationship...but in effect, yes."

Evie nodded and looked up at the closest screen. She tried to translate the German report. Then she turned towards the woman on her right, "Where does it go from here?"

"No one knows—not even the citizens. This vacuum makes Germany more susceptible to unwanted influences."

Evie looked down at her notes and scribbled the words *vacuum* and *influences*. Then she leaned back.

For days, as the hours ticked off and the general election loomed ever closer, Evie, like most Germany watchers, feared a catastrophic event. Yet when nothing happened, an eerie calm filled the air. Evie exhaled. Nothing of disruptive significance occurred—no mass protests turning into unchecked riots, no intimidation of voters at polling locations, no overt involvement of foreign nations in the sovereign politics of Germany. There was a clear and orderly process and the voters cast their ballots. Of the sixty million eligible voters, seventy-six percent participated in the democratic process, and no bolts of lightning scurried the event. The efficient and orderly undertaking, however, caused Evie a great deal of consternation. Like an iceberg, she feared the unseen dangers that lurked just beneath the surface.

***

Munich, Germany

The two brothers, ages six and four, huddled together on foam mats in the basement of a home in Nymphenburg. The neighborhood was best known for its historic castle and splendid gardens. It was also close to the city center, yet, surprisingly, it was undiscovered by both tourists and residents alike. This suited the captors' low-profile agenda.

Martin, the older boy, reached out to console his younger sibling, but could only stretch to the limit of his padded ankle brace. The brace itself was shackled to a long steel cable which in turn was fastened to a wall-mounted metal lock box. This gave each of the boys four feet of maximum circumference, and permitted them to touch.

"Please, Martin," said the youngest in tears. "I want to go home."

"So do I, Garrin, but you can't make noise." The older boy tried to quiet his younger brother. He stretched his arms sideways.

"I want to go home," said the youngest, sobbing aloud. "I want Mommy."

"Shhh," said Martin. "The woman said she would spank us if we made noise."

"I want Mommy," said the four-year-old again, "I *want* Mommy…" He broke into a loud blubbering release.

Then, Martin started to shake. He was also afraid but unable to comfort his brother. He worried that the woman would hurt them for disobeying.

Chapter 46

Munich, Germany

The six women sat around the oval dining table in the large apartment in Gartnerplatz. There was a sense of satisfaction in the room, an air of success. It was the type of smug but quiet confidence that surfaced when a group committed to a common goal, worked very hard, and then experienced the sweet taste of victory. It was justification for all the late nights and personal sacrifice.

The home's owner looked at her fellow conspirators. "The election results are complete and we have won a mandate. The AfD, the far right party, has earned a startling fourteen percent of the vote—that is nearly three times the minimum threshold for seats in parliament."

"Four years ago, the AfD did not exist. Today they have over a hundred delegates," said the leader.

"Your son is to be commended," said the youngest woman to Frau Fuchs. "His oration made the difference."

The leader leaned forward. "Our time is now. The world is changing. It started with the American elections, then the Brexit vote, and now here, with the anger over immigration and national sovereignty. Gerhardt has become the voice of the German people."

The apartment owner raised her hand to make a point. "We took our delegate votes from the two dominant parties. The chancellor has lost her majority and she must try to cobble together a shaky coalition. It will fail and we will be ready to step in and calm the chaos that follows."

There was a pause, and then the lady across the table asked, "What is the status of our list?"

"It is nearly complete. It's important that we include the most influential names."

There was a series of open-handed taps on the table top. It was a demonstration of agreement between the women.

The youngest cleared her throat and spoke. "For the first time since the 1950s, there are six political groups entering parliament. This fragmentation that we have caused will help us more accurately assess candidates."

Gerhardt's mother set down her coffee cup and glanced around the table. The leader caught her eye and nodded. "Frau Fuchs, you have a comment?"

"Ja," said Fuchs as she twisted in her chair. "As you all know, the government is using the Emergency Acts to search for my son. They are casting a broad net." For a moment she glanced around the table at her associates. Then with a nod from the leader she continued. "We have had to take executive action against one of our financial supporters. It was unfortunate, but necessary."

The other members digested the context of Fuchs' words. Then the home's owner leaned forward. "Perhaps now, those in our network will rethink discussions with outsiders. Our action should temper their behavior."

***

Munich, Germany

Terry carried Ronja over to his bed, removed her shoes, and covered her with a blanket. She appeared exhausted, and like so much in Terry's world, he needed to make a judgment call on the mother's veracity. She certainly appeared to be a parent under stress, emotionally distraught over the status of her sons. However, Solak knew that in the world of espionage, people were not only accomplished actors, but they were also inveterate liars. Terry's gut told him that Ronja's concern was genuine. Maybe das Netzwerk had put her up to a charade, or maybe the organization had truly become her adversary and snatched the brothers as leverage. Solak needed to play out the script to see which way the milk spilled.

Terry paced around the hotel room, putting together a plan of action that he could use to ferret out likely members of the women's group. In so doing, he also hoped to get closer to identifying the location and the background of the mystery orator named Gerhardt.

Solak moved the cushioned chair and ottoman to the center of the hotel room where he could easily view both the door and the bed with a quick turn of his head. Then he double-bolted the latch and stacked two aluminum waste baskets in a leaning tower just inside the door. The makeshift configuration served as an early warning device. Finally, he nudged Ronja's foot until she awoke.

"Ja," said Ronja looking at Solak with bleary eyes.

"Do you want my help?"

She nodded.

"Then I need you to stand up and remove your coat."

The mother stood and tugged off her short leather jacket. Terry stood four feet to her front. He took the coat and motioned for Ronja to turn around and face the wall. Then he proceeded to give the coat a quick but thorough search, paying extra attention to the collar, the lining, and the cuffs before tossing the jacket on the bed.

"Place both hands on the back of your head," said Terry, "and lace your fingers together."

Ronja obeyed, resisting the urge to turn and face Terry. She felt him close the distance. Then he placed one hand on her laced fingers and proceeded to weave his free hand through her mid-length hair.

Solak continued with a quick but thorough frisk, methodically moving down Ronja's frame, paying special attention to bulky portions of her clothes. To her credit, she appeared unfazed at his practiced search. Terry was all business, not shying away from her genitals, well aware that wires and weapons were most commonly hidden in 'off limits' underwear. If Ronja was embarrassed or offended, it didn't show. Her demeanor allowed the security process to proceed faster.

"Okay," said Solak as he stepped back to his original position, "you can relax."

Ronja lowered her arms and turned in place. Then she refastened her pants waistband and snugged her bra, both of which had been checked.

"What now?" asked Ronja.

"Get some rest," replied Solak, pointing at the bed. He turned and walked back to the chair. "I'll let you know when I am ready to move."

Chapter 47

Berlin, Germany

The group of twenty sat in the conference room on the eighth floor of the chancellery building. Each was analyzing the results of the recent national election, and paying specific attention to how their organizations performed. The collective result, whether from luck or preparation, was that despite some minor disturbances, the nation experienced a calm and orderly elective process.

Nonetheless, there were surprises, and though the chancellor herself won reelection, her party had lost a governing majority. The far right AfD was the new power broker. Six political groups had been elected to enter parliament.

"Let's get started," said the VP of the domestic security agency. He glanced across the table at Geiger of the Federal Uniform Police. "Herr Director, you are to be commended on the vigilant placement of specialized personnel at several locations. It was instrumental in offsetting potential problems."

Geiger tilted his head in acknowledgment of the compliment.

"And you, Holger," said the VP, continuing the accolades as he swiveled to face the state police official, "are to be commended for the quick response to several polling stations. This prevented the activities of would-be disrupters."

The Landespolizei deputy nodded.

"But we are not out of the woods yet," said Frau Steir.

All eyes turned to the powerful aide de camp. Steir's boss, the chancellor, had just won her fourth consecutive national election, but this time the loss of a party majority signaled tough sledding ahead. Steir motioned towards deputy Ludwig of the federal criminal investigative police. He seemed to sit more erect in his chair as he consulted his notes.

"As of yesterday," said Ludwig, "we have arrested, apprehended, or taken into custody eight hundred forty-one individuals from all over the republic.

They are being held under various means of incarceration and house arrest, pending a continuation of the Emergency Acts." The deputy looked up from his notes and caught his breath before continuing. "Many of you know, the individual states have somewhat different by-laws regarding periods of confinement."

"The important point," said Geiger, "is that known agitators and radicals from both the left and right were kept from disrupting our general election."

"Yes," replied Ludwig, "and in the process we were able to develop detailed profiles for many of the agitators in custody."

"What about the biggest agitator?" asked Holger of the State Police.

The VP of the domestic security agency stood, using the opportunity to stretch his arthritic leg. "Actually, we have good news on that front."

"Oh," said Steir. She seemed caught off guard by the admission.

"Yes," replied the VP. He glanced around the room, and cleared his throat. "We have it, on corroborated sources, that Gerhardt is actually hiding right here in Berlin."

A sudden hush fell over the group as they digested the important piece of information. Steir turned in her seat. "Are you sure?" she asked.

"Yes," answered the VP. "Although we read the IP address as Munich, our engineers have penetrated the dissembling program that was used. We are double-checking the leads and hope to have the orator in custody in the next twenty-four hours."

Steir looked at the VP with a surprised expression. Then she nodded. "That is very good news. The chancellor will be most pleased."

***

Munich, Germany

Terry gently shook Ronja's hand. It took a few seconds before she stirred from her deep slumber. There was a moment of confusion and then she focused on Solak who sat patiently at the corner of her bed.

"Is everything okay?" asked Ronja. She rubbed bloodshot eyes.

"Time to go," replied Solak.

Ronja threw the blanket aside and swung her feet over the side of the bed. Then she put on her shoes. "Where are we going?"

"You'll see," said Terry. He repositioned the SIG Sauer pistol in the small of his back.

Ronja stood and fluffed her hair. She checked her wristwatch. "You know that it is two o'clock in the morning?"

"Yes," answered Terry. He took Ronja by the wrist and guided her towards the hotel door. "One last thing," he paused and fixed Ronja with a serious gaze. "If you lie to me or interfere in any way, I will kill you."

Ronja swallowed, not expecting the threat. Then she nodded.

Terry led Ronja from the room, down the elevator, and into a taxi summoned by the nightshift doorman. "Bogenhausen," said Solak, watching Ronja's expression as the driver shifted gears and pulled away from the curb. Her surprise was evident. The cat and mouse game had begun. He had suspicions about Ronja and worried that the whole children's abduction scenario was a ploy. He would play things tough, push the envelope, and bully, bribe, or cajole anyone in his path. If Ronja was sincere about the disappearance of her sons, then she would support *any* action that would lead to their safe return. If her story was a pretense to separate Solak from the true facts, then she would soon be exposed.

Solak guided the cab driver from the rear seat, dictating turns and changes in direction by memory. Despite her knowledge of the neighborhood, Ronja remained silent. They drove for ten minutes.

A block from Hedda's mansion, Terry had the driver pull over. He settled the fare and led Ronja down a side street, hand in hand like a couple, until they reached the villa's high stone wall. Solak pointed at Ronja.

"Call Rolfe. Speak only in English. Tell him you are *here*, and you need to see him right now."

Ronja gave Terry a strange look and then pulled out her mobile phone and complied. It took three rings.

"Hallo," said a sleepy male voice.

"Rolfe," replied Ronja to the manservant. "It is Ronja. I am outside. I need to see you."

The manservant began to protest in German, objecting to the time of night and the inappropriateness of the request.

"English," said Terry in a whisper.

Ronja repeated Solak's demand. She held the phone in the air between them, on speaker, so that Terry could hear the conversation. It took Rolfe only a moment to realize that Ronja was not alone.

"Proceed down the side street to the delivery entrance on the west wall."

Rolfe disconnected.

Three minutes later, Ronja was buzzed through a heavy, oak door reinforced by steel plates. They entered a hallway that opened into a supply room. The manservant stood alone, dressed in pajamas and slippers, his hands tucked into a monogrammed bathrobe. He looked at Ronja and then Terry—whom he immediately recognized.

Rolfe led them into an adjoining lounge on the ground floor and motioned at several empty chairs. "You are here about Frau Eckhart?"

"Yes," answered Terry taking the lead. At any moment he expected a couple of private security guards to enter the lounge. His eyes scanned the room for signs of closed-circuit cameras or listening devices. "Where are your security personnel?"

Rolfe studied Solak before answering, "I gave them the night off. It has been a difficult two days. Frau Eckhart's grown children are expected tomorrow."

"Where are they?" asked Terry.

"The daughter was traveling in Asia, and the son was away at university."

Ronja had a hard time sitting still. Her face was drawn and turgid. She shook her head. "I don't understand. How is she?"

The manservant looked at Ronja with a confused expression. Then he looked at Terry. "Does she know?"

"No," said Solak. He had not shared the final important piece of Otto's information. Ronja was still under the impression that Hedda was sick and hospitalized.

"Know *what*?" asked Ronja in an irritated voice.

"Frau Eckhart is dead," said Rolfe in German.

"English," said Solak with a snap.

The German obliged.

Ronja seemed to be surprised by the news. "Dead?!" There was a look of incredulity on her face.

"Who told you?" Terry asked the manservant.

"An old friend of Frau Eckhart."

"Someone from the SKAT game?"

"No," answered Rolfe.

"The friend wasn't there?"

"No."

"How did she know so fast?"

Rolfe paused and then shrugged.

Terry glanced at Ronja, and then shifted his eyes back. "What is her name?"

Rolfe hesitated but did not answer. It was clear to Solak that the dapper manservant knew more than he was revealing. In addition, it was apparent that Ronja was confused by the events surrounding the kidnapping of her children.

He pressed forward. "Why did you close the boutique and send everyone home?"

"She told me it would be best."

"What is her name?" asked Solak again.

As the seconds ticked off, Terry reached behind his back from a seated position, extracted the SIG Sauer, and swung the pistol in a short arc. The metal barrel smashed Rolfe in the knee.

The ferocity of the attack stunned Ronja as the manservant howled in pain and crashed to the floor, gripping his leg.

"I am not a patient person," said Solak in a whisper. He glanced at Ronja who was stunned and confused by Terry's actions. Then he plucked a pen and notepad from the coffee table and handed them to Rolfe. "I want a name and an address."

Solak stood and moved around the lounge as Rolfe scribbled on the pad of paper. Terry kept shifting his gaze between the doors at either end of the room. Then he placed the muzzle of his pistol against Rolfe's head. "Last question, where are Ronja's boys?"

The manservant took several deep breaths. "I don't know," said Rolfe pleading for mercy by holding up his hands in submission.

"Who has them?"

"The same people who murdered Frau Eckhart...but I don't know their names."

Terry reached forward and grabbed Rolfe's scribble, and pocketed the notepad. Then he pulled on Ronja's arm and led her from the lounge.

Chapter 48

Berlin, Germany

The telephone in the living room of Gerhardt's condominium rang. Nora looked up from the news story she was watching on the television. The pitch of the telephone alerted the blonde. It was a different sound, intentionally, and although it was unlisted, it was rarely used.

Nora bounded across the room and plucked the receiver from the cradle. "Guten tag," answered Nora in a conversational tone.

"Evakuieren," said a mechanical voice. The sound was electronically altered to obscure identification. The word 'evakuieren' was repeated and then the line went dead. Nora cradled the telephone and immediately launched into action.

She charged into Gerhardt's study where he was prepping a speech for video release. Nora half-pulled, half-pushed Gerhardt to his feet. "We are leaving," she said in an excited tone, "right now." She yanked at her lover's sleeve and motioned. "Put on your shoes, there is no time." She snapped her fingers several times to emphasize haste.

"What is it?" asked Gerhardt, his attention drifting back to the computer screen.

Nora leaned forward and gripped his head with both hands and looked deep into his eyes. "Focus…we must go, *now*!"

She pulled him from the chair and pointed towards the rear hallway. Then she shut down his computer, folded the laptop under her arm, and nudged him from behind. "Emergency exit," said Nora.

Gerhardt grabbed two coats from the rear closet and plugged a series of numbers into the wall-mounted security system. A thick metal door clicked open as Nora spoke into her cell phone. "Two cars, emergency exit, immediate pickup, evacuation procedures."

Four minutes later a Mercedes-Benz S-series sedan pulled up and retrieved the waiting Gerhardt and Nora. Then, as the first sedan sped away using an auxiliary road that paralleled the Spree River tributary, a second sedan arrived. Three men exited the car and bounded up the emergency exit stairs carrying fire accelerants. They entered Gerhardt's condominium.

***

Munich, Germany

Terry had two options for a quick escape—either hot-wire a car or hijack a car. Neither were great choices, yet walking the streets in the wealthy enclave of Bogenhausen at three o'clock in the morning did not suggest a harmless local.

Solak was not concerned with Rolfe calling the police. He did assume, however, that the manservant would warn das Netzwerk of the intrusion. If the name and address Rolfe gave Terry were accurate, then the manservant was walking a tightrope. For this reason, Solak had intentionally turned violent. He needed to impress upon Rolfe that Terry was an equal adversary, and someone to be feared.

The problem, of course, was that Terry was operating with a shortage of resources and equipment. When pressed against the element of time, Solak needed to make less than perfect tactical decisions. He played out the options in his head. The name and address of Hedda's 'old friend' could be real or subterfuge. The manservant could be lying about the woman, and could be setting Solak up for an interception and confrontation. What Rolfe knew was that if das Netzwerk could kill a rich and connected Hedda Eckhart, they could certainly get to her hired help.

Terry had two threads to pursue. He took Ronja by the hand and asked, "Where does your nanny live?"

"Au-Haidhausen," answered Ronja. She looked a bit numb, confused by how events were unfolding.

"Is it far?" His eyes scanned the street, analyzing different cars parked along the various driveways and gated entrances.

"What are you looking for? There are no taxis roaming at this hour."

"I know," replied Terry. "I need a twenty-year-old Volkswagen."

"What?" she looked over at him in the darkness. "Why?"

"If I'm going to hot-wire our transportation, I need an old and inexpensive model…everything else over the years has been manufactured to resist theft."

"This is Bogenhausen," said Ronja, reciting the obvious. "Rich people do not drive old, inexpensive cars."

Terry and Ronja continued to walk through the neighborhood while hugging the main artery of Ismaninger Straße which connected Prinzregentenstraße to the south with Mittlerer Ring in the north. She held his hand, playing the role, avoiding confrontation. She seemed a little trance-like, focused on her sole priority, which was the rescue of her two boys.

They approached the A94 Autobahn traffic zone and Solak quickly assessed his second option for vehicular transportation—a carjacking. "Remember what I said," whispered Terry. "Don't object. Go with the flow, and we will find your boys."

Ronja nodded.

Several cars slowed as Solak entered the inside traffic lane and waved down the closet vehicle, a Porsche Cayenne. The SUV carried an elderly man, driving alone.

Terry was following the template. Cultural tendencies stressed that the 'safest' approach in a hostile environment was an older man; children were unreliable, women were gender taboo, and young men were prone to betrayals of ambition. An elderly man, by contrast, was more set in his ways and therefore less likely to upset the status quo.

Terry bent over as the driver lowered the passenger side window a few inches. "Please," said Solak, adopting a nervous demeanor, "my car." Terry pointed over Ronja's shoulder.

The elderly driver peered past Terry into the darkness. It gave Solak the chance to extract the SIG Sauer from the small of his back and thrust the pistol through the opening.

"Put the car in park," said Solak, "and unlock the doors."

The driver followed the instructions. Ronja jumped into the rear and Terry slid into the front seat next to the driver.

"Do you want to live?" asked Solak as he waved the pistol in an ominous fashion.

"Yes," replied the driver. "What do you want?"

"For now," said Terry, "your assistance." He looked at Ronja in the rear seat. "Guide him."

She started to parse out street directions to the elderly man without revealing their exact destination.

Chapter 49

Evie broke the telephone connection and removed her wireless headset. She pushed back in her chair and took a deep breath. She had just ended a call from Terry. He had taken a few minutes to bring her up to speed using the live contact to serve as a situation report. Events were moving very quickly on his end, and he wanted to assure that Evie had the opportunity to tie together any threads he may have missed.

Something didn't quite fit, and Solak's information caused her to hesitate. She made notations and chronicled his update with her historic timeline. It was Evie's take that the post-election scenario was new. She felt that it was an intentional lull more than a political reshuffling of an old deck of cards. It was also more than adding a couple of wild cards to the mix. Evie felt that this political turn to the right signaled a cultural shift; a new direction for the country, and that everything until now had been to set the stage.

What troubled Evie the most was that prominent people were being eliminated—not government officials, but well-known citizens; Frau Jokols of Landsberg, Herr Dieter of Heidelberg, and Hedda Eckhart of Munich. This created both a cultural void and a sense of fragility. When respected, non-authority figures suddenly died, the populous grew restless. It fluttered their equilibrium. It left the voters with the feeling that violence could happen to anyone at any time, and what Germany lost in the process was the perception of calm, the aura of order.

Evie considered the immediate aftermath of the election. The conservative voters had won the battle of the ballot box. They had forced the chancellor into a caretaker administration pending her efforts to cobble together a coalition with enough votes to govern. Evie studied her notes and compared Solak's information updates to the Nazi template of the 1930s. She continued to feel that percolating under the surface was more than a political shift in the wind. It was a power grab that would affect Germany, and by extension, the entire European Union.

Evie looked up and casually twirled a lock of her hair under the hijab. Looming behind all the suppositions was the long shadow of the ever-present right wing orator Gerhardt, a man who claimed pure and direct bloodlines to Adolf Hitler.

***

Munich, Germany

Friedel Schulz and Frau Keller sat in the beer garden of the Augustiner am Dom restaurant. The casual inn was popular in a cozy sort of way, with a wonderful view of the Frauenkirche Cathedral and a regular clientele who enjoyed the Bavarian cuisine.

The ladies sipped coffee, waiting patiently until Sharif Ali entered the beer garden from the patio. His two body guards slipped into an empty table to the left as the prince joined the women and turned his back to the boisterous crowd.

"Thank you for being punctual," said Frau Keller. She tilted her head as a courtesy. "We have the information that you requested."

The prince smiled in an uncharacteristic fashion. "That is good news." Sharif bent at the waist and leaned forward.

Friedel Schulz reached into her handbag and extracted a crumpled paper napkin wrapped around a data storage device. "This is a flash drive," said Schulz. She hesitated before giving the Saudi the crumpled napkin. "The information is complete for a first run. We expect there to be changes as the list develops."

Keller lowered her voice as Schulz pulled back the flash drive. "It is important to us that you demonstrate some flexibility," said Keller.

As if on cue, a waiter approached their table and set a sample platter of finger food in front of the prince. It included several types of sliced sausages, ham, cheeses, and soft pretzels with mustard. Then the waiter placed a tall, cold Bavarian beer from the historic brewery on the table.

Schulz sat with the crumpled napkin in her lap. She watched Ali as her friend spoke.

"You should try our local Bavarian food," said Frau Keller. "This restaurant is quite traditional."

The Saudi inspected the food and beverage. It was not lost on him that the two women were well aware of the Islamic prohibition against eating pork or drinking alcohol. He touched his chest with an open hand and politely declined the offer. "My thanks," said Ali, "but I ate a late lunch."

"Are you *sure?*" asked Schulz. "This food is quite good. It gives one a sense of Germany."

Sharif looked across the table at the two women. He knew this was some type of test. He wondered if he had somehow inadvertently offended the women when they previously met at the Ozdeveli restaurant. These actions were too subtle, even for the Saudi prince who was incredibly well-traveled—albeit in the bubble of an uber-rich existence.

"The Turks are Muslims as well," said Keller.

Ali shrugged, well aware of the nuance.

"It has been our experience," said Friedel Schulz, "that many Turks are willing to relax the Islamic dietary standards to bond with their adopted country."

"As in Saudi Arabia," said Ali in a diplomatic tone, "some citizens are more religious than others."

"Yes," replied Keller, glancing at Schulz, "we had hoped you might make a small exception."

Sharif Ali looked across the table at the two German women. Then he reached forward, picked up a toothpick, and speared a piece of roasted sausage. He hesitated as they watched, and then Ali popped the sausage into his mouth. The prince chewed the pork, savoring the taste before swallowing. Then he reached forward a second time, picked up the stein of frothy beer and took a long drink of the cold lager.

Ali set the beer stein back on the table and wiped his lips with a handkerchief. "It's very good." Sharif sat in silence and waited.

Finally, Friedel Schulz reached forward and passed the flash drive to the prince. "Thank you for your flexibility," she said.

The two women stood and Keller spoke. "Please stay for a few minutes before leaving. Take your time. Enjoy the food."

Chapter 50

Munich, Germany

Ronja guided the elderly man to a vacant lot in Schwabing, a neighborhood on the far side of Munich, in the opposite direction from their destination.

During the short trip, Terry continued to look over his shoulder as if they were being followed. He made several comments to Ronja to support the deception. The drive took fifteen minutes.

Solak took the man's mobile telephone and spoke in a reasonable tone. "One hour." Terry checked his watch. "That's what I ask. If you do *not* leave this parking lot, I will telephone the police, with the location of this car, and your telephone will be inside. Do you understand?"

The elderly German looked at Terry with a quizzical expression. "You want me to stay here?" He checked the empty parking lot. It was attached to a mini mall of small businesses. All were closed.

"The decision is yours," said Solak in a matter-of-fact tone. "The time is zero four-thirty. If you leave or try to contact someone for help—before zero five-thirty—I will know. Then I will burn this car and your phone. Do you understand?" Terry didn't explain how he would know, only what the consequences would be for disobedience.

"I do not want your money or your car," continued Terry as he outlined the plan, "I only want to *borrow* this car for one hour." He held up his index finger to emphasize his point. "If you do as I say, the police will recover this car in perfect condition with your cell phone inside. Do you understand?"

The elderly man nodded.

"Get out," said Terry, "and step away from the vehicle." Then he raised his burn phone to his lips and made a pretense of speaking with someone for a few minutes. Finally, Solak slid into the driver's seat and lowered his window. "You are being watched. Stay here. One hour." With a twist of the steering wheel, Terry floored the accelerator and the Porsche Cayenne sped across the empty parking lot.

"Guide me," said Terry over his shoulder, "on the quickest route to your nanny's home."

As soon as they were out of sight, Solak lowered his window and dropped the elderly man's cell phone on the side of the road.

Ronja directed Terry out of Schwabing, back across Bogenhausen, into Haidhausen. He was careful not to speed or drive too aggressively. For her part, she watched him handle the unfamiliar SUV with ease. He seemed to be a man that could adjust quickly to changing situations, and she never quite got a handle on where he drew the line. He had an ability to keep her off balance.

"Do you think he believes you?" asked Ronja as she met Terry's gaze in the rear-view mirror.

Solak shrugged. "It's worth a try. We need time."

A pause ensued, and then Ronja looked again into the rear-view mirror. "Would you have killed him?"

He looked at her before answering. "Maybe."

Ronja leaned back in the rear seat, not sure if she should believe him. Unsure if she wanted to believe him. "You lied about the mobile phone."

"Yes, too easy to track."

The ride was uneventful. It was the dead time of the night, when people with normal work hours entered their deepest sleep and were prone to fuzzy thinking and easy confusion.

Terry parked the SUV between two stationary cars three blocks from the nanny's apartment. He walked half the distance and then pulled up short.

"What's wrong?" asked Ronja.

"I want to watch the street for a couple of minutes. Tell me about your nanny."

Ronja turned and said, "She's eighteen years old…been with me for almost two years."

"What are her work hours for you?"

"Every school day from two in the afternoon until I get home from work after closing the boutique, maybe around six at night."

"What does she do before working for you in the afternoon?"

"She attends Gisela Gymnasium," answered Ronja. "It's a secondary school, a type of high school."

Terry's eyes roamed the street as Ronja answered his questions.

"Does she live alone?"

"Yes."

"Does she have a steady boyfriend?"

"I don't think so," replied Ronja.

"Okay…remember what I said, no interference, no hesitation…are we clear?"

Ronja swallowed and nodded. Then Terry turned and led them down the quiet street towards the front door of the nanny's apartment building.

***

Berlin, Germany

Gerhardt concluded the taping of his next video release. It had been a tumultuous few days following the sudden evacuation of his condominium on Corneliusstraße. The team around him, led by his paramour Nora, had reacted instantly to the evacuation alert. Reliable sources believed that the orator was in immediate danger of apprehension.

He inserted a new flash drive and played the newest—yet to be released—video. Gerhardt checked the oration, the tone of modulation, the physical mannerisms and the patterns of speech. He was every bit the embodiment of his grandfather in both visual presentation and emotive passion.

Nora entered the room and peeked over his shoulder. Their new home was an apartment in Mitte, the borough at the very center of Berlin. There was nothing fancy about the new condo except the location. Mitte residents shared space with monuments, government buildings, upscale businesses, and the private home of the recently reelected chancellor. The tactical advisor for das Netzwerk had used the evacuation procedure as an opportunity to confuse the authorities. Internet babble and false leads crossed the airways with 'reliable' sightings of Gerhardt in several Bavarian villages. The whole country sought the orator, and a huge cat and mouse game commenced—mostly at the expense of the established order.

The beauty of the location, of course, was the hiding of the increasingly popular Gerhardt right under their collective noses. It was the ultimate flick of the thumb at the authorities. The police and security agencies scoured the countryside searching for Gerhardt, and he challenged their ineptitude with his very presence in their midst.

"It looks very good," said the blonde. "We must make sure that it crystallizes the emotions. Germany voted for change, and we *will* have change."

"Of course," answered Gerhardt, nodding as he continued to watch the video. "The message must be clear: to those who stand in our way, to those who would impede our progress, there *will* be consequences."

He paused in the oration, realizing that Nora was an audience of one, and she did not need to be convinced of the importance of their pending actions. He stopped the video and looked up. "I need to call Mutti."

"Of course," replied Nora, "but keep it short. We are so close."

Gerhardt picked up the new burn phone and drifted towards the far end of the small apartment to call his mother.

Chapter 51

Munich, Germany

The most difficult aspect of a forced entry was negotiating the defense in depth. One had to clear the external door of the apartment building before one could focus on the internal apartment door.

Old buildings in European cities rarely had extensive security measures, and when they did, it was generally outside a student's price range. Ronja's nanny was no different.

Terry pressed the security button on a half dozen different apartments and, true to form, three of those responded under the incessant irritating buzzer that interrupted their sleep.

The latch clicked in the door and then the portal popped open. Terry guided Ronja into the foyer, taking a quick glance and then leading her up the stairs by the hand. It took them thirty seconds of climbing before Ronja paused outside the nanny's flat. She nodded at the door, and Solak stepped back before hugging the wall beyond peephole range.

"Gerty," said Ronja in a quiet voice with a knock on the door. "Open up."

A woman's voice filled with sleep, responded from inside. "Miss Ronja?" asked the voice.

"Ja, Gerty, open up."

They heard a bolt turn and then a chain lock slid open. As the portal cracked a couple of inches, Terry threw his shoulder at the door and smashed his way inward.

The nanny stood stunned, and then Solak took three steps forward and pointed the pistol at the woman's forehead. "On the floor," said Solak in a threatening whisper. He pointed down at the hardwood surface. "Sit on your hands."

Terry paced across the room, ripped a table lamp from the electric socket, and grabbed a sturdy wooden chair from the kitchen area.

As Ronja closed and re-bolted the apartment door, Solak pulled out his Buck knife. He cut the electric cord to the lamp and pointed at the empty chair. "Sit."

The nanny again complied with his instructions and started to cry when Terry tied her wrists and bound her to the chair. She kept looking across the room towards Ronja, hoping for a touch of empathy. Ronja ignored the young woman, which only served to increase Gerty's anxiety.

Terry started to circle the chair in a counter-clockwise fashion. "I'm going to ask you some questions, and you are going to answer them…if you lie, I will know…and I will hurt you."

The nanny shivered. She was tall, pretty, with blonde-brown hair, dressed in a short, cotton nightgown. He saw the goosebumps form on her bare legs as the crisp nighttime chill of a Bavarian autumn penetrated the building. "Are you cold?" asked Solak.

"Yes," answered the nanny. "May I get a pullover?"

"No," answered Terry in a curt voice. He wanted her both physically and psychologically uncomfortable. "What is your name?"

"Gertrude," answered the nanny. "But I go by Gerty."

Her eyes followed Terry as he paced.

"How old are you?" asked Solak.

"Eighteen."

"Where do you work?"

"I go to school."

"Where?"

"The Gisela Gymnasium in Schwabing."

"Where's your boyfriend?" asked Terry. He had intentionally disregarded the information supplied by Ronja on this matter.

"My boyfriend? I am not seeing anyone."

Solak took a moment to look over the nanny's shoulder. Ronja stood to her rear and shrugged with a confused expression.

"Are you sure?"

The young woman began to cry. She knew something was very wrong. Her big concern was Ronja's demeanor and the status of the boys. But Terry saw the development of having the two women together as an opportunity to flush out some facts. He needed to determine if they were acting alone or as a team.

"Your boyfriend," said Terry again. Then he whirled towards the nanny, yanked a lock of her hair, and snapped with the knife. The speed of the action startled Gerty without actually hurting her. Solak held up a fistful of her blonde-brownish hair so that she could see his handiwork. It was intimidation without physical pain.

"Please," said Gertrude as she tried to turn and look to Ronja for help.

Terry changed course midstream. He leaned forward and spoke into her ear. "Tell me *where* the boys are." Then he pulled his face back and stared into Gerty's eyes. "Where?"

The nanny started to crumble in place. The hot-cold approach when coupled with Terry's threats aided by the time of night all contributed to a young woman caught in a serious game beyond her ability. "Please, Miss Ronja..." said the nanny. She tried to turn in her seat and look to Ronja for assistance.

"She will not help you," said Terry in a confidential tone. "She wants me to *kill* you for taking her boys."

"No," replied the nanny. She was growing more aware of her deteriorating situation. The tears were flowing.

"She trusted you with her boys," said Solak. He permitted Gerty to swivel enough to peek over her shoulder. Terry stood and walked several paces while looking back for emphasis. "She is reckless with her anger...Ronja wants me to do terrible things, to make you pay."

The nanny broke into an anxiety-filled moment as Solak twirled his knife. "It's about her sons," Terry said.

***

Berlin, Germany

The group of twenty gathered again in the eighth-floor conference room of the chancellery building. The news of political paralysis following the elections grew by the day. The reelection of the chancellor to her fourth term in office did little, in the face of mounting tensions, to assuage the frustration of the citizens. Even as the chancellor herself grew impatient with the demands of the far right, she was unable to reach consensus on a workable platform. She was unable to govern and, as the days ticked by, the country faced the prospect of having to call snap elections in the spring for the first time in years.

Germany was the European Union's largest economy, and a loss of confidence followed as the preeminent power started to plunge into a deep political abyss. It caused a high level of civil unrest. To make matters worse, the elected officials of the AfD, the country's newly-powerful far right party, were fanning the flames of discourse, confident that they would benefit even further from another general election held in the near future. All the while, lurking in the midst of the instability that had gripped the nation, sat the coup de grâce; the irrepressible, dangerous orator named Gerhardt, ready to pounce.

Holger of the Berlin State Police spoke first, bringing his counterparts up-to-date on the efforts of his Landespolizei to control the malaise and frustration that infected the populace. Angry people were dangerous people. "We continue in our efforts to identify and isolate the most virulent provocateurs."

Director Geiger leaned forward and folded his hands together on the conference table. He looked at the VP of domestic security. "Perhaps," said Geiger in a deep voice, "we could be brought up-to-date on the status of our *most* dangerous provocateur?"

"We will, Herr Director," answered the VP, "but I was saving my report on the matter until we conclude our other business."

"Of course, but we were led to believe that an arrest of Gerhardt was imminent." Geiger glanced around the table at his peers.

It was obvious that the others in the group preferred an immediate update on the planned apprehension of Gerhardt as well.

"Very well," replied the VP. He shifted in his seat to relieve the pain in his arthritic leg and motioned to his right.

Deputy Ludwig of the criminal investigative police cleared his throat and began. "Three nights ago, at nine in the evening, a team of federal investigators attempted to serve a warrant under the Emergency Acts at a condominium located at Corneliusstraße five-D here in Berlin. They were supported by a SWAT team from the Berlin State Police and a detachment from the Federal Uniform Police."

Ludwig took a sip of water before continuing. "When the police arrived, they confronted a fast-burning, internal fire that quickly enveloped the building. It destroyed most of the apartments in the block. When arson inspectors arrived later, they identified accelerants and the selective burning of personal possessions to include desktop computers, written notes, and partial timelines."

"Gerhardt escaped?" asked Geiger.

"Yes," replied Ludwig.

The attention in the room shifted back towards the VP. He let the information settle and then made a comment. "But all is not lost. There is one piece of good news."

"Do we have a lead?" asked Geiger.

The VP shook his head. "Not exactly." Then he turned towards his chief of internal security and nodded.

The man reached forward and touched the 'play' button on the tabletop console. It activated a surround sound audio system tape recorder.

"This is 's'," said a familiar voice in a clear tone. "Activate evacuation procedures immediately…an arrest is imminent…I repeat, activate evacuation procedures immediately."

The taped message ceased and the VP of domestic security looked up to see all of his counterparts looking past him to the woman two seats to his left.

Frau Steir of the chancellor's office closed her notebook and stood. Then two investigators from the Federal Criminal Police entered the conference room. She looked around the table. Nothing needed to be said. It was Steir's voice. They all now understood that the source of the leaks that had stymied their efforts for weeks had emanated from the chancellor's own senior staff. It was a betrayal of unfettered proportions.

Everyone watched in collective surprise and confusion. The two investigators escorted Frau Steir from the conference room and closed the door. A pause ensued as everyone looked at the VP of domestic security.

Director Geiger held up a hand in quiet acknowledgment of the VP's work before asking, "How did you know it was her?"

The VP bit his lip and said, "I didn't, I've been monitoring everyone in this room for over two months."

Chapter 52

Munich, Germany

The six women sat around the oval table in the apartment on the far side of the city. The owner turned towards Gerhardt's mother. "Is your son ready?"

"Yes," said Frau Fuchs. "He has been preparing for this day for his entire life."

"He understands," said the leader, "that by injecting himself into the activities by his rhetoric, the authorities will seek to arrest him by using the Emergency Acts."

"Yes," replied Fuchs, "Gerhardt accepts he could be located and imprisoned. If it should occur, he expects they will exert all manner of pressure."

There was a moment of silence, and the leader set down her teacup. "We are settled then." A series of nods around the table and some affirmative table tapping ensued.

Then the leader consulted her wristwatch. "It is now six thirty-seven in the evening…" All of the women checked their timepieces. "…in one hour and twenty-three minutes, we commence Operation Blackbird."

***

Munich, Germany

Terry's head spun. The more disjointed and uneven the facts appeared to be, the more connected and contrived the web of deceit became.

Gerty, the nanny, was complicit in the abduction of Ronja's children. She was compelled to cooperate with the assurance that Martin and Garrin would be safe. Nonetheless, she had misgivings. It left a door opened, and Gerty sensed that her best option now was to oblige Ronja and the dangerous man that accompanied her.

"They swore to me," said the nanny between gulps of air, "that the boys would *not* be harmed."

Terry spun the knife in an ominous fashion. Gerty had blurted quite a bit of information that Solak needed to get his arms around. He needed to make sense of the stream of assertions offered by a nanny who was confused, afraid, and emotionally exhausted. The trail of this kidnapping was littered with competing influences that seemed to lead back to the women's organization, das Netzwerk.

Solak glanced at Ronja, and then he stepped to the far side of Gerty's apartment and tugged out his cell phone. He speed dialed Otto in Berlin, well aware of the unseemly hour.

"Helios," answered the German foreign intelligence officer. "Where are you?"

"Down south," replied Terry remembering Otto's description of Munich, "in the belly of the beast. I'm with the mother and the nanny."

"Ahh, now I understand…how is she doing?" asked Otto referring to Ronja.

"Pensive, concerned, but under control."

"Do you think she is part of the plan?"

Terry took a moment to consider the clues. It was the question that haunted them from the beginning. Otto and Terry shared a fear that they would become sidetracked following a useless stream of chaff. "I'm not sure, but my instincts tell me that she's out on a limb by herself—more concerned with what the women will do, than aware of what I might find out."

"Do you think she's a delaying action?"

"Maybe, but I'm now less inclined to lean that way." Solak looked first at Ronja, and then at the tearful nanny. "What do you know about the Gisela Gymnasium?"

"Gisela…that's a prestigious secondary school. It was named after an Austrian duchess. Why?"

"It seems that the nanny is a student there, and one of the school administrators set up the abduction of the two boys."

"Not a surprise," said Otto with a sigh, "it has one of those connected histories."

Terry paused and looked again at Ronja and the nanny before asking, "Can you give me an example?"

"During World War One, the school building was used to house an army engineering battalion. Many of the students volunteered for military service."

"So, a conservative school. One with a proud lineage."

"Yes," answered Otto, "and in the 1930s, with the rise of the Nazis, they sponsored numerous student organizations such as the Hitler Youth and the Jungvolk. There was a good deal of political indoctrination of the students."

"I see," replied Terry, as he considered the information. "So this is all plausible?"

"Very. A school administrator could expel the nanny and prevent her from receiving her *Abitur*...that is quite a bit of leverage in this country."

"Abitur?"

"A German diploma, a secondary school certification. No Abitur, no university."

"Is it really that significant?"

"Yes," replied Otto. "And the Gisela is unique in that it is funded by the city of Munich itself, *not* the Free State of Bavaria. It depends for money upon a special charity: The Friends and Supporters of Gisela, or some such name..."

"So none of this surprises you."

"Only that I didn't see the connection earlier," said Otto. "The tentacles and control would go back to the time of the nanny's admission to the school— that is the style of das Netzwerk. They are patient. They have been laying the foundation for eighty years...are you in a secure location?"

Terry looked around the nanny's apartment. "For now."

"Get me the name of the administrator at the Gisela school, and I will call you back."

Chapter 53

Duisburg, Germany

The telephone in the parlor at the rear of the home rang. The home's owner, a widowed woman in her sixties, stood and walked to the side table. She looked down at the landline and waited until it rang a second time. Then she plucked the receiver from the cradle.

"Hallo," answered the woman.

"Blackbird, Blackbird, Blackbird," said the voice, "confirm."

"I confirm," replied the woman. "Blackbird."

The line disconnected and the voice was replaced by a dial tone. The woman cradled her receiver and walked back across the parlor to a large mahogany china cabinet. She opened the lower left-hand drawer and pulled out an envelope containing a short, typed list of names followed by telephone numbers. Then she reached deeper into the same drawer and pulled out an unused burner cell phone. With telephone and list in hand, the woman sat at her small desk and began to replicate the process.

***

Munich, Germany

Otto delivered. It took an hour, but given the time of night, the speed of the intelligence officer's response was commendable. Everything was on a compressed schedule. The advantages of using an outsider to probe inside Germany were matched by the disadvantages. Terry had freedom of movement and flexibility to act, but his operational presence alone was illegal. If apprehended by the German police, it would create a very loud, but very short, diplomatic tussle

185

that would quickly end with Solak being shipped out of the country under cover of darkness.

The flip side for Terry was that, although he operated with impunity, he was without reinforcements or resupply. His sole contact in country was Otto, a foreign intelligence officer who placed himself in considerable jeopardy to provide assistance. They were all treading on dangerous legal ground.

A quiet knock on the nanny's door caused Terry to stand and glance at his wristwatch. It was half past five in the morning—less than an hour to sunrise. He withdrew his pistol and checked the peephole.

"Helios," said the visitor.

Solak opened the door and two men entered. The first man gave Solak a nod and pointed to the side. Then his associate stepped into the room and proceeded to free the nanny from her lamp-wire binding before securing the young woman with nylon flex handcuffs. A moment later Ronja stepped forward from the corner and the first man addressed her. "Are you the mother?"

"Yes," she answered.

He motioned at Terry and the two men receded to a corner of the flat where they could talk in quiet tones but view the room.

"What's the plan?" asked Solak.

"I have two cars downstairs with drivers. The nanny goes with my associate to our safe house. We hold her for questioning and then hand her over to the state police."

"How much time can I get?"

"I can buy you two days."

"Okay, and the administrator?"

"I will take you to her home now. Let's go, we will update you en route."

The associate wrapped Gerty in a coat and slipped her into a pair of shoes. Then the five people filed from the small apartment.

On the street, the first sedan sped away carrying the second man and the emotionally fraught nanny sitting alone in the rear seat.

Inside the second car Ronja turned towards Solak. "What will happen to her?"

"She'll be interrogated for a couple of days by Otto's people and then the police. Kidnapping is a crime."

Ronja looked at Terry in the glow of a new morning. The sun began its laborious ascent upward over the horizon. "You didn't hurt her."

Solak shrugged. "No need. She told us what she could." He smirked. "But I think I ruined her haircut."

Ronja studied Solak with a curious expression. She couldn't read him. On the one hand, he scared her. On the other, she felt safe with him. He seemed able to shift his demeanor at will, and she couldn't quite tell if his comportment was contrived for effect, or he was actually as dangerous as he appeared. Ronja settled back for the short ride.

Chapter 54

Berlin, Germany

It was a quiet Sunday morning in Mitte as the unmarked white van cruised along Kupfergraben. It pulled to a stop beside the canal, hugging the metal fence that served as a bicycle rack, and the side door slid open. Stepping to the curb was a cameraman, a sound technician, two body guards and Gerhardt.

The orator wandered out into the middle of the street, and dodged the occasional vehicle as he looked back towards the Pergamon Museum. He was dressed in a dark business suit, a fedora, and sunglasses. The cameraman zoomed in on Gerhardt's face, catching his uncanny resemblance to Hitler in a close-up, filming as the orator removed his hat and glasses. He was the spitting image of the long-deceased Fuhrer.

Gerhardt started to speak, and a flash crowd gathered in the street. Several locals recognized the speaker. He built a steady stream of logic with his words and shaped an argument that promoted German control over Germany's destiny.

Fingers were pointed and questions were asked. A perfect head and shoulders frame of the orator squared against a yellow building to his rear. It was a familiar building to Germans. The five-floored, six-windowed, wide structure at Kupfergraben six was the private residence of the recently reelected chancellor. Two uniformed policemen stood outside and watched the multitude of pedestrians multiply. Curiosity provoked more curiosity.

Gerhardt engaged the live audience in a conversation that warned of civil strife as the ruling political class strangled the people's government with bureaucratic ineptitude. The inability of the politicians, to find a consensus and to form a coalition, frustrated the citizens. Throngs of migrants demanded privileges in the face of social changes.

Inside the van, a video engineer watched and listened as Gerhardt elevated his cadence, speaking in louder, more impassioned phrases, imploring support for the right wing populace movement. In minutes, there were several hundred pedestrians gathered in a semicircle around Gerhardt, his profile planted firmly in the public space, with the chancellor's yellow apartment building as a backdrop over his shoulder.

The two policemen stepped closer, crossing the street as they now recognized the visage of Gerhardt from a distance. One of the police made a call on his radio as the second backpedaled to post outside the front door of the yellow building.

Gerhardt promised a new order, a return to German rule for a German people. Cell phones snapped photographs of Gerhardt, selfies of the audience, and pictures of the private residence. The apartment building across from Museum Island left little doubt as to the very public location selected for the oration.

Several sirens sounded in the distance. It shattered the low-key calm of the Sunday morning. As a crackling energy penetrated the air, the crowd listened to Gerhardt who then challenged the political order with a threat to accept the populace themes.

"Those elected officials who *fail* to follow the dictates of the election, who ignore the peoples' priorities, who regard Schengen, the European Union, and the Muslim migrants as deserving of our munificence, who demand equality as non-citizens of our nation, *will* pay a price."

The sirens grew louder as the police reinforcements approached. More pedestrians, tourists, and local residents joined the quickly assembling mob.

The white van turned from the canal and rushed towards the crowd. The side door slid open and Gerhardt paused, facing his audience. Then he raised his right fist in the air. He spoke in a deep guttural voice. "Put Germany first." With a nod he jumped into the van and sped away.

***

Munich, Germany

Ten minutes into the ride, Otto's man spun in his seat and began to recite facts pertinent to the Gisela Gymnasium administrator. "Frau Thiel is a deputy principle at Gisela. She is fifty-eight years old, divorced, the mother of two grown children, both of whom live up north—one in Bremen, and one in Schwerin." He paused for a moment before continuing.

"Thiel actually attended Gisela herself as a teenager. She completed the curriculum and then attended the University of Munich where she studied chemistry. Upon graduation, she went to work at a pharmaceutical company where she specialized in toxicology."

Otto's associate paused again as the information took hold. Strands of das Netzwerk pulled together. Poison was a favored tool of the women.

"Frau Thiel went back to Gisela as a teacher. She rose through the ranks as a competent and strict instructor."

"How long has she been there?" asked Terry.

"Over thirty years." Otto's man raised and lowered his eyebrows as an expression of suspicion. "She has had a somewhat closed experience by modern standards. She lives alone, in a modest home here in Schwabing, near enough to walk to work in good weather."

"Gisela is all she knows," said Ronja, speaking for the first time.

"Yes, some would call that a stilted existence," replied Terry.

"But one with a purpose," said Otto's man, "and needless to say, she is quite protective of the school."

Solak considered the information as he formulated his approach. "Tell me about security."

"She lives alone and has an alarm system that she rarely uses. Her few friends seem to be former students of Gisela from her youth. She prefers to travel to Austria rather than other parts of Germany, and she rarely sees her grandchildren."

"Why?" asked Ronja, a little surprised.

"She seems to differ with her own children on their methods of parenting. She believes their kids lack discipline."

"Sounds like a pleasant lady," said Terry in a sarcastic tone. He stole a glance at Ronja.

Otto's man stifled a laugh and changed the subject. "When I drop you off, you'll be on your own. In thirty minutes, we will leave a rented auto parked a block from Frau Thiel's home." He handed Solak an envelope. "Inside are the keys and the vehicle plate number. You have Otto's number if there's an emergency."

Terry pocketed the envelope. Four minutes later the driver pulled to the curb and pointed at a well-maintained, single-family home constructed of stained wood and cove pattern siding.

"Good luck," said Otto's associate with a wave. Terry and Ronja bounded from the auto and walked the short distance to Frau Thiel's home. In a neighborhood of Jugendstil restored facades, her home was unique in its ordinary appearance.

Following a quick look at the outside, Terry led Ronja around the back of the house using a flagstone walk that opened to a large garden filled with more plants than flowers.

"Wait here," said Solak in a quiet voice. He crept up to examine the rear door.

Ronja had long since stopped trying to analyze his thought process. She waited as he studied the rooflines, the overhangs of the walls, and the shutters. Above, on the first floor, Terry saw two windows, each cracked open several inches for air. Germans, like many Europeans, preferred a natural breeze over air conditioning, and the October temperature was crisp and fresh.

To Ronja's surprise, Terry started to scale the rear of the house as she stood and watched from the garden. He gripped and tested several handholds and footholds that could bear his weight until he grabbed at a roof overhang that permitted him to crouch abreast of the hall window. He stood one floor above the ground and peeked inside. Then he slid the window open and climbed over the sill. He was in.

Seconds later a bedroom door opened, and the administrator exited. Terry rushed forward just as Frau Thiel started to scream. He tackled the older woman, grabbed a fistful of hair with one hand and covered her mouth with the other. Then he shoved his pistol into her neck until she gasped. Half asleep, Frau Thiel was unprepared for the dawn attack. Solak guided her down the stairs in a controlled movement, keeping her close, shifting his eyes in search of other occupants. In the ground floor hallway, he unlocked and opened the rear door. Ronja rushed forward.

Chapter 55

Munich, Germany

The administrator's eyes bulged at the sight of Ronja, the kidnapped children's mother.

"If you make any noise," said Terry, "I will hurt you."

Solak sat her in a chair away from the windows in the ground floor parlor. Then he motioned at Ronja, who seemed to intuitively understand her part of the process. She unplugged a table lamp and used Terry's Buck knife to cut and prep the long wire cord the same way she had watched Solak do at the nanny's apartment. Then, still holding the knife, she guarded Frau Thiel as Terry lashed her to the chair.

To her credit, the administrator appeared more angry than afraid. Her face was stern, and her short gray hair unruffled despite Solak's strong grip.

"We want the boys," said Terry.

Ronja was in operational mode. She cut a broad piece of curtain and then gagged Thiel. There was a glow in Ronja's eyes. She leaned forward and whispered in the administrator's ear, but rather than cower, Thiel gave Ronja a defiant look.

It was a mistake. Ronja had grown increasingly impatient through the evening's activities. She had turned desperate. She wanted her sons. In a blur Ronja stabbed the administrator in the upper arm.

Thiel made a muffled scream through the gag, as a surprised Solak backed Ronja away from Thiel.

"What are you doing?" asked Terry. He noted the look in Ronja's eyes and realized the tide had turned. Ronja was over the edge and past the point of being rational. She would be difficult to control now, so in a moment, Solak switched gears and decided to use Ronja's emotions. He became the reasonable captor

192

in the good-cop, bad-cop scenario. He replaced the pistol at the small of his back and knelt close to the administrator. Then he spoke in a quiet voice, but loud enough for Ronja to hear.

"She's desperate, and I don't think I can control her."

The administrator hesitated and Ronja stabbed her again, choosing the fleshy portion of Thiel's other arm.

A second muffled scream as Thiel bounced in the chair. She was now bleeding from both of her secured arms.

"*Where are they?*" asked Ronja through clenched teeth. There was a flicker of tension in her voice.

"Please," said Solak again, "she won't stop…she doesn't care."

As if on cue, Ronja stepped forward and stabbed the administrator a third time. She chose the outside of Thiel's thigh.

The woman jerked in pain as the tears flowed, but she was tough, almost resolute in her demeanor. She blurted between gulps of air as Terry loosened the gag.

"It doesn't matter," said Thiel. "You're too late…"

Ronja's eyes widened in dismay and she raised the knife again, ready to strike. Solak shot his arm forward to impede Ronja's thrust and asked, "What is too late? Are the children dead?"

The administrator looked at Terry as if they were on two different wavelengths. "What? No, the children don't matter because they served their purpose."

"What purpose?"

"Blackbird. The operation has begun," Thiel looked at Solak with an edge of superiority. "and you can't roll it back."

"Blackbird?"

"Watch and learn," said Thiel. She winced and then spoke between gulps of air. "The children are irrelevant."

"Are they alive?" asked Terry in a demanding tone.

The administrator gave him a sneer, and Ronja stepped forward in a rage, thrusting hard at Thiel's chest. Terry was able to deflect most of the stab towards the administrator's shoulder, but received a laceration on his forearm for the effort.

"What the fuck," said Solak, growing more perturbed by the minute. He sidled up to Ronja and led her across the room. "Dead people don't share information—use your head and get under control or you will have yourself to blame."

Solak spun and paced back across the parlor. He stopped in front of the bleeding Frau Thiel, but continued to stand, forcing her to raise her head to meet his eyes. His voice took on an authoritarian edge. "Where are the boys?"

"Who are you?" asked the administrator. "You are *not* German."

"Are they alive?"

Thiel squirmed in her chair. She was in a great deal of pain, but only bleeding at a reduced rate.

"What is Blackbird?" asked Terry to keep her talking.

"You will see," replied Thiel.

"Are you prepared to die for it?"

"If necessary," said Thiel. "You people don't understand commitment."

"Are you prepared to die for children as well?"

"The boys have served their purpose," she said.

"Where are they?"

Thiel seemed to be analyzing the options. She glanced over her shoulder at Ronja who stood ten feet away, shifting her weight nervously from one foot to the other. The mother still held the knife.

"Nymphenburg," said the administrator.

***

Langley, Virginia

Evie stood at her desk and picked up several file folders packed with information. She exited her cubicle and paced down the hall to Bob Colman's office. His door was open, but Evie was halted by the SAD chief's assistant who mouthed the words, 'on phone.'

Evie stopped, but did not sit. She walked in a tight circle, making an oval treadmill of the space between the assistant's desk and Bob's door until she heard Colman bellow from inside, "Enter."

The collection manager abruptly stopped, turned, and veered sideways into the office.

"Bob, you need to see this," said Evie who started to lay out several manila file folders on Colman's conference table.

The SAD chief stood and walked around his desk to join Evie at the conference table. She had created two vertical columns, side by side, of four folders each. As Bob cleaned his eyeglasses with a handkerchief, she began.

"Thirty minutes ago, I received a verbal sitrep from Helios on a burner phone. In his brief, he referred to Operation Blackbird." She paused and looked at Bob. He shrugged. Evie then turned her attention to the manila stacks. She

194

pointed at the top left folder and flipped it open. The title read 'General Election 1930.' Then she reached over and flipped open the corresponding file from the right column. The title read 'General Election 2017.'

Evie paused and held out her index finger for emphasis. Then she flipped open the second file in each column and read aloud the titles, "Reichstag Burns…Brandenburg Gate Bombed."

Bob leaned forward over the conference table and read several lines from each open folder before nodding and stepping back.

Evie flipped open the cover of the third row of manila files and quickly read aloud the titles. "Enabling Act…Emergency Acts," she took a breath and opened the last files. "Operation Hummingbird…Operation Blackbird."

Colman spoke, "So everything matches?"

"Yes," replied Evie, "the template is complete—except that the last step has yet to occur."

"Blackbird."

"Correct," said the analyst.

"Hummingbird rings a bell, was it a Nazi operation?" asked Bob.

"Yes," answered Evie, "from 1934. And if true to form, 'Blackbird' is the modern equivalent to 'Hummingbird.'"

Bob looked at Evie as he waited for the final piece of the puzzle. She cleared her throat and said, "Operation Hummingbird is often referred to by historians as 'The Night of the Long Knives.'"

Chapter 56

Wuppertal, Germany

The recently elected member of parliament scaled one of Wuppertal's numerous staircases. High stairs, low stairs, circular stairs, rainbow-colored stairs—all merged together in steel, stone, concrete, and wood to connect the streets and cross the hills. He was excited, lost in political thought, considering all the new opportunities that lay ahead as a delegate to the German Bundestag. He followed the staircase as it angled left and then started to descend.

The MP came to Germany as a migrant nine years earlier. He was a skilled machinist from Poland, who met and married a local girl, became a citizen, and settled down with two small children. He did not notice the woman or the three men to his rear.

As the MP hit the bottom step of the crossover staircase, the woman signaled with a subtle wave. Then she peeled off to the left, increasing her distance from the MP as they walked in opposite directions.

The two closest men increased their speed until they stood directly behind the MP. He turned—suddenly alarmed—and watched in a blur as they pulled out matching P8 automatic pistols. The shooters squeezed the triggers in rapid-fire mode, unleashing a hail of gunfire at point blank range, alternating bullets between the politician's head and chest until he collapsed sideways. Then they stepped over his body and turned down a street to the right.

Finally, the fourth member of the wet team, the cleaner, paced past the lifeless torso of the MP and dropped a miniature red flag embroidered with a white crescent and star on the corpse.

It was the national flag of Turkey.

***

Munich, Germany

Terry turned towards Ronja outside the administrator's home. "Do you know how to get there?"

"Yes."

He handed her the car keys. "You drive, I have to make another call."

It was the second burner phone call in three minutes. The first call made from the huge garden in the rear was to Langley. He always wanted the Agency to have the most up-to-date info lest things went bad. At least that way someone could react to whatever intel he had uncovered. The 'Blackbird' lead seemed promising, if for no other reason than the administrator acted downright smug in her demeanor.

Terry climbed into the passenger seat and speed dialed Otto.

"Helios," answered the foreign intelligence officer. "What is your status?"

"We are leaving the administrator's home now," said Solak as he took a peek over his shoulder. "She's in tough shape, she'll make it, but I would send someone out there soon."

"Was she helpful?" asked Otto.

"Reluctantly. She's a mean one."

"As we suspected...how is the mother?"

Terry stole a sideways glance at Ronja before answering, "On edge."

"Will she hold together?"

"For now." Terry leaned back in the seat and considered the sequence of events. Each lead had brought them a bit closer to Ronja's sons, yet it also appeared to spill some information related to a significant operation. "Does *Blackbird* mean anything to you?"

There was a short silence on the line. "No," replied Otto after a few seconds. "How did it come up?"

"The admin boasted of it several times...said that it was already in motion...she also confirmed that the children were a throw off."

"A misdirection?"

"Classic," replied Terry.

"I will dispatch a team to the admin's home right away...in the meantime, did you get a new location?"

"Yes," replied Terry, "it's in Nymphenburg. I will text you; we are about ten minutes out." Solak disconnected.

They drove in silence for a minute before Ronja spoke. "Was that Otto," she asked while keeping her eyes on the road.

"Yes."

"How is he?"

"Worried about you," said Terry.

Ronja blushed, unsure of her own capacity for violence, but accepting of the fact that she would take any action that could produce the safe return of her children. "I doubt that," replied Ronja. "Otto is not the sentimental type."

Terry shrugged as Ronja slowed the car. She pointed at a modest, stand-alone home a stone's throw from the palace.

"Drive by," said Solak, "and circle the block." Terry started to look in all directions as he made a quick assessment of the neighborhood.

It was now nearly nine in the morning, and the city was awake and bustling. They had followed several leads of interest, each one peeling another layer from the onion, but clearly the kidnapping of Ronja's sons factored into the end game. The women's group, das Netzwerk, had an agenda, and they were methodical in following some type of timeline.

Terry pointed, and Ronja parked the car two houses down from the target address. "Can you keep it together?" he asked.

Ronja fingered the Buck knife under her coat and nodded. He had permitted Ronja to keep the folding knife, conceding an element of control and trust to the frazzled mother. She nodded.

"You will approach the front door alone. Make up a story. Mention that you were sent here by the administrator. If she hesitates or anything appears out of place, signal me."

"Where will you be?"

"Close behind. I only need them to open the front door a crack. Do they know you?"

"I doubt it. The boys were taken while they were with Gerty."

Terry leaned back as he considered the information. Then he patted her wrist. "Let's go."

Chapter 57

Berlin, Germany

The VP of the domestic security agency kept his head tilted forward as he scanned the typed itinerary. This was the first meeting of the group of twenty since the revelation that Frau Steir had betrayed both her position and her responsibilities. During the ensuing days, the senior appointees of the chancellor's office came under incredible scrutiny. Everyone was suspect. It opened the door to a massive dose of political paranoia. Gerhardt, the Hitler orator, the father-like figure, stepped visibly into the void. He actually met with citizens in the middle of Kupfergraben, right in front of the reelected chancellor's private residence. The most wanted man in Germany was standing in the center of Berlin, on a bright Sunday morning, discussing politics with the locals and the edited video was posted online for millions to see.

"It was an impromptu speech," said Holger of the Berlin State Police.

"In broad daylight," replied Geiger of the federal police, "on a Sunday morning in Mitte?" The tall police director slapped the table with an open hand to add emphasis. "It was planned to insult us."

"I agree," said Ludwig of the federal criminal investigative police in a sharp tone. "They framed it against the chancellor's private residence to make a point."

"To embarrass us," said Holger.

"To emphasize the failure of our government," replied the VP.

"He is hiding here," said the deputy Minister of the Interior. "Right under our noses. We are made to appear inept."

"No," said Holger. "We are inept…in the eyes of many citizens, change is the only solution." He leaned forward and lowered his voice. "We must be careful here, frustration prompts violence."

"The deputy president is correct," said Geiger. "History is filled with radical change replacing long-accepted practices."

"Gerhardt is challenging the constitution," said the VP. "He is in open violation of the law. His rhetoric has gone too far."

All eyes at the conference table looked past the VP towards the empty chair two seats to his left.

"Have we learned anything from Frau Steir?" asked Holger.

The VP stood and rested his hip against the conference table. This served to lessen the arthritic pain in his leg. He spoke in a quiet voice. "We have questioned her for several days. Steir has proven to be as disciplined as she appears. Obviously, our methods must be above reproach...having said that, she has hinted—in less taciturn moments—that there is something major afoot. But, our information is sketchy at best."

***

Munich, Germany

Ronja knocked on the door, and to her surprise, it was answered by a man. He was a hulk; huge, fleshy, and bald, adorned in finger rings and tattoos.

"Ja," said the sentry.

"The administrator sent me," replied Ronja as she passed a hand signal to Terry. The man studied her for a moment and then started to turn as he closed the door. Solak burst forward from the blind side and rammed his shoulder against the portal. The wooden frame smashed against the huge man's forehead, temporarily stunning him, and sending his body backwards several steps deeper into the foyer.

The brute recovered and charged Terry. Solak drew his pistol and fired twice. The nine-millimeter bullets penetrated the sentry's chest, center mass, and he tumbled in a heap.

"We have to move fast," said Terry as he pulled Ronja into the home. "The jig is up." Solak closed and bolted the front door. The element of surprise was now lost. Gunshots caught people's attention—either in the house or in the neighborhood.

Ronja nodded in understanding as she pulled out the Buck knife.

Terry led her in a fast, but thorough, inspection of the ground floor, more due to fear of other occupants than the expectation of imprisoned children on the primary living level. He approached every closed door and open archway as if it would discharge a defender. They swept through several hallways, rooms, and closets without incident. Ronja tailed Solak by several feet, holding Terry's knife at waist level, providing an extra set of eyes and ears to the search.

Finally, Terry tugged open the final closed door off the kitchen. He pulled with a flourish, only to confront a darkened stairwell leading down into the basement. Solak nuzzled up to Ronja's ear and whispered instructions. She nodded and let Terry descend. He gained several steps of separation until he reached the bottom. Then she snapped on the overhead light. Solak crouched in a two-handed shooter's stance and scanned the now illuminated cellar. He swiveled the pistol in a horizontal arc. There was no movement.

Terry motioned for Ronja to join him. She descended the stairs and took up a position several feet to his rear. They moved together, using the available light to differentiate people from furniture.

To the front, a noise, more like a murmur, and then the realization that it was joined by a child's sniffle. Ronja's eyes widened. They passed a long storage cupboard along the left wall, leading toward the noise. Suddenly it popped open and a small woman leaped at Solak, slashing his flank with a pair of scissors. Terry spun, wounded, aiming his pistol as the attacker tumbled to the floor. Ronja reacted, stepped forward, and stabbed the woman in the back. She slumped and Ronja stabbed her a second time.

Solak recovered, and pulled Ronja away from the dying attacker. "Focus," he said, motioning towards the sounds of children. He ignored his wound, alert for more occupants in hiding. *We need to keep moving.*

Across the basement, the far corner had several long blankets draped like curtains in a makeshift room.

Ronja nodded as she regained control. Her adrenaline was pumping. Solak's instinct was to keep penetrating deeper until they had recovered the children or searched every corner of the private residence.

Terry motioned several times with a flat hand. He was coaching Ronja to proceed under control, since they never know what other surprises may exist.

Another murmur from the corner was followed by several sniffles—the unmistakable crying pattern of a child. Solak waved Ronja to his rear so that he could take the lead with the pistol. He took a final scan of the partially lighted basement and then ripped aside the makeshift curtain wall.

A thirty-year-old brunette backpedaled towards the corner. She held a young boy against her chest, shielding her torso with his body, pressing a box-cutting razor to the captive child's throat.

Chapter 58

Langley, Virginia

Evie accompanied Bob Colman to the seventh-floor SCIF at CIA headquarters. She set down several file folders in organized piles and looked around the conference room. It was full. As post-election problems in Germany grew, so too did the meeting participants. There were a number of interested parties, many of whom Evie recognized from her time in the German election situation room. The Director's Brief attracted a crowd, and everyone wanted a piece of the action. It was beneficial for an analyst to be noticed and to make a positive impression; unlike field operatives who produced more measurable information from a distance.

Germany, due to its geographic location, but also because of its population, financial prowess, and EU status, sat at the top of the hill. It mattered, and if a foreign power or group wounded the German republic, then reverberations would follow.

The Director entered the SCIF at a fast pace and waved everyone to remain seated. He pointed at the deputy director for Analysis who worked the electronic console and sealed the room.

"Let's get started," said the Director, looking first to his left and the supervisor of the German desk.

"In the past forty-eight hours," said the woman, "there have been ten murders in Germany. This caught our attention, as proportionately it is a high number. Also, however, these were execution-style killings—six by handguns, two by poison, one a knife attack, and one victim was thrown off a bridge." The supervisor paused for a moment before continuing. "Each of the victims was recently elected to the nineteenth Bundestag."

"All members of the new parliament?" asked Arthur Kent.

"Yes," nodded the desk supervisor, "and in ten different cities—smaller metropolitan areas a little off the radar."

"For example?" said the Europe Division chief.

"Essen, Leipzig, Wuppertal, Bremen…" the supervisor rattled off the secondary size cities by memory. Then she shifted in her seat to squarely face the Director. "The handgun killings all used standard nine-millimeter ammunition."

"Anything else of note?" asked Kent.

"Yes," answered the desk supervisor, "a miniature flag was left at the scene of each murder."

"What type of flag?" asked the Director.

"The Turkish flag, which is also the flag of the Ottoman Empire."

"So now we are back to attribution, a bit too obvious isn't it?"

"Yes, Director," replied the supervisor, "plus photos and CCTV film indicate that all of the hit teams appear to be staffed by bearded, dark-haired, Mediterranean types."

"We are running down matches on our in-house data bases," said the staffer from counter-terrorism.

There was a pause in the conference room as the Director shifted his gaze around the table. He settled on Bob Colman and raised an eyebrow. "Bob?"

The SAD chief looked at Evie and gave her a nod. She took a sip of water before speaking in a clear voice. "It's a live-fire test."

The SCIF fell silent before Kent leaned forward and pressed Evie. "Can you elucidate?"

"A test, but not a dry run. There is no wasted motion and no turning back. A live-fire test forces them to cross Checkpoint Charlie."

"What do they gain?" asked the Director.

"Multiple goals: they monitor the police response, the logistics tail, and the public pushback. Most of all, they create rampant fear in the political class." Evie sat forward and opened several dossiers. "Operation Blackbird," she said, "is a plan of extrajudicial executions against select members of parliament and other government officials all at the same time. The targets are developed from a list of pre-determined enemies of the right."

"But there are nearly six hundred seats in the new Bundestag, with another hundred-plus overhang or leveling seats," said the desk supervisor. "How can the government protect that many people?"

"It can't," answered Evie. "However, the German electoral system of mixed member proportional representation only needs to fill the vacancies from the same states."

"And the selection of new members will only be considered in light of the obvious physical threat to the candidates," said the deputy director of Analysis.

"That's it," said Evie, "the stagnation of the government in the face of Article thirty-eight of the German Basic Law will create conditions ripe for massive civil unrest."

"A civil war," said the Director at the far end of the long conference table.

"Yes," answered Evie, "and then a savior rides into the chaos. A man with a plan, a following, and a lineage…"

"A man," said Bob Colman, finishing her thought, "named Gerhardt."

***

Munich, Germany

Ronja followed Terry into the makeshift room and gasped. His free hand was raised in the air, silently advising her to halt. Martin, her oldest, was in the clutch of a very intense female captor. The woman held a box cutter with a razor edge against his carotid while slowly backing away from Terry.

"Don't move," said Solak in a calm voice. He watched the woman's eyes dart between himself and Ronja. They stood abreast, separated by five feet.

"I'll kill him," she said.

"I believe you," answered Terry, "but there's no need. We have a new objective."

She studied Solak for a moment. "Who are you?"

"A friend," lied Terry. "I was sent by Frau Thiel." His use of the Gisela administrator's name gave the woman a moment of doubt.

The woman gripped Martin tighter and pressed the sharp razor edge against the six-year-old's neck until it drew a trickle of blood. Terry watched her, waiting for an opening, hoping that his disinformation would give her pause.

Martin sensed the shift in seconds. To his credit, the young boy understood that a sudden move could be fatal. He glanced over at his baby brother, just as Garrin realized it was his mother entering their captive area.

"Mommy!" said the child in an excited voice. Garrin was on his feet running toward Ronja despite his ankle being attached to a long steel cable.

Ronja stood, frozen to the floor, her eyes shifting between Solak, the woman, and her two sons.

"I'll gut him like a hog," said the woman captor. "Stop!"

"Please," said Terry holding up his Glock for inspection, "no problems." He made a point to aim the pistol at the ceiling. A sudden move could spook the captor into a death cut that could drain young Martin of blood in minutes.

Then Garrin gave Solak his chance as the child shrieked in delight at reaching his mother. Ronja fell to her knees and scooped up the four-year-old in an emotional embrace.

The act caused the captor to look over and relax her grip. Martin jerked sideways and the slight separation caused a space between Martin and the woman.

Terry reacted by clasping his hands together in a double grip shooter's stance. He aimed and squeezed the trigger. The nine-millimeter parabellum bullet penetrated the woman's forehead and she tumbled backwards, dead.

Martin stopped, mid-distance before the steel cable attached to his ankle could yank him back.

Solak inspected the dead woman. Then he walked across the area to touch Ronja on the shoulder. "We have to go."

The mother was on her knees, smothering her youngest in kisses and hugs, while also reaching out to touch Martin who stretched to the end of his own steel cable.

Terry scanned the basement and noted several rows of garden tools stacked in an organized fashion along the cement wall. He grabbed a claw hammer and proceeded to rip the steel cables from their wall sockets. Then he gathered the excess cables, still attached to the boys' ankles, and pointed at the stairs. "We *need* to move."

Terry led Ronja and the two boys up the basement staircase. He pulled out his burner phone and called Otto.

"Helios," said the foreign intelligence officer as he answered the call. "What is your status?"

"We've got the boys. We are leaving now, but you need to send cleaners."

"Are there removals?"

"Yes, three, plus you need to sweep for information, I don't have time to check."

"Understood. I will text you the address of a safe house. Take your cargo there. I will meet you." The cell phone disconnected.

Chapter 59

Karlsruhe, Germany

The VP of the domestic security agency winced as he climbed from the front passenger seat of the BMW sedan. His arthritis was in a flare-up, and he struggled to not let the condition affect his ability to function. For, more than any other federal department, the collection of attacks, political turmoil, and national destabilization fell in his lap. His BfV was expected to uncover and defuse internal threats to the republic before they occurred.

The VP paused outside a municipal building in the city center, near the tower to the eighteenth-century palace. He was accompanied by deputy Ludwig of the federal criminal investigative police, Holger of the Berlin State Police, and a deputy Minister of the Interior. They had all read the transcripts of Frau Steir's multiple interrogations, which proved to be a useless exercise in disciplined propaganda.

In most cases, crimes in Germany were investigated and prosecuted by each of the sixteen different state police departments. The exceptions were acts of terrorism, espionage, and treason. These cases were prosecuted in Karlsruhe, under the federal jurisdiction of the Public Prosecutor General whose office was located in the city alongside the country's two highest courts; the Federal Constitutional Court and the Federal Court of Justice.

Frau Steir was under house arrest in a municipal lock-up in town. All of her interrogations and interface with the nation's levers of power would occur under the watchful gaze of the public prosecutor. Just as well, thought the VP. Berlin was a cacophony of noise, from the political parties jockeying for position, to the news media trying to get a sensationalist edge to their reporting. It all served to escalate the unrest and sense of chaos. The embarrassing distinction behind the involvement of the chancellor's *own* senior staff only compounded the discord. Berlin by population and prestige did not need the extra visibility afforded by Frau Steir's moment in the spotlight.

The four men were met outside and escorted to a secure setting in the basement. They inspected Steir's private cell with its toilet, sink, bed, desk, and television. It was not a five-star hotel, but it was extra suitable as an incarceration facility close to the public prosecutor's office for an alleged traitor being held in pre-trial confinement.

The VP and his associates were led into a special interrogation room complete with a large conference table, several chairs, a two-way mirror, an audio system and closed-circuit television. Steir was then escorted into the room in ankle chains and wrist handcuffs. Despite the situation, she carried herself with dignity and calm.

"Are you here to check on my accommodations?" she said, and then took a seat at the table. "We don't want anyone back in Berlin thinking I receive special treatment."

"By the looks of it," said the VP answering for the group as he sat, "one would surmise that life—despite the loss of liberty—was reasonable."

Holger, Ludwig, and the deputy Minister of the Interior all took their seats at the table.

"I seem to be outnumbered," said Steir. "Are we going to do more interrogations?"

"No, we've read all the reports," said the VP. "It's more about our confusion."

Steir tilted her head at an odd angle. "What has you confused?"

"The why," replied the VP.

"The why?" Steir leaned forward in her seat as an expression of wonderment crossed her face. She shifted her gaze, looking from one of the men to the other. "You *really* don't get it, do you?"

"Explain it to us, Frau Steir," said Holger.

Steir smirked and made a flip motion with her right hand. "Herr Holger, this is a federal matter now. Do you even have standing here?"

The answer irritated the deputy president of the Berlin State Police. He grimaced before answering. "I assure you, Frau Steir, that I have special standing in this matter."

She laughed, and it served to antagonize Holger further, but the VP leaned inward. He winced and Steir noticed.

"Still fighting the arthritis?"

"It will keep," replied the VP in a dismissive fashion. "The question I asked was, why?"

"To save Germany," said Steir.

"Save Germany?"

"From the folly of the bureaucrats. The world is coming apart at the seams. We *must* act while we still can. We see that."

"We?" asked Ludwig.

"My friends and I," replied Steir with a nod.

"You mean, your women friends," said the deputy Minister of the Interior.

"Das Netzwerk," said the VP.

Frau Steir shrugged and folded her hands together on the table. "Something like that."

"Tell us about Operation Blackbird," said Ludwig.

"It's too late," replied Steir. "I tried to warn the chancellor, but she was filled with ego and self-righteous indignation. She was going to lead Europe with Schengen—despite the burden and pressures manifested on our citizens."

"Are you saying she was wrong?"

"Of course she was wrong! She didn't listen to her constituents. She heard what she wanted to hear, and now Blackbird is in motion, and she *cannot* stop it."

***

Munich, Germany

Friedel Schulz and Frau Keller took a sidewalk table at the Frischhut Schmalz-nudel Café. The popular bakery was renowned for a special fried dough made fresh each day. The women ordered cappuccinos and pastries.

A few minutes elapsed and the umbrella tables gradually filled as a couple in their thirties managed to snag the last open seats. All of the patrons separated into private conversations. The young couple seemed to ignore the two women, focusing on each other, nuzzling face-to-face, and whispering unheard pleasantries until their order arrived.

After a short interlude, Frau Keller raised her eyebrow and motioned towards the Rosental side of the street. Sharif Ali walked alone, his eyes scanning the popular bakery, his two bodyguards several paces to his rear. He caught Keller's eye and she motioned toward the empty seat they had reserved at their table. The Saudi prince joined them.

The new arrival was mostly unnoticed by the other customers with the exception of the couple in their thirties. They exchanged a look and then the female repositioned her pocketbook on the table angled towards the two German women and the swarthy visitor who joined them.

"Guten tag," said the Saudi as his two bodyguards faded into the background.

Both women nodded in return. "Were you followed?" asked Friedel.

"I don't believe so," said the prince. "We were careful." He motioned to the waiter by pointing at Schulz's coffee, and then circled his hand in the air as an inclusive gesture.

Several patrons came and went as the women leaned in towards the center of the table, straining to hear the prince as he lowered his voice to a whisper.

"The live trial went well. We were able to analyze the police response, as well as to identify several small logistical issues."

"Yes," replied Schulz, "and the initial shock value of attacking members of parliament has proven very useful."

"Nothing gets people's attention," said Keller, "like personal risk."

"Everyone is watching and waiting," said Schulz.

The Saudi paused before saying, "Yes, and this brings us to the situation in Ankara."

"The president of Turkey has purged the military, the judiciary, and their media," said Keller.

"And talks on Turkey's accession to the EU have effectively been frozen," replied Schulz.

"I agree," said Ali, "but we need more."

"The billions of euros in financial support to Turkey have not materialized," answered Keller, "and visa liberalization is dead."

"Still," said Sharif Ali, "Turkey has an expansionist policy. Ankara is establishing both military and economic beach heads on the eastern flank of the Arabian Peninsula. This is our backyard."

"We understand," answered Schulz.

"Blackbird is in motion," said Ali. "It has been timed to allow for these last-minute changes. Do you have the final update?"

The two women exchanged a look and then Keller reached into her handbag and extracted a USB flash drive wrapped in a paper napkin.

"The final list," said Keller, reaching across the table towards Ali.

The prince palmed the crumpled napkin and leaned back in his chair.

The activity of Ali and the two women went unnoticed by the other customers of the bakery, with the exception of the young couple. They had followed the two German women all morning. The female pushed a button on the flip side of her pocketbook, and a camera shutter clicked several times. The lens was hidden in the exposed brass clasp facing the Saudi. After a few seconds, the couple paid their bill and left the café.

Chapter 60

For six hours, Ronja did not let her children out of her sight. Most of that time, she literally kept them within arm's reach. As the minutes ticked off, they were bathed, fed, and seen by a medical doctor, a child psychologist, and a foreign intelligence officer. Otto's network of assets rotated through the safe house one by one, as he sought to retain every advantage afforded by the successful rescue operation. Two security officers in the apartment checked on the arrivals and departures of the rotating staff.

Finally, a lull fell over the activities just as the physician finished suturing Solak's wounds. Ronja placed her two boys together in the nearest bedroom with the door partially ajar. Then she took a seat at the kitchen table across from Terry where she could also keep an eye on the bedroom. It had been a harrowing experience by any standard, and the mother took the opportunity to finally sit.

She looked at Solak, who seemed to be miles away in his own deliberations. After a couple of minutes, he glanced over at Ronja. "You doing okay?"

"Yes," said the mother. "Thank you."

Terry stood and grabbed a bottled water from the fridge. "You thirsty?"

"No," answered Ronja. She looked at him with a sincere expression. He could see a tear creep into her eye. "I mean it," said Ronja. "Thank you."

She reached across the kitchen table with an open hand and gestured towards Solak. He leaned forward and took her hand in his own. Then Terry saw Ronja's pretty face brighten, and she cracked a smile.

"It isn't over," said Solak. "They are going to need to talk to the kids, and there will be several debriefings."

"I understand," replied Ronja. "I expected as much. The good news, as such, is that they don't appear to have been physically abused."

Terry paused for a few seconds before positioning the rescue in the context of the German issue. "Emotional barriers," he said, nodding towards the mother. "The whole ordeal was traumatic, but accept that the kids may have valuable information that they are unaware of—impressions, memories, overheard conversations."

Ronja acknowledged the premise with a detached attitude. "As long as I am present during the questioning." She made a point of reaching forward to touch the newly sutured wound on Terry's forearm. "Sorry about this."

Solak made an admonishing gesture. The wound was the result of deflecting her kill stab on Frau Thiel, the Gisela school administrator.

"I overreacted," said Ronja.

"You think?" said Solak sarcastically. "She was our best chance at gaining the children's location. You almost doomed our whole effort."

A tear rolled down her cheek as Ronja touched the fresh dressing on Terry's side where he had been gouged by the scissor-wielding woman. "You've done a great service for my family, and I need you to know that I will never forget."

Ronja squeezed Terry's hand as he made a gesture to downplay his efforts. "Maudlin doesn't suit you, but I understand."

A moment later one of the security personnel entered the kitchen and nodded at the door. Otto stepped forward followed by several new associates. "Helios," said the foreign intelligence officer, "sorry about the delay. I got tied up in Berlin." Then Otto turned towards the mother. "I am glad that this worked out, Miss Ronja. We have much to discuss. How are the boys?"

"Good," answered Ronja. "They are sleeping."

Otto pulled out his unlit pipe and studied both Ronja and Terry with a practiced eye. He noted their wounds, their blood splattered clothes, and their exhausted expressions. He pointed towards the bedroom. "Take a nap, Miss Ronja, I need to speak to our friend first."

She stood, and with a final touch to Terry's shoulder, Ronja angled towards her children's bedroom, entered, and closed the door.

***

Langley, Virginia

Germany faced a constitutional crisis. The chancellor was unable to cobble to-gether a coalition that enabled her to govern, and all the while the Bundestag receded into parliamentary stagnation. The republic was at a crossroads, and fear of the unknown, when coupled with the inherent danger in visibility, coaxed most politicians and government officials to lay low. Those that could summon police or security service protection did so, because it had become dangerous to walk the streets. Mobs of competing interests had turned on each other, and the country fought to maintain a sense of order in the midst of chaos. Civil and criminal arrests skyrocketed and the prison population bulged.

Through it all, the internet filled with videos and media blasts. The name, the voice, and the photos of Gerhardt were everywhere. Graffiti sang his praises. He had become—by popular acclamation—the emotional connection to all things German. Yet despite the tentacles of government, the appendages of power, no one had been able to locate the man who claimed to be the grand-son of Adolf Hitler. He remained elusive.

Evie took a seat in the situation room. Once again it had become the pivot point, serving as the base to monitor developments in Germany.

"An update on the federal republic…" said the desk supervisor, "…there are now roving bands of neo-Nazis attacking Muslim businesses—especially those of Turks. As a group, the ethnic Turks have become the focal point of the migrant issue; much of this we believe is due to the symbolism, the flags, attached to the recent murders, as well as the deep-seated frustration at decades of Turkish immigration."

"I would also suggest," offered the European division analyst, "that the rhetoric by the Turkish president did not help."

"Agreed," replied the desk supervisor. "His involvement in their election was totally inappropriate…but now we have some additional information…"

The dozen analysts, supervisors, and collection managers sat forward.

"…we believe they have initiated an operation to intimidate or eliminate select delegates to the Bundestag."

"You refer to the recent series of killings. Is that Operation Blackbird?"

"Yes," said the supervisor. "We have it on good information, that the re-cent spate of executions, was a live trial for a major purge of MPs that are un-favorable to the far right agenda."

"Who has the infrastructure to mount such an operation?" asked the room monitor.

"Good question. A highly secretive, deeply embedded organization that goes back decades. It's known as 'das Netzwerk.'"

"German based?"

"Yes, Nazi sympathizers. We believe they are sponsoring the Gerhardt phenomenon, and that they also have external assistance."

"State sponsored assistance?" asked an analyst.

"Possibly." The desk supervisor used the opportunity to flick her remote control. A slide of Friedel Schulz and Frau Keller appeared on the screen. "Ever since the declaration of the Emergency Acts, the BfV, the German domestic security agency, has placed many citizens under surveillance. They believe that these two women are charter members of das Netzwerk. The BfV has requested any and all assistance in identifying *this* man." She flicked the remote control again, and several close-up photographs of Sharif Ali meeting with the women appeared on the screen. "We believe he is of Middle East origin, most probably a Gulf state. It is crucial that we identify *this* individual. Our ability to forestall the full implementation of Operation Blackbird may hinge on that effort."

Winter 2017

Chapter 61

Munich, Germany

Terry and Otto huddled in the corner of the kitchen sipping beers. Solak was bone tired and in need of a nap, but he understood the value of being debriefed sooner rather than later; recollections changed, memories faded, and impressions softened. Otto's ability to nudge and explore while activities were fresh in Terry's head helped to focus his attention. They considered the ambiguities now that he was a step beyond the heat of the moment.

"They took us on a long ride down the rabbit hole," said Otto, "and it ate up a good deal of time."

"That was the intent," replied Solak. "It was a well-planned diversion that gave the women an opportunity to execute their game."

"Multiple targets in multiple locations."

"Our best chance to interrupt the event is to somehow identify the targets beforehand," said Solak.

"Which means we need a copy of the list."

"I sense," said Terry, taking a long swig of beer, "that the ladies of das Netzwerk have placed themselves in the center of the timeline. They are patient and methodical."

"If history has taught us anything about Adolf Hitler," said Otto, "it's that he knew the value of propaganda. Goebbels was a genius. They were deep into symbolism—what is said, what is done, how it is said, and how it is done." The foreign intelligence officer fumbled with his unlit pipe before looking at Terry. "Which brings us back to Gerhardt."

"Yes," replied Solak in agreement.

"Hitler and Goebbels were the masters of emotive speech, signs, and visual images," said Otto. "Success in an operation as complex as Blackbird would

217

send a message far beyond the numeric importance of murdered delegates. It is the message received and perceived at a point in time—destiny for a people on edge." Otto placed his elbows on the kitchen table and exhaled. "It's either the list or the orator. We need to locate one or the other."

***

Langley, Virginia

Evie leaned back in her chair and let her attention wander. To her front she had positioned several file folders on top of the long extension to her cubicle desk. Her eyes darted back and forth, shifting between the files, collating the data contained in each folder by memory. Evie was more convinced than ever, that her unsheathing of the Blackbird Operation was moments from zero hour.

Unlike Evie, many of the specialists following the events in Germany were schooled in the customs and culture of the modern republic. They often thought alike, because they had been groomed alike, and only possessed a passing appreciation for the dark days of the Weimar Republic.

Evie, on the other hand, was a novice on German politics, and therefore had no predisposed opinions. Everything was open to debate and consideration. In her mind nothing was inconceivable. Nothing was off the table. She believed that the template was real and that there was historic significance to the pattern. Evie was convinced that just as Operation Hummingbird compiled a hit list in the 1930s to intimidate and eliminate adversaries of the regime, so too did the current Operation Blackbird plan a political purge of delegates to consolidate a hold on power.

The quickest way to short-circuit the success of Blackbird was to acquire the list and interrupt the planned assassinations.

Her telephone rang, and Evie twisted in her chair, alerted by the distinct ring of her personal mobile. She looked over and noted the California area code as she answered, "Hello?"

"Havva," said the male voice.

"Amir?"

"Yes, Havva," said the older brother.

"Is everything alright?"

"No, it's Baba. He is in the hospital."

Evie sat forward at her desk and pressed the cell phone closer to her ear. "What happened?"

"A heart attack."

"Again?"

"Yes, fortunately Baba was at the store and his cashier called an ambulance. He was rushed to Hoag Hospital. He is now in intensive care. You must come home."

Evie hesitated for a moment before fumbling through a response. The sudden news jolted the collection manager. She was torn between her commitment to her family and the responsibility to Helios—all at a critical juncture.

"Amir," said Evie finally, "it is not so simple."

"Of course it is," replied the brother with a touch of exasperation. "It is Baba...he is dying, and he is asking for you."

Evie squeezed her eyes together. "Let me make some arrangements," she said. Then she stood and looked down at her piles of analytical data. "I have to go."

A minute later, Evie placed her work product into the desk safe that was bolted to the floor inside her cubicle. She turned in place, retrieved her pocketbook and suit jacket, and exited. She then carried one thin manila folder down the corridor.

Bob Colman's door was half open and Evie motioned to Marge.

"You okay?" asked the assistant. "You look frazzled."

"A family emergency," answered Evie. "I need to clear my absence with Bob. I hate to be away at this critical point in the mission."

Marge waved a hand dismissively. "Bob would say that if it's an emergency you have to go."

"It's my dad," said Evie. "He just had a heart attack—his third one—and he's in intensive care."

Just as Marge started to respond Colman swung the half-closed door open. "Evie, what's up?"

"My dad," replied Evie, trying to compose herself. She gave the SAD chief a quick outline of the father's medical condition and status.

"And you're worried about being away during the Helios probe."

Evie swallowed and nodded.

"I appreciate your professionalism, but you have to go. It's your father. If you don't, then you will regret the lost opportunity." Colman leaned on the door. "Take a burner phone. If you get an opportunity, check-in and let us know how he is doing."

Evie relaxed a little. "Thank you, Bob, I really..."

"You need to leave right now," said Colman as Evie handed him the one thin manila folder. He accepted the file and pointed. "You'll miss your flight, we'll talk later."

Chapter 62

Ten uniformed federal police quietly exited two unmarked Volkswagen Tourans. They were accompanied by a Bavarian State Police SWAT Team (SEK), a federal criminal investigator, an officer of the State Police Investigations Bureau, and an agent of the domestic security agency. The combination of federal and state police agents and officers fanned out into pre-determined positions and surrounded the quaint home in Altschwabing near the Englischer Garten.

An authoritative rap on the door was immediately followed by SWAT team members breaking down the front door and barking out their commands in sharp, concise sentences.

The sudden intrusion caused Friedel Schulz to drop her coffee cup as she looked up at the black-clad Bavarian SWAT team. "What do you want?" asked the widow in a defiant tone.

"Friedel Schulz," said the investigator from the Federal Criminal Police stepping forward, "you are under arrest for conspiring to commit high treason against the constitutional order of the federation, section eighty-one, of the German criminal code."

For a moment, Friedel Schulz sat still, her hands in plain view, as she stared down the federal criminal investigator. Then the agent of the domestic security agency stepped forward accompanied by the State Police investigator, and they waited as the federal criminal investigator produced both arrest and processing warrants.

Friedel Schulz stood, turned slowly, and walked to her foyer closet to retrieve a coat.

Two kilometers to the east a similar scene was taking place at the home of Frau Keller. She was arrested by a team of federal and state investigators, in a very loud and public manner. It was overkill with a purpose, hoping that word of the arrests would rattle both the neighborhoods and the members of das Netzwerk. The authorities had leaked word of the pending arrests just in time for news outlets to arrive and record the action. They counted on the display causing a circus-style media event to expose the arrests.

***

Langley, Virginia

Bob Colman leaned back in his chair and gave a cursory look at the pile of folders stacked on his desk. Due to the nature of black ops, computer files of current operations in SAD were the last pieces of information to be updated into the Agency mainframe. If someone had 'need to know' information on a sensitive op, they were delivered in a hand-written file that was then locked in an office safe. The operational information and after-action reports were later typed into the master computer file with special access codes. The Agency had years earlier accepted the fact that the most sophisticated computer systems could be hacked by prying eyes.

Bob plucked the manila folder from the top of the pile and read the code-word. Then he set the file down on the left corner of his desk, thereby starting a new stack of folders. Next, he lifted the second, third, and fourth files sequentially from the top of the pile, read each codeword, and restacked them in the new pile to the left. SAD had so many black ops in progress around the globe, that Colman's job became one of intelligence triage. Just as an emergency room physician would instantly classify and focus medical attention on the most critical situations first, Bob became the experienced arbiter that honed the Agency's prodigious reach on sensitive operations.

It wasn't until Bob got to the seventh file that he paused. It was the thin file left behind by Evie before she dashed off to catch a flight to California. He read the codeword: *Blackbird*, and opened the file. She had printed him a note on yellow sticky paper. Inside was a full-size photograph of Sharif Ali, with a question: *Who is this man?* in bold letters.

Bob held up the picture and studied the face. There was something familiar, but he couldn't quite place the resemblance. He flipped over the photograph and the remainder of the file was empty. He frowned. Colman knew that Evie had compiled a huge amount of work product on the Helios probe operation, yet she made a point of narrowing Bob's attention to a single photo identification. Why? Something had caught the collection manager's attention, yet without time to explain, she opted to grab his focus.

Colman stood, file in hand, and walked out to his assistant's desk. "Marge, get ahold of your contact in DS&T and have them scour their facial recognition database until they can tell me who this guy is."

The assistant took a glimpse inside the thin folder, noted the photo of the Saudi prince, and stood. "Front of the line?"

"Yes," replied the SAD chief, "before Germany breaks into civil war."

Chapter 63

Munich, Germany

Otto rushed into the safe house with a burst of energy. His demeanor was noticeably upbeat. "Helios," said the foreign intelligence officer, speaking in a loud voice as he searched for Solak.

"Over here," answered Terry, hunched over a cup of coffee. He sat up and waited as the tall German entered the kitchen.

"We may have finally caught a break," said Otto. The German motioned for Terry to follow, then turned and exited the kitchen heading for the small den at the opposite side of the apartment.

"A break?" asked Terry, repeating Otto's words as he took a seat on the sofa.

"Yes," replied the foreign intelligence officer with a grin. He immediately tugged open his briefcase and placed a stack of black and white photos on the side table. Then he spread them out so that Terry could see separate pictures of Frau Keller and Friedel Schulz.

"Who are they?" asked Solak.

"Two women known to my German counterparts at the BfV."

"The domestic security agency?"

"Yes," said Otto in confirmation, "and true to the BfV's charter, they never deviate from judicial control."

"Which means," replied Terry, "that these women have become involved with foreign influences." He started flipping through the photographs.

"Yes, the domestic security officers are drilled to stay clear of matters that can be challenged in court. Without strong, verifiable legal grounds, *any* invasion of privacy is a serious undertaking in Germany."

"And now their surveillance has developed a potential foreign agent."

"So they contacted us for help," said Otto, "thereby keeping their legal precepts in order." Otto leaned back in his chair and watched as Terry studied the pics.

"Are these two women part of das Netzwerk?" asked Solak.

"We believe so," said Otto, "even though domestic security will not confirm our suspicions."

Solak placed the final photographs on the side table and shuffled his feet. "They mean nothing to me," said Terry, "sorry…"

Otto withdrew his unlit pipe and then reached back into his briefcase for a smaller stack of separate photos. "Try these," said the German.

Solak looked at the first picture of Sharif Ali and noted a familiarity—but he couldn't place the face. He rotated through several photos of the prince having coffee with Friedel Schulz and Frau Keller. Then he paused to study a full-frontal, head and shoulder photograph of the Saudi prince. It was frustrating. Terry's probe mission in Germany for the past six months introduced him to dozens of Middle-Eastern ethnic men. It became a blur, especially as many men with Mediterranean blood tended to grow facial hair for religious and cultural reasons. This complicated Solak's memory.

"It seems," said Otto, "that the domestic security agency is seeking an identity to this man."

"What's his take?" asked Terry.

"We don't know," answered the foreign intelligence officer. "But there is a sense of extra concern that these two women are long-standing Nazi sympathizers, who have both the resources and the contacts to be involved in Blackbird."

Terry bit his lower lip as he gazed at the full photo of Sharif Ali.

"For the record," said Otto, "the two women have been arrested."

Terry nodded. "If he is a foreign agent, then his involvement would suggest that Operation Blackbird has both external state sponsorship as well as internal domestic support."

"Yes," replied Otto, taking the opportunity to fill his pipe. "A rather disconcerting thought."

***

Berlin, Germany

The Gerhardt video hit the internet with a thud. It was another surprise when least expected. Flash crowds simultaneously appeared in twenty German cities,

224

in the most public spaces, carrying signs and placards that stressed pride in Germany and an end to Schengen migration.

The sheer number of cities that produced mobs in various popular squares throughout the republic startled the police. Each location managed to play the video by blaring the audio over a hidden public address system while projecting the visual images against a preselected building or wall.

The video itself was a bit of Hollywood subterfuge. Nora planned another ruse. She used the gifts of modern technology to convert a green screen backdrop into a chroma key video of Berlin's Tiergarten. The setting had been filmed earlier that week and then superimposed with the overlay of Gerhardt, who, to video observers, appeared to be delivering a live monologue while strolling the lush lawns of the former royal hunting grounds.

Gerhardt stood ramrod straight, dressed in a modern military uniform which notably displayed no rank. It did exhibit several similarities to the modern Bundeswehr service uniform which consisted of a light gray, single-breasted coat with dark gray trousers, a light blue shirt, black tie, and black shoes. He held a peaked visor cap in his left hand, assuring that no part of the incredible likeness to his proclaimed grandfather was obscured from the camera. It looked to the whole world as if Germany's most wanted man was on a relaxing walk through the popular inner-city park, discussing politics.

As Gerhardt delivered the oration, the Berlin State Police converged on the huge Tiergarten from every direction, using dog patrols, helicopters, cruisers and a detachment of Federal Uniform Police as back up—all to no avail.

His speech condemned Turks in particular, Muslims in general, Schengen, the European Union, and liberal politicians as he wandered amidst the lush vegetation, the tree-lined paths, the laughing children, joggers, cyclists, and sunbathers. Yet, once again, the orator's ability to slip arrest, to arrive and depart without detection or apprehension, stoked his appeal. He had the command of logistics. The police could not locate Gerhardt. He seemed to evaporate into the forest, when in fact he was never even there.

After ten minutes of suspense-building oration, Gerhardt paused and turned to face the camera in a full-frontal view. He looked squarely into the lens and spoke. "Some politicians must go. The bureaucrats that clog our system, waste our money, and ignore our demands no longer speak for the people…" He raised an index finger to eye level, "…for this reason, they will be replaced. All delegates to parliament are *now* under our review." Gerhardt elevated his voice in a deep guttural pitch as he extended a closed fist. "Germany first, we *will* protect the fatherland."

Chapter 64

Irvine, California

In some ways Evie Khazemi's sudden departure to the west coast was a respite. Not in a traditional sense, because a family health issue was anything but a positive, but it did force her to slow down, shift gears, and adapt to a change in focus. She felt a huge pressure lift from her shoulders as she sat in the hospital at her father's bedside, holding his hand as several medical monitors recorded each and every beat of his failing heart.

His eyes opened and he looked at his only daughter, thirty years old, unwed, alone in the world, involved in a career of which he disapproved. "Havva," said the father in a quiet voice, "you came."

"Of course, Baba," said Evie squeezing his hand. Her eyes teared up.

"You are so beautiful," said the father, "but I fear I will not be able to walk you down the aisle." He sat forward and coughed up some spittle before taking a moment to clean his lips. "Where are your brothers?"

Evie sat forward. "Amir left about an hour ago while you were resting. Hamid left this morning when I arrived. He was here all night."

The father nodded. "Are you still doing that job in Washington?"

"Yes, Baba, and it's not just a job, its important work."

"Yes, yes…" replied the father, uninterested in continuing the conversation.

Bob Colman was right of course, the only viable option for Evie was to 'just go' to the west coast and visit with her father. The Helios probe could wait—or at the very least, do without her services. It gave her some time to reconsider the various aspects of the mission in a light that cast a different glow. Had a virulent strain of neo-Nazis partnered with an external force to disrupt the government of Germany? Was the republic the sole target, or was it a proxy for the whole European Union? If the EU failed as an economic trading block, what would happen to NATO? Over the years, the military mutual defense treaty had become more closely aligned with the EU and the European Central Bank.

If the populist movement rising in so many countries had the effect of breeding a vibrant nationalism that threatened the EU, the common currency of the euro and, by extension, the collective military defense of Europe, then it all came back to Hitler.

Evie leaned forward and affectionately rubbed her father's wrist. "You will be okay, Baba. I am not getting married soon, so you will be with us for a long time."

Her father managed a smile and forced a wink. "I am holding you to that," he whispered. The father drifted off to sleep as Evie leaned back in her chair.

The Gerhardt presence was disconcerting. His existence progressed a cult of personality that transcended eight decades of turbulent history and posed a rallying cry for a populous insurrection. Now, in addition to the self-proclaimed grandson of the long-dead Fuhrer, there was also evidence of state sponsored interference.

Evie moved to a corner of the hospital room and called headquarters on the burner cell phone. She wondered as to the identity of the sole photograph in the thin file folder she had left back at Langley with Bob Colman.

***

Munich, Germany

Terry stepped from the shower and wrapped a towel around his waist just as Ronja pushed open the bathroom door. She only glanced at his half naked body, holding his ringing cell phone at arm's length as he faced the mirror. Then he turned, took the burner phone, and with a mumbled thanks exited the bathroom. He was unaware of the look on Ronja's face as she studied the vicious scar on his back.

"Helios," answered Terry as he sat in the den.

"It's me," replied Bob Colman. The SAD chief gave Solak a moment to digest the unexpected voice. "You good?"

"Yes, how is my new Point of Contact doing?"

"She's doing well, but she got hit with a sudden emergency and had to leave on short notice."

"Work related?" asked Terry.

"No, a family matter."

"Got it," said Solak with a touch of relief. He had grown to rely on Evie's intuition and reliability during their short time working together. For most SAD officers, the collection manager was often their only contact to Langley. This created a wide swath of trust between special operators and headquarters. The link assured SAD officers working without official cover or diplomatic immunity that someone knew, and hopefully cared.

Before continuing their cryptic dialogue, Colman let the dust settle on Evie's absence before saying, "She left me with a file just as she departed. It had a photograph that needed identification."

The SAD chief let the conversation wane. A few seconds passed in silence as Terry waited out his boss, before offering, "Okay."

"It is an acquaintance of yours," said Bob, "a Gulf-state type."

Solak shifted in his seat as he drip-dried on the cushion chair. "Lots of those ethnicities here," said Terry.

"Yes," replied Colman, "but this is someone you met far away from your current assignment."

"Another country?"

"Another continent."

There was a pause on Terry's end as he tried to recall recent mission postings. "It's all a blur," replied Terry, "but…"

"It was Mali," said Colman.

In a flash to Otto's stack of photographs, Terry recalled and placed the familiar-looking picture of Sharif Ali, the Saudi prince that had met Solak halfway around the world in Timbuktu. "You're kidding."

"Afraid not," replied Colman.

"You think the kingdom is involved?"

"Why not, someone is. We know that Turkey is a problem, but they're also probably a false flag."

"What does Otto think?" asked Terry.

"He said the domestic security people corroborate the contact between the women's club and the prince. They initiated the all-points identity search."

"So they have no idea."

"None. We will help them with the ID, but we are not prepared to open our books on the Mali operation."

"Understood…how do you plan on playing this?" asked Terry.

"Close to the vest. We now know that in addition to the internal domestic issue, there is also state sponsorship. So, we will let Otto take the lead. I'll be back to you."

Colman's burner phone disconnected.

Chapter 65

Berlin, Germany

The city was in virtual lockdown, not declared, but in effect. The flash point violence had escalated to the level that people just stayed home. Those that needed to venture out, did so, but often while in view of police escorts and patrols.

By contrast, provocateurs and trouble makers sought out pockets of serenity for the sole purpose of fomenting trouble. Anyone and everyone was a target; politicians, police, migrants, and Muslims—with a special emphasis on Turks.

A federal sedan started down the access road outside the chancellery when the sole occupant in the rear seat, Police Director Geiger, motioned to the driver. A mob had gathered between the admin wings, directly in front of the main building. A dozen uniformed federal police in riot gear formed a semicircle perimeter in front of the sliding steel fence. This effectively separated the protesters from the glass front doors of the modern chancellery. Geiger stepped to the pavement and dismissed the car. In seconds, a surprised police inspector emerged from behind the police line and reported to the director. They exchanged a few words and then the inspector turned and immediately relayed Geiger's instructions over his FM radio transmitter. Within minutes, two dozen additional uniformed police appeared from the east wing and reinforced the original perimeter. Despite the effort, the crowd continued to grow at an exceptionally fast clip.

Geiger paced back and forth behind the cordon, his hands clasped at the wrist, his square jaw jutting forward in a rigid pose. The tall, erect bearing of the police director with the gold wreath and stars epaulets on his shoulders stood out in his dress uniform and peaked cap.

An open lorry truck pulled up at the access road and stopped. A dozen men jumped off the back and started to unload basket after basket of rotten vegetables and spoiled eggs.

The crowd extended lengthwise and four-deep, offering visual protection as the concealed refuse was passed from one end of the protesters' line to the other. The mob continued to expand. Geiger snapped at the inspector, seeking information on the basket contents. The thirty police officers now confronted several hundred protesters who seemed to be cradling some type of weaponry in their midst.

Geiger, who had arrived at the chancellery to attend the group of twenty meeting in the eighth-floor conference room, had seen the mob, and inserted himself in the middle of the confrontation. Suddenly, a silent volley of eggs and vegetables arced through the air, soaring over the four-deep column of protesters, splattering the smelly, decayed food atop the police. A rotten egg smashed on Geiger's shoulder, dripping his meticulously cleaned and pressed uniform in an odorous yoke of black and green goo stuck to the splintered shell.

From above, the VP of the domestic security agency turned from the huge picture window and summoned the other attendees to the conference table. "I think that Herr Geiger will be delayed," said the VP. "We should plan on starting without him."

***

Munich, Germany

In the three days that passed, Terry caught up on his sleep and his body repaired with the help of Otto's physician. The wear and tear took a toll, but Solak was conditioned to the process and learned how to pace himself on little food, less rest, and constant shifts in direction.

Otto stood at the kitchen door and motioned for Terry to follow him into the den. "I have important news," said the foreign intelligence officer. He pulled two photographs from the stack of surveillance pictures. They were the same photos he had shared with Solak a day earlier. "This man," he held up the pictures of the prince, "has been identified as Sharif Ali, of the General Intelligence Directorate of the Kingdom of Saudi Arabia."

"Really..." Terry looked surprised. He had already been briefed by Bob Colman on the identification of the Saudi prince, as well as the need to play dumb and not reveal the previous operation in Mali. "Saudi Arabia?"

"Yes," replied Otto as he fumbled with his pipe.

"Who confirmed the identity?"

"Your people. They responded to an identification match to all western sources put on the wire by our domestic security agency."

Terry appeared to digest the information. "Now what?"

"I have a fix," replied Otto. "We were able to determine his location here in Munich."

"That was fast."

"Not so difficult really. We recognized that the kingdom has a very lean presence here in Germany. This precluded a suitable base of operations for the prince."

Terry laughed. "Yes, the Saudis do expect their creature comforts."

"They do. So, we narrowed the list. A high-end rental would make sense, but it's hard to hide issues from the staff."

"So, a hotel?" asked Terry.

"Yes, the next best choice for the prince to work and stay low-profile. We narrowed the search to the five most expensive hotels in Munich and worked our contacts. Registrations were checked, extended stays and repeat reservations noted."

"What is the BfV's position on this?"

"They informed us of the prince's true identity. He is a foreign national. Given that my people are operating with limited resources in the country, domestic security is still unaware of your involvement with us."

"It's getting sticky."

"Yes," answered Otto. "We'll eventually bring them into the loop, but not yet."

"Do you have a plan?"

"I do," said Otto, "but I'm not sure you will approve."

Terry's eyebrows raised in surprise. He shifted on the sofa and then waited for the foreign intelligence officer to lay out his thought process.

"The prince is here without his typical entourage—just a couple of bodyguards, no staff and no escorts."

"Makes sense, fly under the radar," said Solak.

"He has a roving eye."

Terry caught the gist of the comment. "He likes the ladies?"

"He does," said Otto. "I can get an attractive professional, but this matter is much too sensitive for someone I don't know. I'm thinking of a chance encounter rather than a paid professional."

"Present a challenge?"

"Yes," said Otto. "Let him stroke his ego. A sure thing is a release but not a victory. The prince is a trained intel officer, and a prostitute would immediately retreat to her strength. He would notice. A professional is too pliant, sex is the end game, but we need a deeper hook."

Solak sat back and took another look at the photos of Sharif Ali without his beard. He was a handsome man, lean, swarthy, and well-groomed. This was a rich prince who carried himself with a confidence born of family ties, wealth, privilege, and education. He fancied himself a man of the world, polished and irresistible to women.

"It may work," said Terry. "You need someone who can think on their feet, a moody seductress."

"Well stated."

"Do you have someone in mind?" asked Terry.

Otto nodded, and then let his eyes drift over to the first bedroom where Ronja slept with her boys.

Terry looked across the apartment before catching the reference. "You can't be serious?"

"Who else can I trust on such short notice?"

"After what she's been through?"

"She's tested and reliable," said Otto. "We are doing our part protecting her and her children. She's very attractive; a blue-eyed, blonde, ice queen from Germany. A real ego stroke for a privileged prince who knows he can pay, but doesn't think he should have to."

"What about her kids?"

"We depart here and they stay in a new safehouse protected around the clock by my people."

"Will she accept that?"

"Why wouldn't she? It's a whole lot safer than sending everyone home. The Nazi women would be all over her family."

Terry looked off across the room. "I think you are pushing the envelope. You're putting Ronja in an untenable position."

"Due to my organization's focus, I have better resources outside the country. Internally, domestic security holds all the cards, and they play by the book. Where do I turn? Sharif Ali is a target, and the republic needs to survive."

Chapter 66

Berlin, Germany

The VP of the domestic security agency sat in the corner of the Dicke Wirtin beer pub in Charlottenburg. Small, cramped, and inviting, the authentic décor suited both tourists and locals alike, and complemented the chance for a quiet conversation between the VP and Herr Ludwig of the federal criminal investigative police.

"Thank you for meeting me away from the government crowd," said the VP. He paused until the waitress had delivered two frothy mugs of lager.

Ludwig nodded in reply.

"The chancellor's new deputy is bringing me in for a chat, and I hear you will be next on the list," said the VP.

Ludwig swallowed his first sip before setting the beer mug back on the table. "My sense is that she is looking for someone to hold responsible for our inability to locate and apprehend Gerhardt."

"That is the political way," said the VP, "take credit for the good, lay blame for the bad, and stay neutral until the winds shift."

A minute passed in silence. Ludwig sat forward in his chair. "I never did get your opinion on the grandson," he said.

The VP fingered the rim of his beer mug and then shrugged. "I'm a bit conflicted."

"How so? Do you believe it?"

"I don't know. It certainly sounds plausible the way it's been framed."

"We've all heard the stories," said Ludwig. "The escape tunnels under Berlin all the way from the Fuhrerbunker to the airport, followed by a mass exodus from Tempelhof."

"With eight planeloads of Hitler possessions. It sounds intriguing."

233

"It explains how the Soviets could not capture him," replied Ludwig.

"But if he *did* escape to Spain, and then to South America with money and support, doesn't it seem likely that he would have a mistress with children somewhere in the Argentine jungle?"

"Which brings us back to Gerhardt and the Braun sisters. Eva was incapable of having children, but Gretl was clearly fertile."

"There is no sample," said the VP, taking the opportunity to savor a long swig of beer, "by which to procure a DNA match."

"Then how," said Ludwig, "does one prove Gerhardt's DNA sufficiently replicates Hitler's to claim a lineage."

"That's the conundrum. How does one disprove a negative? You cannot prove that something never occurred, if it never occurred."

Both Ludwig and the VP leaned back in their chairs and considered the duplicity inherent in the Gerhardt phenomenon.

"Going forward," said Ludwig, "the danger is in the acceptance of a truth. People believe what they want to believe, because the conditions for belief are present and it fits a desired mold."

"The best lies," replied the VP, "are always couched in truth."

They both took another sip of beer, before the VP stood. He let the arthritic pain in his leg subside before dropping a ten euro note on the table.

"Thanks for the willing ear. I'll let you know how my meeting goes."
He walked from the pub, noticeably favoring his bad leg.

***

Irvine, California

Evie leaned back in her chair and held her father's hand in a reassuring manner. He popped one eye open and then smiled to himself. He seemed to relax and drift into a quiet sleep.

She looked down at her iPad and then at her notebook that sat on her father's bedside table. She had been quietly doing some research as it pertained to Germany's most notorious figure. This kept her mind focused in between bouts of her father's wakefulness. Keeping busy kept her mind sharp, but she was careful to avoid information or discussions that touched classified or sensitive data.

"How is he doing?" said a voice.

Evie looked up to see her older brother, Amir, who leaned over her shoulder as he surveyed their father. "Restless," said Evie, "but when he sees me, he calms down and then nods off to sleep again." A tear crept into her eye as she looked at her father's diminished capacity. It was difficult to align her memory of the once robust man she knew growing up, with the shell of the man she now saw.

Amir looked down at Evie's notebook and read aloud, "AH had notoriously poor teeth, with extensive dental work to include complicated dentures and bridges…who is AH?" asked Amir.

Evie closed her notebook and gave her older brother a perturbed look. "No one you know."

"Is it for your work?"

"No," replied Evie. "I'm in a book club, and we were working on a project. It keeps my mind off of worrying about Dad."

Suddenly a beeper sounded, and the various cardiac monitors and vital sign systems started ringing their alarms in a cacophony of disturbing noise.

Evie jumped up from her seat as Amir ran to get medical assistance. The staff were already in motion. A team of doctors and nurses rushed forward and surrounded her father's bed. The lead physician snapped orders as Evie and Amir were shuffled to the rear of the cardiac care unit and resigned to helplessly watch as their father died.

Chapter 67

Munich, Germany

Ronja climbed into the rear seat of the sedan and frowned. She brought an air of frustration into the car, and it all came to the surface as she faced Terry. "So, I guess you're on board with this new foray?"

"I agree," said Solak offering a different perspective, "that something has to be done."

"It's that serious?"

"Yes," answered Terry, "but I don't necessarily agree with the method."

"So you disagree with Otto pimping me out?"

Solak turned to face Ronja. "You're a very attractive woman, but that doesn't give us the right to choose your bed partners."

Ronja paused, not quite sure how to interpret Terry's backhanded compliment. She took a long, hard look at the man she knew only as Helios. There was some relief that this man she had learned to trust would not use her body as a piece of furniture. "I'm Otto's asset, so it's his decision?"

"Yes. If he has something to offer that would entice your willing participation, then fine...but I did make it clear that using your sons to apply leverage was out of bounds. Did he?"

Ronja hesitated and then shook her head. "No, he promised protection to my boys regardless of my decision."

"Good. I told him I would ask. If he crossed the line, I was out."

"Out?"

"Packing up and going home. At this point he needs me as well."

"Home to the States?"

Terry shrugged, but did not answer.

"You are from America, aren't you?"

"Does it matter?" asked Solak.

Ronja didn't answer, but rather reached over and touched Terry's forearm wound. Then she settled back in the rear seat and started reciting Otto's logistical details. "He is setting up my reservation at the Hotel Vier Jahreszeiten. I am a sales consultant for a German cosmetics company in Bonn. We drop you off and I go clothes shopping for an appropriate wardrobe." She paused before continuing. "I understand that you will be there."

"Not at the same hotel as you and the target, but close."

"The only preconditions I had with Otto was protection of my children, and that you had to be involved. I don't trust him."

"I understand," replied Terry. "I will be nearby." He thought to himself for a moment. "Any information you gain will be helpful. Don't discount anything. Take the seduction as far as you are comfortable. If it doesn't work or you want out, then break contact. Otto will just have to try a different approach."

Ronja remained silent as she studied Solak. Then she spoke in a quiet voice. "I know what you are capable of, but considering your line of work, you act like a decent man."

Terry listened without comment.

"Otto, on the other hand," said Ronja, "finds it easy to make me feel like a whore."

***

Berlin, Germany

Director Geiger entered the Platz der Luftbrücke and paused. He turned in place, slowly rotating his body in a counter-clockwise fashion, absorbing the sight lines from each direction. The police commander noted the entrance to the former Tempelhof Airport, the memorial to the Berlin Airlift, and multiple government buildings including the headquarters for the Berlin State Police. The landmarked square was at the junction of two major traffic arteries that connected the U-bahn station and the east-west and north-south roads of Berlin. He motioned, and then led his team to the station entrance at the north end of the square. He descended the steps escorted by a detail of black-clad, heavily armed, GSG-9 police from the crack anti-terror unit of his Federal Uniform Police (BPOL). For security reasons, their identities were obscured by balaclava face masks.

For some time, Geiger had pondered the logistics tail of the Gerhardt success. It gnawed at him that the Hitler protégé seemed to evade arrest with each appearance, managing to stay a step ahead of the prodigious German police machine. This, in effect, sent a very clear message to supporters and aspirants alike, that the Gerhardt phenomenon was real and they could deliver on their message.

For Geiger, the egg and spoiled food protest had coalesced the movements of the right into a study of speed. Somehow the mob had appeared in front of the chancellery building. They had produced five times the number of people as the police in a short period of time. How?

Geiger thought back to his schooling at the military academy in his youth. A study of Julius Caesar, one of the great generals of history, emphasized the Roman's penchant for getting to the battle first, with the most. Caesar believed that the first combatant to the battle selected the time and place of the actual fight. It also offered the maximum opportunity to deploy troops to his own advantage.

Geiger then determined that the weak point of the state's control of the city was the visibility. The authorities controlled the air and the ground, but the proletariat controlled the tunnels. Berlin was a city where forty percent of the structures were below street level. These included sewers, brew cellars, U-bahn lines, S-bahn lines, railroad tunnels, old pneumatic dispatch systems, World War Two bunkers, air raid shelters, East German escape tunnels, and new electrical communication wiring. It all existed in the subterranean refuge of the underground world, sharing the space with people traveling in multiple directions. The flash crowds would appear with effortless invisibility. It hampered the police effort to control the situation. Geiger determined that Gerhardt and his adherents had mastered the speed and secrecy of the tunnels in Berlin.

This brought the federal police director to a consideration of the ever-divisive and ever-elusive Hitler progeny. Somehow, he moved with impunity, and appeared with aplomb. He had followers who understood and guided his use of the tunnels to include false walls, hidden entrances, and secret exits. Geiger wanted to get into the head of Gerhardt, just as the proclaimed Hitler grandson used symbolism to recruit wave after wave of populace protesters.

In full police director uniform, and accompanied by the GSG-9 detail, Geiger walked the brightly lit, long, double-quay platform of the U-bahn 6. His eyes wandered over crevices in the high vaulted ceiling, searching for a clue, something that would imbue them with the ability to arrest the orator as he traveled the vast underground network of buried passageways.

Chapter 68

When Frau Keller and Friedel Schulz were arrested, Sharif Ali immediately changed venues. From the beginning, the Saudi prince had maintained a suite of rooms at two different hotels in Old City, each under a different name and passport number. It wasn't lost on the prince that his contacts to the Nazi women's group known as das Netzwerk had, at the very least, been under suspicion. In the German government's growing panic, they were lashing out under the pervading fear that something very big was due to happen, and they needed to interrupt the momentum.

At the same time, Otto's assets in country were stretched to his limit. He had a foreign intelligence surveillance team staking out the Vier Jahreszeiten Hotel on Maximilianstraße waiting for the prince to return, while Ronja sat in the rear seat of an airport limousine offering the cover that she had just arrived. The sudden switch to the second location, the Mandarin Oriental Hotel on Neuturmstraße, complicated her opportunity to make an entrance that the prince would notice.

In many ways, Ali possessed an arrogance born of his family. He would at times get lazy about operational security. The prince believed that between his diplomatic status and his personal bodyguards, he was immune to problems while on assignment. In this mode, Ali tended to prefer the Vier Jahreszeiten as a personal residence. The arrest of the women, however, forced Sharif to revert to his other choice at the last moment.

Solak tailed Ronja's limo as it followed the prince's sedan. Then Terry spoke to Otto over his cell phone. "Abort drop off, redeploy team to second location."

It took only seconds before Otto's experienced team folded up shop at one hotel and changed their focus to the second hotel. Fortunately, both establishments were nestled in the Old City section of Munich, and thus physically within a short walking distance of each other.

Four minutes later Ronja stepped from her airport limo just as the prince entered the opulent lobby of the Mandarin Oriental Hotel. She looked stunning. The bodyguards noticed her first, stepping to the side as Ronja passed the winding staircase en route to the recessed reception desk. Her appeal extended outward and she acted very much at home without appearing impressed.

It was an interesting transition for the working mom. Just as she was naturally attractive, she often chose to play down her beauty in the rush of daily responsibilities. Grooming came easy to Ronja, yet she rarely devoted much time to the effort.

Ronja wore a clingy skirt suit; professional, dark colors and only slightly cut above the knee. It was enough to show her shapely legs when paired with high heels. Her jewelry was tasteful for business, and she offered an impression that she knew how to dress for day or evening with equal grace.

The prince watched as Ronja entered the lobby followed by a doorman carrying her two pieces of luggage. Then Ali paused again as he waited for the elevator with his two bodyguards and watched Ronja as she checked in. When the elevator door slid open, the prince took a last look at Ronja. She made brief eye contact, and the prince mumbled something to one of his bodyguards.

After Ronja cleared reception and was escorted with her bags up to her room, a man from Otto's team entered the lobby carrying a newspaper. He took a seat in a position where he could observe everyone entering and exiting the hotel lobby.

***

Berlin, Germany

The VP of domestic security turned and faced Director Geiger of the Federal Uniform Police.

"Herr Geiger," said the VP, turning in his seat. "We understand you've been inspecting various U-bahn rail stations in the city. Is that correct?"

"Ja," said Geiger, taking a seat at the large conference table.

"Do I understand that you are traveling with a detail of GSG-9 police commandos?"

"Ja," said the police director again, unfazed by the line of questioning. He glanced across the table at his long-standing adversary, Holger of the Berlin

State Police. "This is my prerogative." Geiger took a moment to brush a piece of lint from his shoulder epaulet. The motion served to draw attention to his rank.

"Yes, it is," replied the VP. He looked over at Holger, the source of the information. "But they may be a bit intimidating for most civilians."

"By design," replied Geiger.

"Yes," said the VP, phrasing his questions. "Was there a potential terrorist threat?"

"Always in these current conditions," said Geiger. "One must troll for migs where one can."

None of the other members of the group of twenty understood Geiger's use of an old, slang military term used by U.S. Navy pilots during the Vietnam War.

"I am not sure we understand the expression," answered the VP after a glance around the table.

"Suffice to say," replied Geiger, "that GSG-9 is the best we have, and therefore, it allows us to convey a sense of *calm* to our citizens, while at the same time performing important inspections to our mass transit facilities."

"It alarms the population."

"I disagree," said Geiger. "People want to know, they *need* to know, that we can protect them. They crave a sense of *order*."

"And if we don't provide that feeling?"

"They will turn to others to satisfy the emotion. Gerhardt succeeds because they trust him. He tells them what they want to hear, and then he provides the framework by which to feel safe."

Holger of the Berlin State Police leaned forward and jabbed a thick finger in the air. "You are overstepping your charter."

"Someone," said Geiger, leaning forward to match Holger's seated posture, "must do the job that the Landespolizei cannot seem to handle."

"How dare you!" said Holger in a fit of rage, as the VP shot an arm in the air to cut off the pending argument between the two police officials.

Then the VP of domestic security defused the tension with a quiet comment to Geiger that everyone could hear. "At your discretion, Herr Director. These are dangerous times, but do consider the perception of our citizens as you," he paused, "*troll* the tunnels of our rapid transit system."

Chapter 69

Munich, Germany

Ronja sat in a cushioned chair, cupping the cell phone in her hand. She hated the waiting. Like the military or police work, intelligence operations were often quite punctuated. It was hurry up and wait, and then suddenly there was a burst of energy and everything seemed to be moving at once.

She had unpacked her luggage, freshened up, and changed clothes from a business suit into more dinner-casual attire. Much like she supposed a German cosmetics consultant from another city would approach their stay in Munich.

Ronja dressed in a skirt with low heels and a V-neck style blouse with a sweater draped over her shoulder for a late-night chill. Her eyes took a moment to wander the opulent hotel room. She looked confident and poised, comfortable in her attractiveness and business acumen. The type of woman who posed a challenge, but not a threat, to a prince used to having his way. The difficulty was in presenting a chance encounter as a coincidence.

Sharif Ali was in motion, and although Otto had several of his surveillance team prepared to walk while others used vehicles, they had to adjust to the prince's movements on the fly. Any number of variables existed, and in so far as the team did not know the Saudi's plans, they were prepared to adapt. The key was to open a door for an introduction in hopes that the prince would take the bait.

Otto's goal was to find out how deep the prince, and by extension Saudi Arabia, were involved in Germany's election issues, and the rise in influence of Gerhardt, the purported grandson of Adolf Hitler.

The foreign intelligence officer had considered various electronic devices. The risks were obvious; if Ronja wore a wire on her torso, or managed to plant a wireless microphone in Ali's suite, her efforts would be open to discovery.

242

Otto had intentionally kept Ronja in the dark as it regarded the prince, his identity, and his nationality. She only knew the prince as a wealthy, foreign investor. Whatever bits of information Sharif shared—most of which would be dubious—would present to her as new intel. Better to keep the operation simple, and her instructions clear: get him talking and remember everything, regardless of its banality or perceived importance.

Ronja's cell phone rang and Otto spoke. "He just left in a private car, and we didn't have a chance to cross paths again in the lobby."

"Are you following him?" asked Ronja as she smoothed her skirt and put on her low heels.

"Yes, we have two cars en route. He often eats alone with his bodyguards watching from a short distance. We are waiting to see where he ends up. Go down to the lobby and I will pick you up."

"Okay," replied Ronja. She took a last look in the full-length mirror, grabbed her pocketbook, and exited the hotel room.

Otto's two surveillance cars played hopscotch as they tailed the prince around the Old City neighborhood. They drove for fifteen minutes, playing at the rudimentary elements of vehicle security before Sharif Ali's private sedan pulled up in front of the Little London Bar & Grill. It was less than a three-minute walk from the hotel.

Otto, turned in the rear seat of the third car and faced Ronja. He motioned. "Our target has entered an expensive restaurant just around the corner. We will have you walk by yourself." Otto gave Ronja the simple directions and then added, "If you are each seated alone for dinner, then make innocent eye contact."

"I understand," said Ronja.

"Remember, better to hold back. Be hesitant. Let him make an effort. He will feel less suspicious if he's the pursuer."

"Yes," replied Ronja.

At the corner of Hockbrucke and Herderstraße Otto tapped his driver on the shoulder and pulled their car over.

"You'll walk from here," said Otto. "Take your time. You don't have a reservation, but say the concierge recommended it. It's a top steak house." Otto frowned, "Nothing but the best for our target."

Ronja nodded and climbed from the sedan.

***

Irvine, California

Evie caught the red-eye flight back to the east coast. She was bone tired, as much due to the emotional turmoil of losing a close family member, as to the jet lag and long hours of sitting at the hospital. Her dad had died, his weak heart finally giving out despite the best efforts of modern medicine and a committed hospital staff.

Evie shifted in her seat. Her mind was a muddled collection of disjointed facts and memories of growing up as the only daughter in a Muslim household with a traditional father. Nothing came easy. Fortunately, she had two older brothers to blaze the trail. Amir and Hamid made their Baba proud, but everyone knew that Evie was his favorite.

In accordance with Sharia, or Islamic law, they followed appropriate Muslim burial traditions. The sons bathed their father, shrouded his body in white cotton, and said Salah over his corpse. The Janazah, or funeral, was completed within twenty-four hours. When they lowered his coffin into the ground, they made sure to face Baba's head in the direction of Mecca.

The family then invited friends and well-wishers to the father's home to observe the three-day period of mourning. To Evie, it was ritualistic, but comforting because she knew her father would appreciate the effort to adhere to cultural traditions in the face of a generational turning point. A nod to the past, followed by a nod to the future. Evie was caught in the promise of America, straddling the unique cultural traditions that distinguished each ethnic group from the blended whole.

She started to cry. It had been a tough few days, and Evie appreciated the diversion of her work. Her brothers, their wives and their children all asked for Evie to stay longer, but she felt a compelling tug from Langley. So much of her reading had focused on Germany, and the likelihood that something would break loose in the republic. She spent her hospital time reading Persian stories to her father. When he drifted off to sleep, she would research the history of the Nazis and the political chaos that buffered the Hitler rise to power. Evie was not an attorney by training, but she kept coming back to Article Eighty-One of the German Basic Laws, the republic's constitution. She sensed that a manipulation of the roles between the president and the chancellor would surface during a legislative emergency, and the extrajudicial executions spawned by Operation Blackbird on members of parliament would create the climate for Gerhardt's rise to a position of actual political power, from his current status as a wildly popular public orator.

Chapter 70

Ten minutes later, Ronja entered the Little London Bar and Grill. It was early evening, and the maître d' had no difficulty in seating a lone diner without a reservation. He guided Ronja past a lively mahogany bar replete with British paraphernalia and a large photograph of Queen Elizabeth.

A few steps later, they entered into the main dining room and Ronja was seated in a small table beside a printed wall cover that complemented a classic white wainscoting. The restaurant managed to combine a British, masculine, feminine ambiance all at the same time. This in turn attracted an eclectic crowd of both drinkers and diners, and made it easy to interact with others.

Ronja took a glance around the dining room and noticed the prince off to the side, sitting alone. They made eye contact, and he extended a nod. Ronja hesitated, and then she returned the nod with a slight smile. Finally, she used the interruption of the waiter to break eye contact, and order a drink.

For the next few minutes Ronja casually scoped out the dining room, trying her best to get the feel of the restaurant without appearing overly interested. She noted Sharif's two bodyguards, seated together a few tables away, each man focused on a different angle looking away from the prince. Otto reinforced the notion that Sharif was a wealthy financier from a Mediterranean country who had information pertinent to the German situation. Ronja did not care, and she did not question Otto's motives, but she feared his Machiavellian tendencies, and his willingness to exploit others.

Ronja was no prude. Like most Germans, she was uninhibited on the subject of sex, and didn't downplay or overplay its significance in the course of people's lives. That being the case, it was her body, her decision, and Otto's cavalier involvement in Ronja's choices felt like a massive invasion of her privacy. It was an intrusion, and she resented the foreign intelligence officer for pushing her into this corner.

The waiter brought Ronja's drink, a traditional gin martini in a stem glass with three olives, and took a moment to discuss dinner specials, cuts of beef, cooking applications and types of side dishes. Then he handed her a full menu and shuffled away.

Ronja took the opportunity to look over at Sharif again as she picked up the menu and surveyed the items. He glanced her way, and this time Ronja offered a lingering smile that was at once friendly without being seductive. She sipped at her cocktail and then went to the lavatory.

In keeping with the decorum of most top restaurants there was no rush to dine unless requested by the patrons. The waiter returned and Ronja ordered a green salad and a small steak.

Sharif noticed that although Ronja took her time enjoying her drink before dinner, she didn't appear to be waiting for anyone. A few minutes later the maître d' approached Ronja's table. He leaned over and spoke in a quiet voice.

"The gentleman to my left is dining alone, and believes you may be as well. He has extended an invitation for you to join him for dinner. Would you be interested in having company?"

Ronja shifted in her seat to get a clear view of the Saudi prince. He raised a glass of red wine in a sign of toast and she paused.

"That's a kind offer," she replied to the maître d'. "Please advise the gentleman that I accept the invitation."

"Very good, Frau," said the maître d' as he pulled back Ronja's chair. She stood and he escorted her the few feet to Sharif's table. The waiter transported Ronja's martini in kind.

"Thank you for the courtesy," said Ronja as she sat.

"It is my pleasure," said the prince. "I travel quite a bit, and I know how desolate it can feel eating alone every night."

"Yes," said Ronja with a touch of excitement in her voice, "I do hate eating alone."

The prince sat forward to make a point. "I thought you looked familiar, but I could not place your face…then I remembered seeing you at the Mandarin. I believe we are both staying at the same hotel."

"Yes," answered Ronja.

Sharif Ali raised his wine glass again and tilted it forward. "To unexpected introductions. My name is Sali."

***

Berlin, Germany

The long knives fell, and the country was unprepared. Despite the warnings, and the threat assessment system's highest risk category, the first wave of executions overwhelmed the police. Forty-three assassinations of Bundestag members occurred in two hours before police officials collated the common denominators of the victims and realized that the German parliament was under attack.

The means of murder were varied in that handguns, knives, and several bombs were all used to effect the death of politicians. The tie-in surfaced once the federal criminal investigative police determined that, amongst the victims, two of every three were killed by specially trained wet teams consisting of a spotter, two shooters, and a cleaner. Death was by P8 automatic pistols, the standard nine-millimeter handgun of the German military. It was at once organized, efficient, and final, intended as much to intimidate the populous as it was to eliminate specific individuals. The speed of managing the hit list took on a momentum of its own, and as trickles of information surfaced, it became known that the police and security services had received notice of something big brewing, but decided not to alarm the citizens. They kept the information private.

The police had, in fact, told some members of parliament that unsubstantiated rumors warned of potential attacks. Nonetheless, without more specific information, the authorities had neither the resources nor the personnel to protect all elected officials.

By midafternoon of day one, sixty-seven murders dotted the landscape, dominating the larger cities by sheer numbers, but sure to include members of parliament in each of the sixteen states of the republic. It was a full-frontal blitzkrieg, eliminating a broad swath of liberals from the Bundestag in a lightning path across the political map.

As news coverage pieced together what government officials knew of the planned attacks, the decision *not* to warn the public of the pending action only served to increase the resentment of the electorate. The people had a right to know.

"It's the tunnels," said Geiger with an attitude of certainty. "I told you, they have mastered the underground network in this city."

"And what about the other fifteen locations that have nothing to do with Berlin?" asked Holger of the State Police.

247

"Berlin is key," said Geiger. "It is the capital of the republic. Parliament is here. We are here. It stands to reason that if these neo-Nazis, or Islamic extremists, attack an MP in another city or state, it's to make a propaganda point. It's to emphasize the extent of their reach. Yes, it sends a message, but the wheels of government turn here."

"They are grinding the wheels of our government to a standstill," said the VP of domestic security. He stood, so as to survey the entire length of the conference table.

"What do you suggest?" asked the deputy Minister of the Interior.

There was a pause in the conversation and Geiger leaned forward to fill the void. "I, for one, have ordered copies of all engineering schematics that pertain to construction beneath street level in Berlin."

"How far back are they dated?" asked the VP.

"Some of the blueprints are over a century old," replied Geiger. "They are a cumbersome collection of escape tunnels, caverns, U-bahn lines, and bomb shelters. The difficulty is in identifying undocumented, unofficial passageways left behind by the Nazis, or escape networks under the Berlin Wall."

Holger turned towards the VP of domestic security who continued to stand, and spoke in a quiet voice. "Our democracy is literally under attack, in plain view, by some combination of neo-Nazis, Turks, and an unknown nation-state…" He turned in his seat, "…and Geiger wants to study ancient blueprints."

Chapter 71

Munich, Germany

The seduction of Sharif Ali went surprisingly well. The Saudi prince was both engaging and polite in his demeanor. At no point did Ronja feel that she was acting aggressive in her intent. This helped to calm her nerves as she still felt in control of the decision. It was enough to encourage her continued participation because when she was pressured by Otto to perform, Ronja's natural reaction was to pushback.

She took a sip of wine. Ronja had nursed the beverage throughout her meal. She knew it was important to be clearheaded following the rare pre-dinner martini.

Sali, aka Sharif Ali, told Ronja a cover story of being a financier from Malta. She tried to memorize everything the prince mentioned, and Ronja gradually fell into a comfort zone. He was handsome, well-traveled, and appeared successful. There was a certain 'pull' to his aura, and she felt herself being a little smitten.

They enjoyed a pleasant dinner together and then, after an hour and a half, the prince seemed to routinely consult his wristwatch. Ronja noticed that it was a rather ornate diamond-studded Vacheron Constantin from Geneva. A few seconds later, his cell phone rang and he stood, turned and walked towards the mahogany bar. He engaged in a short, quiet conversation. Then just as quickly, he returned to their table. "Pardon the interruption," said the prince. He paused, "It is growing late. May I walk you back to the hotel?"

"Yes," replied Ronja with a smile.

Sharif stood, nodded to his bodyguards, and pulled back on her chair. Then Ali motioned to the maître d' as Ronja took Sharif's forearm. They exited the restaurant.

The walk was short, and Ronja commented on Ali's bodyguards who followed several steps to their rear. She concluded it wouldn't be natural to avoid the obvious and not mention their presence; and given Otto's line of work, Ronja surmised that Ali was more than a wealthy businessman. The prince made light of their presence and excused the escort as a corporate issue.

As they entered the lobby of the Mandarin Oriental, Ronja prepared to engage her new acquaintance in a long night of ardent passion. She looked up at the taller Ali, and offered a dazzling smile. As much as she now expected to consummate their relationship, she decided to follow Otto's advice and hold back, waiting for Sharif to make a move. She sensed the prince had a strong attraction and she wanted him to suggest they continue their evening together.

That is when the prince did a most unexpected thing. He extended to Ronja a hand to shake as he leaned forward and gave her a kiss on the cheek. "I had a wonderful evening. I would like to continue our friendship, but I am afraid I must travel very early in the morning."

"Really," said Ronja in a surprised tone. "Are you leaving town?"

Sharif studied Ronja for a moment. A wave of suspicion crossed his face. "Yes," answered the prince in a cautious voice.

Ronja recovered and stuck to the script, "I was hoping to spend more time with you. I will be here for the rest of the week."

"I'll be back," said Sharif Ali. "I am only going north for a couple days. When I return, I will call."

The prince turned and walked to the elevator.

***

Langley, Virginia

Evie followed Bob Colman into the SCIF on the seventh floor. Several other senior officers and section chiefs entered the conference room and took seats. In minutes there were fifteen people in the SCIF. Then the Director entered followed by an assistant and waved for everyone to remain seated. He pointed at a list that she carried on a clipboard.

"Before we begin," said the former senator, "we need to check your name against Katie's list. This briefing is highly sensitive, SCI, so be patient. There are no substitutes and no fill-ins. If Katie doesn't confirm your name you must step out."

The Director's eyes scanned the room and settled on Evie. He took a few steps forward and leaned over her shoulder. "I am sorry to hear about your dad." He extended his hand to shake. "Are you doing okay?"

"Yes," said Evie with a forced smile. She was surprised by the acknowledgment. She shook his hand.

"Remember, it takes time," said the Director. He straightened and, in parting, reached forward and patted Bob Colman on the shoulder.

Six people were excused from the meeting, and the Director took a thumbs-up from his assistant before settling into the seat at the head of the table. The deputy director for Analysis activated the electronic console and walls started sliding and sealing off the conference room.

"Germany," said the Director in a commanding voice, "is in a meltdown." He pointed at the German desk supervisor.

She stood, cleared her throat and began reading from her notes. "As of an hour ago, there have been eighty-three assassinations in the German republic in two days; seventy-seven were recently elected or reelected members of parliament; four were prominent administrators in left wing parties, and two were well-known, left-leaning political agitators."

"Were the last two some type of message?" asked Arthur Kent, the deputy director for the National Clandestine Services.

"We don't believe so," said the desk supervisor. "We think that maybe there were a few personal scores being settled on the Blackbird list."

Kent nodded.

"How does the German parliament stack up *now*?" asked the Director.

"About fourteen percent of their total of five hundred ninety-eight members' seats are now vacant."

"Can they function?" asked Kent.

"Technically they can establish a quorum. They fine MPs for missing a vote, but the real issue is fear. No members wish to make a point of entering the Bundestag."

"Is the chancellor secure?" asked the Europe mission center chief.

"She's well protected," replied the desk supervisor. "Politically she is elected for a full term, and can only be dismissed by a constructive vote of no confidence…which means that parliament must elect the chancellor's successor at the very same time."

"Simultaneously?"

"Yes."

"That reduces the playing field."

"It is precisely the result of the constant musical chairs during the Weimar Republic. The authors of the Basic Law, the German Constitution, sought to ensure that a potential dictator would never again be able to come to power in the republic."

The Director let the information settle before glancing around the table and motioning towards Colman. "Bob?"

The SAD chief calmly brought the attendees up to speed on the Helios probe, and the fact that it had helped to identify Saudi Arabia as the state sponsor that aligned with neo-Nazis to disrupt the German election and its aftermath.

"So Turkey is not involved?" asked the deputy director of Analysis.

"Only peripherally. They are a convenient false flag."

"But Saudi Arabia, you're sure?"

"Quite," said Bob. "The lead officer is a prince in the House of Saud, and a senior player in the General Intelligence Directorate of the Kingdom of Saudi Arabia. We have had dealings with him."

Colman grew silent, avoiding further discussion on the identification of Sharif Ali, or the operation in Mali. With the exception of Colman, Arthur Kent, Evie, and the Director himself, no one in the room knew about Terry Solak's adventure to Timbuktu.

The Director looked at Evie. "I know you've been busy with personal issues Evie, but did you have any thoughts?"

She sat forward and rearranged her notes. "Actually, I did have an observation, Director." She pulled out her papers. "The desk supervisor is correct in that the German Basic Law was written to avoid the Weimar era rules, where easy dismissal of the chancellor was the constant political ploy."

"And?" asked Kent.

"And I think we should look past the chancellor's position. The German Presidency also has unique reserve powers during times of political instability."

"Such as now?" said Kent.

"Yes."

"Some examples?" asked the Director.

Evie looked down at her list. "The president can propose a chancellor to the Bundestag, appoint and dismiss cabinet ministers, judges, and federal civil servants, dissolve the Bundestag, and declare a state of emergency."

The Director sat forward, "Quite a bit more power than I understood."

"Yes, the president of Germany has many executive powers without a national referendum. They are elected in a secret ballot, with no debate, at a special convention, for a five-year term. They have no party affiliation." Evie leaned back in her chair. "In addition, during a legislative emergency, the president has wide discretion to exercise their official duties." Evie paused to hold everyone's attention and said, "I fear we may be watching the wrong horse."

Chapter 72

Munich, Germany

Sharif Ali took the 6.00 a.m. flight from Munich, making a point to avoid using a private jet. The flight itself was a little over an hour in duration, and following Ronja's recitation of her conversation with the prince, Otto reached out to the domestic security agency for assistance. They needed manpower.

A team of surveillance specialists surfaced at Berlin's Tegel Airport and formed an invisible net around the Saudi and his two bodyguards. They followed him through the terminal building.

The lead from Ronja had paid an immediate benefit, and although minor at face value, it appeared that the prince needed to take a meeting in Berlin, just as the carnage of Operation Blackbird began.

Otto looked across the kitchen table of the new safe house and fumbled with his pipe. "Our ice queen produced a small but important piece of information."

"Going *north* was an ambiguous indicator," replied Terry.

"Yes, but Berlin was a logical guess, given the state of affairs here in the republic."

"I wonder *who* our prince is meeting?" asked Solak, thinking aloud.

Otto blew several smoke rings as Terry sipped at a cup of coffee. Then the foreign intelligence officer leaned forward and spoke in a whisper. "I think that they will make their play."

"This is the time," answered Solak. "It's maximum disarray."

"Yes, the republic is shaking as we speak."

"And the German mind craves order," replied Terry with a touch of sarcasm.

Otto laughed in spite of himself, and then he said in a more serious tone. "The chancellor is fighting for her political life and the people want clarity. This is the time for a strong leader to emerge."

***

Berlin, Germany

Nora entered the small study in Mitte where Gerhardt was preparing the final touches on his nationwide address.

"Gerhardt," she said in an excited voice, "the Minister of the Interior just stepped down. The president accepted the minister's resignation."

"And the chancellor?"

"She has not publicly commented."

"This was expected," replied Gerhardt.

"Yes, someone had to take the fall. The minister took responsibility for the failure of the chancellor's policies."

Gerhardt swiveled in his seat, looking from the computer screen to Nora. "Who will she choose?"

"We do not know, but the president is involved because Germany is under reserve powers. This occurs only during times of political instability."

Nora leaned forward and wrapped her hands around his forearm. "This will work, my love. Write a great speech. Loyal people are engaged. The time is ours."

She stood and with a parting kiss on the back of his head, she whispered, "We will be changing apartments again. Travel light and fast. We will *not* be returning here."

Chapter 73

Munich, Germany

Otto charged into the bedroom just as Terry finished a set of pushups. Solak was back into a daily regimen, exercising in solitude, watching the news, and prepping his mind for whatever would happen next.

In the day and a half since Ronja's dinner with Sharif Ali, she had remained behind at the Mandarin Oriental Hotel, dutifully playing the part of a cosmetic executive in town on business. They both waited in separate locations for Otto's guidance. So much depended on the Saudi prince's contacts in Berlin, and the reports from the German domestic security agency.

"Helios, we are on the move again."

Solak patted his forehead and blotted away the perspiration with a hand towel. "Where to?"

"Berlin, of course." The foreign intelligence officer took a moment to smile as he packed the bowl of his pipe with fresh tobacco. "Have you been watching the news?"

"What I could understand."

Otto nodded. "The Minister of the Interior resigned under pressure—just an hour after our prince from the House of Saud took a meeting at Bellevue Palace."

Solak gave the German a blank expression. "Help me out."

"The president of the republic lives at the Bellevue, it's his official residence."

"Isn't he a figurehead?"

"Yes, but under our constitution, the normally staid presidency takes on extraordinary powers during legislative emergencies."

"And you're saying there is a connection."

"I'm saying," replied Otto, "that the coincidence is a bridge too far."

"So now what happens?" asked Terry.

"The Minister of the Interior is one of the two or three most senior cabinet positions. It is responsible for all of the internal security and civil protection of the constitutional order. They *must* name a new minister."

"From a coalition party?"

"Maybe, it's a plum position, and given the current state of affairs, one of great power."

"Is it the chancellor's call?"

"In theory," answered Otto, "but it would appear that the president also holds quite a bit of sway." Otto held up his hand and motioned. "We need to find out how deep the Saudis have penetrated our politics. I've made arrangements for a private flight, and I'll have Miss Ronja travel north by commercial aircraft."

Terry looked surprised. "Has the prince returned to Munich?"

"No, and in addition, the internet is announcing a major speech to be delivered by our Hitler stand-in. We leave in ten minutes."

***

Berlin, Germany

They descended on 'Alex' from every direction, employing the S-bahn, U-bahn, buses, trains, autos, and foot. They carried placards and posters of Gerhardt, fixing his portrait on walls and across buildings, converting the huge former cattle market known as Alexanderplatz into an open-air auditorium dedicated to the orator. Alex, the square, had not seen such a crowd since the anti-communist protests preceding the fall of the Berlin Wall. The numbers were estimated at well over a million people, effectively marking the evening event as the largest anti-government demonstration in German history.

Lines of police tried to control the points of access, only to be overwhelmed by the sheer volume of people. Several feints occurred at different locations, first at the Neptune fountain, then in front of Galeria, and finally outside the Vapiano restaurant. These well-rehearsed false sightings served to stifle the police control by drawing away their attention. It enabled the disguised Gerhardt to mix in the throng of bodies and enter the packed square without being seen.

Minutes passed and a buzz of anticipation bubbled to the surface. Then darkness fell over Alex and a makeshift stage was erected and surrounded by a partisan crowd of adherents. They squished together, ten-deep in a circle, effectively cutting off access to the frayed police lines, when suddenly Gerhardt appeared. He stood and surveyed the sea of bodies radiating in every direction. His posture was erect, his bearing formal. Television spotlights intersected over the swarm of humanity, playing off the buildings that hedged the square, and then back to the makeshift stage. Gerhardt, the embodiment of Adolf Hitler, nodded to the supplicant crowd as they beseeched him to lead them from the swamp, and restore order to their beloved republic.

He turned in a half circle and the television cameras zoomed in for a close-up. The blaring microphones captured his words and a nation, nay a world, listened to the reassuring opening comments of the now infamous orator.

"Germany is at a crossroads…yesterday, the Minister of the Interior resigned…it is imperative that the chancellor select a German loyal to our values for this position…a man of courage and vision…a citizen who sees the opportunity through the lens of Germany's future…one who craves progress, unity, and order for our citizens…a leader who reveres our past, *and* sees the possibility for our future…"

He paused for a moment as the crowd turned silent. They watched and listened, spellbound, as he spoke. Then he began again, elevating their concerns, tweaking their emotions, inspiring their confidence as the oration picked up speed and gravitas. He would safeguard their families. He would buttress their fears. For ten minutes he coaxed and cajoled them forward. His cadence and tone shaped their senses, as past became prologue, and he became the living embodiment of his professed lineage. Finally, in a right-fisted salute that somehow mimicked both a Roman salute and a Nazi salute without being quite either, Gerhardt summated his position with a final phrase, "Germany is for Germans!"

The crowd erupted, half raising their right arms at an angle with a closed fist, the other half turning on their cell phone flashlights. Everyone together began to chant. They bellowed his name in unison, again and again, echoing off the walls, strong, powerful, clear: *Gerhardt.*

Chapter 74

Berlin, Germany

Two levels beneath the square, Director Geiger of the Federal Uniform Police negotiated the tunnels with a blueprint in hand and an enlarged contingent of GSG-9 police commandos in tow.

"Here," said Geiger pointing towards the blueprint, "this tunnel links the Alex station from the U2 to the U5."

The balaclava-masked police captain pointed at a dotted line extension to a sealed steel door. "Can we breach this metal barrier? It's been sealed for years."

Geiger took a moment to scan the connections between the S-bahn rapid transit lines to Alexanderplatz station. "This is the most likely route of escape. This affords him direct access to the Berlin Wall tunnel."

"Let me send for the engineer," replied the captain.

Geiger nodded and took a step back, using the opportunity to survey the tunnel link and orient his blueprint to the layout of Alexanderplatz directly above. "Yes," said the police director to himself, "it would have to be an underground passage ignored by transit workers and construction engineers alike, an access door ignored for years."

***

Berlin, Germany

The escape was a masterful plan in tactical illusion. The crush of bodies that crowded Alex Square was interspersed with thousands of the orator's supporters. For an unsanctioned rally advertised over the internet, the speech drew an almost uncontrollable mob. The citizens craved action and only the populace-driven orator named Gerhardt spoke with clarity.

The police paid attention and arrived in force, but under the guidance of leaders from das Netzwerk, pockets of rough-looking neo-Nazis arrived in bunches to steer the peaceful crowd into human obstacles—keeping the orator and the police separated.

Gerhardt climbed down from his makeshift stage and a half dozen rolls of black, plastic sheeting unfurled outward in six different directions, extending into the crowd, and quickly covering the heads of the boisterous protesters.

At the same time, all of the people in the square were asked to turn on their cell phone flashlights and aim them toward the sky as a single sign of solidarity. The brightness of hundreds of thousands of lights obscured the activities on the ground and helped to cloak the sightlines above. The television cameras and police helicopters were effectively blinded.

As the six lanes of plastic sheeting ruffled towards the teeming mob, a Gerhardt look-alike mounted the stage and motioned towards the far end of the square. The attention of the crowd shifted and immediately police in riot gear started to move in that direction. The fourth lane of black sheeting ended a hundred meters away, near the underground U-bahn entrance. This was then surrounded.

For a few minutes the police seemed preoccupied by the pedestrian lanes, afraid the orator would use the overhead cover to cloak his movements and blend in to the crowd. Instead, Gerhardt moved down to the fourth lane, and just before emerging from the makeshift open-air alleyway, a series of firecrackers exploded to the rear. People panicked, and ten police broke ranks to stem the sudden disturbance. Just as quickly twenty burly men in leather jackets obstructed the split police line and shielded Nora as she raced forward holding Gerhardt's arm. Across the pavement, down the stairwell, and into the tunnel raced the pair. They were surrounded by bodyguards who adeptly steered the other pedestrians into blocks of people. The pure volume of bodies squeezed together to create a human barrier that impeded apprehension. Then the police rushed forward and ordered the crowd to part. Nothing happened. The group of supporters continued to grow and clog the subway platform as Gerhardt, Nora, and their contingent of security personnel faded into the darkness. Then, near the end of the gangway, the Alexanderplatz station lights suddenly extinguished. The blackness startled the crowd, but within seconds the emergency generators hummed, and reserve lights turned on; albeit at sixty percent of the regular illumination.

An eerie glow permeated the station, and Gerhardt's team crossed off the tracks, onto a narrow concrete passage. They paused beside a sealed metal door which opened from inside the north wall. Then the rarely used engineering door was tugged sideways and the escorts turned on handheld flashlights. They guided the contingent along the quay. The tunnel twisted several times, too sharp for a train, which was self-evident as there were no tracks. This was a narrow, concrete tunnel used only as a pedestrian passage. It converted into a major U-bahn link tunnel with an unknown route seldom used since the dark days of the Cold War, a time when East Berliners made their escape through a tunnel, under the wall, to freedom.

After ten minutes at a steady pace, the escort team halted in front of a black, wrought iron fence. It opened to an anteroom and a second iron door. Four bodyguards entered ahead of Nora and Gerhardt and once the men pushed through the second door, a series of stun grenades exploded at their feet.

Chapter 75

Six employees sat in the SCIF on the seventh floor when the Director entered.

"Sit, sit," said the Director with a wave of his hand. His quick wit and superior intellect were masked by a folksy charm that he retained from his time in the Senate. He eschewed formality, preferring a pragmatic approach to problem solving.

He pointed at the deputy director for Analysis. The motion was a signal to start. The deputy activated the security procedures and the conference room began to electronically seal itself. Then the Director looked across the table at the German desk supervisor. "Let's begin."

The woman leaned forward over her notes and cleared her throat. "Yesterday, the Minister of the Interior resigned his cabinet position."

"Was the resignation under pressure?" asked Arthur Kent.

"So it appears, but it's common knowledge that he did not agree with the chancellor's Schengen policy."

"Did the German president play a part?"

"We are not sure," said the desk supervisor, "but we do know that he has taken a number of meetings with Bundestag members."

The Director leaned forward. "Given his responsibilities, is that unusual?"

"No sir, but he has also taken several meetings at the Bellevue Palace with foreign nationals."

The Director sat still and gently bit his lip as he pondered the information. Twenty seconds elapsed, and then the Director spoke in a quiet voice. "Continue."

Evie sat in silence next to Bob Colman, idly perusing her notes as she waited for her turn.

"Who will get the nod?" asked the Director.

"Not sure, sir," replied the supervisor, "but the supposition is that the chancellor is being coaxed to broaden her base of support."

"By the president?"

"We believe he is exerting influence."

"How far will it stretch?"

"We think," replied the supervisor, "that she may be forced to go outside her current coalition to fill the cabinet vacancy."

The Director ruminated on the observation for a moment. Then with a twist of his head he faced the Europe mission center chief. "Tell us about the Gerhardt speech."

The center chief flipped a page on her notebook file and pointed with her pen at several entries. "They estimated that a crowd of over one *million* descended on Alexanderplatz at dusk. The announcement of the speech was all over the internet, but as in previous speeches they never filed for a political rally permit."

"Did they arrest him?"

"No," replied the center chief, "true to form, Gerhardt arrived in secret, gave a nativist tinged speech, fired up the populist base for fourteen minutes, and then managed to fade away."

"He escaped," said the Director in a frustrated tone.

"Yes, sir," replied the center chief.

The Director looked around the table before settling on Bob Colman. He nodded at the SAD chief.

"Helios is in Berlin with his German foreign intelligence contact," said Colman. "They followed the Saudi prince north."

The Director leaned forward and spoke in a solemn tone. "Germany is fighting upstream against a uniquely German problem. We need to help identify a solution for them. If we don't, they could have a political chain reaction."

"Our goal?" asked Arthur Kent.

"Find Gerhardt," said the Director without pause. "This Hitler look-alike, this Houdini...find the purported grandson before Germany implodes, followed by the European Union, followed by NATO."

***

Potsdam, Germany

The four-car caravan sped along the A10 motorway, often referred to as the Berliner Ring. In the rear seat of the second sedan sat Police Director Geiger.

The other three cars contained a dozen federal police in plain clothes on special duty. The traffic was sparse, and the caravan made the fifteen-mile trip from center-city Berlin in thirty minutes.

Potsdam offered the safe house de jour. It was a secluded mansion, nestled between the interconnected lakes and landmarks that dotted the pastoral formal residence for kings and kaisers. Potsdam's spacious parks and preserved palaces spoke to the prestige of royalty in a bygone era. It helped to complete the picturesque dream of a life of distinction to special 'guests' of the federal republic.

The caravan turned off the motorway and took a series of gentle twirls to arrive in the very quiet enclave. People in the neighborhood were familiar with wealth, power, and privacy. It came as second nature to the locals.

The vehicles then turned into the secluded drive and semi-circled up to the side entrance. A senior police officer inspected the occupants before settling on Geiger's face. A courtesy nod was exchanged and all the car doors opened at once. The tall frame of Police Director Geiger stepped to the pavement in a navy-blue suit. His arrival was conveyed over an ear plug wireless transmitter to the occupants of the home.

Inside, Geiger was met by the shift commander and guided down a hallway to the rear study. They paused outside the door. "How is our guest?" asked Geiger.

"Physically he has some tinnitus, and a few burns that the doctor said should heal over time," answered the commander. "His appetite is good, and he has taken several naps."

"Is he cooperating?"

"He is polite, but restless," answered the commander.

Geiger nodded. "And the woman?"

"She is difficult."

Geiger considered the answer before pressing the issue. "Has she made threats?"

"Only one. She *demands* to see him."

"You have not accommodated her." Geiger made the statement sound like a question.

"No, sir, our instructions were clear."

The police director nodded and motioned at the door. The shift commander escorted Geiger into the study.

Gerhardt looked up and then stood from behind the desk. He crossed the room to greet Geiger face-to-face. "Who are you?"

Geiger towered over Gerhardt, by standing at the full breadth of his six-foot, two-inch frame. The orator noted the gray hair, the erect bearing, and the piercing blue eyes of the police director. "I am your host," answered Geiger.

There was a pause as the police director absorbed the deep resemblance of Gerhardt to the long-dead Fuhrer. From an arm's distance, the acute likeness was a bit unnerving.

"Why am I being held captive, I have broken no laws. Am I under arrest?"

"You are our guest," said Geiger in a quiet voice.

Gerhardt squinted, studying the much taller police director for twenty seconds before he said, "Well at least I am at the disposal of a true Aryan."

Geiger nodded and then motioned to several cushioned chairs at the other end of the study. "Let's talk."

When both men were seated Gerhardt asked, "How is Nora?"

"The woman is in good health. She will be extended every courtesy if she cooperates."

Gerhardt crinkled his short mustache.

"Needless to say," said Geiger, "we have plans for you. Let me explain the situation."

Chapter 76

Berlin, Germany

Berlin, the city of spies, had a legacy. Therefore, it was no surprise to Terry that the German foreign intelligence service—with no charter to operate within the borders of their own nation—would still have a half dozen safe houses in their capital. Such was the nature of intelligence work; need to know, and a lack of trust in a very untrustworthy world.

Otto breezed into the sitting area of the third-floor walkup in Wrangelkiez. Two security officers protected the premises through Otto's revolving door of assets, as various specialists arrived and departed at different times. At one point, Solak received a brief personal note from Ronja who stayed at a second safe house a kilometer away. It was a personal touch permitted by Otto to keep Ronja pliant.

"What a nasty piece of deceit this assignment has become," said the foreign intelligence officer with a grimace.

Solak looked up to see Otto tap on the stem of his pipe. "You've been busy," replied Terry.

"The Bellevue has become a cesspool of politics and infighting. Gossip and speculation rule."

"This is over the new interior minister?"

"Yes," answered Otto.

"Isn't this the chancellor's decision?"

"In theory, but given the very weakened state of the chancellor's coalition, the president is fully engaged in the selection process." Otto sat and crossed his ankles in a frustrated pose.

Terry moved closer so they could talk in quiet tones. "Does he have the leverage?" asked Solak.

"He does when operating under emergency powers," replied Otto. "The president can challenge—even pressure the chancellor to bend. He can add quite a bit to the political debate. Remember, he has the power to sign-off on laws, *and* to veto laws." Otto tapped the spent tobacco from his pipe.

"Sounds like there is room to maneuver," said Terry.

"Yes, given the current state of affairs. The chancellor runs the government, but the president safeguards the state."

"So it's open to some interpretation?"

Otto offered a grudging nod. "The influence is subtle when all is calm, but pervasive when things go awry."

Solak paced around the room for a few seconds, assimilating the information and insights from his counterpart.

"In theory," said Otto, "all cabinet ministers are equal with a slight exception for the finance minister. Of course, everyone knows that *some* ministries are more important than others."

"So, the pressure is on to name a new interior minister from the chancellor's own party, the Christian Dems."

"Yes," answered Otto, "or at the very least, from their sister party, the Christian Socials."

"And the Alt for Germany Party?"

"The far right," said Otto, "the surprise spoiler of the election and now the primary opposition to the chancellor. They want a cabinet seat."

"Will that happen?"

"A week ago, I would have said no…but this version of the grand coalition is so shaky it could splinter at the slightest provocation."

"So everyone is playing the angles," said Terry.

"Including the president. In the last two days he has met with several foreign delegations at the palace."

Terry paused before saying, "That wasn't reported in the news."

"No," said Otto in agreement. He tapped his tobacco pouch and filled his pipe bowl. Then he looked up at Terry but did not elucidate.

"Cabinet positions are important," said Solak.

"They are prestigious and powerful," replied Otto. "The Alt for Germany Party seeks legitimacy."

"Their political platform reads like a neo-Nazi guide book," said Terry. "They sound like a party for Gerhardt."

"Yes, they do, except the orator declares no party affiliation. He has broken no laws," said Otto, "but of course, one could argue he has come very close on several occasions."

266

"Speaking of Gerhardt," said Terry, "where is he?"

"We don't know. He seems to have disappeared again," replied Otto. "Candidly, his ability to elude apprehension is becoming an embarrassment."

They lapsed into a brief silence, and Terry stood and took several steps in a small circle before changing the subject. "Do you think that there is a hidden alliance between the chancellor's sister party, the Christian Socials, and the Alt for Germany Party?"

Otto looked at Terry. "That's an interesting question. Consider this: the Christian Socials are a distinctly Bavarian party. The Alt for Germany Party espouses an almost identical platform but are even more conservative." Otto paused before saying, "Our president was born in Furth and raised in Nuremburg, which is just a short train ride to Munich." Otto hesitated for a moment to add emphasis. "The heart of Bavaria."

***

Berlin, Germany

As head of state, it was expected that in the performance of his duties, the federal president would meet with foreign dignitaries, diplomats, and political leaders. In addition to his parliamentary oversight, he was also expected to take a broad interest in overlap issues that impacted Germany on an economic, social and cultural basis.

The Office of the Federal President houses one hundred and eighty staff members in a four-story glass and stone building beside Bellevue Castle on the border of the Tiergarten. Official receptions occurred at the palace, and unofficial meetings took place at the executive offices of the president's staff.

For the second time in five days, Sharif Ali arrived to see the German president. This time, however, he was not acting as a member of the royal family on a diplomatic mission, but as a senior officer in the General Intelligence Directorate of the Kingdom of Saudi Arabia. He was offering information pertinent to the rash of political murders enacted during Operation Blackbird.

The prince was met at a side door, and guided to an anteroom on the third floor. Unknown to Sharif Ali or the German president, the arrival sequence was filmed and recorded by the German domestic security agency.

The prince's two bodyguards were accompanied to a separate waiting area and offered refreshments as the state secretary engaged the Saudi in polite conversation. Six minutes later the German president arrived.

They spent a moment exchanging pleasantries before Sharif said, "Thank you for your willingness to see me on such short notice, Mister President."

The German president brushed at his thick white hair. "You made it clear that you had information that was of critical importance to our republic." He offered Sharif an open hand.

"Since we last spoke a few days ago," said Ali, "much has happened."

"Yes, we face several challenges," replied the president in a calm manner. He was an experienced statesman, and if the president had concerns, they didn't show.

The prince nodded, "The kingdom of Saudi Arabia wishes to offer irrefutable proof of the involvement of Turkey."

The German president adjusted his thick-framed glasses. "There have been multiple pieces of evidence to this effect. Do you have something conclusive?"

"We do, Mister President, and in return, we would request certain considerations."

The German president leaned back and concealed a frown, hiding his attitude towards the duplicitous nature of nations. Then he motioned for Sharif Ali to continue.

"At our first meeting, Mister President, I discussed how deeply offended we were by Germany's pro Iran policy shift of the past year. As you know, Saudi Arabia and Iran are bitter enemies. We hoped that we could put a thaw in the frosty relations that developed between our nations because of the Iran issue."

"What do you propose?" asked the president.

"To begin, a lifting of business sanctions," said Ali. "As you know, previous to this freeze, Germany was Saudi Arabia's top European trading partner."

"Yes," said the president, "until in May of this year, when Riyadh halted all new business contracts to Berlin. The door was closed to German business."

"Yes," answered the prince. He took a moment to clear his throat, "But now Germany offers business to Iran and Turkey—two countries in the triangle of evil."

"We adjusted to your provocation," said the president. "Now you claim to have exclusive evidence of Ankara's involvement."

"Turkey is not the friend of Germany," said the prince. "Make no mistake, despite the long history between your countries dating back to the guest-worker's program, the autocrat in Ankara involves himself very directly with *your* elections."

The president shifted in his seat and then asked, "Would we be considered for the vision twenty-thirty project?" The Saudi construction project was a plan to reduce the country's dependence on oil and to diversify its economy.

"Yes," answered the prince.

"And the construction of Neom?" Neom was a planned city and economic zone close to the Egyptian border.

"Yes again," replied the prince. "In return, we ask that you publicly change your posture towards Iran and Turkey, *and* begin the process of using Saudi oil as an alternate source of energy."

The president sat back and absorbed the request. They were both aware that Germany received seventy percent of their energy needs from Moscow, and together with Saudi Arabia, Russia controlled twenty-five percent of the world's crude oil supply.

"That is a very serious petition," replied the president, "not so easily done."

Sharif Ali nodded. "Yet it makes sense to adjust the equation. We are offering you an alternate plan to protect your future acquisition of oil."

The president leaned forward. "We will have to see the information you offer."

"Of course," said the prince. "But make no mistake, Ankara is heavily involved in the recent violence perpetrated in Germany. The Turkish president is outspoken against the established order here in Berlin. He is an autocrat who condemns the West and seeks to reinstate the caliphate."

They lapsed into a moment of silence as the state secretary received a cell call. He excused himself and walked to the far end of the anteroom. Then he took the call before circling back to the president. He whispered in his ear.

The president nodded and stood. "Thank you, your highness, we anxiously anticipate the delivery of this information."

Chapter 77

Berlin, Germany

Otto entered the safe house followed by Ronja and a second woman. He had decided that a frontal engagement was in order. They needed to risk the incongruity of a second meeting in a second city between Ronja and the prince. Events were cascading against the government, and a lack of viable options pressured the foreign intelligence officer to push the envelope. He pointed towards the living room with the stem of his pipe.

"I took your advice, Helios, and decided that Miss Ronja offers a more plausible excuse if she encounters our target while accompanied by a friend."

Terry nodded as Otto introduced the second woman.

"This is Frau Richter," said Otto with a hand motion. "She is on loan from domestic security." The woman was thirtyish, brunette, and attractive in a pleasant sort of way. "I have briefed her and Miss Ronja on their cover stories and our goal for this impromptu meeting."

Solak took a few seconds to make eye contact with Ronja who made no secret of her delight in seeing Terry again after a short separation.

"The target has been very busy these last two days. Something is afoot, and we are out of options," said Otto.

"Is the target under active surveillance?" asked Solak.

"As we speak," replied Otto. "Frau Richter's team has been involved since his arrival here in Berlin. He is checked into the Adlon Kempinski Hotel. We'll make our move there."

Terry sidled up to Ronja as Otto turned to lead them from the living room.

"The boys are okay?"

"Yes," answered Ronja. Her face brightened and she grabbed at his forearm in a gesture of appreciation. "Thank you for asking."

"Into the breach," said Otto, adding a touch of levity to break the pre-operational tension. Then he smiled and led them from the safe house.

***

Berlin, Germany

The state secretary for the Office of the Federal President sat at his desk in the executive building, next to the Bellevue Palace. He was a busy man. In a nation filled with layers of civil servants, the state secretary was the first amongst equals by virtue of his position running the supreme federal authority.

As the state secretary to the president, he was tasked with advising, inform-ing, preparing, and executing all issues before the office, to include presiding over thirteen federal divisions organized into three directorate generals. In ad-dition, he also ensured the task functions of the communications unit, the pres-ident's policy planning team, and the liaison officer for the Bundeswehr (German armed forces).

The secretary was a very competent, experienced, and powerful technocrat who assured that the grinding gears of German government continued to func-tion.

There was a knock on the door, and a middle-aged woman in a cafeteria staff uniform entered pushing a stainless steel trolley. "Herr Secretary," said the woman, "your afternoon coffee."

"Danke," replied the secretary returning his attention to the stack of docu-ments on his desk. "Where is Frau Weber?"

"Sick at home," answered the woman as she prepared the secretary's coffee with one sugar and a dollop of cream. "She should be back tomorrow."

The secretary nodded in an absentminded fashion. Then she placed a fresh scone of deep-fried dough covered with honey butter on a plate next to the cup of coffee at the corner of his desk.

"Anything else sir?" asked the waitress.

"No," said the secretary immersed in the reports. He looked up and mo-tioned. "Thank you."

The waitress left the bone china plates, coffee pot, and cup on the desk and exited the office.

Ninety minutes later, the secretary sat up straight, gasped for air, clutched at his chest, stiffened, and slumped over his desk.

Chapter 78

Potsdam, Germany

Police Director Geiger entered the mansion by the side door. He was dressed in a gray business suit, and accompanied by two men also dressed in civilian attire. Inside, he paced down the hall and entered a door that led to the basement stairs. They followed.

There were several rooms in the converted bomb shelter, each with concrete walls, padded ceilings, a shower, toilet, sink, and small refrigerator. There were no televisions, radios, telephones, or reading materials in the rooms, just a single bed with a mattress and a pillow. There were no windows.

Geiger stopped outside the first room and studied the lone occupant through a two-way mirror. "How is she?" asked the police director. He watched Nora pace the small cell-like room, her eyes shifting suspiciously from side to side.

"She has been difficult," said the shift supervisor.

Geiger nodded in understanding before saying, "She has had the opportunity to cooperate." He turned. "We are moving her to an off-site location."

The supervisor motioned towards a locked medical cabinet mounted on the wall outside the padded room. "Should we medicate her?"

Geiger considered the question before answering with a motion towards the cabinet.

They prepared a syringe filled with ketamine and then the supervisor and the two men with Geiger entered Nora's room. She immediately stepped back, wary, her eyes searching their faces, and then she saw the syringe. Her eyes popped wide in fear and she cried out in a defiant tone: "No!"

Nora leaped towards the open door but the men caught her mid-air. They carried her back to the bed, even as she struggled, and forced her face down on the mattress. Then they pulled down her pants to expose her derriere, and the supervisor injected the drug into her buttocks.

A few seconds passed and Nora seemed to calm. Then the three men backed out of the room and relocked the cell.

The supervisor turned to Geiger and spoke in a quiet voice. "It should only take about five minutes. It's fast acting and powerful."

"Use the underground garage and the van to affect the transfer," said Geiger.

"Yes, sir," replied the supervisor.

He motioned and the two men in civilian clothes led the police director back up the stairs towards the main living quarters of the mansion.

***

Berlin, Germany

The hook was timed. Ronja entered the lobby of the Adlon Kempinski Hotel with Frau Richter of the domestic security agency. The women had been briefed by Otto, and their role-play was that of two co-workers who met for a social lunch between work engagements.

The goal was to reacquaint the prince and Ronja in a neutral setting, and by so doing, rekindle their flirtation. It was apparent to Otto and Terry that Sharif, as a senior intelligence operative of his country, was involved in nefarious intentions towards Germany. They hoped Ronja might find something out.

Minutes later, Sharif Ali paused under the hotel's distinctive red awning and looked west. The carnage of Ali's car bomb on the distinctive façade of the Brandenburg Gate stirred a sense of pride in the prince. He had attacked the symbolic heart of the nation by defacing Berlin's most distinct edifice. Germany must suffer for their support of Iran and Turkey, two spokes in the 'triangle of evil.'

The prince turned and entered the lobby followed by his two bodyguards. For all appearances, the two women were engrossed in a warm, light-hearted conversation. They were positioned just inside the entrance, making it difficult to avoid their quiet voices and light laughter as one entered the hotel.

The Adlon, like all hotels in the prince's orbit, was of the highest quality standards for location, service, and furnishings. It had an old Europe feel, complete with bergère armchairs, velvet sofas, and a huge chandelier from the Venetian island of Murano. Everywhere there were touches of cherrywood, mahogany, and marble.

Ali nodded politely as he tried to squeeze behind Frau Richter. Then as he made polite eye contact with Ronja, the prince's face brightened in a genuine expression of surprise. "Ronja?"

"Sali," she replied, and returned his delighted expression. She used the name Sharif offered when they had first met in Munich several days earlier. "What brings you here?" asked Ronja.

"Business of course," replied Ali as he recovered from the mild shock and hastily introduced himself to Frau Richter. She played her hand like a seasoned professional. The surveillance specialist adjusted to take the emphasis away from Ronja. "We work for the same cosmetic company," said Richter, "and I invited my old friend up for a quick visit before she flies home."

"How long will you be here?" asked Sharif, looking at Ronja with interest.

"A couple of days," said Ronja. "I never spent much time here in the past." She nodded towards Richter. "Now I have a tour guide."

"And there is so much to see," said Richter leaning forward to speak in a conspiratorial whisper.

"We just had a wonderful lunch," said Ronja with a smile.

"There is lots of gossip to discuss," said Richter. "Our business is changing *so* fast."

Ali nodded at the polite shop talk before asking, "Have you made plans for dinner?"

"Not for this evening," said Ronja as she motioned towards Frau Richter.

"I have a commitment for tonight," said Richter. "It's a long-standing family obligation." She looked up at Ali with a hopeful expression. "But possibly you could join Ronja for dinner if you were free?"

"Oh no," answered Ronja offering the prince an opportunity to beg-off. "I wouldn't want to impose."

"It would be my pleasure," said Sharif, with a smile directed at Ronja.

Richter smiled as well and then injected a thought. "I would hate for her to feel abandoned her first night here." Then she turned towards Ronja, "And tomorrow we can go shopping, there are some really interesting new stores."

"It is settled then," said Ali. "I will meet you here in the lobby at seven o'clock."

"Lovely," replied Ronja in an upbeat tone, "I will see you then."

Sharif shook hands with both women and continued across the lobby towards the elevators followed by his two bodyguards.

Ronja and Richter made small talk for a few minutes before Richter turned towards Ronja and gave her a subtle wink. "Well done," she said in a quiet voice. "You played that perfect." She gave Ronja a platonic hug as Sharif's bodyguards turned and gave the women a final glance.

Chapter 79

Langley, Virginia

The Director entered the seventh-floor SCIF in a brisk walk and waved everyone to remain seated. The familiar electronic measures began and the room sealed just as the German desk supervisor started her update.

"Seven hours ago, the German chancellor announced several cabinet changes as a result of the recent resignation of her interior minister." The supervisor paused, "the Economy and Energy Minister, from her own party, steps over to take Interior." She let the information settle before adding, "and the transportation minister from her sister party takes Economy and Energy."

The desk supervisor allowed a few minutes for everyone to absorb the information.

"This leaves an opening at Transportation," said Arthur Kent.

The desk supervisor nodded and held up her index finger. "Yes, and *that* ministry will be filled by the leader of the Alt for Germany Party, the AfD."

The conference room hushed into a surprised silence as Kent asked, "Aren't they the far right party?"

"Yes," replied the desk supervisor. "This is their first cabinet appointment. They did not exist as a party in parliament four years ago."

"Will this breakup the chancellor's coalition?" asked the Director.

"The gamble is that it will *not*. The federal president is a seasoned negotiator. Reports suggest he has been very involved in the discussions." She took a moment to scan the room before continuing. "The leader of the Alt for Germany Party is a woman, and this helps to balance the cabinet's diversity. In addition, it does not change any of the other postings, especially amongst the Social Dems Party."

"So Interior and Economy Energy stay close to the chancellor, and the 'pride of the populists' attains a cabinet position," said Kent.

The Director looked around the conference table before settling on Bob Colman. He motioned with his left hand. Bob pushed a folded piece of paper towards Evie who knew the message, and pulled out the situation report sent from Terry Solak that morning.

"We believe," she said, clearing her throat, "that there is more to come. The president is key. They call him the 'gray efficiency' due to his ability to manage disagreements beyond the political spotlight."

"You have mentioned him before," said the Director, "is there cause for alarm?"

Evie looked down at Bob who gave her a nod.

"We think there is cause for concern. In previous positions, the German president ran their intelligence services, and their foreign ministry. He has a broad mandate during difficult times. The president has taken several meetings with foreign elements and known provocateurs."

"But isn't that part of his job?" asked the deputy director for Analysis.

"Yes," answered Evie, "but the timing strikes us as odd. It is out of place." She allowed that thought to settle before adding, "And Gerhardt seems to have—yet again—evaded the German police authorities."

"He's disappeared?" asked the Europe mission center chief.

"So it seems," answered Evie. "He is wanted for questioning, but is nowhere to be found."

***

Berlin, Germany

The VP of domestic security scanned the long conference table before speaking, "We should get started."

Police Director Geiger turned from his typical perch at the windows of the eighth floor, watching over the city from the height of the chancellery building. He took his seat across from the VP.

"Official estimates," said the VP, "confirm that the rally in Alex Square attracted over a million people."

"That's a guess," said Holger of the Berlin State Police. "How could we know?"

"By any method," replied the VP, "the crowd in attendance was massive."

Several in the group around the table nodded in agreement. Each member of the group had some jurisdictional responsibility in the matter at hand. Their mission, quite simply, had evolved into a matter of survival for their constitution, their nation, and their way of life.

"Gerhardt," said Ludwig of the federal criminal investigative police, "is still at large. We are at a crossroads."

"He clearly has the popular support," replied the VP.

"This can*not* be denied," said Geiger. "We must acknowledge the realities on the ground. He is being protected."

"He is a Nazi," said Holger with a touch of exasperation.

"Maybe," replied Geiger. "Probably."

"This does not alarm you?" asked Ludwig.

"Of course it does," answered Geiger.

"And the *new* Minister of Transportation is from the far right, the Alt for Germany Party," said Ludwig.

"She is *also* a Nazi," said Holger. "Think of what is happening here."

"We need to pull Gerhardt in and defuse the situation," said Geiger.

"How?" asked the VP before the discussion became heated.

Geiger shrugged.

"What do you propose?" asked the deputy Minister of the Interior.

"If we arrest Gerhardt without clear legal grounds," said the VP, "all hell will break loose. He is much too popular."

"That discussion is academic," said Geiger. "First, we must locate him."

"So much for trolling the tunnels," said Holger in a snide manner.

Geiger gave Holger a dirty look before saying, "He inflames passions. We need to assure Gerhardt that his concerns are *not* falling on deaf ears."

"How do we have that conversation?" asked the VP. "We cannot even find him."

"This is preposterous," said Holger in frustration. "He is a Nazi, we give him no quarter. What choice do we have?"

"Certainly *not* fascism," said Ludwig.

"Then socialism," replied Geiger.

"What? We are a benevolent capitalistic society," said the new deputy from the chancellor's office, "as is most of Europe."

"Really," said Geiger. He leaned forward and rested his elbows on the conference table. "So, you believe we should continue this erratic Schengen policy and open our doors to the world?"

"With some constraints, of course," said the new deputy.

"But open doors *is* the policy of the chancellor. You seek a continuation of this process. This socialism as dictated by the communists in Brussels at EU headquarters."

"Socialism is *not* communism," answered the deputy. "We are not Russians."

"Indeed," said Geiger with a thoughtful expression. "Then please explain to me the difference."

The deputy did not answer. Instead he remained silent.

"You cannot," said Geiger with a mischievous grin, "because it is the *same*."

"It is not..."

Geiger cut him off before offering, "I have studied Marx and Engels—two enlightened Germans on this issue. I have also read the dissertations of chairman Mao, Lenin, Ho Chi Minh, and Che Guevera. They *all* quote the same ideology and revolutionary rhetoric. They wish to destroy our way of life by controlling the mechanisms of government and the means of production. They wish to replace benevolent capitalism with socialism—which is code for communism. Look at Venezuela, Nicaragua, or Cuba. It *does not* work."

"But we have the EU," said the new deputy.

"For how long?" asked Geiger. "The socialism model is imploding. EU members are turning on the Schengen policy. Immigration is at the forefront. Look at Brexit in the UK, and the Five-Star Movement in Italy."

"There are a few weak states," said the deputy. "The strength of the EU is not in Hungary, Poland, and Slovakia."

"Then look to Austria, Sweden, and Switzerland," replied Geiger. "Are you unaware of what is happening?"

"Herr Geiger," said the VP in a calm voice, "possibly there is a way."

"We deal with our electorate *now*," said Geiger, "or we suffer the consequences."

"I will *not* have a fascist Nazi in the cabinet," said Holger.

"You have no choice. The federal president negotiated this compromise with the chancellor," replied Geiger.

"You don't know that."

"I know that we either deal with the fascists in our government that we *can* see, or we deal with the hidden communists that we *cannot* see. Pick your poison," said Geiger with an impatient snarl.

The police director leaned back in his chair and folded his hands together on the conference table.

Chapter 80

Berlin, Germany

They sat in a quiet room at the rear of Ronja's safe house. Otto and Terry discussed the plan, taking turns in poking the setup for weaknesses. For her part, Ronja appeared calm and ambivalent towards consummating her relationship to the prince. The quicker this ended, the better.

Otto kept repeating his essential elements of information, trying his best to assure that Ronja remembered their key points of interest.

Frau Richter of the domestic security agency was on hold. Her work was temporarily completed, and therefore she spent the night monitoring radio transmissions. This operation had become, at face value, a throwback to honeytraps, where an attractive, seductive woman would use her sexuality to pry information from an unsuspecting or smitten target.

The 'Mata Hari' mystique was well earned. The ego of men coupled with the allure of an attractive woman paid regular dividends. It reinforced the 'knowledge was power' bubble, and the prince had all the prerequisites; money, good looks, and charm. Otto's primary concern was that Sharif Ali, known as Sali to Ronja, had penetrated the protective walls of government service in the daily grind of German politics.

One of the safe house security officers interrupted the three-way briefing and whispered in Otto's ear. The intelligence officer's eyebrows raised in surprise. Then he pulled Terry away from Ronja and spoke in a quiet voice.

"We just received a report that the state secretary for the president's office died."

"Isn't that an important job?"

"Very," answered Otto. "It's a top civil service position."

"When did it occur?"

"An hour ago. Attempts to revive him were unsuccessful."

"What happened?" asked Terry.

"Heart attack."

"Did he have a condition?"

"Not to anyone's knowledge," replied Otto. He gave Solak a perturbed look.

"Where was he?"

"At work, sitting at his desk."

"Was he alone?"

"Yes," replied Otto.

Terry turned and considered the information before asking, "Will they do an autopsy?"

"Yes, complete with a toxicology report, and tissue tests to include fluids, blood, urine samples, a mass spectrometry, and immunoassay. Needless to say, I don't like the timing of this at all," said Otto. He looked at Terry before saying, "Don't mention this to Miss Ronja. We do not need to confuse her with extraneous details."

"Agreed," replied Solak. "It's all related, but she's got enough conspiracies to worry about. We need to keep her focused."

Otto nodded and Terry recrossed the room towards Ronja.

"Sorry about the interruption," said Solak.

"Everything okay?"

"Yes," replied Solak in a casual tone. "Same stuff, different day. How are you holding up?"

"Fine," shrugged Ronja. "A little impatient to get things going."

Terry smiled. "I'm sure he's quite charming. At the very least, you'll have a nice dinner."

Ronja's face broke into a mischievous smile. "He is quite charming...and handsome...and apparently very successful..."

"You mean *rich*," said Solak.

"Yes," said Ronja with a laugh. She leaned towards Terry, "But if it was my choice, I would prefer to be dining with you." She touched his wounded forearm.

"Well, when this is over, we'll have to do something about that," replied Terry. Solak stood and gave Ronja a peck on the cheek. "I'll be out of sight, but close by. Take it only as far as you are comfortable, it's *your* call."

"Thank you," said Ronja in a quiet voice. She appreciated Terry's words. They reinforced her sense of choice in the matter. Then Ronja nodded, stood, and exited the room.

***

Berlin, Germany

The domestic security agency was in full surveillance overdrive, pushing the process, and utilizing every questionable legal loophole to gather information.

They assembled an array of parabolic reflectors, both handheld and vehicle mounted, and trained the dishes on the prince's hotel windows. They also aimed directional condenser microphones at anyone the prince spoke to, hoping to catch a phrase or comment that would help to reveal his plans.

On the street, a control van with fake corporate markings guided both the mounted vehicular teams and the pedestrian 'foot' teams deployed at various intervals.

Finally, a black bag team of specialists surreptitiously entered the prince's hotel suite, and strategically placed multiple wireless, voice-activated audio recorders throughout the rooms. Sharif Ali, ranking officer in the General Intelligence Directorate of Saudi Arabia, was being watched under danger-close observation.

Chapter 81

Langley, Virginia

An emergency session was called for the Director's Brief. Events had sped up the pace and rapid changes were now affecting the government of Germany. The vestiges of democracy were preserved and decisions were made within the framework of a functioning republic. However, every knowledgeable political observer knew that the core of the political class was crumbling. Germany was at a dire crossroads, a dilemma not seen, not contemplated, since the end of World War Two.

The Director pointed at the desk supervisor. She leaned forward and began checking off bullet points of information for those assembled. "Seven hours ago, the state secretary of the Office of the Federal President died of an apparent heart attack. He was arguably the top civil servant in the country with vast experience and responsibilities. Politicians come and go, but this man knew where all the levers of power existed."

"What are the chances," asked Arthur Kent, "that it was *not* what it appears?"

The desk supervisor nodded before referring to Evie.

The collection manager shifted in her seat to better face the Director. "We received a sitrep from Helios an hour ago that contradicts the 'official' public statement on the state secretary's death. Internal police and intelligence sources confirm a classified toxicology report. They use of a poison known as aconite was present."

"Aconite?" asked the Director.

Evie nodded, "A plant-based poison found in Northern India. It is sometimes referred to as wolf's bane or monkshood. It is highly toxic and has symptoms that mimic those of a cardiac arrest." She paused as the nine people in the

283

conference room listened with interest. "Helios stated that that poison is a favorite tool of das Netzwerk, the neo-Nazi women's group. In addition, they believe this particular drug was used to eliminate an asset in Landsberg several months ago."

"So why kill the secretary?" asked the deputy director for Analysis. "He's not an elected official."

"No," replied Evie in agreement. "It's about power. They need internal players for their agenda."

The Director motioned, a signal that she should continue.

"Operation Hummingbird, the *template* for Operation Blackbird, was primarily about consolidating power for the Nazis. By eliminating a powerful civil servant, they accomplish two things: they send a warning—that no one is safe—and they create a critical vacancy for their own selection."

"But Germany would *never* permit a Nazi to return to power," said the desk supervisor. "Given their past, its unthinkable."

"It's already happening," said Evie. "The new transportation minister holds extremely conservative positions on immigration, Muslims, and the EU. Her appointment to the cabinet was *not* a fluke. It was a calibrated event."

"And in these turbulent times," said the Europe mission center chief, "how far will they take it?"

"The path is open now," answered Evie. "A populace, nativist revolt is in progress throughout Europe. Germany, due to her population and economic prowess, is the most visible."

"And most susceptible," said Bob Colman speaking for the first time.

"Because of her history?" asked the Director.

"That, and the fundamental leanings of the players. The chancellor hails from East Germany, and the president grew up in Bavaria."

***

Berlin, Germany

The dinner with Sharif Ali was relaxed and simple. The prince made reservations at one of the hotel's four restaurants, the renowned Michelin two-star known as the Lorenz Adlon Esszimmer. Ronja and Ali reacquainted like a couple of old friends which allowed for easy conversation and unpressured dialogue. She revealed trivia about her cosmetics job, and he amplified on his success as a financier who traveled the world. Neither appeared to be playing a role, yet both carried the discussion with equal aplomb.

"And after Berlin," asked Ronja, "are you off to another adventure?"

Sharif hesitated and then made a noncommittal shrug, "Wherever my consortium sends me." He topped off her glass of wine. "My strength is in finessing through the final details of the negotiations."

Ronja smiled. "So, will you be available at all tomorrow?"

"Maybe," replied Ali. He offered her a confident look.

Ronja studied the prince. He was every bit the charmer, easy-going in demeanor, but with an air of superiority. It sometimes made him overbearing.

They worked their way through dinner but when Ronja politely refused dessert, Ali said, "I have a bottle of champagne being chilled upstairs. Would you join me?"

"I cannot handle too much bubbly," answered Ronja with a modest smile.

"Nor I," replied the prince, "but it was a gift and I would hate to drink it alone. Will you join me for a toast?"

Ronja offered a gentle nod, and they both stood. For a moment she thought about Terry, the man she knew only as Helios. He promised to be near, but out of sight.

Sharif motioned for the maître d', and they exited the restaurant followed by Ali's two bodyguards who were seated off to the side.

The luxury suite was impressive, a large multi-roomed layout filled with lavish furnishings, including a baby grand piano and a spectacular view of the Brandenburg Gate.

Ronja excused herself and entered the toilet. The prince's two bodyguards immediately made a quick walkthrough of the suite. They checked every corner, closet, and blind crevice before finally one of the men pulled out a small handheld countersurveillance detector, and started to sweep the suite before Ali gave him a curt wave. He stopped, and with an obedient nod, the two bodyguards retreated to the adjoining room and locked Ali's double doors behind them.

A few minutes later, Ronja exited the bathroom and joined Sharif at the panorama windows. The Brandenburg Gate was lighted in partial ruins, and Ronja looked in awe as she saw, up close for the first time, the carnage wrought on the German national monument by the terrorist attack. He handed her a flute of expensive champagne.

"Dom Perignon," said Ali. "For you, nothing but the best."

They raised their glasses in a silent toast, yet Ronja couldn't help but feel it was somehow out of place. Then the prince leaned over and gave her a gentle kiss. It was the icebreaker, and Ronja responded, kissing him in return but feeling more mechanical and less enthusiastic about the encounter than a short time earlier.

Sharif took her glass and set it on the side table before leading Ronja across the room to a huge king size bed. He kissed her again, this time with more intensity, and then he laid her back on the bed and started to caress her shoulders as she removed her clothes.

Chapter 82

Berlin, Germany

The hit team consisted of ten people, a combination of mixed couples and singles. They entered the expansive lobby from either end, one couple settling into cushioned chairs near the reception desk, the other ordering cappuccinos near the elephant fountain. Their interlocking vision covered all angles of entrances and exits into the ground level of the posh hotel. Minutes later, four single men dressed in business suits entered from various directions. They were alone and apart. Two made their way to the suite level using coded room keys to summon the elevators.

Gradually, over a ten-minute interval, six of the hit team made it to the prince's floor, while the other two couples remained behind. The latter's job was to provide active surveillance of the hotel's response and to cover and assist in the shooters' escape. The lone woman on sight above was positioned to offer a softer look for hotel employees or other guests that might frequent the suite floor.

The shooters fanned left and right, keeping their eyes on the fire escapes and the elevator doors, while listening to continuous updates by the reconnaissance teams posted in the lobby.

Upstairs, the woman knocked on the outside room door of Ali's suite occupied by the two Saudi bodyguards. She held a specially embroidered mahogany box up to the peephole and smiled. The other five men hugged the walls to either side, standing well beyond the peripheral view of the security slit as the woman spoke in German, acting the part of a senior hotel employee.

"A special gift from the hotel manager."

"Leave the gift," said one of the bodyguards in accented English through the door.

"I cannot," replied the woman. "My instructions were quite specific. It must be hand delivered."

She waited patiently as a small discussion took place between the two bodyguards inside the room. Then she heard the bolt lock open and gave a gentle nod to her co-workers.

The bodyguard swung the door inward and the woman thrust the mahogany box through the crack. She held tight as the five men, in unison, stormed the outer room door and forced their entry into the suite of Sharif Ali.

***

Berlin, Germany

They sat in the control van on the street directly outside the Adlon Kempinski Hotel, sipping coffee, and talking softly. Surveillance work was often boring and repetitive routines spliced by moments of brisk activity. A short lull permeated the air as the panoply of sophisticated eavesdropping equipment blinked and stirred in silence.

Suddenly Frau Richter sat forward and snapped her fingers in the air. Then she cupped her right hand over the hearing shell on her ear. "Gunshots."

Terry and the other domestic security officers leaned forward as Richter raised the speaker volume for the others to hear. Seconds later a woman's voice, a sharp scream and a muffled but distinct popping sound filled the van.

"Silenced weapons," said Terry as he stood and slip open the van door. In seconds he was on the street, running towards the side maintenance exit of the hotel.

"Go with him," said Richter in a demanding voice. Several domestic security officers jumped up and gave chase. Then Richter alerted the mobile members of her team that had infiltrated the common areas of the hotel, and gave them a series of short, concise orders.

Chapter 83

Berlin, Germany

Two Mercedes-Benz stretch sedans pulled up to the gate leading to the four-story executive office building of the federal president. They passed through the checkpoint and circled through the shadows to an obscured side entrance of the glass and stone structure; well-hidden from the street by a forest of deep trees and thick vegetation. They were at the edge of the imposing Tiergarten.

The sedans stopped in front of the entrance that led to a special elevator that offered private access to the third-floor anteroom. The doors on the first Mercedes opened and four plainclothes federal police officers exited. They formed a tight perimeter around the rear of the second sedan as Director Geiger stepped to the blacktop. Then he was followed by a second passenger of average height wearing glasses, a fedora, and a high-necked collar to his coat. He was escorted through the door into the elevator, his face indistinguishable to onlookers; the darkness of the hour and the tree-lined campus aiding the secret arrival.

Inside, Director Geiger and the visitor were brought to the anteroom where they waited in silence. All was quiet in the executive office building, as the normal workday had long since ended.

After ten minutes, the internal door opened and Geiger and the visitor were brought into a large study-like office. Sitting at the desk was the unmistakable portrait of the federal president of the republic, looking up from the papers on his desk, his thick white hair and dark framed glasses the countenance of a serious politician.

The president stood and circled his desk, taking the opportunity to acknowledge Geiger before addressing the visitor. Then the visitor removed his hat and glasses, and turned down the coat collar.

The president stopped two feet to the visitor's front and gasped.

"I am Gerhardt," said the visitor, fixing the president with a steady gaze.

The resemblance to Adolf Hitler was unsettling, and the normally unflappable president took a moment to swallow before motioning at a sitting area off to the side.

"Thank you for meeting with us," said the president in a slightly deferential tone.

Gerhardt nodded in courtesy, "Yes, we have much to discuss."

***

Berlin, Germany

Terry barged through the partially opened suite door and stepped over a dead Saudi bodyguard. Then he saw the second Saudi protector lying face down in a pool of blood ten feet to the side.

One of the domestic security officers recovered an automatic pistol with an attached noise suppressor, from beside a dead assailant. Then he pointed towards the open doors to the prince's inner chamber, and with a nod, he and Solak stormed the bedroom together.

Another security officer quickly entered the bedroom and started searching through the carnage. Blood and spent bullet casings were all over the suite. It was clear that a very brief, but very violent firefight had taken place.

As Terry paced forward, he saw the torso of Sharif Ali lying on his back, his chest heaving in discomfort. The prince looked at the standing Solak and pointed. "I know you," said Ali. He beckoned Terry closer and whispered. "Have we met?"

Solak knelt over the prince as the Saudi gurgled blood from his throat.

"Helios," said one of the security officers to Terry, calling from across the room. He pointed down at Ronja's body in the bed.

The name caught the Saudi prince's attention. He grabbed at Solak's hand and looked off into the distance as he mumbled the codename to himself. "Helios...yes...we met...where?"

Solak let the question settle, debating internally about whether to break protocol and answer the dying man's question. Then, in a gesture of charity, he leaned over Sharif's body and whispered in his ear. "We met in a land far away, where dusty streets now cover rosewater-flowing fountains."

A glint came to Sharif's eyes and he forced a smile before nodding. A moment of clarity injected into a confusing situation. "Mali," said the prince.

Terry winked and patted the Saudi's wrist before standing and moving towards the bed.

Ronja lay on her back, naked, her torso partially covered by a sheet, staring up at the ceiling with wide-open eyes. She had two bullet holes in her chest and one in the middle of her forehead.

Solak stood to the side of the bed and checked her carotid pulse. Then he turned away and grimaced.

The security officer with the dead assailant's pistol held it up for Terry's inspection. "Do you recognize the model Helios?"

"Yes," said Terry turning his head sideways to view the silenced weapons held at an awkward angle. He frowned. "That changes the playing field."

The German nodded and wrapped the weapon in his handkerchief.

"Helios," said the security officer across the room as he held his cell phone, "Orders from the van, you must leave—immediately."

"I can't," replied Terry, "Please advise Frau Richter that…"

"Nein," answered the domestic security officer, "the orders come from Otto."

Terry gave the security officer a frustrated look, but before he could continue his objection, the man raised a hand and pointed towards the door. Solak nodded and took a last look at Ronja. He touched her on the cheek. Then he turned and exited the hotel room followed by the security officer.

Chapter 84

Langley, Virginia

The Director's Brief commenced as soon as the physical security barriers were activated in the SCIF.

"Before we get to the other agenda items," said the Director, "we have some updates on the German situation."

Bob Colman shuffled some notes on the table and waited for the signal to begin. The Director motioned.

"Nine months ago," said the SAD chief, "at the request of our allies, we rendered assistance to our German counterparts in the form of a special ops officer. His assignment was to imbed himself with certain known domestic organizations that threatened the sovereign status of the German republic."

"He was on loan?" asked the deputy director for Analysis.

"For lack of a better term," replied Bob. "He was under operational control of a seasoned German intelligence officer. They needed a fresh face."

The deputy director nodded. The other attendees were enthralled at the peek under the lid of the black ops world. They seldom were involved in the mechanics of SAD operations, given the 'need to know' protocol.

"This involvement led us, and by extension our German allies, to identify the nation of Saudi Arabia as the perpetrator of a cabal to affect the German national elections."

Bob took a moment to catch his breath before continuing. "This information stood in stark contrast to the evidence that strongly suggested elements of the Turkish diaspora in Germany as the perpetrators of the wave of violence."

"But the Germans have also identified members of domestic neo-Nazi groups having involvement," said the desk supervisor.

"Yes," said Bob with a nod, "that's correct. We have identified a relationship between the Saudis and a domestic subversive underground pro-Nazi organization known as das Netzwerk."

"So, the Turkish angle is a false flag," said Arthur Kent of the clandestine service.

"Yes," said Colman to his boss for everyone's clarity, "there are still pockets of anti-German resistance amongst the Turks, but the evidence holding them responsible is fabricated information. Our own source *confirms* that the Saudis were aligned with the neo-Nazis for political gain."

"So what about the recent wet work at the hotel in Berlin?" asked the Director.

Colman turned towards Evie and motioned.

The collection manager gathered her notes before beginning. "We received a sitrep from Helios followed by a formal intel update from the German domestic security agency. At approximately eleven p.m. Berlin time two days ago, a kill team of at least eight, and possibly as many as twelve, trained assassins entered the Hotel Adlon Kempinski in Berlin and executed Prince Sharif Ali, a member of the royal family as well as a senior officer in the General Intelligence Directorate of Saudi Arabia."

"Who was the prince with?" asked the Europe mission center chief.

"His two bodyguards and an unaffiliated local German woman who appears to have been a guest of the prince."

"Bad luck," replied Arthur Kent, "wrong place, wrong time. Any witnesses?"

"None that have surfaced," answered Evie. "The operation was fast, clean, and thorough. Very professional."

"Was it the Turks getting even?" asked the desk supervisor.

"No."

"Who then?" asked the Director.

"Moscow," said Evie in a flat tone.

Several people sat forward.

"You are sure?" asked Kent.

"One of the assailants, a member of the hit team, died in the altercation with the prince's bodyguards. The German response was so fast that there was no time to sterilize the location. This provided ample opportunity to process crime scene evidence, to include autopsy, DNA match, weapons recovery and expended brass bullet casings. The dead assailant's handgun, recovered at the scene was of particular note."

"Classic GRU Spetsnaz team equipment," said Colman.

"What if it is a setup?" asked the Director. "Another false flag."

"Possible," said Evie, "but highly doubtful."

"Why?" pressed the desk supervisor.

"Several reasons." Evie paused to take a breath before outlining her response. "One, the methodology of the attack was textbook Russian training manual for the GRU using multiple shooters, surveillance teams, and target access." She paused and looked around the conference table. "Two, the recovered weapon, a silenced Russian Makarov PB pistol, which is a ballistics match to nine by eighteen caliber bullet rounds removed from the victims, is a specialized pistol developed and used by Russian operators. Three, the DNA match and fingerprints confirm both a Slavic ethnicity and body scars previously identified in file postings of a GRU military intelligence officer. Four, Moscow has the most to gain if the partnership between Saudi Arabia and Germany fails. With the addition of the Baltic Sea pipeline, Russia will control eighty to ninety percent of Germany's energy needs. Conversely, if the partnership for energy between Saudi Arabia and Germany *succeeds*, then Russia loses a vast source of reliable cash flow—which it desperately needs—and Russia also loses a piece of significant leverage over the continent's dominant member. And finally," said Evie, "five, it was a typical, bold Russian move. We believe Moscow was sending Germany, the EU, and NATO a stiff challenge."

The Director swiveled his attention from Evie to Bob Colman. "Bob, when is our agent-in-place due home?"

"Soon, Director," said the SAD chief. "He's just wrapping things up with our German counterparts."

"Good," replied the Director. "I'll want to meet him when he gets back."

"So will I," said Evie in a quiet voice, reminding Bob Colman that she and Solak had never actually been introduced.

Colman laughed and then turned his attention to the typed agenda. "I predict," he said with a wink, "that you and Helios will get along famously. By the way, his real name is Terry."

***

Berlin, Germany

They sat in the kitchen of a safe house in Wilmersdorf, an upscale residential neighborhood known for restored pre-war buildings and eclectic foodie crowds. Terry sipped at a beer as Otto turned off the desktop tape recorder. The German intelligence officer fumbled with his pipe before speaking. "That's enough for now, debriefs can be so tedious."

"I agree," said Solak.

The quiet time allowed the two intelligence officers from different countries a moment to disengage from the actions of the last several days while they considered the crosscurrents of their efforts.

"Any regrets?" asked Otto.

"For what?"

"Your involvement in this decidedly European affair."

Terry leaned back and shook his head. "No, I try not to overthink the assignment. Germany is an ally."

"So you go where you are sent," replied Otto, filling his pipe bowl with fresh tobacco.

"Pretty much. The political fallout doesn't faze me. I accept that my actions are part of a bigger picture, and that I—by design—don't have all the information."

"A true operator," said Otto with admiration.

Terry stretched. "I trust that smart people will get it right. I seldom question the *why*."

Otto lit a match and fired up his pipe. He puffed through several plumes of smoke before asking, "And Miss Ronja?"

"A loss," answered Terry. "I liked her. She was a little intense, but true. I think she caught a raw deal."

"I agree," said Otto with a nod. "In any event, I think she was sweet on you."

Solak shrugged. "Well, I guess we will never know." He set down his beer and folded his hands. "Is there anything you can do for the kids?"

"Not officially," replied the foreign intelligence officer, "but we may be able to parlay a small satchel of money for the boys' future. It would be a one-time, off-the-books entry."

Terry leaned back and frowned. "That could help. It's the least you could do. She was a citizen, and she helped you expose the foreign sponsor *and* the neo-Nazi group. Who would have thought of Saudi Arabia?"

"I agree," said Otto. "It's worthy of discussion. At least now we have up-ended the Riyadh connection and put our foot on the brake of the Nazi objective. We can rest easy."

Terry gave Otto a quizzical look. "Can you?"

"My country has had some difficult moments, but we exposed Sharif Ali and his government, as well as the rudiments of our own domestic Nazi problem," said Otto.

"What does that tell you?" asked Solak.

"That due to our history, we are overly sensitive to the Hitler mystique. I now believe that we have it firmly under control."

"It doesn't concern you?" asked Terry.

"I don't accept," replied Otto, "that it could happen again."

Solak leaned back and laced his fingers together before bracing them behind his neck. He looked at Otto with a clear gaze. "Do you remember Frau Jokols?"

"Of course," replied the German, "our Jewish historian from Landsberg. She was poisoned."

Terry nodded. "The last thing she said to me when I left her home, was don't believe *anyone* that denies that it could happen again."

Chapter 85

Munich, Germany

The six women sat around the oval table in Schwabing. It was a sunny day in January, and the brisk cold of a Bavarian winter had forced the temperature below freezing.

One of the members passed a pastry dish to Frau Fuchs with a nod. "Something sweet on a special day."

The spry seventy-year-old smiled and pushed at her short hair. "Danke," she answered before stealing a glance around the room.

Everyone was nervous, anticipating an important event, politely engaging in small talk as they waited for the news to be reported.

"It's live," said the home's owner, entering the room in a rush and pointing at the blackened flat screen of the television. "Turn on the news."

The television blinked several times and then the group sat looking at the easily recognized profile of the federal president, his thick white hair and dark eye glass frames a distinct fixture on the national news coverage.

"Turn up the volume," said one of the members, as they caught the politician in the middle of a prepared address.

"...therefore, at the nomination by the chancellor, and with my support, we are adding one advisor to the new grand coalition cabinet. He is a man of vast insight and proven loyalty to our nation...Germany and all of Europe is undergoing a stressful debate on the issues relating to migrants, refugees, and asylum integration within the European Union...we seek a man who has the confidence of the people and the insight for skillful compromise..."

The six women sat enthralled, as the home's owner squeezed Frau Fuchs' hand.

"…for this purpose, we are expanding the cabinet to include Herr Adolphus Gerhardt Fuchs as the Federal Minister for Special Affairs."

The president turned from the podium and motioned. All the cameras shifted to the shadows and then Gerhardt stepped forward. The purported grandson of Adolf Hitler stood on the stage next to the federal president of Germany.

It was a moment in time. The camera lenses zoomed in on Gerhardt, focusing on the forty-year-old with straight brown hair, and the distinct mustache that suddenly stopped inside the edge of each corner of his upper lip. He stood erect, his jawline fixed, his greenish-brown eyes shifting to a lifeless gray as he surveyed the crowd of reporters.

The women around the oval table erupted in boisterous jubilation. Two members leaned forward to congratulate Frau Fuchs and several others slapped the table in unison with open hands.

The frame of Gerhardt froze on the television, as the news analysts debated the announcement of the populist's appointment to the chancellor's cabinet as a new Federal Minister.

"We succeeded," said the leader of das Netzwerk in a quiet voice to Fuchs, "your son is now a cabinet minister."

"He is without portfolio," replied Gerhardt's mother.

"For now," replied the leader. She smiled and patted Fuchs' hand. "When combined with our new transportation minister, we have made great inroads." She motioned at the television screen and the parting portrait of Gerhardt. He was the very embodiment of Adolf Hitler. "We have waited a long time, but the republic has finally come full circle." Her lips parted in a subtle smile. "The Fourth Reich lives."

Acknowledgments

As in any heavily researched endeavor, I owe a special thanks to several individuals; first, to Lutz and Goekcen Domeier, good friends, world travelers, proud Berliners, and astute observers of the German people.

Next, to Lauren Longenecker, my long serving, ever-reliable content editor, and finally, to Ian Andrew and the team at BRE for their patient and insightful efforts at bringing this novel to fruition. You make 'Five Eyes' proud.

About The Author

Steve Dimodica was born in Boston and raised in Massachusetts. The second of six children, he grew up in a suburban neighborhood with many young families having the dual focus of school and sports. After college (B.S.) and graduate school (M.S.), Steve joined the Army with the intent of exploring foreign countries before settling into a domestic career. Instead, he found a greater challenge.

Steve spent the next 20 years on Active and Active Reserve Duty in the U.S. Army Special Forces and Military Intelligence. Following three mission deployments to North Africa where he served as a Weapons Leader and Medical Specialist on a Special Forces A Team, he received a Direct Commission as a Military Intelligence Officer.

For the next fourteen years, Steve had numerous mission deployments to Europe and Central America, serving as both a Counter-Intelligence Officer and a Detachment Commander on the Special Forces A Teams.

Steve lives in the Philadelphia area with his family.

Also By
Steve Dimodica

Covert Matters (2008)
The Einstein Proxy (2015)
Vile Means (2016)
Accidental Evils (2017)

CPSIA information can be obtained
at www.ICGtesting.com
Printed in the USA
LVHW041136251119
638400LV00006B/964/P